NAK

Judi James was a model before running a Chelsea, discovering and training models as Naomi Campbell. She then became a management consultant and now lectures to businesses on presentation skills. She lives in North London and *Naked Angels* is her fifth novel.

JUDI JAMES

Naked Angels

HarperCollins*Publishers*

HarperCollins*Publishers*
77–85 Fulham Palace Road,
Hammersmith, London, W6 8JB

A Paperback Original 1995
1 3 5 7 9 8 6 4 2

Copyright © Judi James 1995

The Author asserts the moral right to be
identified as the author of this work

A catalogue record for this book
is available from the British Library

ISBN 0 00 649046 8

Typeset at The Spartan Press Ltd
Lymington, Hants

Printed in Great Britain by
HarperCollinsManufacturing Glasgow

PROLOGUE

London 1995

THE MODEL

Even when she was dying she was still counting the calories: none in the hot water toddy at breakfast, ten in the Extra Strong mint on the way to the shoot. She licked the insides of her teeth, savouring everything.

The model's changing room was shared. Two males and herself. The sour but tasty stench of quick-tan and the sick-sweet perfume of hashish. She watched them push tissues down the front of their trunks while her stomach gnawed painfully. Too much padding? One less? Why not go for it? They laughed easily. Their pubic hair had been waxed. They looked gleamily good. She weighed less than seven stone but she still looked crap. Too fat – too much around the hips.

She listened to the male models laughing and thought they were making fun of her. Paranoia. She knew she was right, though. She gave her grave face a few little smacks to raise some colour onto it. It was six a.m. She sighed and lit her fourth cigarette of the day.

The litany continued in her head. Two dry biscuits for dinner. Three Strawberry Pop Tarts yesterday, even if she did throw them up later. Her last binge had been over a week ago: chocolate spread sandwiches on thick white bread with butter, yellow-cream rice puddings, Alpen, pink-iced cakes, and cheese triangles on warmed rolls. It had taken her an hour to be sick afterwards and she'd lain exhausted on the bathroom floor feeling the linoleum tiles cool against her cheek.

The make-up made her skin hurt. She'd studied it like a

science and knew exactly what it was doing to her flesh – every liposome, every nanosphere, every trace of phyto-bium. She winced and the make-up artist halted.

'The sponge – it's a bit scratchy. Have you got a softer one?'

He smiled but his teeth formed a set line as he went to fetch a new one. She closed her eyes and relaxed a little.

The set was bare – just the model and the guys. The photographer was firing instructions at her. She had so much oil on her body she slid off the male models like an eel. They touched one another breezily between shots, swapping muscle tone.

She'd do it that evening, definitely. She didn't want any more of this.

Back in the changing room she stared at herself in the mirror. Six feet tall. A freak, dressed in two-hundred quid fishnets and denim cut-offs with the bum sagging. And the shoes – velvet stiletto tart shoes with diamante toe-caps – she liked the shoes, they were pretty.

She was fifteen years old, yet she felt three hundred and nine. Fifteen seemed a long time to have lived. She wanted to be young again. She wanted an end to it all.

THE ILLUSIONIST

The photographer sat before his computer screen, the model's image flickering and dancing in front of his face. The room was dark. His face was half lit and eerie. The model was perfectly reflected as a pair of tiny twins, trapped in the round orbs of his Calvin Klein wire-rimmed glasses.

'It's a conceptual shot,' he told his assistant.

'You mean it's shit.'

'It's O K,' the photographer said, 'it doesn't matter. It's the concept – the concept is sound.'

'She looks bad,' the assistant said, studying the model's image.

'Bad as in good?' the photographer asked.

'No, bad as in *bad*. Really bad. I thought she was supposed to be a name. What's the matter with her, her face looks like Emmenthal. Is she on something? I thought she was special.'

'The client wanted her,' the photographer told him, 'it's OK, I told you.' He lit a cigarette and pushed it into the side of his mouth. Smoke billowed from his nostrils and arched around his head.

'I'm so disappointed,' the boy said.

'You won't be,' he was told. 'A little computer enhancement and we will have created your true goddess for you again.'

He pressed a few keys and pulled the model's face into close-up. He felt as though he was a true artist, creating a perfect image with a few finger-flicks: less darkness under the eyes. Bleached pupils. A small mark removed from the cheek. He added warmth and tone to her pallid cheeks and widened her distressed-looking smile.

'What d'you think?' he asked. The boy leant forward. Both faces were lit gleaming and frog-like by the flickering colours on screen.

'It's cheating,' the assistant said. He laughed, though. The model looked the way he knew her now. She looked like the face everyone saw in the magazines. Healthy. Glowing. Fuckable.

The photographer shook his head. 'No,' he said, 'it's art. Total empowerment via VDU. We've become the creative force we always yearned to be. Look at that fucking face – I created that face, just like Leonardo created the Mona Lisa.'

He sat back in his chair, scratching himself, swinging gently. 'It's all illusion, son, playing tricks with images. Digital imaging – fucking brilliant. Photographers have been cheating for years, only now we can do it all with a finger-twitch.

'Did you know one of the first patentees of the photographic process was a prize illusionist?' he asked. 'There's some history here, it's a tradition – only now we've got it down to an art form. Don't you like what you see?' He

7

turned to his assistant, the light in his glasses obscuring his eyes. 'Don't you like it?' he repeated.

The boy smiled.

'Does it matter that what you see doesn't exist?' the photographer whispered. 'Do you think many of the punters have a hope in hell of meeting her in the flesh anyway? It's trickery, son, hocus-pocus, jiggery-pokery. It's alchemy – turning basest metals into gold. And she is gold, isn't she? Look at her – shit, man, look at her. We got rid of all her faults. We made her perfect.'

He looked back to the screen, stroking his stubble. 'Maybe a little more leg,' he said. His assistant nodded his approval.

THE PAPARAZZI

Flaccid had to be the saddest word in the English language. The snapper shifted sagging weight from ossified femur to atrophied tibia. Never fuck a fashion hack – why had no one ever told him that? Or maybe they had. Maybe he just forgot.

The incense made his nose itch. When he moved again he could just glimpse the faux-snakeskin linoleum behind the post-modernist Conran headboard. She should take the Hoover round there more often, he thought – there were dustballs the size of large rats down by the marble-effect skirting. Or were they rats? Jesus!

That season the fashion hack was into Tantric Sex. She slid deftly into the Lotus position, opening her mouth and sticking her tongue out like a Maori rugby player prior to a match. He'd bought her dinner at Quaglino's but she'd barfed it all up in the john half an hour later to balance her inner toxins.

He was so bored it hurt but she was Lavender Allcock-Hopkins, just about The Biggest Name in the Fashion Business, so he gritted his buttocks and pressed on with the Chi Gung. When the portable phone chirruped from beneath the herb-stuffed continental pillow he could have fucked that instead, he was so relieved for the interruption.

'Where are you, you bugger?' It was the editor of the *Sunday Slimes*, sizzling and shouting as though Edison Bell were just a figment of some ad-man's imagination. The snapper held the phone near the open window so the traffic sounds fizzed down the wires.

'Kensington Palace,' he yelled, 'down at the gates. There's a bit of serious to-ing and fro-ing down here and word is out the prince . . .'

'Sod the prince!' his editor screamed. 'Get down to Piccadilly. There's some sort of awards night going on and Spike says they've just smuggled some celebs in by the tradesman's. Are you on your bike?'

The snapper grunted. In his haste he'd shoved two feet into one leg of his Gaultiers. He scowled across at Lavender but she was into her forty-fifth inner-vaginal orgasm and so barely aware he was AWOL from the Futon.

There were hideous whale sounds playing on the CD. The flask of amyl nitrate he'd brought lay untouched atop the Jeff Koons Retrospective catalogue. That little gift had been received with all the enthusiasm of a box of Quality Streets on a first date.

''Bye, lover,' the snapper mouthed, quickly syphoning Givenchy beneath each armpit before picking up the keys to his Harley and tossing them twice into the air. Lavender was silent but the whales hooted their eerie farewell.

THE KILL

It was raining – but then the rain always drizzled on a true paparazzo. They stank of the rain – it steamed from their anoraks and snaked through their hair gel, bubbling like mucus. Without the rain they would have lost the kudos that came with the cupped cigarettes and the serious body-hunch.

As the snapper strolled across to join the straggle they quickly banded together, staring like meerkats spoiling for a fight.

'Who is it in there tonight?'

'Fuck-knows.'

'Again? We did him last night.'

'Very funny.'

'You think so?'

'No, actually.'

'It's Paul Daniels, I saw him go in.'

'Buggeroff.'

'Buggeroffyerself.'

Some even claimed it was the patter and camaraderie that kept them loyal to the job.

The snapper tried to shin a low wall but slipped and scuffed his trainers and grazed his palm into the bargain. He swore and scowled at the nearest of the pack, daring him to laugh. He didn't.

There was a sudden surge around the entrance to the hotel and the heartwarming sound of a scuffle breaking out. The paparazzi moved as one beast, pressing forward, pushing, lining up for a sniff of their prey. Someone moved from the darkness out into the street-lights and a volley of silver flashes greeted their arrival. A huge meatball of a bodyguard appeared from nowhere and a small guy in a new pair of Timberlands had his nose crushed to a crimson coulis by the lens of his own Leica.

They all had stepladders ready in case it was Prince. In the event the ladders were superfluous because the man who finally stepped into the glare of the lights was tall enough to be seen in any crowd.

'Who the . . .?'

'Shit, give us some space for Christssake. I was here first you know . . .'

The jostling became violent as the bodyguard leant his full weight to the crush. Squeezed like lemons, the paparazzi oozed a collective odour of Key West. The snapper's foot found someone's calf beneath it and he used it as the lever he needed to haul himself onto the wall behind.

The man in the middle of the crowd turned full-face and he recognized him at once; the chill wind of jealousy blew throughout his vitals.

'Mik-Mak!' The whisper went round. The paparazzi virtually slobbered with glee. Mik Veronsky, super-snapper. Exclusive, elusive and charismatic enough to be worth a few bob in the next day's papers. The pages of *Vogue* and *Tatler* had been liberally peppered with shots of his face for the past month but now he was about to be captured for the benefit of the nation's chip-wrappings and cat litter-tray linings, too.

The snapper swallowed hard and his camera dropped waist-high as his colleagues moved in for the kill.

Supersnapper – what the fuck did that mean? All it meant was that Mik Veronsky charged more to do less. And got to screw all the best women. It meant he was top barker in the whole pack of snivelling hounds. It also meant he was flavour of the month with the fashion journos. Mention his name to Lavender Allcock-Hopkins and a greedy, syrupy little smile would gather across her suet-white face. He raised his camera reluctantly and faffed around with the focus instead.

Mik had lost his rag now – he was really raging. He'd grabbed a nearby journo and was trying to tear the poor sod's epiglottis out with his bare hands.

What was it that women saw in him? He was taller than necessary with wide shoulders and a skinny, demi-starved frame. His skin was vampire-white and his hair as black as the long coat he always wore. His outfit was de rigueur supersnapper: boots, jeans, acres of ethnic jewellery, stupid fucking hand-woven hat that looked like it had been stolen from some passing Kurd or other. Hair extensions? Did normal men have hair that far down their backs? And hadn't it been cropped short last season? Eyes like angry dark stones.

Mik wasn't handsome in the pipe-and-knitting-pattern sort of style, but he was, in a casual way, incredibly beautiful. Arty-farty, the snapper thought. All high fucking cheekbones and flared bloody nostrils. Then, of course, there was the voice. The accent: what Lavender Allcock-Hopkins described as multiply orgasmic.

The snapper looked back through his telephoto. Mik's eyes were so dark you could barely see the definition between pupil and iris. There was a soft dent above his top lip and a small scar near his left eyebrow.

'I don't know what they all bloody see in him,' he announced to anyone within earshot. He looked back again. There was a locket hanging around Mik's neck, a plain silver one, nestling just along the watermark where the chest hairs started. Lockets weren't in that season — everybody knew that. Press-prattle had it that it held something dear to Mik — something even that cold-hearted bastard cherished as a memento.

A body moved in front of Mik, blocking the snapper's view, and he swore under his breath. He looked up to see who it was. Another photographer. It looked as though the prat was going to ask for a bloody autograph. The shame of the concept turned the snapper's face scarlet.

A car backfired. Twice. Mik's hair seemed to explode with the shock, rising up behind his head in serene and stately slow motion. The crush of bodies parted like the Red Sea. Mik stood alone now, frozen in grey space. The thought flashed through the snapper's mind that maybe the pack had given up at last. Maybe a sense of the injustice of it all had finally permeated their crusty skulls. Mik had no talent as a photographer. He'd screwed his way to the top. He couldn't tell a Nikon from a Box Brownie if his life depended on it. The game was up: the pack had rejected Mik Veronsky and all his hype.

The snapper watched with glee as Mik disintegrated with the lights of the press no longer upon him. People moved further back. Mik lurched towards them. He looked startled and amazed at their apparent lack of interest. His mouth opened and he screamed a name:

'Andreas!' There was an echo from other empty streets. Nonsense. Crap. The guy was all to pieces. Then the word was replaced by something else – something dark that spewed out of his mouth, splattering the bystanders. People moved back quickly in disgust, checking their clothes, wiping stains off their anoraks. All you could hear now was the shuffling and squeaking of Timberlands on wet pavement. There were a couple of screams, too.

Mik seemed to trip over nothing and began to fall, crumpling onto the concrete without a sound. Silence after that, total and profound.

Then suddenly the flashes began like applause after a great performance; not a quick volley of shots this time, but a barrage. No gaps between the silver light. The snapper's mouth fell open but his hands would not move. Something seeped from beneath Mik's fallen frame, something thicker and darker even than the rain.

The snapper knew then that his moment had come and passed him by: that split atom of a millisecond that fate offers up to everyone at some time in their meaningless little life, the one chance we all get either to make it or not. The photographer had blown it. He could have been famous. He could have been rich.

The moment had been his. He'd had the best view, the best angle, the best picture in his viewfinder. The irony of it was exquisite. Someone cannoned into his back and his camera rolled to the ground. He felt like jumping on it. Mik Veronsky had just been shot and all he'd done was stand there like a dickhead and watch.

THE PHOTOGRAPHER

It was good watching her work in the studio. Very good for an hour or two. Then maybe not so good for a while. After ten hours it was a clear descent into hell.

The trouble was, she was a perfectionist and perfect took time. Time cost money. Clients went from mildly nervous to deeply tense to totally, frenetically, bizarrely apeshit.

13

They knew she was slow – everyone in the business knew she was slow – she was famous for it, but very few people knew exactly how slow. That was when the torture began.

Legend had it one client went completely bankrupt by the second day of a shoot. He could have stopped her, of course. He could have stood up there and then and told her that not only had his budget run out half-way through day one, but also that his entire year's profits were at risk – yet he didn't, and nobody blamed him. It would have been like stopping Michelangelo mid-brushstroke to explain your cash-flow problem as he painted the ceiling of the Sistine Chapel. Sometimes it was just easier to stock up on the Prozac and sweat it out.

She was rich, famous – she'd made it. Trading on past successes, maybe, but still a big name. Her studio complex was the size of an aircraft hangar and you got agoraphobic just walking round it. Like all true talents, though, she specialized in looking broke.

Watching her work you noticed the round bones of her spine that showed through her faded t-shirt like strung marbles as she hunched over the loaded camera. You saw how her long, wild sun-streaked hair got pushed dismissively back into an old rubber band she got from one of the paper boxes. When she was concentrating she would often pull a strand of hair down from the band to chew.

You heard nothing because she very rarely spoke and if she did it was in a whisper and you couldn't hear what she said. After a while the soft puff and squeak of her sneakers as she crept almost soundlessly across the varnished floor, moving from pools of light into total darkness, would get on your nerves.

What you saw when you booked her for a shoot was a tall, youngish woman – not ugly, not plain, but not quite beautiful either – in the throes of an intense, all-consuming relationship with a handful of strobe lights and a beaten-up Rolleiflex. What you got was an illicit love affair with light that made you feel like a snoop even to be watching.

At thirty-five she had been at the top of her profession for several years, having hung there precariously owing to a mixture of driven ambition, technical perfection, and perpetual motion. Her name was legendary in the business and even photographers who trashed her work were in awe of her skill and her knowledge. She was not an instinctive worker — her pictures excited by their composition rather than their content.

She would frown all the time when she worked; it was only when she was finished that she would flash the famous grin, but by then you were too emotionally and financially drained to catch it.

The client that day was Japanese. He'd been warned about her working methods but his company was one of the largest in Japan and well up to the financial challenge. Besides, they wanted the best. The guy had foresight. He had a small roll-up bed with him, a portable TV for the Teletext and the number of an excellent local Japanese restaurant that delivered.

An hour after he'd settled behind the set the news of Mik's shooting had flashed onto CNN and less than an hour after that he was informed his own shoot was in the can. No take-away sushi and no flies on the Futon.

His initial astonishment soon turned to anger, but when he went to speak to the photographer he found her staring into space and completely oblivious to anything around her. She looked so unwell he feared she might have had a stroke, but then the studio manager came to spirit him away and assure him that all was well and the job fairly completed. When he looked back the photographer still hadn't moved. Maybe it was merely a display of the type of artistic behaviour the Americans were prone to. If the shots were no good he could always sue. But he still wasn't sure she hadn't had a stroke or a breakdown.

He bid her farewell and good luck just in case, and was extraordinarily relieved when she finally looked up and smiled and politely wished him the same in almost perfect Japanese.

1

Budapest 1981

The child was intrigued by a small speck of light that
danced away somewhere deep in the heart of the darkness.
He had been scared many times before but never so much
that it hurt.

He wore a small plastic submarine pinned to the inside
of his vest which was a medal for valour given to him by
Father Janovsky for beating the shit out of Istvan Gosser,
even though the boy had been armed with a knife. The
trophy meant nothing today, though. Today his mouth felt
like it was full of pitch and his heart was trying to punch its
way out of his chest. If he had encountered Istvan Gosser
down there in the dark he would have greeted him like a
long-lost friend, and meant it, too.

The light squirmed some more. Perhaps it was a ghost —
the soul of one of the newly dead. It might even be Andreas. The thought turned the boy's knees to sponge. The
place smelt funny. He wished he were somewhere else,
somewhere with proper light. Anywhere. If he could have
remembered his prayers he would have said them. Then a
door opened from nowhere and he thought he would die
from the shock.

The sudden glare startled him. The darkness felt almost
better now. Dark was bad but that bright glare was a
million times worse. Someone — not a ghost, because
ghosts don't wear rubber aprons and smell of tobacco —
pushed past him and the door fell back almost shut again.
The boy was quick, though, pushing his fingers between
the crack and preventing the door from closing properly,

17

even though it hurt. When the corridor was quiet he prised the door open. Then, with a quick glance around first to check he was unseen, he stepped inside.

The local mortuary was one vast, watery-smelling place that was tiled and lit like a public convenience. The bare bulbs strung in a line overhead made everyone look like a corpse whether they were dead or not. If the boy could have seen his own reflection in a mirror right then he would have made himself jump.

His face was whey-white with guilt and his hair, in contrast, looked black. The lights bleached the grime and dirt on his body so that he looked almost clean and his mouth had shrunk into a slit. It was hard for him to imagine he was above ground in that room. It was harder still for him to imagine he would ever get out of there alive.

There was a noise. There were other people in that long room. The boy fled to hide, scuttling across the floor like a rat.

Joszef Molnar farted and Laszlo Kovacs giggled. It was the echo that made it so funny. Whistling was good for that, too. The corpse that lay between them on a trolley did nothing, of course. Not that you could always rely on a corpse to play dead. Sometimes they moved, sometimes they even sat up – it was something to do with the escaping gasses as they decomposed. Joszef and Laszlo had seen it all in their time.

The corpse was covered in the regulation green rubber sheet but attached to the sheet were two pink balloons and a badly hand-written card that read: 'Happy Birthday Lisa'.

Lisa Janus was the local pathologist, a great heifer of a woman who was, nevertheless, the nearest thing to a sex object either man was ever likely to meet. They had been courting her half-heartedly for over a decade and the smell of Lysol was now like an aphrodisiac to them both.

18

As they heard her galoshes squeaking down the dark labyrinth of outer corridors both men assumed appropriately sober expressions. The aprons they wore covered their police uniforms and that was a shame, but it was the rules. Molnar cleared his throat in readiness and Kovacs licked at his moustache to make it neat. Not that it needed further neatening; he'd spent fifteen minutes on it already that morning, trimming it into a straight line with his wife's toenail clippers.

Lisa Janus was not an ugly woman, although she could have been taken for one as her face puckered with annoyance at the sight of the two policemen. Every time those two brought a body in they behaved like fishermen displaying a catch. Then her eyes moved down to the rubber sheet and she noticed the pink balloons for the first time.

'Is this supposed to be a joke, gentlemen?'

A grin broke out on Inspector Kovacs's face.

'Ta-daa!' He pulled the rubber sheet back with a flourish. The sudden movement caused the corpse's head to roll to the side and he straightened it quickly.

Lisa Janus let out a gasp and the two men smirked.

'We thought you'd be impressed,' Kovacs said. 'The doctor was keen to get his hands on this one but we saved him for you.'

The body was that of a young man, not more than twenty years old at the most. He was tall and slim but — most of all — he was extremely, outstandingly beautiful. His fair hair lay curled and plastered around his face. His skin had yellowed but it was a clear complexion, showing that he had, at least, eaten good food at some time in his upbringing.

Looking at his slender corpse was like admiring one of the white marble statues in the National Museum. Earlier on, Kovacs had tied a red ribbon around the young man's penis but then thought he might be taking the joke too far and removed it. Molnar had been disappointed at that — he had thought the red ribbon a hilarious touch.

19

'Who is he?' Janus asked. She was impressed. Her voice had shrunk to a whisper.

Molnar shrugged. 'Who knows? Lowlife. We found him collapsed in the street. No one has missed him – can you imagine that? What a loss to womankind, eh?'

'Someone might miss him,' Kovacs said. He twisted the corpse's arm a little. 'Look.' The name *Paulina* was tattooed on the white forearm. 'I should imagine this proves he had at least one girlfriend.'

'It might be the name of his mother.' Janus leant closer, fingering the tattoo gently.

'Can you work out what he died of?'

Lisa Janus tutted softly. 'Drugs,' she said, 'he died of an overdose.' There was no question in her voice.

The two men shared a quick glance over her head.

'No.' Inspector Kovacs sounded equally sure. 'No drugs, Dr Janus.'

'How can you tell?' She sounded tired rather than angry.

'No syringe nearby, no needle marks. I checked. The boy is clean. He must have had a weak heart, or a fit, or something.'

The pathologist gazed at him. Her eyes were a watery shade of hazel. Brown eyes. That meant she was not a true blonde. That meant . . .

'Would you be prepared to risk money on your theory, inspector?' she asked.

Kovacs sucked in his top lip. A bet? That was different.

'Look.' Janus leant forward and the men leant forward too, because her overall had gaped a little at the top. There was a sweepstake back at the station over whether she wore underwear beneath her gown or not. Confident of a captive audience, she held the corpse's upper arm with both hands and squeezed. To the policemen's amazement a tiny teardrop of red blood appeared at the inner elbow.

'No *apparent* needle marks,' Janus said. 'He used a sharp syringe and most likely he was not an actual junkie. I suspect I could do the same trick with the other arm. He

20

probably injected heroin in one and cocaine in the other. I believe they call it a Speedball in the United States. I dare say the heroin was too pure. There is a batch doing the rounds at the moment. We had a similar death in here last week.' She smiled then, for the first time that day. 'Never take appearances for granted, inspector,' she said, 'they can easily be deceptive, you know.'

'He didn't use drugs! He wasn't a junkie!'

Anger had overcome the young boy's fear and guilt and he stepped out into the full glare of the light for the first time. They all turned to see who had spoken. For a second they looked shocked. He stared at the adults' faces; for a while *they* appeared guilty, then they started to look angry too.

He had a round, shining face, like an angel, and his eyes were swollen with tears. His nose was running because he had not dared to move in order to wipe it. His clothes were clean enough – cleaner than him, at any rate – but they were old clothes, well out of style, and looked strange, somehow not right. The policemen tried to gauge the boy's age. Kovacs guessed eleven and Molnar thought maybe twelve. They knew his sort straight away; the streets were running with them in parts of the city. Lisa Janus did not know his type. She thought he just looked very young and very sad.

'What are you up to, son?' Molnar asked. He had three kids of his own at home and they all got up to tricks but none of them would have been stupid enough to hang around a mortuary for fun. Then he noticed the boy was shaking with fear.

'I was sent here,' the boy said. 'I came to identify . . .' He pointed to the corpse on the trolley in front of them.

'You know this lad?' Kovacs asked.

The boy nodded slowly. 'He's my brother.'

Even in the bright lights he could see the policeman blush. Kovacs looked down at the balloons. He prayed the boy was lying.

'How can you tell?' he asked. Perhaps he *was* lying. After all, he could barely see from where he stood.

'I can smell him,' the boy said. 'I can smell his cologne. I could even smell it in the corridor. That was why I came in here. I knew he was here. I found him myself. He's my brother. I would know him from his smell. He's dead, isn't he?' He tried hard but his voice broke on these last words. Until you say it you don't have to believe it. Now he had said it. Andreas was dead.

Molnar and Kovacs looked at each other.

'How long have you been standing there?' Lisa Janus asked the boy.

'A few minutes. Before you arrived.'

The pathologist tugged the balloons off the sheet and threw them in the policemen's faces.

'Aren't you ashamed of yourselves?' she whispered. 'At least let him come and see if he's right, poor little fellow.'

Kovacs motioned the boy forward. He had to stand on tiptoe to see the body properly. The policemen stood back, their faces grave. Then the boy leant across and kissed the corpse full on the mouth.

Molnar looked away with an expression of distaste.

'Peasants!' he muttered, and Lisa Janus gave him a stern look.

Kovacs pulled the boy away, noticing it took quite a deal of strength to do so, even though the kid felt like a sack of bones underneath his clothes.

The boy was fighting for breath. He had to get some answers out of him before the tears started in earnest.

'What's your brother's name, son?' he asked.

'Andreas.'

'And *your* name?'

The boy stared at his brother's body. He felt dead inside himself, now. Did it matter who he was? Would they arrest him for what he had done? 'Mikhail,' he said,

22

though he had not heard his full name used for years, 'Mikhail Veronsky.' There was no point in lying now. Andreas was dead. Nothing mattered any more.

2

Boston 1966

The day they moved the old windmill from the cowfield behind Mrs Jackson's house to its new home looking out over Saul Peterson's cranberry bog, the local school turned out to cheer its progress down past the wild apple trees along the high street and around Jeakes's corner. The truck doing the towing took the corner a shade too sharp, though, dragging strips of vine down off the white clapboard walls, and a smell of sour grapejuice filled the air along with the stench of the diesel.

Summer was sweet that year. The children ran barefoot down the old dirt track, skirting vast uncut fields that were thick with golden-rod and clicking with grasshoppers, and making for the cooler air that hung around the lower marshes. They waved at the workmen and the workmen waved back, and the sound of the World Series came at them from the radio inside the truck's cabin, mingled with plumes of grey smoke from fresh-lit roll-your-owns.

One child did all the route-planning for the others. When Evangeline Klippel grew up she grew ugly-attractive. At six, though, she was just plain ugly – but that didn't matter so much because she was rich enough not to have to notice.

Ever since the youngest of the O'Connell boys got expelled for doing things to Chimney, the school dog, Evangeline could claim quite fairly to be able to spit further and out-wrestle any of the boys in her class.

She cut a fearsome enough sight, running wild through the emerald marshes, her shock of crinkled brown hair

24

bouncing with each beat of her small thumping feet and the sun glinting off her gleaming silver braces as she smiled her gummy, victorious grin.

She had grass stains on her dress, which would mean trouble at home that night. Not big trouble, just a grumble or two, maybe – and if Patrick jumped up at her the minute she got in, like he usually did, she could say it came off his paws instead.

No one ever scolded Patrick because he was easily the oldest hound the town had ever known – maybe even the oldest hound alive – just like no one scolded her baby brother Lincoln, because he was too little and wouldn't understand.

Last month Evangeline had loved Patrick the most but the sun was no friend to old dogs and made them smell pretty bad. It was this month baby Lincoln had gone and learnt how to smile, too, and so Evangeline loved him far the best for the moment. His grip was getting good, as well – she tested it each morning with her finger. The way he was growing she reckoned they would be climbing the cedar outside the nursery window together by the fall, easily.

As Evangeline stood squinting in the sun Ryan Hooley landed panting at her feet and she squished mud into his ratty hair for losing the race so badly. At that moment Miss Starmount – the crabbiest teacher with the grey-flecked moustache – caught up with them, her face as red and shiny as a rose hip.

More winded even than Ryan Hooley, she was unable to speak and could do no more than stare. Evangeline smiled her gimpy smile at her as Ryan wiped cowpat off his shorts. No one scolded Evangeline because of who she was. Her parents were famous; not world-famous, maybe, but local-famous. They had even been in the papers and on the television.

Darius and Thea Klippel were Boston's golden couple. Both respected artists, though Darius retained the celebrity tag while Thea was an also-ran for her occasional sculptures, they were every bit as beautiful as they were talented. Darius was beautiful; Thea was beautiful; baby Lincoln was drop-dead beautiful, even Patrick the dog was beautiful – in an old kind of way – which made Evangeline the odd one out, though everyone was far too well-meaning to mention it.

Besides, the whole town knew she was not Darius's real daughter; he had adopted her soon after he'd married her mother, so that explained things, somehow. Evangeline had never set eyes on her real father but she knew he must be double-ugly, or she would never have looked as she did.

She had to shoe-up and walk back to school hand-in-slippery-hand with Ewan Goodman, which was punishment enough for running off because his father was a butcher and he smelt of raw meat.

They got back to the school by pick-up time, which meant parents were waiting and the drive was full of cars. Evangeline searched about but there was no sign of her mother's dusty Oldsmobile, which was odd because Thea was always on time, even when she was sculpting.

Evangeline sat on the gatepost in the shade and waited. When the last car had left she was still there, too, shooing a bluebottle and kicking whitewash onto her sandals. A small speck of fear had started to itch at the back of her throat and she had begun swallowing a lot to keep it in check. If no one came she would walk. It wasn't so far, after all – a couple of miles, maybe. She could go past where the windmill had come to rest for the night and see if the workmen would let her have a poke around inside.

It was quiet now, in the drive. She knew the duty teacher was watching her like a sea-hawk but she felt lonely, all the same. When did it start getting dark?

'Did your mother say she'd be late, Evangeline?' It was the same teacher that had chased them across the marsh. Her face had cooled down now and her cheeks were back to mottled purple-white.

'Did she have a meeting or something?'

Evangeline just looked. Why make things easy for her? She must know someone would come for her eventually. There was no point kicking up a fuss. Her mother was always there.

Miss Starmount stared down the road, looking annoyed. 'We'll have to phone,' she said, after a while.

She led Evangeline into the school, clutching her hand in a grip tight enough to mash corn. Thea's phone was engaged. Damn it. Evangeline's mother was getting her into all sorts of deep trouble.

'I guess that means I'll have to drive you home myself,' Miss Starmount said, but she didn't sound as though she cared much for the idea.

Her car was old and the insides smelt musty – a bit like Patrick did before Darius bathed him.

'Do you own a dog too, Miss Starmount?' Evangeline asked. The teacher shook her head. She was having some sort of fight with the clutch. There was no air conditioning in the car and you had to wind the windows by hand if you wanted more. Evangeline felt too hot, but didn't want to wind the window without asking.

The journey was a long one and Evangeline thought about her supper. Then she thought about her father. When he was working at home Darius would always wait by the gates to surprise her when she got back from school.

'Yoo-hoo!' he would yell like a crazy man as she and Thea drove past, and they would both yell, 'Yoo-hoo!' back – at the top of their lungs – then he would climb in and sometimes tickle Evangeline until she begged for mercy. Darius was red-haired and wild. One time he had Mickey Mouse ears on and Thea had gunned the car right past him, fast, and that had made them all laugh till they wept, watching him race up the drive behind them, trying to catch up with the stupid old mouse ears on his head.

They'd put the ears on Patrick later, for a photo, and then on baby Lincoln, too. Evangeline had the photos of

27

Lincoln and Patrick wearing the ears stuck in the wallet of her school bag.

No one yelled, 'Yoo-hoo!' today, though. The drive to Evangeline's house was blocked with cars and the iron gates were hanging wide open. Was there a party? Miss Starmount pulled on the handbrake and got out to look. Evangeline watched her bottom wobble as she walked from the car and back again.

'Come with me,' she said, holding out her hand.

They squeezed past the cars and up the drive. Something was badly wrong. Patrick should have got her scent by then because he had been a hunting dog in his youth and could still smell familiar flesh a mile off. Maybe all the cars had scared him off. Miss Starmount snagged her skirt on a fender and tutted.

The big old house that was Evangeline's home gleamed in the late afternoon sun. The summer before Saul Peterson had taken time off tending his cranberries to paint the whole place afresh and he had done it all white with black shutters, which was the old colonial style, according to Darius, who knew a thing or two about local history — maybe more than old Saul himself. You couldn't see much gleam today, though, for all the people that were standing about outside.

The front door of the house was open, which was strange. Miss Starmount looked quickly down at Evangeline and her expression changed to one of embarrassment. There were blue lights everywhere and blue ribbons around the porch. They pushed on closer but a policeman stopped them. Miss Starmount whispered something into the man's ear and they had a conversation, and then she let go of Evangeline's hand and gave her an odd sort of look. So did the policeman.

People had begun to turn and stare. Someone held a camera out and a flash went off in Evangeline's face, then everyone started pushing.

Things were wrong – really wrong. It was then that the

small speck of fear in Evangeline's throat started to grow out suddenly until it was choking her and, without knowing what she was doing or worrying whether it would scare anyone, Evangeline Klippel threw back her head and howled her longest, loudest-ever howl.

3

Cape Cod

Grandma Klippel made Miss Starmount look like the Sugar Plum Fairy. It wasn't that she was bigger, exactly – or that she was uglier, either – but if it had come to a frowning and squinting competition then Grandma Klippel's expression would have won the cup hands down every time.

The first thing Evangeline had to learn about her grandma was that she was rich – richer than Croesus – and then some. Grandma Klippel was so rich she'd even had holes put in her ears so she could hang her diamonds from them. She was nothing like her son Darius, who would wear baggy-kneed trousers and washed-out t-shirts. Darius had money, even Evangeline knew that, but Grandma Klippel was something else again.

She was smart, with perfect stockings and a buttoned-up cardigan, and she looked taller than she was. She had pale powdery skin on her face and freckled skin on her arms. Her teeth looked false but good, like a row of cultured pearls.

Evangeline had been Lincoln's age when her grandmother last paid a visit, so there was no way she could recognize the old lady who arrived at the house and insisted on taking her off. Nor did she realize exactly how far away 'off' was. If she had done she would have fought to the death to stay right there in Boston until her parents got home and explained the joke.

It had to be a joke. They would never have left her there otherwise. It had taken her a while to realize – at first she had even been frightened – but once she cottoned on to the prank she had laughed until her eyes watered. It was a hoot, all right. They were hiding from her, waiting for her to find them.

Darius loved playing tricks and he'd fooled her many times in the past. This was a good one, though – the best. She just wanted him to get on with it and jump out from where he was hiding. She didn't mind losing, just this once, but she wished they'd come out, that was all.

Evangeline had supposed they'd all be lurking somewhere in the house. She'd wandered off to hunt for them but a policeman had stopped her and taken her downstairs.

'Where are you off to?' he'd used the sort of kind tone people who have no kids of their own use when they talk to children. Evangeline had stared at him. It was *her* house. She had no need to explain. Thea never stopped her if she wanted a wander. She hadn't been stopped since she was three years old and unsteady on the stairs.

'I'm hunting for my parents,' she told him. 'They're hiding here somewhere. It's a game.'

The policeman's expression changed. 'Aren't you the Klippel girl?' he asked.

Evangeline nodded. The man looked sick suddenly, taking off his cap and running a white handkerchief over his forehead.

'You'd better run on downstairs, honey,' he said in a funny voice, 'your mommy and daddy aren't hiding here.'

It was not long after that that the Bentley arrived and Darius's mother climbed out of the back with her tight little smile and her leather high-heeled shoes that matched her handbag, and stole Evangeline back to her house in Cape Cod. She had nipped her up like a pinch of snuff and stolen her away right from under Miss Starmount's nose and the teacher had not said a word, just sobbed and waved a hankie as the car had driven off. Evangeline had always thought teachers were there to look after you until your mother arrived. She hoped Thea would give the woman a good hiding as soon as she got back and discovered what she had done.

'I can't stay long,' she told her grandma as they drove off. 'I have to get back for my tea.'

The old lady said nothing. She was sitting so straight her back never touched the seat and her eyes were runny-looking, as though she was trying hard not to laugh. Every so often her body gave a little shake, as though a snigger had finally leaked its way out, but when Evangeline looked she was never actually smiling.

'You may eat your tea at my house.' The answer had been so long coming Evangeline had forgotten the question. Grandma Klippel's voice sounded thin and scratchy, like wire wool.

Evangeline looked troubled. 'Do you have banana cake?' she asked.

'Thea allows you to eat cake?' The old woman sounded surprised.

'Every day.' Evangeline needed to clear these points up. She'd heard about kids who only ate cake and sweets as a treat. She had never been one of them.

'Anything,' she added, for safety. 'I'm allowed to eat anything. Whatever I like. So is Lincoln.' She didn't want her brother going short, either.

She expected an argument but Grandma Klippel was looking out of the window and had some sort of lace material pressed against her mouth. Maybe she got travel sick, like Patrick.

'Evangeline, you're going to have to learn to be good – very good,' was all she said, and it came out in a whisper.

'OK, Grandma.'

'I can't abide lying, Evangeline. You must always be truthful, dear. Whatever else you do you tell the truth at all times, do you hear?'

Evangeline nodded. She studied the boils on the back of the chauffeur's neck for a while. Perhaps it was the sight of *them* that made the old lady queasy. She'd better not hang around Patrick in the winter, then, because the old dog would get lazy in the cold and mooch about the house all day, and that brought on boils that made the chauffeur's look like mere pimples in comparison.

They drove on in silence past the bleak-looking sand flats, and the sky turned to slabs of slate, so that Evangeline wondered if it was night coming or a storm. A black crow circled the car for a while, making her shiver. She wasn't scared of crows, not unless they got too near, but she was a bit scared of storms. She began to dig in her school bag.

'What are you doing?' Grandma Klippel perked up a bit, though her voice still sounded as though it came from far away.

'Looking for my lucky picture.' She pulled out the shot of Lincoln in the mouse ears. 'Look.' It just *had* to make the old lady laugh. That picture made everyone laugh, guaranteed.

Grandma Klippel took the photo from Evangeline. Her arm smelt of perfume, which was strange, because Thea only wore perfume when she was going somewhere special. She watched the old woman's face. It was a while before she could turn her eyes towards the shot and when she did she didn't laugh, she looked as though she'd been kicked. A bit of her mouth sort of crumpled away and her eyes got thinner, like stick-beans.

'He doesn't mind people laughing,' Evangeline told her, in case she thought it was rude or something.

The old woman raised a finger and touched it to the part of the photo that had Lincoln's face on it. The crow swooped so close its wing touched the window. Evangeline cried out and when she looked back the photo was back on her lap and her grandmother was gazing out at the sea again. Only this time the hankie was stuffed harder against her mouth.

Evangeline was asleep by the time they reached the house and she only woke up as the chauffeur tried to lift her out of the car seat. She wriggled a lot. She didn't want to be lifted. She wasn't a baby. Then she took one look at the house and she knew more than anything that she wanted to go home.

They were absolutely in the middle of nowhere. There was the house and the car and there was them and then – nothing, just the sand and the sea and a handful of gulls overhead who screamed as though they were being gutted alive. Evangeline hated the sea. She turned to look up at her grandmother. This couldn't be true. This couldn't be her home.

'You live *here*?' she asked. She didn't mean to be rude, she just wanted to check the facts.

Grandma Klippel nodded. 'Will you come inside? It'll get chilly out here soon.'

Evangeline swallowed. 'I think I ought to be getting back.' No wonder they'd never had the grandmother to visit – she'd have melted away in all the noise and doggy racket of the house in Boston.

The old lady looked down at her then, looked her right in the eye for the very first time: 'This is your home now, dear,' she said. 'You must live here, with me.'

Evangeline looked back at the house. The place was huge. There must have been over a hundred windows staring back at her. She could see the sky reflected in those windows – flat and grey, like curtains that needed a rinse. Saul Peterson would have needed a whole month off tending the cranberries to paint a place that size.

It was made of clapboard that was painted a dirty blue colour, like the sea should have been, with white around the windows and the doorway. Someone had made an ugly garland around the porch by pressing clamshells into cement. In front of the house were sand dunes and behind the house was the sea. It looked as though the house had turned its back on the ocean altogether because there were no windows on the lower floors on that side. The view from everywhere but upstairs would be of the grass-spiked dunes out front.

'Patrick won't like it here,' Evangeline said. The sand would blow into his eyes and between his paws. They'd taken him onto the beach last year and he'd come back whining with sores between his pads. There were no trees to climb, either. She'd promised Lincoln they'd be climbing trees before the fall. What were her parents thinking of, moving out here?

Her grandmother was going into the house anyway. Evangeline picked up her school bag and ran after her.

4

By the fifth day the joke was wearing thin. Evangeline's family was not hiding in the house; the place was huge but she'd checked it all over and anyway she would have heard Lincoln yelling at night, the rooms were so quiet. Which meant they were on their way, coming for her.

Maybe the clue was in the bit about being so good and truthful. Her grandma had said she had to be good and tell the truth, always. Good children always got their reward; she'd been told that at school often enough. Maybe they were seeing just how good she could be before they came back and surprised her. Being good would be hard, then, because she didn't feel good, she felt mad that they'd gone at all.

Grandma Klippel lived mainly on her own, apart from a handful of staff. As well as the chauffeur, who lived in, there was Mrs O'Reilly, an elderly Irish woman bent up with arthritis who nevertheless hobbled the length of the beach each day with a bag full of half-dead flowers for the house, to cook and serve the meals. The flowers were always anemones. Grandma Klippel liked vases full of them all around the place. By the first day their heads would start to droop and by the next they were powdering tables and mantelpieces with their pollen. Mrs O'Reilly was a good person, even though she'd once been bad. Mrs O'Reilly had been good for many many years now, according to Grandma Klippel, and she didn't seem to have that much to show for it.

Then there was the woman's son, Evan. Evan was simple, like a child, but he could polish like a demon and came up for an hour each morning, just to clean the place. When he cleaned he made a racket with his breathing, like an old man. Evangeline wondered whether he was allergic to all the pollen he dusted.

Evangeline waited for her parents, watching at the window of her room, where she could see for miles. Few cars came by, though, and none ever stopped, apart from the vans with deliveries.

Twice a day a small plane flew by and either buzzed over the house or trawled along the shoreline like a lazy fly. Mrs O'Reilly swore it was Evan's father flying the plane and Evan himself waved at it sometimes and did a mad frenzied sort of hopping dance along the beach after it. But Grandma Klippel told Evangeline it had nothing to do with Mrs O'Reilly or her son. She said Evan had no father, which was why he was simple.

The waiting made Evangeline cry a lot. She wasn't scared, exactly, but she was tired and impatient and her head ached because it was full of so many questions.

The house was mainly hollow inside and a lot of the rooms stood empty. The ones that didn't were filled with old things – dangerous things that broke if you only looked at them. Darius had brought home a few antiques once but these rooms were crammed with them. They were mostly too fancy for Evangeline's taste; she liked new things you could play with. Grandma Klippel's belongings made her feel jumpy and nervous. She wondered how Evan, who was fat and hopped about almost as much as Patrick, ever got by without breaking much as he polished. Then she discovered that Grandma Klippel stuck the ornaments down with tape each morning before he came.

The sea made her twitchy, too. Sometimes she would wake up frightened that it had come right up to the house. It might seep in through the doors and flood the cellar. She could hear it in the dark like a whispering, and often she thought she could make out whole words.

'They're not coming back,' the sea whispered one night.

'What?' It woke her. She stood shivering at the window and watched it heaving. Her eyes were popping and her ears almost fell off her head, they were straining so hard.

'They're not coming back.' Did she hear right or was she dreaming? What did *it* know? She listened till her ears actually ached with the effort. When you listened so hard to silence you thought you could hear anything. She even thought she heard her grandmother crying away in her bedroom.

'They're not coming back.' The idea was ridiculous. Parents didn't just leave their kids — not responsible parents, like hers. Besides, she'd been good for weeks and she'd even picked a spot on the bed for Patrick to sleep on. Sleeping on the bed at night might make up for all the sand.

Grandma Klippel was difficult company. Despite living alone she still carried on as though she had a house full of people, minding all her manners and dressing properly for dinner. Maybe she did it for Mrs O'Reilly and Evan. Evangeline had never dressed up for dinner before, except at Christmas and Thanksgiving. Now she did, though, because Grandma Klippel insisted on it. She also insisted Evangeline sit up straight all the time and she corrected her grammar when she said something wrong.

They said prayers before they ate and more prayers at night. Mrs O'Reilly told Evangeline her grandmother had been a regular at the church along the coast for many many years. That was how they met, Mrs O'Reilly said; she tended the flowers there and Grandma Klippel played the organ on Sundays and did good works during the week. She'd stopped going since Evangeline came to live with them, though. The day before she'd left for Boston was the last day they'd seen her there for prayers. The priest came to the house several times for visits, but Grandma Klippel had never once set foot in that church again.

Evangeline began to wonder how Darius ever grew up so normal.

'Did Darius live here when he was a child?' she asked her grandmother over breakfast.

The old lady always looked surprised when she spoke, as though she'd forgotten she was there, and she always paused a long while before answering, too.

'He most certainly did,' she told Evangeline.

'Did he mind the sea?'

'Mind it? He loved it. It was his passion – sailing, swimming, fishing for crabs down by the old rocks.'

She touched Evangeline on the arm. 'Darius was a very special child, dear. Very talented. Very beautiful. So was your mother. You have a lot to live up to, you know. You have to be special too, Evangeline. Better than all the other children. It would please me so much. Do you understand?'

Evangeline looked thoughtful.

'Is that why Darius wants us to move back out here again?' she asked. 'Because he misses the sea?'

The old lady sniffed. She had blue veins and brown spots on the backs of her hands and sometimes you could see her wrinkles through her make-up.

'Darius is not coming back here, Evangeline,' she said slowly. 'They have gone, dear, all of them. My son, your mother. The baby. Even the dog. I'm sorry.'

'Gone where?' Evangeline looked at her boiled egg and the toast that Mrs O'Reilly had cut into strips. The egg was hard in the middle and dented when she poked the bread into it. Also there was no salt, there never was. For some reason Grandma Klippel would not have the stuff in the house. If you wanted salt you got it outside all right: salt on your face that the sea-spray spat up, salt on your mouth if you forgot to keep it closed, and salt caked onto just about everything that lay in the sea's path.

There was a long silence before Evangeline looked up.

'*Gone where?*' she repeated.

Her grandmother dyed her hair, she was sure of it. When you dyed white hair chestnut what you got was orange.

False teeth and dyed hair. The old lady's hair was the colour of pine pollen.

'Gone . . . away,' Grandma Klippel replied. Her mouth was tugging at the corners again. Evangeline just stared, even though she wasn't allowed to. The tickle of fear had started in the back of her throat. She wanted to go on eating egg but the tickle wouldn't let her.

'How long for?'

Grandma Klippel sighed. 'For ever. I'm sorry.'

Evangeline nodded. A sliver of yolk managed its way down the back of her throat after all.

'Are they on holiday?' she asked.

The old lady shook her head.

'They just went, dear. You must understand that they are not coming back. Ever. They just had to go away, that was all.'

'Without me?' It had to be asked. The yolk was slipping back up again, like snot.

'Without you.'

'I won't see them again?'

'No.'

'But I was *good*!' It came out choked, like a wail.

Grandma Klippel closed her eyes. 'Then you'll just have to be better,' she whispered.

Then all the egg and all the tears and all the snot seemed to well up and ooze in Evangeline's throat at once, so that she didn't know if she wanted to cry or be sick, and she choked and hiccuped but she could suddenly neither breathe nor see.

Her grandmother stood up.

'No tears at the table,' was what Evangeline thought she heard her say. Maybe she was scared she'd make a mess on the white linen tablecloth.

The fog came down the following night and it stayed for a week or more, rolling mournfully around the house and making the sunsets look as though the whole sky was on fire.

When Evangeline stood on the back porch in the evening the sea's voice was muffled, though its smell was sharper than ever. It smelt of decay, despite all the salt. She imagined it heaving with dead fish, wood from sunken boats, empty quahog shells and a gull's corpse that floated on the tide with one filmy eye turned towards the sky that it could no longer soar about in.

The fog was so heavy her hair got wet just standing there and she had to dry it by the fire when she got inside again.

She was going to look for her parents once the fog lifted. There was no doubt about it, Grandma Klippel was wrong and the sea was wrong. Nobody went away like that. Nobody left little girls alone, it just didn't happen. Someone had made a terrible mistake and it was up to her to sort things out. Maybe her teachers could help if she could just get back to her school. Or a policeman. Darius had always taught her to go to the police if she ever got lost while she was out.

She didn't go to her own school any more. Grandma Klippel said it was too far away and sent her to a small private place a mile up the coast instead. She missed her friends – even Ewan Raw-meat Goodman. The new kids acted almost as though they'd been told not to speak to her. Her grandmother had her booked in under a different name, too. Evangeline Cooper – it had been her grandmother's surname before she'd married Mr Klippel, the owner of the local bank. Walter Klippel had died so long ago there were no pictures of him in the house, just a chair Evangeline's grandmother never used because he'd sat in it a lot.

Then one night, when the fog was at its thickest, Evangeline heard a noise like a dog howling and she knew it had to be Patrick. The waiting was over; they'd come back at last. She felt mad with her parents as well as pleased they were back. She opened her window full out and the howling grew louder, and even though it sounded as though it

41

came from miles away – from another country, almost – she just knew he was telling her they were on their way and she would not have to wait much longer.

Excited to the point where she was leaping on the spot, she decided to go down and meet them. Pulling a big warm jumper on over her nightgown and an old pair of boots onto her feet Evangeline ran out of her room and down the landing, yelling to her grandma as she went.

'They're here! Grandma Klippel, they're here, they're outside somewhere. I heard them, I heard Patrick howling, they're here!'

Everything was right all of a sudden. The world stopped tipping crooked and straightened out at last. She didn't care who she woke with her shouting, she was just relieved that the waiting was over. Her legs worked like pistons and she took off down the stairs without once needing to grip on to the banister.

'They're here, I heard them!' Opening the front door was a problem but it was her time at last and she knew she was on a roll, so the catches slipped back without too much fumbling and then the cold wet air hit her face and made her laugh with relief.

'Patrick! Mommy! Daddy! Lincoln!' She knew they'd never left her really and she was too pleased to be mad with them for disappearing like that.

'Evangeline!' So she'd woken her grandmother after all. 'Evangeline!' The old girl could holler louder than she'd thought. Her voice had a high, rasping quality that made it more like a scream than just a yell.

Evangeline took off down the sand flats, towards the sound of Patrick's howls, her brown frizzed hair streaming out behind her like a banner.

'Evangeline!' She wished her grandmother would be quiet so she could hear the dog instead. She'd forgotten where the sound was coming from and she couldn't see further than a few feet in the fog.

The sand was wet and sucked at her feet. She ran until

her legs were tired and then she ran some more with them aching. Her feet got heavy with the sand and then suddenly they were heavy with water. She stopped.

'Patrick!'

There was water on her legs. It hit the top of her boots and then – colder even than ice – it fell inside the boots with a rush.

'Oh my.' It was all she could think of to say and it came out in one word, like a sigh. She looked back, but there was no back any more, it had all gone in the fog. The smell of the sea overwhelmed her and the hiss of the surf was all around. Her bones began to ache from the cold but she wasn't scared yet.

'Yoo-hoo!' she hollered, so Darius would know it was her, and at that moment there was a sharp tugging at her legs as the cross-current came to take her away.

It was the chauffeur who snatched her back, as naked as nature intended, because Grandma Klippel had not given him the option of dressing after she tipped him out of his bed. The man had plunged into the surf like an athlete and wrenched Evangeline up just as the boots were being pulled off her legs by the current.

She popped straight up like a cork from a bottle, unable to differentiate between dark and light and the sea and the shore. He carried her off roughly, hurting her arms.

Her grandmother was waiting on the dunes, her hair as wild as the marsh grass. Her teeth were missing. She carried a storm-torch in her hands and she shone it full into Evangeline's face.

'What in God's name were you up to, child?' Her voice sounded spitty and stretched out and thin with anger and concern.

'I heard them, Grandma, they're coming back. I went to look for them in case they missed me.'

'You *heard* them?'

Evangeline was suddenly short of air. 'I heard Patrick, Grandma, he's barking out there somewhere in the dark. I think he smelt me, you know. He used to be a hunting hound and he can smell . . .'

Her grandmother dropped the torch suddenly and seized Evangeline's face in her white hands. '*Listen*,' she said. '*Listen* to what you heard.'

There was a noise, a noise somewhere out at sea. A lonely noise. The noise Evangeline had taken for Patrick's howls.

'It was a foghorn,' Grandma Klippel said angrily, 'just a foghorn. They're not coming back. Now why won't you believe me?' Her voice sounded like the sea's voice; whispery and tired and dull. 'Evangeline, I told you you *had* to be good,' she said, sadly. 'I thought you understood.'

The chauffeur shook water off himself like a dog and droplets flew out from his body.

On the slow walk back to the house Evangeline looked out across the beach. 'I know you're out there somewhere, waiting for me,' she whispered to her parents under her breath, 'I know you're just lost, that's all. I'll be good and I know I'll find you, don't worry. I promise.'

5

Budapest 1981

The first metro train of the morning rattled slowly out of
the terminal at Vorosmarty ter, waking the boy up. His
nose was running and his bones felt as though they had
been cemented in the night. Andreas was dead. It was the
first thought of the day every day. It came followed
closely by self-pity and then, as he woke properly, by
unbearable, crushing guilt. The guilt was like a large balloon in his chest that got inflated every morning. What
had he done? Why was he alive? He had no right, no right
at all, now that his brother was dead.

He saw Andreas every day. His brother was haunting
him. The thought made him shake, but he knew it to be
true. His brother never came close – he was always hiding
in crowds and dodging round corners – but he'd confront
him one day, Mikhail was sure of it.

He had no one else. His mother was gone. Once he had
thought about her a lot, but now he no longer knew what
it was he should be thinking. Andreas had been his only
parent and he had loved him all the more for that. Then
he had done the terrible thing, and now he was scared of
him.

Someone was watching. Maybe it was the police at last.
He knew they would come for him. He wanted to pee but
instead he stood up slowly, shoving his hands deep inside
his trouser pockets, and mooched off casually. His black
hair looked wet with grease and his face was so pale you
could see veins through the skin. He walked quickly but
he didn't run. If you ran you looked as though you were

up to no good. Walking with your hands in your pockets looked like you were just on your way to somewhere else.

He could hear music playing – a violin or a cello. The sound came from the railwaymen's huts nearby. There was a smell of fresh coffee, too. Mikhail felt his stomach begin to contract with hunger. The men in there would be shaving. He thought he could smell the soap – lavender, maybe. It was as though the balloon in his chest had burst. Beads of angry sweat appeared on his forehead, even though it was winter and well below zero outside. He sobbed out loud and kicked at the wall as he passed it, and a lump of china tile fell off onto the ground.

The metro was old. The place was crumbling. The smell of the coffee wouldn't go away, even though he had passed the last of the huts now.

The station was not a deep one and there were only a few steps to the pavement. The air that hit him was so cold he almost urinated where he stood. He set off for the old fruit market to steal some food.

They had made him go to a hostel at first, after Andreas's death. The place was warm and the food first-rate, but he had found he couldn't stand the fear of waiting all the time to be arrested. They would have come for him before long, he was sure of that. The two policemen at the mortuary had looked at him as though they'd known something was up. He couldn't just wait for them; he'd had to run away.

He'd gone back to the room he'd shared with his brother, but the locks had been changed, which didn't surprise him. He'd tried with his penknife, just in case, but the padlock held firm. Maybe it was just as well – they would have come for him there too, sooner or later. He'd wanted to get inside for a little while, though, just to check; to make sure things had really happened as they had.

So now he was living on the street. Andreas would have been mad with him – it was the one thing they'd always avoided. He pushed off down Vaci utca and past all the old pastry shops. The wind was cold but he wore his brother's coat and it was a good one; it kept him almost warm.

He had always envied Andreas's heavy coat and now it belonged to him. It had been lying around at the mortuary and he'd taken it, just like that. It was too big but that was all the better because it kept his legs warm, too. That was the other thing about the hostel: they had made all the boys wear short pants and he had felt stupid in them, like a child. He was twelve years old, nearly thirteen. No one of his age should be made to wear short pants, it was ridiculous.

He pulled one of Andreas's cigarettes out of the breast pocket of Andreas's coat and lit it with a match from Andreas's box. The smoke kept his mouth warm. He cupped his hands over his face and inhaled as deeply as he could.

6

Cape Cod 1966

The Bentley was a pretty good drive – maybe even better than the Oldsmobile. Evangeline had made quite fair friends with the chauffeur on the school run and she knew the car had power steering and a sixteen horse-power engine – which meant that even if you had sixteen real horses harnessed to the front of the chassis the car wouldn't have gone any faster than it did.

Grandma Klippel had paid good money to get her into that school. She could tell from the other grand cars in the drive and from the way the kids spoke without moving their lips much, but despite all that money they still had sneers and secrets leaking out of those mean little mouths.

Evangeline knew something else, too – a secret not even the know-all-miss-snotty kids knew. A secret even her grandmother wasn't aware of. A terrible thing. She knew that her parents were dead.

They were all dead: Thea, Darius, baby Lincoln – maybe even Patrick, too, though she wasn't sure about that. The chauffeur had told her by sheer mean mistake. He hadn't meant to, she knew that. It had sort of slipped out while they were talking one day. It wasn't his fault and she never found out how he knew, because Grandma Klippel had no idea – she knew that for sure.

'My grandmother told me they'd gone away,' she'd said. Grandma never lied; it just wasn't possible.

The back of the chauffeur's neck had glowed strawberry-patch red.

'Maybe that's what she thinks,' he'd told her after a

while. It had been difficult for him to say it at all. The words seemed caught somewhere in his throat.

'Maybe she's right.' Evangeline didn't know what was worse: that they'd gone away or that they'd died. There didn't seem a whole mess of difference if they were never coming back. Dead sounded worse, though. She felt that snot in the back of her throat again, distorting all her words when she tried to speak.

'Maybe,' the chauffeur echoed.

'But they are dead.'

'Yeah. I'm sorry. Don't tell your grandmother. Please.'

It was a while before Evangeline could talk at all. Dead: like the fish and the seagull, and empty, like the quahog shells. Floating on the oily surface of the water with their eyes all white like pearls, and blind.

'Did they drown?' she asked.

'I doubt it.' So he didn't know either.

'Why doesn't my grandmother know?' she asked.

The chauffeur shrugged. She could see his eyes in the rear-view mirror. He looked scared.

'Maybe because she's old. Maybe the shock . . .' his voice faded away. Evangeline nodded. The shock would make her ill. The thing was to keep it from her. It sounded like a useful plan. Darius would be proud of her when he got back. She was confused, or was she? She still *felt* they were all coming back, that was the problem. She still felt it as much as when she knew they were gone. It just didn't happen. Nobody left their kids alone for too long.

The good thing was she hadn't cried properly – not in front of the chauffeur and not in front of the other kids, anyway. The chauffeur would have been embarrassed about telling her all over again if she had. She didn't want him feeling awkward over such a stupid mistake. It could have happened to anybody. And she definitely didn't cry in front of her grandmother. Keeping it secret was important; if she'd cried as much as she wanted to the old lady would have known something was up and maybe even have died herself.

She'd known the other kids were watching her at school, she could feel their squinting eyes on her back throughout each and every class. Did they know too? She always sat up straight as a post, just like her grandmother had been teaching her, and she never let anything show on her face. She knew they felt cheated, somehow, and she was glad. The secret made her special; important, even. She had to be special, Grandma Klippel said that over and over. Make Darius proud of her. Make Thea proud of her. It was something to do. It was a way of working to get them all back.

Evangeline watched the coastline go by as they drove back to the house. The sea looked so different with a slick of sun on it. It didn't scare her when it looked like that. She didn't think her parents were on the other side of the sea any more, either.

'Do you know if Patrick died too?' she asked.

'Who?' the chauffeur's voice started to sound queer again.

'The dog. Patrick.'

The chauffeur cleared a frog from his throat. 'Maybe. I don't really know. Sorry.'

Evangeline nodded again. That made sense. If they were all gone then Patrick would have gone with them. Otherwise he'd have sniffed her out by now. It was worth asking, though. He might just have been roaming the grounds of their old house somewhere, howling and looking for her. At least he wasn't lost somewhere, starving. A sudden thought came to her.

'Old Mr Carstairs's heart gave out when they told him his wife had died,' she said. 'I think maybe that's why Grandma's been told they're all away on holiday somewhere. I wouldn't want her to be sick too.'

If the chauffeur said anything in reply then Evangeline missed it. His neck was getting hotter by the minute, though. She could fry eggs on that neck now, she thought, with all that grease there, too. You could see the grease in a line on his collar. She wanted to pull her photo of Lincoln out of her school bag to look at but she didn't dare because she didn't want to cry in front of him.

When they got home Grandma Klippel was outside waiting for them. At certain times it was hard to imagine how tough the old lady could be, and this was one of those times. With her linen skirt flapping about her knees and her skinny, saggy-fleshed arms hanging out of her cardigan sleeves, she looked almost frail. The light was going and her expression was hard to gauge. There was a smell of beach plum blossoms and Evangeline remembered it was nearly spring.

There were circles of dark skin around her grandmother's eyes, as though she'd been rubbing, or reading without her glasses, or something.

'Hello, dear. And how was school?' she asked.

Evangeline looked back at the chauffeur. 'Fine.'

Grandma Klippel smiled. 'Do you know you are at the same school that my son went to? Darius was at that school for four years and he adored every minute of his time there. I used to wait for him to come home each afternoon just like I am standing here waiting for you. Isn't that wonderful?'

She was the only person Evangeline knew who could smile without looking happy. She tried to smile back but the right look just wouldn't come. When she started to shiver she pretended to her grandmother it was the wind making her cold, even though they both knew there wasn't any more than a breeze blowing that afternoon.

She fell ill on that day; the fever lasted a week or more and she was off school for a month. When she got up again it was almost summer and her grandmother took her on a berry hunt just as though nothing had ever happened.

On her first day back at the school Evangeline got sent home early for fighting. She'd got angry over nothing much other than her unhappy life and she'd jumped on the girl with the

51

most know-all face in the class for little more than the fact that the girl had a father and she did not. When she jumped the girl went down like a pile of old paper, instead of fighting back. So the car had been summoned to pick her up.

The chauffeur's name was Cecil. It was a strange name and she didn't know if she dared use it. He came from Manchester in England, which was why he talked so funny. He had a colour photo of his family in his glove compartment. She wondered if he missed them as much as she missed her own.

This time Cecil stopped the car. Not quickly, but just slowing down onto a verge as though stopping to point out some tern that dotted the sky overhead. The windows came down automatically and they both sat there a while, listening to the wind cutting through the dune grass. There was a rock nearby that was covered in creamy-white shells dropped by the gulls. Beyond the rock was a lonely-looking yellow sandbar that the tide was busy trying to cover up.

Evangeline's nose caught the smell of fresh smoke and when she looked around Cecil was drawing on a weedy-looking roll-your-own.

'Do you mind?' he asked, and she shook her head, flattered by his manners. He had lowered the glass between them so that his voice didn't sound so funny. It was nice, sitting there quietly. After a while Evangeline started to cry but he didn't make a fuss, or try to stop her. He just let her cry until her eyes were empty of tears and then he took his own hankie down to the water and brought it back wet, so she could wash her face with it.

'She might know, you know,' he said, meaning Grandma Klippel. Evangeline shook her head.

'If she knew she'd have said. She never lies, she told me so. She wouldn't say anything unless she believed it. Why do people die?'

'God knows.' Cecil spat a fleck of tobacco. He was not a philosopher. Evangeline thought the answer was fair enough. She never asked the question that was really troubling her, though: why did they die without her? Why hadn't she gone as well? Didn't they want her with them? Thea, Darius, Lincoln and Patrick. All together. Without Evangeline. The thought came into her head that they had hated her. Why? Was it her school grades? Was it because she was so ugly? It just didn't make sense unless you looked at it that way.

Maybe they did hate her, after all. She would never have considered doing anything without them.

'Why don't you take a run on the beach for a bit?' Cecil asked. 'Your grandmother's not expecting you back yet. Get a bit of colour into your cheeks.'

She took Cecil's advice, running wild till her legs ached, and the air did feel good. Then they drove back to the house.

'We have whole baby chickens for supper, Evangeline, with herby gravy,' her grandmother said. 'Go and wash up, there's a good girl.' She was wearing a lilac-flowered dress and a matching duster coat, as though she'd been out. She never told lies. She would have said.

7

Nothing was spoken, then, and as Evangeline grew a little older the question 'Why?' hung constantly in her head, like a small bird on a perch in an empty cage, pecking away all the time. When she got a little wiser she asked Cecil how he knew and he said he'd just known, that was all, which seemed to her a stupid kind of an answer.

Then she thought about it properly and she started feeling better. If Cecil had 'just known' they were dead then maybe she knew that they just weren't. Maybe you could sense these things and Cecil was wrong. She tried not to think about it too much. It had made her ill the first time and she didn't want to be ill again.

It was as though a fog slowly settled around the whole affair and as time pushed an ever-widening space between herself and her parents she began to despair of ever finding out the truth.

And just as Evangeline grew older, so Grandma Klippel seemed to grow younger. She was not such an old lady, after all. When she had first come to the house Evangeline had thought her grandmother to be about ninety years old, but now she knew she was nearer fifty. Maybe Darius's disappearance had made her younger because she spoke a lot about when he was a boy and acted half the time as though she were just a young mother again.

Shock over the deaths created some sort of malfunction between Evangeline and her grandmother. She needed the old lady's sympathy and pity, but she knew she could never seek it because that would have meant giving away the secret that was so important to hide.

They lived in the same house, then, and her grandmother was kind, but that was all. Each of them was too empty inside to nurture any real affection. Grandma Klippel would not allow crying in public, though Evangeline heard her grief at night sometimes, when she was alone in her room. She wanted to please her grandmother. Most of all she wanted to please her parents, wherever they were. It was as though they were always there somewhere, watching and waiting; holding their breath until she did something they could be proud of at last. Darius and Thea: beautiful and talented. All of them, some place special, some place she couldn't reach because she wasn't special enough.

Evangeline felt like a ghost. She grew to realize that wishing she were with her family was the same as wishing she were dead too, but that was all she could think about. It was impossible not to imagine that they were having fun somewhere without her. Every bone in her body ached to join them.

When Cecil left to get married, another man took his place. The new man was older and Evangeline imagined out of boredom that he was in love with her grandmother. Unlike Cecil the new man knew nothing about her parents. He spoke little English and he went home at night. They would be all alone in that house then, with just the sea for company.

Evangeline thought about Darius as a small boy, playing happily in the surf. She even tried it herself a few times. The beach was OK in the summer. The sand would be warm on top, though it got colder and wetter the further your feet sunk. She liked the white driftwood and even took a few pieces home, which pleased Grandma Klippel for some reason. She remembered Cecil telling her he'd seen a whale swimming off the coast and that the next day it had been dead and washed up on the beach. Maybe that was how she'd find *them* one day – Darius, Thea and Lincoln, lying in a row on the sand, bleached and blistered by the sun and the salt in the water. She became afraid to go down onto the sand at all after that fancy.

For Evangeline's eighth birthday Grandma Klippel had organized something extraordinary, though she refused to say what. Things stirred in the old house at last. Two rooms were decorated, which meant there was some life in the place as local handymen arrived along with radios, kettles and twenty cans of apricot-coloured paint. Even when the rooms were finished the smell of paint lingered for a couple of weeks.

On the morning of her birthday Evangeline went to school as usual, but when she got back there was someone waiting on the porch with her grandmother. The woman was small with wiry black hair, and dressed in clothes that reminded Evangeline of her mother.

Grandma Klippel was beaming.

'Today is a special day, Evangeline,' she said. 'This is Miss Clayburg and she's to be your tutor, stopping with us for the whole of the summer.' She bent down closer, to be on Evangeline's level. 'You remember what a famous artist your father was, Evangeline?' Her breath smelt of violets. 'And your mother, of course. They had great talent, both of them. I told you. Never forget that.'

The small plane buzzed overhead, drowning out some of her words, but Grandma Klippel ignored the noise. It was almost as though the plane was eavesdropping. Evangeline looked upward. The sun had caught the plane's wings. There was a white trail winding behind it, like a long smokey cloud.

'I know Darius was not your father by blood but I believe somehow you may have inherited his talent. I have seen the green shoots in you already and I want to nurture those shoots. You are to learn to paint, Evangeline. Miss Clayburg is an art tutor from one of the greatest schools in New York. We can thank God she has been kind enough to come all this way out here and take you under her wing.'

Miss Clayburg smiled. She had crooked teeth but they were white, like the driftwood.

'It was no kindness, Evangeline,' she said. 'When I received your grandmother's letter and read who your father was I felt honoured to have been asked at all. I was Darius Klippel's greatest devotee. If he has passed on half his talent you will be a very special little girl indeed.'

Grandma Klippel had more in store. 'Close your eyes,' she told Evangeline.

Evangeline closed her eyes and felt herself being led inside the house. They laughed as they took her up the stairs, counting each step out loud and warning her to take care on the last one. Then they went up again and again, towards the attic.

Evangeline had never been to the top of the house before, Grandma Klippel always kept those doors locked. She could hear the key turning now and then she felt the sun on her face and a greasy smell of oil in her nostrils.

'Open!' Grandma Klippel exclaimed.

The sun was dazzling, blinding. Evangeline squinted, trying to make out the shapes in the room. Miss Clayburg took her by the arms and turned her about slowly. They were in an artist's studio, much like the room Darius had worked in at home, only bigger. The light came from the roof, which was all windows, and the smell came from the tubes of paint, which were lined up in their hundreds, ready for use. There were canvases and easels and several unfinished paintings of Darius's, piled up along the walls.

Grandma Klippel clapped her hands together.

'Well, Evangeline?'

Evangeline had stopped breathing. The smell of the oil paints was like a knife cutting into her soul. Every time she breathed in she was back in the studio in Boston and Darius was fooling around and making her laugh.

Sometimes he put paint on his face. Or he would do lightning scribbles with charcoal and draw funny pictures of Lincoln with his eyes crossed. Once he let Patrick loose with a paintbrush between his teeth and framed the result. Her mother used to joke it was the best work of art in the house.

Not breathing was difficult but she didn't want to know that smell any more, it hurt too much.

'What do you think, dear?'

It wasn't Grandma Klippel's fault, she wasn't to know. She was looking happier than Evangeline had ever seen her. Miss Clayburg looked as though she was in the throes of ecstasy.

Evangeline smiled. 'It's an artist's studio,' she said.

'It was Darius's studio, dear, when he was at home,' her grandmother told her. Her eyes looked pale and filmy with excitement and memories. 'Now *you* are to use it.'

'But I don't paint.' It seemed like a simple truth.

Grandma Klippel was busy looking round. 'We'll see, we'll see,' she whispered. 'I know you have the flair, Evangeline. Look at the driftwood you bring home, just like my son did when he was your age. He used to spend hours gazing at the shapes. You have an eye for beauty and that is an important start. Miss Clayburg can teach you the rest.

'Knowing that this place will be used again has made me happier than I can imagine.' She was speaking to Miss Clayburg now, above Evangeline's head.

Miss Clayburg must have seen her expression, though, because she smiled down at her.

'Don't worry, Evangeline,' she said, 'we'll treat it as a game at first – just have some fun messing around with all the colours and things. Look,' she took Evangeline across to a table covered with paintboxes, 'did you ever see a rainbow? Yes? Maybe we could create one on this sheet of paper here, using these colours. Do you remember how it looked? Draw the shape.' She pressed a pencil into Evangeline's hands.

Evangeline reached across the vast expanse of white paper. It was important to do well. It was important not to make a mistake. She had to be good. She had to be careful.

People were watching. Live people. Dead people. She leant across and slowly drew a neat but teeny arch in the middle of all the white, being more careful than she had ever been before in her life. Miss Clayburg's smile became a little more squeezed.

'Good,' she said, 'but wouldn't you like to make it bigger? How about filling the whole page?'

Evangeline reached for the rubber and erased the first arch, making sure all the marks were gone and the page was clean as a whistle again before drawing a slightly larger second one in its place. She used her elbow to make sure the arch was perfect in shape. She was careful again and took a long time about it. Any bits that went wrong would be rubbed out right away. In the end Miss Clayburg took the eraser away from her altogether. Evangeline was aghast. The picture would never be perfect now.

She watched the tutor wet a brush and sloosh paint all over the arch. Nothing looked right now. The colours ran into one another. Warm tears welled in the back of her eyes. Miss Clayburg should have known better – anyone could see she'd made a mess. Evangeline began to cry more but she kept the tears balanced inside her eyes, so they didn't spill.

'What do you think?' Miss Clayburg said.

'It's very messy,' Evangeline told her in a small voice. She tried to sound polite. Miss Clayburg smiled.

'Look,' she said, pointing to some of Darius's paintings. The paint was all over the canvas. Colours clashed. Edges had been blurred. Nothing looked like anything. 'You don't have to be neat to be an artist.'

'Maybe,' Evangeline replied, but she didn't sound convinced. She wanted to be neat. She wanted to be perfect. Then her parents could be proud of her and Grandma Klippel would go on smiling the way she was now.

8

Budapest 1983

Mikhail had decisions to make. He had lived on the streets for over a year and the truth was he was not a natural survivor. Lots of boys were. He thought of them as corks, floating along on the surface of all deprivation while he was sinking, slowly but consistently going under.

He ate but he was still starving. In the winter he froze and in the summer he was ill. He felt unwell all the time. Sometimes he even thought he was dying. The idea terrified him, but after a while things got so bad that he thought it was what he wanted, after all.

He had not spoken to anyone properly since Andreas's death, although sometimes he addressed himself to Andreas personally. At first the lack of companionship was the hardest thing to suffer but before long he almost relished it. He was a dark shadow on the streets; in a way it was rather romantic.

He had grown a lot in the last couple of years, despite the lack of proper food, and his brother's coat was no longer too big for him. Although he was still only fourteen people had stopped reacting to him as though he was a child, which made him feel safer. A child alone got relentless hassle from the police. A young man, though, was largely ignored, as long as he broke none of the laws.

Despite his deprivations, Mikhail was methodical about reading a newspaper. Sometimes he stole them and often he just took them from litter bins, but always he read as many as he could lay his hands on, as they were his only link with the proper world. When you stopped knowing what was happening in the world you were no longer a part of it. Andreas had read a lot. It was he who had taught Mikhail that.

Mikhail was doubly pleased if he could get the *Daily News* since he could still read a little English as well as Hungarian. Andreas had learnt English at school and he had taught Mikhail too, for he said it was the language of America, where he was bound when he became famous. These things were important, Mikhail could see that. Keeping in touch was important and so was speaking another language. Their mother had made Andreas learn English and, although Mikhail spoke it badly, he needed to remember what it was he had learnt, otherwise he would know he had given up. Giving up was like waiting to die.

When he caught sight of himself in mirrors he was always shocked. His hair was longer and darker. He asked one of the other boys he met to cut it with his knife but the boy turned on him and stole fifty filler from him instead.

Sometimes he did make friends of a kind. There was a boy with the nickname of Tincan he sometimes met down in the metro. Tincan had given him useful advice about where to sleep without being bothered too much. And then there were the men.

Mikhail was approached on average twice a week in winter and as much as three times a day in the summer. They all wanted to help him and they all wanted to be friends. It was Tincan who told him to be careful. The religious ones were the worst, he said, the ones who said they'd pray for you and show you a warm hostel where you could sleep the night for nothing.

'Nothing is for nothing,' Tincan told him, though even he had a couple of regular men friends he would disappear with now and again.

There was one man Mikhail saw a lot, around and about the city streets. Sometimes he would find Mikhail on a bench in the park and just sit chatting, and sometimes he would pass him in the street and nod his head as though they were old acquaintances. The man seemed pleasant enough and even Tincan appeared to like the look of him. He was shortish and middle-aged but smart and well-dressed, like an ordinary businessman.

The man's worst fault was that he appeared to be a little shy, which made him rather boring at times. Mikhail felt safe enough with him, though – the man had never tried propositioning him. The most he had ever done was to share his sandwiches one day when Mikhail was too hungry to refuse them.

Tincan told him the man was wealthy.

'How can you tell?' Mikhail asked.

Tincan shrugged. 'His haircut. The cologne he wears. And did you see his watch? Tell me it's not real gold and then let me tell you you're a fool.'

'I wonder where he lives?' Mikhail asked.

'Dunno,' Tincan said. 'Why don't you follow him if you're so interested?'

That winter the sleeve of Andreas's coat split open and Mikhail grew still more depressed. Too dispirited even to steal food or new clothing, he would often mooch up to Castle Hill and look down on the city and its river and dream of hot pork stew and chocolate and nut pancakes.

Tincan grew desperate at the state he was in.

'You must get money, Mikhail, or you'll starve! Look at you – you don't wash, you don't eat. What's the matter, don't you want to live?'

Mikhail did not have the words to explain how he felt. To Tincan existence was all; the good life lay in the future, and if he could just get through the winter then things would pick up by spring. He told Mikhail he was going to become a famous actor and he never voiced any doubts over the possibility of a sparkling career.

'Take money where you can get it, Mikhail,' he said. 'Don't be a fool. Stupid men die, you know – it's the clever ones that survive.'

Tincan survived by meeting men under the iron bridge in the park.

'You just have to wait there, that's all. They give you money, Mikhail, it's OK. Some give a lot – look.' He held some notes out for Mikhail's perusal.

'I don't want to get money like that,' Mikhail said.

'But you don't argue when I offer you food it has paid for,' Tincan said.

'I don't need your food.'

'Don't be stupid!' Tincan grabbed him by the arm. He had hair the colour of linen and a line of matching fuzz across his pale top lip. His eyelashes were nearly white. 'Look, Mikhail,' he said, 'it's not that bad, you know, what I do. What do you think? You don't have to like it, you just have to do it. Tell me, do you masturbate? Ever? Eh? Of course you do. Well, do you hate yourself so much for that? No. Well think of this as being similar, only with someone else, that's all. I do it only to live, Mikhail. It's not so important – life is what counts. One day I'll be working in the film studios in Hollywood and I'll look back at all this and laugh and be glad I was so crafty. Then I'll remember my poor stupid friend Mikhail who died of cold and starvation because he was so foolish and stubborn. That's how it is, you know, that's what will happen.'

Tincan took Mikhail to the park the following evening. At first it was half-light and there were children around, so they smoked a cigarette and shared stale cake until it got darker, and then the children were gone and the whole park fell silent.

Tincan went off for a piss and Mikhail almost bolted. There was a wind hissing through the trees and the branches creaked overhead. He was afraid of ghosts and glad when Tincan got back. Then he saw that his friend was followed and his heart leapt with a greater fear.

The man kept his head down. He wore a knitted cap and his hands were firmly stuffed into the pockets of a greatcoat. He cleared his throat a lot but didn't speak.

'This is Pepe,' Tincan whispered, 'I call him that because of the moustache. He's a policeman but I'm not supposed to know that. He comes here once a week when his wife visits her mother. He's a bit shy of the bathroom so try not to breathe in too much, but apart from that he's not bad. He won't speak in case anyone recognizes his voice.'

Mikhail stared across at the man, who was hopping from one foot to the other in the cold. White breath rose in a plume from his nostrils. His head nodded once. OK.

Tincan had evaporated, though Mikhail could hear his rasping breaths from behind one of the metal posts. The thought that his friend was within earshot made him feel even more awkward.

He walked across to the man. Tincan was right, he smelt of stale fish and cabbages. He was chewing something – tobacco maybe – and he spat it out as Mikhail arrived.

'Have you got the money?' Tincan had told Mikhail to ask first. The man held his hand out; there were coins in his palm, glinting in the lamplight.

It was the clumsy attempts at tenderness that appalled Mikhail more than the lust. The man pulled his face closer beneath the lights, and tried to kiss him on the cheek, but Mikhail turned away. The man's eyes looked regretful. He sighed a deep sigh and unzipped his flies, exposing a thick white cock. He gripped Mikhail's shoulders as he was masturbated and Mikhail worried that Andreas's coat might tear.

Tincan was right; it was nothing, really. The man came quickly, with a grunt, and his knees buckled heavily, which meant he almost pulled Mikhail over. He looked different when he had finished – the sadness had gone from his eyes to be replaced by a cold look of disgust. He pushed the coins into Mikhail's hand in a business-like way and pressed his cock back into his trousers.

There was a splash of white semen on Andreas's coat. He walked quietly down to a small pond and washed it off with his handkerchief. He thought he saw Andreas's face reflected in the dark water, smiling back at him, and he almost screamed. The water was ice-cold. He took a mouthful without caring how dirty it might be, rinsed his gums, and spat it out. It made his teeth begin to ache.

The man stayed in his mind; his sad eyes, his smell, the grunting he had made. He wanted to wash the memory away, too. He wanted to cry for his mother, even though he had never really known her. When Tincan came over, though, he stood up and laughed instead, flicking one of the coins into the air.

'What did you have to do?' Tincan asked. He looked cold through from the waiting.

'Nothing much,' Mikhail told him.

Tincan grinned. 'See? I told you it was easy money. OK?'

'OK,' Mikhail said.

Andreas had told him about the parties their mother used to have after the last stage show on a Saturday night, when there would be huge plates of gleaming salami and cold sausage and bottles of Bull's Blood to wash it all down. Mikhail had never tasted wine but he thought it sounded wonderful.

Sometimes he would stand alone on the ridge of Castle Hill for hours, until it grew dark. He liked watching the floodlights come on along the bridges because they looked like diamonds strung across black velvet and this, for some reason, also reminded him of his mother.

He had never seen his mother dressed up, though, except in his imagination. The one thing he wanted was what he knew he could never have, which was to go back in time and live happily with his mother and Andreas, in the days when she was a successful club act and not living in prison, which was all he could recall of her.

Tincan still worried about him.

'You look ill, Mikhail. You should take care. I saw you yesterday, just wandering about in the cold. Now that sort of thing will kill you, don't you know that? Stay where it's

65

warm, Mikhail. Eat plenty. Beg if you have to; the money is good in this weather because the people feel their consciences prick when they see us standing there, blue with the cold. I got fifty forint in half an hour yesterday, did I tell you?' He grabbed Mikhail by the shoulders and stared him full in the face. 'Do well, Mikhail,' he whispered, 'we are going places, you and I. We're special. We have been marked out for importance. Take it how you can and when you can and don't worry how you get there. Just do it, OK? You think too much. Thinking can kill you.'

But Mikhail was no longer interested. When Tincan tried to cut him into his drug dealing schemes he left the shelter of the metro altogether and never went back.

The businessman approached him just as he was sure he would die of it all. At first they just chatted as usual but then the man leant across closer and Mikhail could smell the expensive cologne Tincan had noticed.

'You look a little unwell,' the man said quietly. 'May I offer you a bed for the night?'

Mikhail looked at him. The man's face had turned pink with embarrassment and his eyes looked comically mournful. How could he turn him down? He had no choice. It was either go with him or die out here.

The man talked nervously and cleared his throat a lot as they walked. His name was Claude and he came from Switzerland, though his Hungarian was almost perfect. He was not enormously wealthy – Mikhail saw that the minute they entered the building he lived in, which was in a small shabby street off a modern square behind a synagogue in Obuda. He had three locks on his wooden door and once they were inside the apartment he reached up to close a large bolt on the inside.

Claude did not live alone in the apartment. His father, a bedridden invalid, lived in a room at the far end of the passage. The old man was deaf but not so deaf that they could afford to talk in anything above a whisper. All the curtains were drawn because the old man was allergic to prying neighbours. Mikhail didn't mind this so much, though, because it meant the place was warm. He felt as though he had never been so warm before in his life and he took Andreas's coat off for the first time that winter.

Claude made them tea and then talked about his job. He worked in a bank – nothing important, just mundane stuff – but he also worked as a photographer, which excited him, and which he said prevented him from going insane with boredom. He had converted a bedroom in the apartment into a studio and took his shots there, some of which had been subsequently published in various magazines. He was proud of his work, Mikhail could tell by his eyes when he spoke about it.

'I would enjoy doing some shots of you some time,' Claude said. He wore nail varnish on his fingernails. The warmth of the room had overcome Mikhail; he was struggling to keep his eyes open. 'If you don't object, of course,' Claude added.

He cooked Mikhail a meal and ran him a scented bath before showing him where he could sleep. The softness of the bed filled Mikhail with melancholy and he went off to sleep with tears running down his cheeks.

The first morning went well. Claude showed Mikhail proudly around his 'studio' and then he brought out some shots he had taken previously. The walls of the room were painted dark and there was a stained sheet hanging in one corner, as a backdrop. In front of the sheet was a white umbrella on a stand and Claude's camera on a tripod.

The photos were innocent enough: soft-focus shots of a woman with too much lipstick on her mouth, a couple of black-and-whites taken at a railway station, and a shot of a boy a bit older than Mikhail, sitting on a stool and smiling at the camera. The boy was wearing old-fashioned-looking clothes: a cream-coloured nylon shirt and the sort of jumper Mikhail had worn to school as a kid, but he looked pleased enough.

Claude had gone into the kitchen to cook breakfast and the smell of the bacon made Mikhail's stomach start to complain. He mooched around the studio. There was a cupboard with the door half open. Inside the cupboard was a pile of cardboard boxes. He pulled the top one open and there were shots in there of the same boy, only this time he didn't have his cheap shirt and jumper on. This time he didn't have anything on.

Claude was whistling in a dreary style. Mikhail replaced the box and crept out of the studio and along the corridor to the old man's room.

Claude was still whistling. Mikhail listened at the door for a second before pushing it open. He wasn't scared of making a noise; he had developed a talent for moving about silently. The room was dark, apart from a dull light that seeped through the holes in the brown lace curtains. There was a warm smell of sickness and urine and disinfectant.

The old man lay on a large wood-framed bed, his head lolling back onto a couple of white pillows. It was a moment before Mikhail realized his watery eyes were open and looking directly at him. A spasm of fear ran through his gut, even though he knew the old man could do nothing to harm him.

'Fuck off.' The old man's voice wheezed out of a thousand bellows.

Mikhail shut the door quickly and crept back into the studio. Claude arrived a few minutes later with a jug of fresh coffee.

'Did you like the photos?' he asked. 'What do you think?'

Mikhail shrugged. 'I don't know. I wouldn't know good from bad. They look nice enough.'

Claude took the photos from him.

'Do you think you could do better? I could pay you to model for me.'

The coffee was too sweet on an empty stomach. Mikhail took the bacon sandwich Claude offered him and grease ran down his chin as he bit into it. Claude had fed his father first

68

– he still smelt of the sickroom. No wonder he wore such expensive colognes; the stench of illness clung like wet fog. It reminded Mikhail of the mortuary.

'Did you pay that other boy?' he asked. Claude looked down at the shot.

'That one? No. He is a relative. My nephew.'

'How much?' Mikhail asked.

'What?' Claude looked surprised.

'How much will you pay me? For artistic shots?'

Claude pulled a face. 'Twenty forint? You have a roof over your head too now, you know.'

'Twenty-five, or I tell your father.' Mikhail looked him straight in the eye.

Claude looked disappointed. 'OK,' he said, 'if you like.'

9

Cape Cod

Miss Clayburg tried her best and so did Evangeline. They painted rainbows and they painted castles and they even painted the sea, but nothing Evangeline created showed any flair whatsoever.

They went down to the beach together to collect driftwood and then returned to the studio to draw it.

'Your grandmother said you brought driftwood home before,' Miss Clayburg said. 'She told me it was something your stepfather used to do when he was young. Would you like to draw it, Evangeline? Find a nice big stick of charcoal and see what you can do.'

But Evangeline did not use the charcoal because she had found it made the paper messy. She picked a pencil out instead and spent a long time sharpening it. Then she made a few small marks on the paper but proceeded to rub them out. Miss Clayburg smiled but her eyes went narrow.

'I thought I told you not to use the eraser, Evangeline,' she said. 'What is that you are drawing?'

Evangeline turned the page round. It was a tiny detail of a piece of bark.

'What about the shape of the whole thing?' Miss Clayburg asked.

'I'll get to it,' Evangeline told her, leaning over the paper again before she caught the look of exasperation in the tutor's eye. It was no good. They both knew it was no good. Only Grandma Klippel wouldn't be told, and so Miss Clayburg stayed on — for her sake as much as anybody else's. Evangeline looked down. Her sleeve had

70

dipped into some paint and the paint had made a crimson smear across her clean white paper. The smear would never clean off. She began to cry silent tears.

10

Mikhail stood self-consciously on the backdrop, staring at his fingernails. The nails were dirty. The rest of him, on the other hand, was scrupulously clean. Claude had suggested he go for a scrub before the session and he'd spent an hour in the tub, wasting time, trying to delay things.

Claude was whistling again, busying himself behind the camera and pottering excitedly. He'd put Mikhail in a black kimono. Then he'd covered some wooden crates with a sheet and told him to drape himself over them. Draping yourself was more difficult than Mikhail had thought. He felt awkward and stupid, like an upturned insect that can't right itself again.

'What is that song?' he asked Claude. Claude stopped pottering and looked up, surprised.

'What song?' he asked.

'The one you are whistling.' It was getting on Mikhail's nerves. He felt anxious and he hated himself for it. Claude had insisted on having a three-bar electric fire in the small room and Mikhail could feel the sweat running down his back. The lead from the fire was plugged into a lamp socket in the hall and he kept wishing Claude would forget and trip over it.

Suddenly Claude seemed ready. He pushed his glasses to the top of his head and beamed at Mikhail.

'Is everything all right?' he asked. Mikhail nodded. Twenty-five forint. It was all he allowed himself to think of. Living in the apartment meant he could save some of the money, too. How long would it be before he had enough to get away from Budapest? A flash went off and he jumped, squinting.

'Try to relax,' Claude crooned. He waited until Mikhail was still again and then took another picture.

'Why are you nervous?' Claude asked.

'I feel stupid,' Mikhail replied.

Claude smiled. Mikhail had never seen him smile so much. 'You look terrific,' he told him. 'I wish you could see how good you look. If you did you wouldn't worry. Here – this is what you look like.' He held a book out to Mikhail. The book was an old one, the pages yellow at the edges. Mikhail supposed the pictures were works of art. Most of them were etchings of young boys in togas. Their faces were beautiful. Mikhail closed the book and put it down carefully.

Claude took some more shots before suggesting Mikhail have a break. The cooler air in the passage felt good. Claude went into the kitchen to make them some tea. Mikhail followed him.

'What happens next?' he asked.

Claude looked alarmed. 'What do you mean?'

'Is this when you fuck me?' Mikhail had never used the word before but Tincan used it all the time.

Claude dropped a teacup onto the floor. As he bent to pick it up Mikhail noticed that the seam of his trousers had split. Claude reached out for the cup but his hand missed and he stayed there where he was, as though frozen to the spot. Mikhail could not see his face but, when his shoulders started heaving, he assumed the older man was crying.

'Shit!' Mikhail whispered. It was another Tincan word.

Claude moved across the floor on his knees, his glasses misted with his tears. When he reached Mikhail's feet he bent double and kissed them. His mouth felt wet. Mikhail kicked him away and he rolled like a dog.

'Don't hate me!' Claude said. He was sobbing properly now, his belly rising and falling like a child's. He would

73

wake his father. Mikhail put his hand out to stop him and Claude grabbed it.

'Please don't hate me,' he whispered, pressing his lips against the centre of the palm.

'I can't afford to hate you,' Mikhail said quietly. 'If I don't live here I'll die.' He knew that. He had no option. That was the way things were in his life. If you wanted to stay alive there were certain things you had to do: steal; sell drugs; pose for pictures; get fucked by old men. That was how it was, he understood that. Nothing was for nothing – it was a fact of his life.

Claude was groaning at his feet, soft little whelps, like an animal in pain. Mikhail undid his robe and the moans grew more intense. Mikhail blocked out what was happening and thought about the money.

Twenty-five forint. It seemed like a fortune. He would save it all for a plane ticket and then he would fly off somewhere where there was no snow. America was a good place, Andreas had told him that. You could get everything there; everything you wanted. Andreas had planned to go to America to get a record deal for his group. Maybe Mikhail could go there in his place. How much and how long would it take, though?

Claude was kissing his feet again and he kicked him harder, this time in the belly. Claude let out a cry of pleasure. 'Again!' he called. Mikhail watched him squirm on the floor.

Too long, was the answer that came into his head, much, much too long.

It was a whole year after Miss Clayburg had left the house at Cape Cod, and nothing much more had happened other than Evangeline growing another inch and her grandmother having her heart broken for the second time.

The old lady never said a word, but Evangeline knew she had pinned great hopes on her being artistically gifted. She still went up to the studio to try long after her tutor was gone, but one day the door was just locked and that was obviously an end to it. Evangeline would have been relieved, but her disappointment stung like salt on a scratch.

She wanted to do well so badly that it hurt. If Grandma Klippel was searching for another Darius, then she was looking, too, for some special talent to make her worthy of her parents' love, even though she knew they were dead now. Sometimes she got angry rather than sad and wished she had a flair so that they might have realized too late what they'd missed and regret not taking her with them. She even wrote small scripts in her workbook:

> *DARIUS: Did you reelize Evangeline had flair as an artist too, dear?*
> *THEA: No i never new that. she was always such a plain child that i never held out much hope for her. Perhaps we made a misstake, Darius. Perhaps she shuld be here with us now, after all.*

When she had finished writing she would always tear the pages out and screw them up into small balls, just in case. She didn't think Grandma Klippel ever came snooping but if she did Evangeline didn't want her finding out her son and his family were all dead. Sometimes she wished Cecil was still there so she could discuss things with someone. She even asked her grandmother if she had his address, but was told he was back in Britain and wouldn't want to be bothered by letters from little girls he hardly knew.

Then something strange happened.

Evangeline was called out of class one wet September day and sent home early. All the way back in the car she worked over what might have occurred but nothing came to mind – apart from the extreme long shot that Patrick might have found his way back.

When they got to the house Grandma Klippel was not on the porch as usual but waiting in the best lounge beside a tray of tea. Evangeline had not been in the room much before. Someone had taken the sheets off the chairs and there was a fire burning and spitting in the hearth; they had put pine logs on the fire and the smoke smelt sweet. Mrs O'Reilly must have been up earlier than usual because there was the biggest bunch of anemones ever in a porcelain bowl on the centre table.

The room itself was mainly reds and rose pinks, and would have looked jolly enough had it not been for the expression on Grandma Kippel's face. Her nose was as crimson as the wallpaper and she looked like she had a cold. Her eyes were swollen and her hands looked fidgety. When she picked up her cup it danced noisily in its saucer.

There was a man in the room. Evangeline thought he must be the new chauffeur, even though she had no idea the old one was leaving. The man was no taller than her grandmother but he had thick hands that were making heavy work of the bone china. His dark hair was cut short and greased back and he wore a suit that looked wrong for his body. He smelt faintly of frying, as though he had stopped off at the diner on the journey down from wherever he lived.

'Evangeline,' her grandmother said, '. . . dear, this is Mr Castelli.'

He had a good-looking face, even though he was nervous. Evangeline stepped forward to take his hand, wondering why it was so important for her to meet the new chauffeur.

'Mr Castelli is your father, Evangeline, your real father.'

She stopped before their hands touched. The man gave her grandmother what looked like an angry glance before turning back to stare at her. It made her itchy-uncomfortable.

'*Darius* is my father.' She knew she'd used the wrong tense but anything else would have hurt her too much to say it.

Grandma Klippel's face looked funny, as though she wanted to sneeze and was trying not to.

'Darius was only your father because he married your mother, Evangeline. When he adopted you he took you for

76

his own, I know that. But Mr Castelli is your father by blood. Do you understand? He was married to your mother before she met my son.

'I know she told you about him. Darius was always insistent about discussing things frankly. Do you remember?'

Evangeline nodded. She had always known she had two fathers but she'd thought this one didn't matter because she had never even seen him. He had a wide neck, like a boxer. His tie was done up, but the top button of his collar was left undone. Evangeline wished he hadn't done that because she knew her grandmother would not approve. She liked men to look properly smart, it was something she often remarked on. A person's dress was a strong guide to their character, as far as Grandma Klippel was concerned. Mr Castelli would have been tested and found wanting. He had sallow-looking skin and a strong, beefy nose.

'You look just like your mother, Evangeline,' he said.

'No,' Evangeline told him wisely, 'I look just like you.'

Mikhail waited until Claude was at work before ransacking the apartment. Things had got out of hand. Tincan had been right: you had to get on. Nothing else mattered – it was stupid to pretend that it did. He threw things from cupboards and broke plates and glasses against the walls. He found Claude's savings beneath the mattress on his father's bed. The old man had said nothing as he took it, just stared at him with an evil glint in his eye. Maybe he had known Mikhail was living there. Maybe other boys had done the same thing.

Claude's payments had never materialized after the first week. Mikhail had reminded him many times but Claude always came up with an excuse. For a man who worked in a bank he seemed strangely forgetful when it came to cash.

Mikhail counted out the exact amount he was owed and then sat staring at the rest. Put yourself first. Nothing else matters. He took a few notes more, then he put them back. Then he stuffed the whole wad into his pocket. Then he pulled it out again. Was he a thief or not? He couldn't decide.

The long winter was over. As the snow cleared Mikhail had started cleaning the windows of Claude's apartment of all their dust and grime, so that he could look out onto the small square below. He went out so little that his skin was unnaturally pale. He was a little fatter now, and Claude had bought him new clothes.

When Claude went out he would read or sleep and when he came back they would talk or he would pose for more photos. He also liked to take baths – lots of them – because he always felt dirty.

There was a smear on the glass. He licked his sleeve and wiped the smear off with spit. The more the sun shone the more oppressive the apartment had become. Claude would never turn the heating down because he said it was bad for his father's health. When he came home he would take off his suit and wear a cotton kimono instead.

Watching other children in the square below was the most painful thing of all. There were boys of his age down there, playing football and messing about. He used to look at himself in the mirror sometimes, asking himself why he had deserved such a fate.

Claude liked to pose as much as he liked taking photos. Mikhail had discovered this fact while rooting out some photos of him in a suitcase under the bed.

'Show me what to do and I'll photograph you,' he told Claude the next time they did some shots together. Claude had been selling the shots of him now, he was sure of it – not paying Mikhail for the posing, while he was getting paid well himself. He had tried not to think of all the men who must have looked at them.

Claude had looked pleased with Mikhail's suggestion. He had shown Mikhail all the basics: how to set the lights, how to focus, and how to frame a shot. Then he'd sat coyly in front of the camera, beaming, while Mikhail clicked away.

Printing the photographs had been less fun, but Mikhail had persisted. Claude used the bathroom as a darkroom and, with two of them in there, it became over-crowded. He placed planks over the bath to use as a table and there was a red bulb in the socket that gave an eerie glow in the darkness. Claude apologized every time they got squeezed together and Mikhail didn't know what was worse, the touching or the bleating apologies. There was a certain magic in the printing process that enthralled him every time, though. You put paper into a tank of fluid and faces appeared on that paper. He saw Claude's face, weak and beaming, appearing slowly as he slooshed the stuff around.

He could almost stand Claude's simpering smiles since he had come to the decision about leaving. He was not going back onto the streets, though. That much he knew for sure. He looked at the money again. Half of it, that was fair for all he'd been through. Half of it would be enough to teach Claude a lesson. He counted the notes into two piles and then worked out how long he could live on the money. He would need a job when it ran out; or he would need a job straight away if he was to spend the cash on a plane ticket. He stood up and padded into the studio. Claude's camera was still on its tripod.

Mikhail unscrewed the camera carefully and wrapped it in a sheet before stuffing it inside his jacket and pulling up the zip. As he did so he heard Claude's key in the lock.

'Guess what,' he heard Claude holler, 'a robbery at the bank!' He sounded happy. 'Thieves broke in last night, and once we had been interviewed by the police they said we should have the rest of the day off while they cleared up –' He saw the carnage inside his precious apartment and froze in the doorway.

'Holy shit . . .' Mikhail had never heard him swear before. It sounded funny and made him want to laugh. 'Mikhail?' Claude's voice dropped. Mikhail heard him creeping around, looking for burglars. Two robberies in one day! He would spend the rest of his life telling the story.

He reached the studio and Mikhail hid behind the door. Claude's head appeared first, low down, as though he were crouching. 'Mikhail?' he whispered. He sounded genuinely scared.

'Claude.' Mikhail stepped out suddenly. Claude's eyes bulged with the shock and he looked as though he might have a seizure.

'Jesus! Oh Christ, Mikhail, I thought you were . . . what happened? Did someone break in?'

Mikhail smiled. 'No,' he told Claude, 'I'm leaving, that's all. I've taken some money – all you owe me for posing – and I've borrowed a few of your things to see me through. You wouldn't want me to starve, would you?'

Claude's eyes were perfect circles. You could see the red veins all around them. His mouth drooped at the corners like a clown's.

'Leaving?' he asked.

Mikhail nodded.

Claude stared around the room in disbelief. 'You can't leave me, Mikhail,' he whispered, 'not like this!'

'How, then?' Mikhail asked him.

'I don't know.' Claude looked desperate. 'Sit down with me first. Have some coffee. We can talk. I'll pay in future, I swear. I love you, Mikhail. Don't leave me.'

He was on his knees again. Mikhail watched in disgust as he crawled across the floor and grabbed at his legs.

'Please, Mikhail.'

Mikhail nearly lost his balance. 'Stop it, you crazy bastard, you almost had me over!'

Claude looked up at him and his tearful eyes focused on the bulge in Mikhail's jacket. His expression changed suddenly and he reached up towards it.

'What have you got there?' he asked. He ripped the jacket open. 'My camera! No, Mikhail! Drop it, you little bastard! Give it back!' He tried to wrest the camera from

Mikhail but the boy was too quick for him. Mikhail walked towards the door to leave. When he turned Claude was behind him, an iron poker in his shaking hands and his face distorted by anger.

'Give it to me, you bastard!' he screamed. He lifted the poker above his head to strike but Mikhail moved first, ducking out of the way as the thing whistled past his ear.

'Stop it, Claude!' he shouted. 'Are you mad, or something?'

'My camera!' Claude's voice was completely unrecognizable. He lifted the poker again but Mikhail punched him in the face before he could strike. There was a sickening sound of bone being crushed and then a blinding pain in Mikhail's knuckles. The pain doubled him up, and he thought his hand was broken. He shoved it between his legs and let out a howl.

Claude stood very still for a moment and then crumpled to the floor with blood spurting from his nose. The blood seemed endless, it flecked the walls and even reached the ceiling, where it speckled crimson against the white paint. Claude was silent. He sat propped against the hatstand, his eyes open but not moving. Mikhail thought he was watching him but when he stepped out of the way, the eyes stared straight ahead. The blood was bubbling now, making Mikhail feel sick.

'Oh, Jesus, Claude, are you dead?' he whispered to himself. He didn't care so much, except for the fact that it would be another thing the police would come hunting him for.

Claude let out a moan and Mikhail let out a sigh of relief.

'Don't go, Mikhail,' Claude gargled. Blood cascaded from his nose into his open mouth as he spoke. He spat the blood out and some of it peppered Mikhail's jacket.

'You stupid bastard!' Mikhail said. The door opened at the far end of the hall. They both looked round at the same time. Claude's father was standing in the doorway, clutching the wooden surround for support.

'Fuck off!' he said. There was no strength in his voice; it sounded as though he was already dead.

Mikhail looked at the old man and then he looked down at Claude.

Then he left.

Evangeline's real father stayed at the house for a few days, until things got so bad between him and her grandmother that you could see sparks in the air. Grandma Klippel went through the motions of playing hostess but anyone could see it was as though a nasty smell she couldn't quite place was hanging about the house. Evangeline's father, on the other hand, acted as though he couldn't wait to be away, however hard he tried not to show it. Grandma Klippel's wealth seemed too much for him. He didn't sit up straight at dinner and he ate with the wrong fork.

He tried to be friends with Evangeline in an edgy sort of way.

'Don't call me Mr Castelli,' he said the first time they were alone, 'call me Nico – everyone else does.'

'My grandmother doesn't,' Evangeline pointed out.

Nico pulled a face. 'Your grandmother is a very special kind of lady,' was all he would say.

'Are you poor or something, Nico?' Evangeline asked.

He laughed, but he didn't look as though he found her comment funny. 'No, I'm not poor. I might look it next to your grandmother, but then so would fifty per cent of the population, come to that. I just live differently, Evangeline. I have a different style of life.'

He ran out of conversation after that; it was obvious he wasn't used to being around children. Evangeline wanted to help him out but she didn't know how. She didn't know what he was there for, either, though she heard him and her grandmother arguing about money a couple of times. She didn't understand what all the arguments could be about. Grandma Klippel had enough money for all of them.

She got called into the lounge again. Her father's face was red and he looked angry and embarrassed at the same time. Her grandmother was sitting down, staring at her hands so that Evangeline could not see the look in her eyes.

'Evangeline,' she began, 'dear, your father wants to take you back to New York with him . . .'

So it was the painting. Evangeline had shown no talent for art and now her grandmother, too, was fed up with her. She had been one long disappointment to everyone. She sucked in her bottom lip. She hated them all for rejecting her; only she didn't, she loved them, and she hated herself most for loving them and disappointing them.

She was ugly and stupid. There was nothing about her that anyone would want to latch on to. She was disposable, she knew that. She wondered if you could learn not to be, because all this rejection was very hurtful.

Her grandmother was looking at her now. She searched the old woman's eyes for a sign of regret over giving her up. Grandma Klippel looked sad, but not desperate. If someone had come to take her beloved Patrick away when Evangeline was younger she would have fought to the death to keep him.

'You don't have to come, Evangeline,' Nico was saying. She barely heard him at first, she was thinking so hard.

'Do you want me to go?' she asked her grandmother.

The old woman sighed. 'I've got no rights, dear,' she said softly, 'whereas you and Mr Castelli are related by blood. I'm just the mother of your stepfather. I can't keep you here . . .'

'She can stay if she wants to.' Nico's face had become redder. So he didn't want her, either.

Grandma Klippel stood up and faced him. A handkerchief fell from her lap onto the floor.

'You told me that was why you came here, Mr Castelli,' she said. Her voice sounded polite enough but tight, as though she was coiled up like a spring inside.

Nico ran a hand through his hair. 'She doesn't have to,' he repeated.

'Why?' Grandma Klippel asked. 'How else would you get at all the money you think is owing to her?'

'Jesus!' Nico looked angry. 'In front of the kid, Mrs Klippel, have a little charity! Evangeline, honey, go and play outside or something for a little while, will you?' he asked.

But Grandma Klippel was too quick for him. She grasped Evangeline by the shoulders and her hands were shaking hard. 'Do you want to go to New York with your father, Evangeline?' she asked. Her voice softened, 'You know you have a home here for as long as you want.'

Evangeline didn't care any more. New York sounded as bad as Cape Cod. Anywhere was bad without her mother and Darius and Lincoln and Patrick. She felt funny. She didn't want them to know they had hurt her so much. She wanted to cling onto her grandmother and make her love her properly, somehow, but then she wanted to hurt her back, too.

'I don't mind,' she whispered. The little girl inside her was hoping that her grandmother might fight over her. Then she thought suddenly and stupidly that her family might be waiting in New York, that they might have been there all this time; but she wasn't a little girl now, she was nine years old, and she knew better.

'You don't mind.' Her grandmother sounded upset.

Nico looked uneasy. 'Do you know what New York's like?' he asked. He bent down so that he was the same height. He smelt of soap and she could see where he had cut himself shaving. He had big dark eyes. She could even see her own reflection in his pupils, and that was something she had never seen happen before. Perhaps it only happened with people you were related to by blood. She tried to remember if she had seen herself in her mother's eyes, but she couldn't.

'There's no sea there, you know,' he said.

That was it, then. New York it was.

11

New York 1969

Nico called the place home but even Evangeline could see it was just an hotel. It turned out Grandma Klippel was paying for them to stay there because Nico's real home – his apartment – was not deemed appropriate for a nine-year-old to live in. Nico didn't agree with that opinion but he liked the hotel life. He smoked fat cigars and ordered from room service with a golden grin on his face. He told Evangeline they'd be moving somewhere better anyway, just as soon as her money came through.

Being sad in Cape Cod was easy but being sad in New York was a deal more tricky, with no sea to gaze out at and no fog to make you think you were the last person alive on the earth. In Cape Cod Evangeline had felt her parents were everywhere, watching her. In New York, though, she had to carry them in a little pocket in her head, just like she carried Lincoln's picture in a pocket in her bag. Did they know where she was? Had they lost her too, now? The place was full of people but she felt lonelier than ever before in her life.

The loneliness didn't scare her, though; in a way it almost felt good. She didn't want Nico to love her like she'd wanted Grandma Klippel to. There would be no more disappointments or distractions. All she had to do now was work at being herself. Maybe if she tried hard enough she could find something there; maybe if she worked at it there would be something to make people want her.

She wasn't getting any prettier but she wasn't growing

uglier, either. Her teeth were big, but straighter since she had worn braces. Her nose was a funny shape but seeing the same nose on Nico's face every day made it better somehow, because he didn't look too bad.

Grandma Klippel seemed to think she'd forget about Darius and Thea in New York, because she wrote all the time reminding her how they had been and what they were like. The letters hurt badly but she still went on reading them, even when Nico got mad.

Thea and Darius — was she really Thea's child? They were so talented, so successful, so special, and so beautiful to look at. Her grandmother sent photographs of Darius as a child. She wrote:

> *You came from good stock, dear, don't ever forget it.*
> *Thea was a wonderful, talented woman. You were*
> *blessed to have her as a mother. Darius thought of*
> *you as his own, too — just as much as little Lincoln.*
> *Make them proud of you, dear. Don't waste your life.*
> *Darius lived each day as though it were his last . . .*
> *make sure you do the same.*

The letters chilled Evangeline. Make them proud of her — how? *Was* she wasting her life? What was it she was meant to do?

Something else began to trouble her. When she had discovered that her family was dead she had been too sad to wonder why. Maybe she believed things like that just happened. As she grew older, though, she realized they did not. Yet nobody had told her *how* they had died. Perhaps nobody knew. Nico just looked awkward when she asked him, which she did straight away, on the drive from Cape Cod to New York.

'What happened to my mother?' she asked. He had been married to her, so *someone* must have told him.

Nico was silent for a long while. Then he cleared his

throat. Evangeline wondered if he smoked a lot, to get a cough that bad.

'She died,' he said, after a while.

'I know she died,' Evangeline told him. She didn't want to sound impolite but she wanted this thing cleared up. 'Nobody told me how, though.'

Nico coughed again. 'What did the old lady say?' he asked.

Evangeline sighed. 'Grandma? Oh, I don't think she knows, you know. She still thinks they've just gone away. She's old – too old. The shock could make her ill.'

'Who told *you* then?' Nico sounded genuinely interested now.

'The chauffeur.'

'The chauffeur?' Nico punched the steering wheel, 'Fuck!' She had never heard anyone she knew say that word before. He apologized straight away.

'Did this chauffeur tell you what happened?' Nico asked.

Evangeline shook her head. 'I don't think he knew. I don't think he knew anything more than he told me.'

'Jesus.' Nico pulled a cigarette out of a packet in his pocket and flipped it in the air once before catching it in his mouth. Evangeline would have enjoyed that, had they not been discussing what they were. She had a bad feeling she was going to need to pee pretty soon but she realized she didn't know her father well enough to ask him to stop. She crossed her legs instead. She watched him light the cigarette with a Zippo and smelt the petrol before he snapped the lid shut again.

'What do you think happened to them?' he asked her.

'I don't know.' Her voice sounded small. She was trying so hard to think like an adult, but it wouldn't happen.

The car hit a rabbit; it bounced straight up over the bonnet like a tumbler in a circus act and onto the windscreen. Nico didn't swerve once; it was as though the accident hadn't happened. Evangeline saw the rabbit's squashed face before it took off again. There was a red splashy mark where it had hit the glass. She almost wet herself with the shock but Nico didn't mention it.

'Do you know?' she asked him after a while. Nico shrugged and said nothing. The shrug told her she wasn't to ask again. She could see the question made him uncomfortable so she looked out of the window instead. 'What do I call you?' she asked after a while.

'What?' She could tell from his voice that he had been thinking hard enough to be miles away.

'Do I call you Mr Castelli?'

Nico made a noise like a snort. 'Of course not,' he said, 'I'm your father.'

'What, then?'

He took both hands off the wheel and stretched as though he were tired. She had never seen anyone drive without using their hands.

'Father?' he asked. Evangeline bit her lip. 'I told you – Nico, then – hell, I don't care.' Nico looked round at her. 'What's that you're doing? Stop that. How long have you done that for?' Evangeline was biting her nails. She didn't stop because it made her feel better. 'I used to do that,' Nico added, after a pause. 'It makes people think you're scared of them.'

Evangeline stopped.

She thought the hotel looked good from the outside and she preferred the noise of the traffic compared to the constant whispering of the sea. She wondered if Nico would be funny, like Darius. Grandma Klippel hadn't a funny bone in her body. Darius must have got his talent for clowning from some other branch of the family. All Nico ever did was look worried.

After a while Evangeline began to imagine she was living in a palace. She felt wrapped in tissue, like a doll. It was strange, ordering all your food by phone. Nico told Evangeline to ring for whatever she wanted. She thought at first that no one would take notice of a little girl on the phone, but the food arrived, just as she'd asked for it. No one questioned her when she wanted ice-cream at every meal and no one told her to sit up straight at the table – mainly because she usually ate alone.

Sometimes Nico sat with her but when he did he would just sit and smoke.

'You shouldn't do that,' Evangeline told him.

'Do what?' he looked surprised.

'Smoke cigarettes. It's bad for my lungs, especially when I'm eating,' Evangeline told him. She sounded just like her grandmother, even to her own ears.

'Don't worry about your lungs,' Nico said.

'Someone has to,' Evangeline replied.

'Then you quit biting your nails,' Nico stubbed out his cigarette.

'Chewing nails won't kill me,' Evangeline said. 'Smoking can.'

'Yeah, yeah, yeah.' Nico folded his arms and stared at her.

Evangeline almost smiled at that. So did Nico.

She used to cry at night; it was part of her routine. 'Never cry in front of people, always cry in your room,' Grandma Klippel had taught her. She would climb into bed and close her eyes and the tears would always come, whether she was feeling sad or not. Bedtime was a sad time. Thea used to read to her when she was small, or Darius would sing. Patrick used to sleep on her bed. It was difficult to get rid of memories like that. One night Nico walked past her room and he must have heard her crying, because his footsteps stopped. She knew he was listening so she held her breath and he walked on after a while.

The next morning she could feel him looking at her.

'Do you miss your grandmother?' he asked.

Evangeline kept her head down. 'No,' was all she would say. It was just about the truth, too. Grandma Klippel always meant well but she wasn't the sort of woman you could admit to missing much.

'Maybe you should go back to her,' Nico sounded almost hopeful.

'I don't think so,' Evangeline told him. She wouldn't look at his face. She was scared she might see his disappointment. He didn't want her there, she knew that. She wasn't going back to live with the sea again, though, not for anyone's sake.

'Did my money arrive yet?' she asked carefully.

'What money?' Nico sounded cagey.

'My inheritance.'

Nico sighed. 'What did your grandmother tell you?' he asked.

'Nothing,' Evangeline whispered, 'I overheard. You want me here so you can get my money, isn't that right? I don't mind.' Nico was blood, after all.

Nico sat down at the table. He tapped her hand until she looked at him. 'It's your money by rights, Evangeline,' he said. 'Your mother would have wanted you to have it. Your grandmother says there isn't any. I know there is. Your parents had plenty; everyone knew that. It's only right that you have it.'

'Why don't you sue her, then?' Evangeline asked.

'Sue who?'

'My grandmother. You think she's keeping it, don't you?'

Nico ran a hand through his hair. 'Jesus, how old are you? Fifty? What do you know about suing? It costs money, Evangeline — money I haven't got. Do you know how much it takes to bring a court case? No, neither do I, but I know it's more than I have, that's for sure. I mentioned suing — as you've asked — and your grandmother laughed at me.'

'Were you in prison some time?' Evangeline asked him.

He started coughing again. 'Jesus!'

'Only I wondered why you never came to see me when I was small.' She sat up straight now, as her grandmother had taught her.

Nico pursed his lips. 'No, I wasn't in prison, Evangeline. I just . . . kept out of the way, that was all. Your mother had a new life. You had a new father. What was I supposed to be hanging around for? Did you want me to turn up every Sunday and take you out to the zoo or something?'

Evangeline shook her head.

'No, well, there you are. I didn't want that either. Neither did Thea, though she never said as much.'

'Where are they buried?' Evangeline asked. Nico did not have to ask who she meant. He stared at her. A nerve in the side of his face started to twitch.

'You want to know where they're buried?'

Evangeline nodded – yes.

'Why?'

'To visit,' she whispered. 'I think I must have rights.'

Nico nodded slowly. 'OK,' he replied. He didn't say where they were or when they would go, though.

'Did you love my mother?' Evangeline asked.

'Everyone loved your mother,' Nico told her. End of conversation.

Nico worked at night quite often and Evangeline was left alone, which was fine because no one was ever really alone in an hotel. Then Grandma Klippel found out and said things had to change. She phoned one night while Nico was out and when he came back she phoned again and Evangeline watched his face go red as he listened to her. 'OK,' he kept saying, 'OK.'

A girl turned up the following night – a big, fair-haired girl with a funny voice, called Nettie, whom Evangeline didn't care for much. Nettie smiled a lot but she was also a mess-maker, which Evangeline didn't like as she had to follow the girl around the place, plumping up cushions and picking lint up off the carpet.

Nettie had her own smell, too – not unpleasant, but different. When she started taking Evangeline to school she would make her wait round the corner where the other kids couldn't see her, just in case. Then Nico was out more and Nettie just sort of moved into the hotel with them. Evangeline found her sitting there one morning, ordering juice from room service.

'I don't know that my grandmother would want to pay for a stranger in here, too,' Evangeline said, but Nettie just laughed. She wasn't fat but she had a small double chin that was pink, like the rest of her.

Her clothes arrived the following day and Evangeline had to crush up in the closet to give her some space. Her clothes were strange, not useful things at all, just cropped-off trousers and a few little tops, like a kid would wear.

Nico told Nettie to teach Evangeline the facts of life but Nettie had her own way of dealing with little things like that. One night when Evangeline got up for water Nico's bedroom door was pushed wide open and the light was on. Evangeline walked past and saw Nico on the bed with his back towards the door and Nettie sitting naked on top of him, riding back and forward like a cowboy at the rodeo. She waved when Evangeline tiptoed past and that must have been the first Nico knew of it because she heard her father swear loudly and Nettie was gone the next day.

'You didn't have to get rid of her,' Evangeline told Nico over breakfast.

Nico kept staring at the newspaper, though she could tell he wasn't reading. 'I know,' he said, 'it was what I wanted.'

Evangeline squirted syrup over the top of her boiled egg. It tasted quite good, if you didn't mind the feel on your tongue. No one stopped her, and so she did it.

'She smelt funny,' Evangeline said.

'How would you know?' Nico was looking at her now. 'You had the place filled with air fresheners.'

Evangeline nodded, 'Because of her smell.'

'Don't be rude,' Nico told her, 'and stop cleaning the place up. Housekeeping is paid to do things like that.'

'They don't get all the dirt,' Evangeline said. It was important to her. Grandma Klippel didn't have dirt in her house. Evangeline wanted the place nice for Nico.

'Stop biting your nails,' Nico said. He said it even when she wasn't. She let her hair flop over her face and chewed that, instead.

So Nico had to take Evangeline out to work with him. She could see how little he liked the idea but she was overcome with excitement. He wouldn't tell her what he did. When he finally told her she didn't even understand the word.

Paparazzi. It sounded strange, like an Italian ice-cream flavour. It wasn't the only job he did, but it was one way he earned money. The other ways were more boring, like chauffeuring local businessmen to and from their offices. Nico was half-Italian and most of the businessmen were, too. Evangeline looked his job up in the dictionary but what she read didn't seem to fit. Nico just photographed people in a club – ordinary sorts of people. Most of them looked pretty much like Nico himself; dark-haired and itchily nervous in their suits. They stood next to their wives and friends in groups and they all smiled warily as Nico counted to three. When the pictures were over they looked relieved and started laughing.

Evangeline wasn't allowed inside the clubs but Nico got her in anyway. She was proud of him for being able to do that. She would wait by the door while he discussed the matter with a few men in the entrance and then he would grin and wink at her and she'd run in after him. They were never inside for long; just long enough to smell the new carpets and the alcohol, though, and to catch a glimpse of the bands that played on stage in their white tuxedos and orange toupées.

Evangeline loved it all. She loved the noise and the pushing crowds and the perfumes and the heat but most of all she loved it because she knew Grandma Klippel would have a seizure if she knew she were there.

People spoke to her. She became known as Nico's daughter. One man gave her a fifty-dollar note and a pat on the head, and a woman in an expensive satin dress gave her the paper umbrella from her cocktail, which Evangeline liked even more than the money. Nico watched her like a hawk all the time, except when he took the photographs. Then he would sit her on a bar stool and tell the barman to check she didn't move. The barman would wink at her and send a glass of cola spinning down the bar towards her, just like he did with the beers. Sometimes he put a small plastic stick in the glass with two cherries speared on it.

Nico would always be late up the next morning so Evangeline would order breakfast and get out the small paintbox Grandma Klippel had packed with her things. She tried to paint something every day, just as her tutor had told her to. Nothing looked like anything much, they were all small pale shapes in the middle of the page; sometimes she couldn't even remember what it was she was painting.

One morning Nico caught her at work. He began a laugh that turned into a cough and when he had finished coughing he turned the pad around and gazed down at the smudge of pale colour in the middle of the page.

'What's this?' he asked. Evangeline chewed at her hair.

'Is it some fruit, is that what it is?' He held it up to one eye at a time, as though he needed glasses, then he turned the picture around slowly. 'I didn't know you were trying to paint,' he said quietly. Evangeline's hair smelt of cigarette smoke.

'Did your mother teach you?' Nico asked.

'No.'

His eyes looked dark, like the coffee he was drinking.

'Who, then? Darius?' It was the first time she had heard him say the name. It sounded strange. He pronounced it wrong: 'Dar-*i*-us'. She longed to correct him but thought it might have been deliberate, like the way he was always calling Grandma Klippel 'the old lady'.

'My grandmother hired a tutor,' Evangeline told him. She washed her brush in the water-pot and cleaned it carefully on a tissue. She couldn't work with him watching.

'You had proper lessons?' Nico sounded surprised, 'For how long?'

'Months.'

'Months?'

Evangeline nodded. She could feel her eyes filling up but she didn't want to look a child in front of her father, in case he was laughing at her.

'She wanted you to be like your mother.'

'And Darius.'

An angry muscle twitched on Nico's cheek.

'And what did *you* want?' he asked. Evangeline pushed more hair into her mouth. 'Did *you* want this?'

'I didn't mind.' Her voice sounded small. Nico was staring at her.

'Why not, Evangeline? You mind everything else! You mind when there is dust on the table, you mind when I smoke, you mind when the coffee's not warm, you mind when I dent the couch – why didn't you mind something as important as this? Do you enjoy it?'

She nodded. Then she thought. Then she shook her head.

'Then you should stop. Don't be Thea. Be yourself.'

'I want her to be proud of me.' It came out in a small stupid whisper.

'Your grandmother?'

'No. My mother.'

Nico sighed and lit a cigarette. Evangeline wished he had done the trick where he threw it into his mouth, it might have lightened the atmosphere a little. He ran his hands through his thick dark hair. She could tell that he was thinking.

'Come with me,' he said at last.

Evangeline got up. 'Do I need my coat?'

'Bring it,' Nico said, 'bring your whole wardrobe if you like. Only hurry up.'

12

They went round to Nico's apartment. Evangeline had
never been there before and she liked it twice as much as
the hotel. It was in a converted warehouse down a small
side street and they had to use a service elevator to get to
Nico's floor. The building was old and huge and wonderfully empty. You could have got a whole car into the
elevator and the thing was open so you could watch each
floor as it slid by. One floor was just empty space and a
bird flew out when the elevator went by. Its wings made a
whirring sound.

The main door was covered with locks. Nico undid each
one slowly, cursing under his breath when he got the
wrong key.

'I like it here,' Evangeline told him.

'You'd like to live here?' he asked, and he laughed when
she said that she would.

'Just you and a few moth-eaten pigeons, eh? Now how
do you suppose the old lady would like that one?'

Evangeline pulled a face. 'If you got my money we could
live just about anywhere we wanted,' she said.

'I told you, I tried.' End of story. Non-negotiable.

The door fell back, emitting a distinctive smell. It was an
empty smell, a smell of nobody having been home for a
very long time. It was unpleasant at first but after a while
you didn't notice it so much. Eventually you didn't notice it
at all. The apartment was warm and there was condensation on the windows. Nico cursed and went off to see
about the heating. Evangeline snooped around each room
and Nico didn't stop her, which was nice.

'It's OK,' she told him when she'd finished. 'You should clean it up, though.'

'I don't live here now,' Nico said, 'I just come here when I need to.'

Evangeline shrugged. 'It would still be nicer clean,' she told him. 'You never know, after all.'

'You never know what?'

'You just never know, that's all. You might get rats or something. Somebody might break in and see all the mess. I don't know.'

Nico shook his head, tapping his finger against his forehead. 'You know you are a little crazy, don't you?' he laughed. He didn't look comfortable, not even in his own home. He picked up a handful of mail from the mat and began sifting through it quickly.

'There's a room locked,' Evangeline said.

'I know. That's where we're working.'

'Today?'

'Yes, today.'

He made coffee, which drove Evangeline mad with impatience.

'We just had coffee!'

'I know, but I always drink coffee when I work. It's a kind of a rule. Black, too. You'd better get used to that yourself.' They drank black coffee that made her shudder. She washed up and dried before he could pour a second cup.

There was another unlocking ritual and then she was inside her father's workroom. It was small, no bigger than a bathroom, and dark, because the windows had been boarded over.

'What is this?' she asked.

'Why are you whispering?'

Because it was like being in church, she thought: weird, silent. Darkness made your voice sound funny, so it was better to whisper. Nico clicked a switch and a bare red bulb bathed the room in an eerie light.

'You OK?' Nico asked. He didn't know if she was scared of the dark.

'Uh-huh.' He heard her swallow.

There were tables and a sink and some washing lines overhead with metal pegs hanging from them. Evangeline held her hand to her face to see what it looked like in the red light. Nico tossed something into the air a couple of times and then threw it at her. She caught it, which was good. It was a film.

'They're the shots from last night,' he said. 'We're going to print them up. This is my darkroom, Evangeline. This is where I work.'

She rolled the film around in her fingers. 'You work in the clubs,' she said.

'No,' Nico told her. 'I take shots in the clubs. *This* is where I work. *This* is where the magic is done. Did you take a look at the people I photograph? Eh?'

Evangeline nodded.

'Pretty? Yes or no? No. Right. *You* know that they're ugly. *I* know that they're ugly. But what do you think *they* know about it, eh? Well I'll tell you. *They* think they look great. *They* think they look so good it's a wonder the mirror doesn't pay them to look into it.

'What they see when they look into the mirror is not what you and I see, Evangeline. *They* see Tony Curtis and Gina Lollobrigida; what *we* see when we look at them is a baboon's arse, if you'll pardon my French. Now, they pay me to take their photo. What do you think they want to see when they get those shots back? Curtis and Lollo? Or a monkey's arse?'

Evangeline laughed.

'Right,' Nico said, 'so therefore the magic. Anyone can take a photograph, Evangeline. It's making that photograph look good that counts.' He bent his head closer towards hers, 'The old lady wanted to teach you how to paint pictures, Evangeline. She wanted you to be like her son and your mother. Well, you're not, so don't bust your whole life trying. Maybe you have talent, maybe you don't. You're not happy with paint and paint isn't happy with you, that much is obvious.

'But there's more than one way to create pictures, Evangeline. You see an image and you record it for others to see. Then you dress it up a little, make it look better than it already is. That is true of great artists, but it is also true of great photographers.

'Photographers and artists see exactly what we all see, Evangeline, but it's how they translate those pictures that makes them good – understand? Right, let's see what we can do with a group of baboons' arses, shall we?'

She had never heard her father say so much before and she would never hear him speak so eloquently again.

She watched enthralled as he took the lid off one of three large tanks and stuck a thermometer into the liquid inside.

'Twenty degrees.' He spoke to himself but she knew he was teaching her, too. He leant across and switched the light out and the room became the darkest darkness she had ever sat in before. There were a couple of cracking noises as he took the film out of its canister and then he described how he was loading it onto a metal spool.

The spool went into the first tank and she heard a watery sound as he dunked it up and down. Then he put the lid back onto the tank and switched the dull red light back on again.

'I have a timer, see? Like an alarm clock. It all has to be timed, like baking a loaf. Six minutes, maybe more – you get the feel of it after a while, but you still time it, right?' The timer went off as he spoke and Evangeline nearly jumped out of her socks.

The light went off again.

'Right. Now it goes into the wash. Now I drain it and then it goes into the fix – see?' Evangeline nodded even though she could see nothing. 'In the fix for two minutes,' Nico continued, 'then I take a look at it – you learn what to look for – then I wash the film for twenty minutes or so. A bit of wetting agent and then we can hang it out to dry.'

The film strips were hung onto the small washing line. 'I hang them over the radiator here so that they dry more quickly – just enough time for another coffee and some cheesecake.'

'Fruit,' Evangeline said, 'or you'll get fat.'

'Photographers don't get fat, Evangeline,' Nico said, 'we're lean, mean fighting machines. We eat what we will – it's one of the rules of the job.'

After more black coffee Nico showed Evangeline how to work the enlarger. She hopped with impatience while he did a test strip and then finally he came up with a proper print on paper.

'See this?' he asked. She bent over the sheet, chewing her hair. She recognized the faces in front of her. It was a man from the night before and the woman in satin who had given her the paper umbrella from her drink. 'Baboons' arses,' Nico said. They looked gormless and ugly. Nico held up a lady's stocking. 'This is where the magic begins,' he continued. He stretched a piece of the stocking over the lens of the enlarger. 'Or I could blow on the lens to mist it,' he told Evangeline. This time the print came up softer and more film star-like. Nico held the shot up to the light. 'I think she needs a smaller nose and less of a gap between the front teeth,' he said. 'He could do with a couple less chins.'

He took the print into the kitchen and sat down with a small box of pens and inks and razor blades. He worked quickly, bending so low his nose almost touched the paper, dabbing, dotting and gently scraping until the shot was finished.

'There you go.' He held the photograph up for Evangeline's inspection. 'Well?' he asked.

He was right – it was magic. He had made the couple look like film stars. Evangeline was speechless.

'You don't like?' Nico looked confused.

'How did you do this?' Evangeline asked. Nico's expression relaxed into a smile.

'You saw how I did it. I showed you.'

'But this is special. This is perfect. You made things perfect, Nico.'

'No, Evangeline, it's just hard work. If you know what you're doing it's not difficult. And I'm not that good — there are many more tricks than I'll ever bother to learn. Look.' He pulled a book out from under a pile of photographic paper boxes. The book was a large one and full of photographs. Nico sat and drank coffee while Evangeline looked through it.

'You like?' he asked. The book was full of shots of old movie stars. Evangeline studied each one closely.

'You think they'd look like that if you passed them in the street?' Nico asked. He was smiling at her. He leant forward, pointing: 'This photographer who did these shots, he was an artist, Evangeline,' he said. 'He took the photograph, yes, but then the true work was done. Retouch, retouch, retouch. The man was a genius. I see him sitting over his desk at night, a box of paints and a few blades, just as I have here, scraping, gently, bleaching, eliminating. He created these stars, Evangeline, he did it himself.'

Nico threw another book down in front of her. 'Never believe what you see in pictures, Evangeline,' he said. 'They say the camera never lies, but that is one of the greatest lies of all time. Famous war photographs — look at them. How many do you think were staged, eh? You see a so-so shot and you turn it into something special with a little staging.

'Do you think Dino Foretti wanted a business portrait of himself squatting in that old cane chair with the holes in it that he works from most days? No. That chair is the truth, but I sat him on a real leather chair, Evangeline, the sort with studs and everything. I draped some satin in the background — red, like presidents use. The result? Not Foretti as he is, but Foretti as he wants to be. Foretti the business tycoon. He was happy, he loved it. Trade in falsehoods, Evangeline, and you have a business. Try to sell the truth, and you end up bankrupt within the month.'

He pointed out one of the movie stars in the first book. 'You like her nose?' he asked. He leant forward and his voice dropped. 'That lady has an invisible wire set up, which is stretched across the set before she is photographed. She leans her nose against the wire and suddenly it isn't so long. Suddenly it turns up at the end, instead of down. Suddenly she looks like the movie queen she is supposed to be. Now that's a class act, Evangeline, take my word for it.'

'It's great,' Evangeline said.

'Good,' Nico sounded as though he approved. 'Now, do you think you're ready to have a go at printing the next batch?'

Evangeline swallowed. 'Sure.' She had never felt so unsure about anything in her life before, but she was prepared to drop down dead before she let her father know that.

For an impatient man, Nico was a surprisingly good teacher. He talked Evangeline through the process and he didn't shout or swear when she made bad mistakes. By the end of the day they were both exhausted and Evangeline had a small print on the table in front of her that was all her own work. The picture was crooked and a little too dark and that made her mad with herself but Nico insisted it didn't matter – it was the best trophy possible for all the effort she'd put in.

'You did well,' Nico told her. He had been surprised to see her so driven and quietly worried by her perfectionism. She was only a kid. Perfection shouldn't matter so much to a kid of her age. It was like the cleaning and the clearing up she was always at. It was as though she wanted everything right. He wished she enjoyed mess more, like most normal kids.

She didn't look up, she just sat chewing her hair, but she was more pleased than she was showing.

'Maybe you'd like to learn how to take shots, too.' She could hear her father smiling at her and she thought she might burst with pride.

'You deserve cheesecake now – proper cheesecake from an Italian deli, not the sugary crap that hotel serves up.' Nico actually put a hand out and ruffled her hair, like she used to ruffle Patrick's coat when he'd done something extra wonderful. Evangeline didn't argue this time. Even cheesecake sounded good. When they'd finished eating he let her cut the end of a cigar for him. The other men in the deli laughed at that and she laughed along with them.

When Evangeline woke the next morning there was a large envelope propped on her bedside table, next to the hotel phone. She wiped her eyes and picked it up. Her name was written on the front in Nico's handwriting. When she opened the envelope a photograph fell out and, when she turned the shot the right way up, she cried out loud as though someone had pinched her.

The shot was the one of Lincoln with the mouse ears, only much, much bigger and much, much fresher. Nico must have done it, he must have taken the shot from her bag and got all the creases out and then copied it just for her. She ran her finger down the baby's nose and a tear landed bang on the back of her hand. Nico was right; photography was magic. Evangeline knew she was smitten.

13

Budapest 1985

Mikhail stood in the middle of Kapisztran ter, beneath the statue of the monk the square had been named after, and studied the tourists. It was a few degrees below zero that morning but the weather was no longer such a problem. He had a new coat around his shoulders and three pairs of good socks on his feet. In exactly seventeen minutes, when the church clock chimed the half-hour, he would go into the coffee house in National Assembly Street and sit amongst the old women with their white hair and pearls and order a hot chocolate with whipped cream and a slice of sweet pancake with nuts on top.

An American couple walked up to the statue he was standing in front of and paused. Mikhail could spot the nationality from the clothes the tourists wore. Furs for the Italians, and always good quality shoes. Trousers for American women and the men always wore a hat. The British wore inappropriate shoes and carried umbrellas, even in summer. Mikhail waited until this couple were busy reading the inscription on the statue before crossing to speak to them.

'Good morning,' he said in English. So polite, so formal. The couple smiled at him. 'Hi there.'

Mikhail pointed at the statue. 'John Capistranus,' he said, 'saint, Franciscan monk and fighter of the Turk.'

The couple's smiles widened.

'He led the armies into the battle of Belgrade. It was a great victory. American?' he asked. The couple nodded. 'Would you like a photograph of the two of you in front of the statue? Both together?' he held his hand out for the expensive camera the American was carrying. The man went to hand it over but his wife dug him discreetly in the ribs. *Keep your camera at your side*, the guide book told them, *Don't let a thief run off with it*. The man was in a quandary. He didn't want to look as though he was accusing the young man of thieving . . .

'I can use my own camera if you like,' Mikhail said, smiling. 'Give me your address and I can have the shot sent to your room by tonight. Cheap, too – not much money.'

The American smiled with relief. 'OK,' he said. They posed nervously for a shot, then paid a very large sum in cash. Mikhail chatted to them a little longer, then stood waving as they walked away. Claude's camera had come in handy. Maybe one day he would even put a film in it and learn how to take some proper photographs.

Tincan was sitting on a bench a few feet away, his hair plastered flat with gel and an ill-fitting jacket around his beefy shoulders. Mikhail sauntered over and passed him the couple's name and hotel address. 'Room 171,' he said. 'They're at the opera between seven and ten thirty tonight.' Tincan would rob the room later and pay Mikhail a little from his takings. Life was almost sweet as long as you forgot the past and tried not to consider the future. As long as you ignored the ghosts, too. Andreas didn't visit so often now and when he did it was only in dreams.

He looked at the camera. Sometimes he thought he could still smell Claude's scent on the plastic. Tincan had suggested he sell it and buy a cheaper one. After all, what did it matter what type he used since it was all a scam anyway? But Mikhail had wanted to keep it. Not for sentimental purposes; his only thoughts of Claude were of anger and disgust. No, Mikhail still had plans to leave Hungary one day for somewhere better and he thought the camera might help to find him a job. He had told Tincan, but the boy had only laughed.

'You'll never get out of here, Mikhail!' he had said.

'What do you think you'll do? Where would you go? Nobody wants the likes of us. You'd be as welcome abroad as a rabid rat.' His own plans seemed to have died in the past year. He still looked like a boy; his face was angelic, with its fair eyelashes and pink lips, but he spoke like a man in middle age. He smiled less, too.

But Mikhail continued to make his own plans. It was better than wishing he were dead. He deserved to die for what he had done, but he kept dreaming that, if he ever left Hungary, his guilt would stay there without him, like an old pair of shoes he had thrown away. But he knew deep down that guilt was not something you could just shrug off. It travelled in your mind, not on your feet.

Sometimes at night he dreamt of his mother and in his dreams she was warm and she smelt good. Andreas had said she had gone off abroad, but then Andreas had said a lot of things. Mikhail could not see the true face of his mother in his mind, but he could see Andreas's face every time he closed his eyes, as sharp as though he stood in front of him. Sometimes it was Andreas laughing but more often it was his brother's face as he lay dead on the slab in the mortuary. It wouldn't go away. And neither would the guilt.

When Andreas's coat had finally fallen into such a bad state that Mikhail had been forced to throw it away, he had torn a small rag off the corner first, as a keepsake. He carried the small piece in his pocket now, along with the toy submarine he had been awarded for bravery as a small child. They were things to look at when he got lonely at night; stupid things, kid's things, but they brought him some sort of comfort. Once the sight of them had made him cry a little but he had learnt to stop all that now.

When Tincan got back from robbing the Americans' hotel room he showed Mikhail a silver locket he had found amongst the jewellery.

'It's not worth much,' Tincan told him, 'too plain. Look.' When he prised it open there was some sort of a typed note inside.

Mikhail read it and shrugged. 'Something medical,' he told Tincan. 'Maybe the husband needed to wear it. Perhaps it says something about tablets he should take.'

'The stupid old fart should have been wearing it then, if it was that important,' Tincan said.

Mikhail turned the locket over in his hands. 'Can I keep it?' he asked.

Tincan shrugged. 'If you want to wear jewellery,' he said, 'maybe Claude's tastes rubbed off on you after all.'

But Mikhail didn't care. He took the small rag from Andreas's coat and folded it as much as possible and, to his immense satisfaction, it just fitted inside the locket. He hung the chain around his neck. He would never lose the rag now. He would wear the locket for ever. The thought made him feel better, somehow.

14

New York 1976

By the time she was sixteen, Evangeline was a whole two inches taller than Nico. She said it meant she could see his bald patch. He told her it was an optical illusion, brought on by the fact that he was heavier than her and generally less tense.

'You look taller because you're so totally stressed out all the time. Relax a little. Take things easy.'

Nico never took things easy; he was out hustling most of the time. After a year in the hotel he'd found them an apartment that Grandma Klippel didn't object to too strongly – though if she'd paid them at least one brief visit and seen the outside of the building she might have had a small seizure. Nico's trick had been to find a block in a neighbourhood that used to have a good name in the fifties, so that the old lady had no way of knowing how run-down it had become since then. It wasn't a bad area but it wasn't exactly good, either. It suited both of them, and that was what Nico said counted most.

Evangeline had insisted on painting the place. Nico had told her to try something bright, like pink, but she'd settled for tasteful pale creams and greens instead. She even tried painting a small intricate frieze around the top of the walls, but Nico had made her paint over it because he'd said it made him feel nauseous.

When Evangeline had finished with the furniture they'd sent a photograph of the place to Grandma Klippel and she'd written back saying nothing in particular – which was as near to approval as they were ever going to get.

Nico gave up chasing Evangeline's inheritance, which was not forthcoming, at around the same time. So there they were; father and daughter. It felt strange when Evangeline thought of it like that. Darius was her father and always would be. She had known what Darius did every day she drew breath – until the end, of course. Nico lived a life of secrets, but that was OK because Evangeline had never known him any other way.

She went to school and he went to work and sometimes when he was late home she would worry that he had gone for ever, like Thea and Darius – though she never told him how she felt. Instead she would whinge at him for having messed up the dinner she had cooked and he would moan, and they'd both end up happy because it was like a little joke – though neither of them laughed out loud much.

Inside she was nervous, though. Sometimes her breathing became funny and she would have to lie down until she calmed herself. Most of the time she was OK but sometimes she just worried too much about things and then this big wave of panic would rear up and overwhelm her. She couldn't help it. She didn't tell Nico, in case he worried too. He liked to see her relaxed and she liked to pretend, for his sake.

Nico taught Evangeline all he knew about taking photographs. What he didn't know she read from books he bought her. Sometimes Nico's advice contradicted what the books said but Nico told her that didn't matter because he was what was called 'self-taught'. By the time she was fourteen Evangeline was telling Nico things about taking shots that even he didn't know.

'You've got the wrong shutter speed for that new film,' she told him one night at the club. Nico had turned to stare at her. The group he was photographing began to laugh.

'Looks like the kid knows more than you do, Castelli!' a fat man in the front called out. Nico laughed but his face had become red. It was the first time he had had a proper argument with Evangeline.

111

'*Don't you ever show me up like that in front of those people again! Understand?*'

Evangeline gazed out of the window of the subway train. There was nothing to see there, only dark flashing tunnel, but it was better than looking at Nico's bulging face.

'What do you mean?' she asked quietly. 'People like *what*?'

'*You know what people – important people!*' Nico shouted. An old woman opposite started to stare.

'You told me they were all lowlife,' Evangeline said. 'You called them scum, remember?'

'Jesus!' Nico ran a hand through his hair. 'Why do you have to do this to me, Evangeline? Tony Corelli is one of the most important men in New York! You made me look small. What'd'you think he was thinking, eh? A man being told his job by his daughter? What were you playing at, eh?'

'You told me the man was just a chauffeur,' Evangeline said.

Nico rolled his eyes. 'Jesus, Evangeline, d'you have to believe everything I say?' he shouted again. The woman opposite had had enough. She started looking around for a policeman.

'You shouldn't tell lies,' Evangeline said, 'it's wrong.'

'Not always it's not!' Nico was losing it now. The thread of his argument had gone completely.

'Grandma Klippel said it always was.'

'Bullshit!' Nico felt a tap on his shoulder. The woman had located her policeman. A grown man yelling at a young girl late at night on the subway; it didn't look good, by anyone's standards.

'It's OK. The young lady is my daughter, officer,' Nico explained. The policeman turned to Evangeline. She had curled into a ball on her seat, chewing a mouthful of fingernails. He'd heard enough father-daughter excuses to last a lifetime. He could write a book on what he heard in the way of excuses and lies. He had learnt to see what he saw. What he saw on this occasion was a guy who could have passed for Tony Curtis on a good night when the lights were low and a tall girl companion who looked like a fresh-faced, long-haired kid, but who could have been a hooker or a victim of molestation, or anything.

'Is that right, miss?' he asked.

Evangeline was silent. Nico turned to stare at her. 'This isn't funny,' his eyes said, 'this is serious.'

Evangeline shook her head. 'He isn't my father,' she told the cop, 'he just followed me onto the train.'

It was a while before Nico spoke to her again. They moved around the apartment independently, neither cooking for the other and avoiding as much contact as was possible in a place so small. Evangeline was pleased, though. She had shown Nico the importance of honesty. Maybe he wouldn't lie to her again. Honesty was important. Grandma Klippel had taught her that.

That summer her grandmother invited Evangeline to the Cape for her holidays. Evangeline hadn't intended going but after her argument with Nico she thought that she would. Then, on the journey down, she felt that she'd made a mistake. She'd forgotten the quiet and the loneliness of the sea. It had been too long. Time had helped to stop the hurt, but going back only revived it. Her body slumped in the seat of the car Nico had hired and she felt sick at the smell of the salt air.

'Stop that with your nails,' Nico said. He had guessed without looking. This time she took her hand away from her mouth. 'What's up?' he asked. He seemed pleased by her discomfort. Maybe he thought it showed she preferred life with him.

Evangeline straightened in her seat. She was breathing too much; the panic was starting. The sky was never that dark in New York. The sky at the Cape always looked mean and heavy – heavier even than the sea itself. A screaming gull brought back all her childhood terrors.

'Do you want to go back to New York?' Nico asked, looking at her from the corners of his eyes.

'No,' she lied. She wasn't a kid any more. She closed her eyes and tried to hold onto her breath.

The house looked a lot older, as though the salt were carving it up to eat. One day when Grandma Klippel wasn't looking maybe the sea would come up and take it off altogether. Evangeline stepped out of the car and then stopped, astonished. Someone had spelt out: WEL-COME EVANGELINE in pebbles on the foreshore.

'I did that.' It was Miss Clayburg, a little chubbier than before but, apart from the weight, looking pretty much the same. Evangeline noticed she had a safety pin holding the fastening of her skirt together. Miss Clayburg saw her observing and smiled. 'Your grandmother's food,' she said, shrugging.

She walked right up to Evangeline and put her arm around her shoulders. 'How are you?' she asked.

'Fine.' Evangeline couldn't think of much more to say.

'It's been so many years, Evangeline. You've almost grown up now,' the tutor said, smiling. 'Your grandmother speaks about you constantly, though.'

Evangeline looked straight into Miss Clayburg's freckly face. Her eyes were all screwed up, as though she were staring into the sun. She looked across at Nico for a second or so and then back at Evangeline.

'I've been staying with your grandmother,' she said. 'She lets me work in the studio. I got sick for a while and the air here does me good. Do you mind me using your paints?'

'They were my father's, not mine,' Evangeline replied. She didn't care that Nico heard her call Darius 'father', she was in that sort of mood all of a sudden. He coughed and sounded uneasy.

'I have to be off,' he said. What he meant was he didn't want to bump into Grandma Klippel.

Evangeline watched him get back into the car.

114

'Phone me when you've had enough,' he mouthed. She waved as he drove off. She wanted to wave more, but her pride wouldn't let her. All the smells of New York went with him in the car. When he was gone there was just the smell of the beach and Miss Clayburg's herbal perfume.

The wind blew about her legs, making the hairs stand on end. Nico had bought her shorts to wear, just as though she was going on a proper holiday.

'Hello, Evangeline, dear.' Her grandmother announced herself from the porch. She held out her arms. Evangeline saw herself through her grandmother's eyes: taller and skinnier, with a mean little expression on her face, buttoned up and hostile, because she didn't want to be there suddenly, though she didn't want to be in New York either. Her hair was long now and there were frizzed bits where she chewed it.

She wore the childlike shorts Nico had bought her with a crochet tank-top she'd picked up at a flea-market. She'd bought the knitted hat there, too, and the army greatcoat she'd thrown over the top in case she got cold. Her new glasses were the granny-style all the kids at school wore. Grandma Klippel took the whole lot in and her arms dropped down to her sides.

'Oh my!' She shook her head from side to side, 'Oh my.' Nico had warned Evangeline.

'Did you do any more painting?' Miss Clayburg sounded hopeful. Evangeline pulled the folder out of her bag.

'I did some pictures,' she said. The tutor took the folder and hugged it to her breasts. 'That's great,' she smiled. Grandma Klippel stepped back to let them both inside. The house was dark and dank, like the hull of a ship. The windows and doors creaked when the wind blew in. There were new curtains in the hall and a bright ethnic rug on the floor that must have been a gift from Miss Clayburg.

Mrs O'Reilly took Evangeline's bags and gave them to a puffing Evan, and then they went into the front parlour for tea. While Grandma Klippel poured, Miss Clayburg set

Evangeline's portfolio down on the table and untied the ribbon.

The first shot in the book was a black-and-white of Nico. She had taken it when he wasn't looking and it was her favourite picture. He had a fat cigar in his mouth and powder from the cigar had fallen down his front. He hated the shot and it made her laugh every time she saw it.

Miss Clayburg looked at the shot and then she looked at Evangeline. 'I thought you meant paintings,' she said.

'It's a picture,' Evangeline told her, 'a picture I created.'

'Yes.' Miss Clayburg held the shot up. Her expression was still politely fixed. 'Yes,' she repeated.

Grandma Klippel stayed where she was, watching the two of them.

'So Mr Castelli's got you taking photographs, has he?' she asked.

'Nico says it's as good as doing painting,' Evangeline told her.

Grandma Klippel spilt some milk down the side of a cup. 'Did he, dear?' she asked.

Evangeline could tell she wasn't pleased. Miss Clayburg flipped through the rest of the pages politely. Evangeline had been proud of her work, but now she saw the shots through her grandmother's eyes and thought they looked stupid.

She had photographed things that she liked: flowers, animals, insects, people sitting in Central Park. Worst of all were the shots she had tried to make clever-looking: a reflection in a bottle, the dew hanging on a spider's web, a close-up of Nico's hand. Some of them were barely in focus. Embarrassed, she went across and took the folder from Miss Clayburg and tied it shut.

'They're very nice, Evangeline.' Miss Clayburg looked confused. She had pale downy hair on her face. Her teeth weren't capped, they were yellower – maybe it had something to do with her illness. She kept looking across at Grandma Klippel and rubbing her hands nervously.

116

'Do you like New York, Evangeline?' her grandmother asked.

'It's OK,' Evangeline said quietly.

'*Just* OK?'

'I like it,' Evangeline said.

'You don't sound so sure, dear,' Grandma Klippel insisted. She sounded tired. Evangeline looked her straight in the eye.

'It's fine,' she said.

'It's just that you've changed so much, dear,' her grandmother said.

'I know.' Although she hadn't realized it until that minute. She felt proud, suddenly – proud that she had changed. She phoned Nico that night.

'I want to come home,' she said. There was a pause as she listened to static on the line.

'Give it a couple of days,' Nico told her, 'just to be polite.' She could tell he was pleased.

Evangeline spent the next day with Miss Clayburg. They walked on the beach together and pretended to be excited about finding a few shells. Evangeline took them back to the house in her hat, though she knew she would throw them out before she left for New York. Shells smelt of the sea, tasted of the sea when you licked them, and they even sounded like the sea when you held them to your ear. She didn't want the sea going back to New York with her.

Grandma Klippel didn't appear for tea that afternoon; Miss Clayburg said she had a headache. They sat in the parlour that seemed suddenly empty without the old lady's presence. A clock ticked loudly on the mantelpiece as they ran out of conversation. Evangeline stood up to get some fruitcake, but when she noticed the photograph on the mantelpiece the cake flew from her mind altogether.

She had seen the photograph many times before; it was Grandma Klippel's favourite shot, a black-and-white of Darius and Thea, set in an antique silver frame. The picture had always been there and at times Evangeline had been unable to look at it because it made her so upset. She supposed it was taken on their wedding day. Thea was smiling so much she looked as though her face might split and Darius was holding her and looking at her as though he wanted to kiss her.

The photograph was different now – or at least the frame it sat in was. There was black ribbon wound around it and tied in a bow on the side. Grandma Klippel must have done it herself. Black ribbon meant death. So she knew they were dead, after all. Evangeline felt her hands begin to shake. She looked at Miss Clayburg.

'Did my grandmother find out that my parents are dead?' she asked. A sort of invisible wall came up on Miss Clayburg's face. Evangeline had just caused a problem, she could see from the way the woman's expression changed.

Miss Clayburg nodded. 'She did, yes.'

'How long has she known?' Evangeline touched the photograph gently. There was a small vase of dried flowers beside it.

'Oh, I don't know,' Miss Clayburg said, 'I never asked.'

Evangeline turned round. 'Did she tell you how they died?' she asked.

The tutor suddenly needed something urgent from her handbag. Evangeline watched her rooting and fussing about and knew she was doing it just to stall for time.

'They died in a car accident, dear.' Grandma Klippel had arrived from nowhere. Miss Clayburg looked up from the depths of her bag and her eyes were moist with relief.

A car accident. Of course. Evangeline saw them, suddenly – Darius, Thea, Lincoln and Patrick – all setting out for a fun ride. Patrick would have been leaping about the seats and Darius would have been yelling at him to sit still and Thea would have been laughing at the two of them and complaining about the dog's smell. Patrick had been due for a bath when he died, Evangeline remembered that. She

118

just wished she remembered all their faces better. Darius was just a voice now.

It had been seven years and she'd grown up in the meantime. She tried to imagine her mother, but her face was smudged, like an egg-stain. Looking at photos was no good; the shots she saw were posed. She'd never seen her parents like that in real life. It was like Nico's retouching – there were lies in that shot. False faces. False expressions. Each year that passed they moved further away from her but the hurt was always there, sometimes garnished with a helping of resentment, too.

'Where were they going?' she asked quietly. Grandma Klippel sat down and stared into space, her hands folded across her lap like a pair of newly pressed cotton gloves.

'Do you know,' she said, 'I never asked.'

'You must have done.' Evangeline's voice sounded strained.

Grandma Klippel shook her head from side to side. 'No, dear,' she said quietly, 'I never did. I suppose I never thought it mattered.'

Of course it mattered. They were going somewhere without Evangeline. They were off for a treat together when they should have been picking her up from school. They left her standing there at the gate. Flashes of ragged memories flew through Evangeline's mind.

'How long have you known?' she asked her grandmother, and the old woman shrugged.

Miss Clayburg was out of her seat, to stand next to Evangeline and pat her on the arm. 'Don't get upset,' she whispered, 'it's all so long ago now.'

'I didn't know until later,' Grandma Klippel said. Her eyes were closed, as though her headache was worse.

'They didn't want you to know,' Evangeline said, suddenly contrite. She took one of her grandmother's hands in her own. The hand felt cold and dry. She had never held her grandmother's hand before. 'Maybe people thought the shock would be too much. Is that what

119

happened? Did you just find out by mistake, like me? Cecil told me.'

Grandma Klippel opened her eyes. 'Cecil?' she asked. She was staring at the photograph on the mantelpiece, 'Did he tell you anything else?' Her voice sounded as dead and faded as the flowers in the little silver vase.

The more Evangeline stared at her grandmother the more she realized how grief must have made her slightly screwy. She was not so neat any more. Her blouse had a stain on it and the cardigan was buttoned wrong. Her hair needed some dye where the roots were growing through white. She was being eroded slowly, like the house. Maybe Miss Clayburg was there to keep an eye on her.

Evangeline shook her head. 'I don't know,' she said, 'I can't remember. I don't think anyone said anything to me after that.'

Grandma Klippel's eyes closed again and her body slumped a little. 'I need to go back to my bed,' was all she said before Miss Clayburg ran over to help her out of the room.

When she was alone, Evangeline picked the photograph up and stared at it. They looked so happy. Where were they going without her? No one had mentioned an outing. There was a mist over her memories now, though. Had someone said something? Maybe she'd forgotten. Something was bothering her but she couldn't work out what it was.

She tried not to think of the accident. Had the car rolled? Had Lincoln fallen out of their mother's arms? She hoped not. She hoped they had all died close together. Sometimes people got thrown out of windscreens. Sometimes they fell so far it was days before the bodies were found.

Maybe they were on a lonely stretch of road and not found for days anyway. But she knew that was wrong. The police were at the house. They must have found them that day. Something was wrong.

She woke up that night, crying. She'd seen them all going

over and over, like bodies in a large tumble-dryer. She woke up crying for Patrick most of all because he had looked the most stupid, with his huge clumsy paws flying through the air.

Evangeline had more questions for Grandma Klippel but none she could put into words and, anyway, she was frightened they might kill her. She wanted to go back to New York. She felt as though she would die too, if she stayed near the sea much longer.

She was called to her grandmother's bedroom the next day. Grandma Klippel lay on her pillows like an invalid with her eyes half closed.

'Evangeline, dear,' she began. Evangeline was spooked by the whole scene. Miss Clayburg stood smiling in the doorway, her arms folded across her chest.

'Are you sick?' Evangeline asked. Grandma Klippel shook her head.

'Migraine,' she whispered.

'Maybe you should sleep then,' Evangeline said. She wanted to be away from that room, with its strange smells of lavender and orange water. The blinds were down and the air was stifling. A bluebottle banged itself to and fro between the window and the screen.

'Dear, I have to speak to you,' Grandma Klippel went on. 'I need to tell you things, important things, difficult things. Do you trust me, Evangeline?'

'I know you never lie, Grandma.' Grandma Klippel hated lies. Lies turned into bad fairies that brought you bad luck when you were older – that was what she'd taught Evangeline when she first came to the Cape.

Her grandmother looked as though her head was hurting even more.

'I always wanted the best for you, Evangeline, even though you are not my blood.' Evangeline looked at Miss Clayburg for help, convinced her grandmother was rambling. Miss Clayburg had vanished, though.

'Evangeline . . .' her grandmother propped herself

121

painfully onto an elbow, 'I don't want you to think you weren't wanted. Ever.'

'By you?' Evangeline asked.

'By me or by anyone, dear. You could have carried on living here, you know that. Your father had rights, though. You were his child by blood, not my son's. Are you happy in New York?'

Evangeline sucked the ends of her hair.

'Do you have enough money? I could put you in a better place, if you like.'

'No.' Evangeline's voice sounded childish, 'no, thank you. We just decorated.'

'I don't think I did right by you, Evangeline. It worries me. Darius might have wanted better for you. If only you could paint . . . maybe Miss Clayburg could still . . . what if we . . .'

Grandma Klippel's voice faded as she fell back onto the pillows. Miss Clayburg must have been listening because she bustled in, a finger placed to her lip to hush Evangeline, and led her out on tiptoe.

'She has some pretty strong medication from the doctor for those headaches,' she told Evangeline. 'You mustn't take too much notice of what she says when she's like that.'

'Is she dying?' Evangeline asked. Her chest felt funny, like it was being squeezed. Miss Clayburg laughed.

'Not that I know of,' she said, 'she'll be as right as ninepence once she's had a good sleep. Migraines run in the family, evidently. Her father was a martyr to them. Maybe you should think yourself lucky you're not a true Klippel, Evangeline.'

When Evangeline finally got home Nico thought she was ill. She didn't mention the fact that he had cleaned up the apartment in her honour, and she walked straight past the pizzas he'd ordered in for their dinner and disappeared into her room. He left her a couple of hours before curiosity finally got the better of him.

'What d'you think?' He stood in the doorway with his arms held out. He was wearing a new suit, one he must have had made while she was away. He turned full circle so she could see the back. 'Classy cut, eh?' he asked.

Evangeline nodded. 'It's good.'

'Good? It's great. Old Henry down at Kleinburg's made it up for me. I thought you'd be pleased. I know how much you complained about the old one.'

'Did you throw the old one out?' Evangeline asked.

'Not yet,' Nico told her. 'I thought you'd like to take it to one of those thrift shops you go to, or something. We can burn it, if you like.' He stepped into the room. 'What's wrong, Evangeline?'

She didn't speak, she just sat curled up on her bed.

'Is it your monthlies?' Nico asked, looking embarrassed. 'Did your grandmother explain about all of that? Jesus, Evangeline, I never thought — not after that problem with that childminder. Do you want me to take you to a doctor —'

'It's not that,' Evangeline said.

'Are you ill?'

'No.'

'You sure?'

'I'm sure.'

'Did the old lady upset you then?' Nico looked angry.

'Not really,' Evangeline said, 'not deliberately. She just told me how my parents died, that's all.'

Nico sat down on the bed. His face had turned a shade paler so that it almost matched the paint on the walls.

'She told you?' he asked. 'She told you what?'

Evangeline sighed. 'How they died in a car crash. Nothing more than that. No details, Nico. I don't think she knows any more. She didn't even know where they were going when they were killed.'

'Does that bother you?' Nico asked. His face had grown tight.

'I don't know.' Evangeline chewed at her nails, 'I don't

know if it bothers me or not. Sometimes it seems so long ago. Other times it feels like I lost them yesterday. Did you love my mother, Nico?'

Nico was up like a scalded cat. This was not his sort of conversation. He tried to shove his hands into his trouser pockets but they were still stitched up. He wiped a hand across his mouth instead.

'Yeah,' he said, 'of course.'

'Did she love you?' Evangeline asked. 'I mean, you're so different from Darius. It's hard to see how she could have loved the both of you.'

Nico stared out of the window. Evangeline could tell he was embarrassed. 'She was an art student when we met,' he said, 'and I was a guy in a suit – a little like now, nothing much changes really. I worked in the clubs and I seemed a million years older and wiser than her and it was OK then because she respected me. When she picked up a few brains she was able to realize her mistake. I always knew she could do better than me but it was fine while it lasted.

'That's why I never hung around you in the old days, Evangeline. I knew you could do better, too. You still can – you are – and I'm pleased for you.'

'I don't have to leave you, though,' Evangeline told him. She was crying now, great tears of self-pity were rolling down her face. 'I'm not like my mother, Nico, I don't want anything better.'

When Nico turned around he was smiling. 'You'll go, Evangeline,' he said, 'but it won't be the same. You should go, it's the way things happen. Did you think you'd be stuck in this apartment with me for life? Kids leave – they get on. They earn vast amounts of money and keep their old men in comfortable retirement. That's what it's all about. It's OK.'

Evangeline smiled too. She was as embarrassed as Nico now, but they'd managed to say what needed to be said.

Nico looked serious again. 'Look, Evangeline,' he said, 'I know it's hard and it may sound like a dumb thing to say, but try to leave your memories where they are – in the past,

OK? Don't keep raking them over. Memories hurt and that hurt can ruin the present and the future. You're young, you have your whole life ahead of you and you should start with a nice clean slate. If you keep poking about I'm afraid you'll get hurt so bad you'll never recover from it — do you understand me? Yes? Leave it. Try to forget it. Don't keep asking how or why, just get on with your own life.'

'But it is my life, Nico,' Evangeline said.

He looked mad. 'Not now, not tomorrow, not the next year and the year after that it's not,' he replied. 'Take my word for it, Evangeline, drop it. OK?'

She didn't answer. She couldn't even look at him. Her head felt like some great empty room that ghosts roamed about in. How could she stop it? They were there. They were part of her. Darius. Thea. Patrick. Lincoln. Blurs with no faces, egging her on.

'You have a two-hour-cold pizza outside if you want it,' Nico said.

'I'll re-warm it,' Evangeline told him in a whisper.

'You always say that breeds germs,' Nico smiled.

'Maybe I feel like living dangerously for a change.'

She had the dream again that night, the dream in which her family were tumbling over and over in their car. Their limbs flashed by like dolls' limbs until she could no more make out whose was whose and what leg belonged to what body. She was sitting when she woke up, not lying any more. And she knew something. She had remembered an important fact.

'The car,' she whispered in the darkness. She had seen it clearly, like a snapshot that shock had printed fast on her memory. The day she had not been picked up from school. The day Miss Starmount had had to take her home with that crabby look on her face, because Thea hadn't arrived to collect her.

The drive had been full of cars, but even with all those others there she had made out their own cars among them. Thea's Oldsmobile had been parked right outside the house and Darius's had been half in and half out of the garage. She'd seen them. She'd wondered why they were both there when one of them should have been outside the school, waiting for her. What car had they crashed in, then? She looked at her clock. It was three thirty in the morning but she couldn't wait, she had to know. She crept out into the hallway and telephoned her grandmother.

The line was bad but the phone only rang twice. Miss Clayburg answered, which surprised Evangeline. She sounded whispery with shock.

'Evangeline? Is that you? What's wrong? Are you all right?'

'Is my grandmother there?' Evangeline was whispering too, in case she woke Nico.

'Lord, Evangeline, it's the middle of the night!'

'Please,' Evangeline said, 'it's urgent.'

She heard a noise and then her grandmother came straight on the line. For a moment the idea flashed through her mind that Miss Clayburg and her grandmother had been lying in bed together and that the tutor had just passed the phone across.

'Hello, dear, what's wrong?' Her grandmother sounded neither sleepy nor confused. Maybe they had been up playing all-night bridge.

'Which car were they in when they died?' Evangeline asked.

'Which car?' Grandma Klippel sounded like a long-distance echo. The static on the line sounded like the sea trying to butt in to their conversation, or drown them out altogether. It was like holding a shell to your ear.

'I saw both their cars in the drive that day. It's a real memory, too, I know it is. What were they driving in? Did they hire one, or something? Had they gone out with somebody else? What?' Evangeline asked.

There was a brief silence. She thought she heard her grandmother sigh, but maybe it was the sea-static.

'I don't know, dear,' was the answer.

126

'You *must* know.'

'No. I'm sorry.'

Miss Clayburg came back on the line all at once, whispering again. 'You're upsetting your grandmother,' she said. The nice tone had gone now, she sounded annoyed.

'I have a right to know,' Evangeline told her.

'Rights aren't written in tablets of stone,' Miss Clayburg said. 'You don't have a right to upset an elderly woman. You just accused her of lying, you know.'

'I'm sorry,' Evangeline said.

'That's OK,' Miss Clayburg was smiling again now, she could hear it in her tone.

'Were you in bed?' Evangeline asked.

'Of course,' Miss Clayburg laughed, 'at this time of night. Where else?'

So maybe they were lovers, after all.

When she looked up Nico was standing in the doorway, in his dressing-gown.

'I told you to drop it,' he said.

'Do you know more?' Evangeline asked.

'No. Drop it.'

'I can't,' she told him.

'You have to,' he said, 'you have to, Evangeline. Let it go. There's nothing else. Let them rest in peace.'

Evangeline shivered.

'Do you want some brandy?' Nico asked.

'No.'

'Good, you're too young. And the old lady's too old, incidentally. Go back to bed.'

So now she had her first commission; sixteen years old and she had her first booking. Nico could barely contain his anxiety.

'Stop chewing the rug,' Evangeline told him.

'You have no idea,' Nico muttered, 'no idea at all.'

'He booked me himself. He saw my work. He must like it.'

'Jesus!' Nico lit a third cigarette. 'Let me stay, Evangeline, at least let me stay.'

'No.' Evangeline was adamant. Nico ran a hand through his hair.

'What if you fuck up – sorry – screw up? What if the shot turns out wrong? What then? Eh?'

Evangeline put her hands on her hips and sighed. 'If the shot goes wrong – *if* the shot goes wrong – then I shall tell Mr Cortelli, or whatever his name is, that the film came from a bad batch and would he maybe like to sit again. It's not a problem, Nico.'

'*Corelli!*' Nico shouted. 'His name is Corelli – Jesus, Evangeline, don't pretend you don't know! You've seen him enough times in the club! He's a big businessman, so don't joke about him – it isn't funny.'

Evangeline bent over the table and went back to spotting prints. She pulled a strand of hair down and pushed it into her mouth. 'Don't worry,' she said. It came out muffled. Nico stared at the back of her head.

'Did you check the lights?' he asked. Evangeline didn't move. 'At least let me talk you through exposure times once again,' he tried.

'You told me, Nico, you told me a hundred times.'

'But I don't think you listened.'

'I *always* listen.'

'In a pig's eye you do!'

'Whatever,' Evangeline said. She could feel Nico staring. She hoped he couldn't tell she was laughing.

Antonio Corelli was as fat as a hog and then some. It was really a wonder he could walk at all. When he sat at his desk the chair disappeared. The fat on his neck ran out around his collar like a frilly pink skirt.

'I want a shot for business,' he said. The cigar nodded as he spoke. His eyes roamed around Evangeline's body as she looked at him. His office was on the second floor of a banana warehouse. Antonio Corelli was the Banana King of Manhattan. Evangeline felt her palms grow moist with nerves and wiped them onto the legs of her trousers.

'So Nico told you I was a chauffeur?' Corelli asked.

Evangeline laughed. 'I think that was just his little joke,' she said. The nut on the leg of the tripod was screwed too tight. She hurt her hand trying to loosen it.

'He's a funny guy,' Corelli said, without humour. He was assessing her like prize meat at the market. His hand felt round her buttock as she leant forward to take a light reading.

'He's a good photographer,' she told him. Her face had turned red. The nut on the tripod came loose suddenly and the leg slid to the floor with a clatter.

Corelli sucked on his cigar. 'He told me you were better,' he said.

'He did?' Evangeline looked up in surprise.

It took her an hour to set up and by then Corelli was awash with frustrated sweat.

'You'll need powder,' Evangeline told him. 'You'll look wrong without it, sort of shiny.' She'd hired a girl from the local beauty parlour, just in case. When Corelli laid eyes on her satin hotpants and knitted boob-tube he was like putty in her hands. She put a vast pink floral pinafore around him first, to keep the powder off his suit. By the time she was finished he had a face like a baby's bottom.

The session lasted another hour and three-quarters before Antonio Corelli called it to a close. He had missed two appointments already and now his dinner would be overcooked.

Evangeline told him the shots would be ready by Tuesday and he gave her his business card and told her to phone.

When Nico saw the print Evangeline was sending the Banana King he nearly went crazy.

'No, Evangeline! Definitely, categorically no! Absolutely not, do you understand? *Are you listening, Evangeline?*'

Evangeline put the print calmly back into its cardboard folder.

'It's a great shot,' she said.

Nico started to sweat. 'I don't care if it's a bloody brilliant shot, you *don't* send it, O K?' He was stomping up and down the room now. The old man downstairs would be banging on the ceiling with a broom handle before long. Evangeline could hear his muffled swearing from below and then the thump as the broom handle hit the plaster for the first time.

Nico sat down to reason with her. 'Look, he's in a frock, right? A pink flowery frock, for christsakes!'

'It was an overall,' Evangeline said. 'The beauty girl put it on him to stop make-up getting onto his suit.'

'Jesus!' Nico was up out of the chair again. 'You made him look like a fucking transvestite, or something! He has a frock on and cosmetics on his face! Do you know what this man is like? Do you understand what he can do to me? If I'm lucky I'll be ruined. Is that what you want? You and me in the queue for the soup stall?'

'You're exaggerating,' Evangeline said, 'it's a nice shot, Nico. Look at the lighting, look how I used natural light and then that other small flash as filler. It's O K, isn't it? Look how it lit his face. His features are in perfect focus, too – I looked through the magnifier. Even the cigar is good, I can read the name on it, and then the background is soft. Do you want to know what lens I used? What are you doing?'

Nico had the phone in his hand. 'I'm ringing him,' he said, 'to apologize. Maybe he'll listen to reason. I'll tell him you're emotionally disturbed or something.' He put down the phone before the first ring. 'What the hell can I tell him?' he asked.

Evangeline picked up her folder. 'Tell him what you like, the guy is a prize sleazeball,' she said to her father. 'Tell him I'm on my way round. If he doesn't like it I'll send it to the newspapers. He deserves it if a few people get amusement at his expense. He had his hand on my ass nearly all the way through the session.'

Antonio Corelli was in a meeting with his partner when Evangeline was shown into his office.

'You got the shot?' he asked, offering her a seat. His eyes were still doing it, still lazily stripping her of her clothes. Evangeline nodded. The other man shook her hand politely. The Banana King just stared at her beadily. 'Is it OK?' he asked.

Evangeline smiled. 'It's great,' she said. She passed the picture across the desk.

Antonio Corelli gazed at it long and hard and his expression never changed. Then he looked across at Evangeline and then back at the shot again.

'What's this?' he asked.

'It's an artistic shot,' Evangeline told him, 'I took it while you weren't looking – before you started to pose. It's off-the-cuff. Much more the thing these days. It's modern, different from the sort of thing most people have taken. I thought you'd like it.'

Corelli stubbed a finger at the frame. 'This is art?' he asked. Evangeline nodded. He showed it to his partner. The man said nothing, just raised his eyebrows.

'I'm in a frock,' Corelli said. His tone sounded even enough.

'It's a sort of ironic contrast,' Evangeline told him. 'The biggest man in the area, the man all people respect, not afraid to be seen in a floral wrap. Not many men could get away with it. You must have seen the work of Warhol. It's the same sort of principle.'

Corelli's eyes narrowed to pink slits. 'Are you pulling my pisser?' he asked.

'Absolutely not,' she said.

The Banana King studied the shot some more. 'How much?' he asked.

Evangeline swallowed. 'Two hundred dollars,' she replied.

There was a long silence. Then Corelli looked up at her again. 'I'd like one of my wife,' he said.

'No problem, sir.'

She ran all the way home to tell Nico.

15

Budapest 1987

Mikhail kissed his silver locket for good luck and walked into the foyer of the old Art Deco building on the corner of Dimitrov ter. He felt nervous somewhere in his stomach. The building was not impressive but it housed the offices of a local daily newspaper and Mikhail had decided to apply there for a job. To get to the building he had walked through the market hall and the smell of the vegetables had made him hungry.

He was eighteen years old now, grown full height, with pale skin and the shadow of a dark beard around his jawline. He wore black, which was the fashion, although he wore it because it showed less dirt. Not that he didn't wash; he was in a flat now and had a good supply of water, but the place was sparsely furnished and of course there were no wardrobes, and clothes got marked when you had to leave them lying on the bare floor all night.

Mikhail had been taken to the flat by a girl he had met on the streets. Her name was Elise and she had short brown hair that was cut like a boy's. She was a student; her accent was good and she came from a good family, but she preferred living rough with the rest of her friends. She was not the first girl Mikhail had made love to but she was the first one he had stayed with for more than a few hours.

Elise smelt of the patchouli oil she dabbed onto her arms each morning, after she had washed. Mikhail had been in the flat two nights before he screwed her and even then he wasn't sure that he had not made a mistake. Not that it mattered much; people were just people to him now, and if

133

he had to screw someone to get a good bed then it was better she was clean and attractive, at least.

She had a pretty face, a little like a kitten's, with small, white, inward-pointing teeth. He liked watching her eat with those teeth. His own were not so good; he had never seen the inside of a dentist's surgery and in the winter they sometimes ached and kept him awake at night.

She spoke very little, which was good, and she never asked questions, which was even better. When she was naked she looked like a child. The first time they had sex she came to Mikhail's bed in the middle of the night. At first he barely woke, but when he felt the warm flesh around his cock he threw the sleep off at about the same time that he climaxed.

'Why did you do that?' He was angry. He felt humiliated. He should have made the first move. He only fucked girls he chose and he hadn't made his mind up about this one yet. He glared at her in the darkness.

'I'm sorry,' she whispered. Her eyes looked enormous, like lamps. 'Don't you like women?' He watched her light a cigarette. 'Your friend Tincan said you used to fuck men for money. I thought maybe your tastes had changed. You're beautiful, Mikhail. Tell me Tincan was joking.' She exhaled a stream of smoke and bent forward to take his damp cock in her mouth. She ran her tongue around the tip and it was hard again. She looked up and smiled. Her ears were pierced and a small silver crescent glittered in each lobe.

Mikhail pulled her down and kissed her, tasting tobacco and toothpaste mixed. The skin of her face felt soft and wet with saliva. She was laughing beneath his kiss. He stopped.

'I knew Tincan was wrong,' she said.

This time he took her properly, like a man. It was a cold, soulless sort of coupling that made his marrow feel chilled like ice. She laughed all the time – quietly at first, but getting louder – so that he had to force his hand over her mouth to keep her quiet, which hurt and frightened her.

134

She came in silence then, stifling her own screams, and when she was finished he came too and then slept straight away, more exhausted than he had felt for months.

When he woke he was shivering; there was snow again outside and she had taken his blanket. He wrapped himself in the undersheet and felt the stiff patches of dried semen scratch against his legs. She returned with tea and cigarettes, his blanket still around her shoulders.

'You're a lazy bugger, Mikhail, you never get up before noon.'

She was laughing again, laughing as she spoke to him and laughing as she lit their cigarettes. 'I brought you some cakes too,' she said. She ate daintily, pulling small pellets of yellow pastry off one at a time before pushing them into her mouth. When she had finished she licked her fingers clean. 'What do we do now?' she asked. The word 'we' depressed him.

'Can Tincan live here too?' he asked. She smiled and shrugged.

'Do you two screw together?' she asked.

'No.'

'He's just your friend, then, is that it?'

'Maybe.' He'd never thought of things that way. Tincan was just around most of the time. He'd helped Mikhail and now he could be helped in return. Mikhail tried to imagine that he didn't care either way, but when he thought about Tincan he realized that he reminded him of Andreas. It was stupid really, they weren't even alike.

There were three other photographers trying to work his patch with the tourists now. He had been beaten up twice by their gangs and he was afraid for his life if they caught him next time. The money he earned was good but competition was fierce and he knew it was time to move on, which was why he had decided to try for a job with the local paper.

He knew what he was risking; he would have to lie about everything, including his age. Tincan had said he could get him the necessary forged documents, though, and he knew he had no alternative. His only options would be a life spent

135

starving and sleeping rough or palling up with a man like Claude.

Claude or Elise: he found little difference between them. Sometimes his lack of emotion troubled him, but then he thought of his dead brother and the pain was as acute as it always had been. He would never love anyone else, they were merely his means of survival.

He had Claude's camera tucked inside his jacket when he went for the job and he pulled it out for effect. There was a main desk which was empty, and he waited a few minutes until a commissionaire arrived. The man's uniform made Mikhail uncomfortable. When he saw uniforms he thought of the police. He cleared his throat.

'Yes, sir.' The man looked polite enough.

'I've come for a job,' Mikhail told him, 'a job as a photographer.'

The man smiled. 'You'll need references,' he said.

Mikhail pulled an envelope out of his pocket. Tincan knew what was what; he'd got Mikhail's references typed up by a friend the day before.

'And they'll want to see some of your work, of course.'

Mikhail wondered whether the man was just playing him along, though he could hear no sarcasm in his tone.

'My work?' he asked.

'Sure, shots and things,' the man said. 'I don't know, I'm just on the desk here, but most guys who come in have a folder full of their work.'

'Mine got stolen,' Mikhail lied, 'on a flight. Baggage handlers, I suspect. You know how it is.'

The man nodded. 'Are your references good?' he asked.

'Sure.'

'Then I'll get the picture editor down to see you. He might give you a go – he usually takes a chance if he finds you'll work cheap.' He picked up the phone.

He made Elise take him to the most expensive café in the area.

136

'Tell me now,' she said, clutching his hand, 'did you get the job, Mikhail, yes or no?'

Mikhail pulled his arm away. The waiter brought soup and some rolls. 'Yes and no,' Mikhail said. 'They want to see some shots. If they're OK I'll be in. They lost one of their photographers just last week – a part-timer – he died of a stroke. He was old, he'd lied about his age to keep his job. They showed me a photograph of him. He'd dyed his hair to look younger; it was obvious. He must have been desperate. Can you imagine?'

'You need some shots?' Elise said. She stared at the tablecloth for a long time. 'My brother knows someone,' she said, eventually. 'He knows a photographer, a guy he went to college with. You could take his shots along and pass them off as your own.'

'I didn't know you had a brother,' Mikhail said, stretching lazily. He smiled at Elise; maybe she had some brains after all. He lifted her hand and sucked the tips of her fingers.

'I'll find out,' she said. Her face had turned pink.

Elise went off the next day and when she returned she was looking scared but she had the photos tucked underneath her coat.

'These are good,' Mikhail said. They were press shots – nothing too special, but professional enough to impress a local paper.

'He doesn't know I've got them,' Elise said. She looked awkward.

'You stole them?' Mikhail asked.

'Sort of. Not really. I had to – he wanted to do things . . .'

'You screwed him?' Mikhail asked her. Elise nodded. He was impressed. She'd even stopped laughing. Maybe things were finally turning out for the better.

He took the shots and returned an hour later with a small bunch of anemones wrapped in tissue. Elise looked as though she had been crying, but she smiled when she saw the flowers.

'You got the job,' she said. Mikhail nodded.

'Mikhail!' She was so excited. He wondered how she could be so thrilled since it was he who had the job, not she. He could never have been so pleased on someone else's behalf. He wanted to smash the flowers into her face. She fussed about, just like Claude, pushing her way into his head and into his life. He needed her, though, he knew that and the thought stabbed like an aching tooth.

'How much?' Elise asked him. 'How much will you earn?'

Mikhail pulled a face. 'I won't get much and what I do get will be for results, not a wage,' he told her. 'The better the pictures the more the money. I just have to make sure I'm in the right place at the right time, that's all. There's a man in the lab there who says he'll do my printing for a few filler. All I have to do is take the snaps. I learnt enough about that from Claude. Everything's OK, Elise. Don't worry.'

'I wasn't worrying . . .' Elise began, but her voice faded.

Sex was better that night. Elise was quieter and more preoccupied and Mikhail was gentler because he had fewer troubles on his mind. As he fucked her she lay beneath him murmuring quietly and when he looked up and out of the window he saw the sky was as dark as velvet and the moon as thin and pale as a toenail clipping.

As he rocked backward and forward the silver locket with the scrap of fabric inside banged softly against his chest. The anemones he had bought for Elise stood in a beer glass on the floor beside the bed. The room was warm and smelt of Elise's soap. He thought of his mother and he thought of Andreas. He saw himself as a small part of a total universe and when he came he felt almost peaceful.

Elise talked in her sleep. He would have quietened her but the noise was OK, it didn't trouble him. She spoke to her father, sounding like a little child. Her father must have beaten her; she was begging his forgiveness. A tear slipped down the side of her face. She looked ghastly in the moonlight; her pupils rolled beneath their blue-veined lids and her silver-grey lips trembled over a stumbling fountain of meaningless words. When dawn came he knelt astride her sleeping body and let his lifeless cock rest against her belly until it was hard again. Then he fucked her awake, as she had once done to him.

'Papa!' She was still dreaming as he pressed himself inside her, though her legs parted and rose in a reflex action and wound around his waist. She never opened her eyes once, but her expression changed from troubled child to soothed adult in an instant. Sex was so necessary but always so sad. He could hear someone in the next room having a pee. There was a smell of bacon fat from the flat downstairs.

'Mikhail!' Elise shuddered beneath him. They made love four more times before cooking their own breakfast and each time was sadder than the last.

16

New York 1977

Nico was amazed at the number of commissions Evangeline got – amazed and proud. He bought a diary to log them into, despite the fact that there were seldom more than a couple a week and Evangeline would have remembered the details without having to look them up.

Sometimes she went to her sitters' offices and sometimes they came to the apartment, where Nico would entertain them with coffee and cigars while Evangeline set up the lights in the spare bedroom at the back.

They mostly came because Antonio Corelli said she was good and no one argued with the Banana King. They turned up in their suits and sat sweating self-consciously beneath the lights until Evangeline was ready to start shooting. Sometimes they brought their wives and often they came back with their mistresses. The women were mostly fat and dark-haired and smelt of talcum powder, which was caked beneath their armpits. Evangeline took the portraits and Nico painted out the moles and the moustaches when the prints were done.

One of the wives did a sitting with seven of her children and, to Evangeline's horror, they all had the same ugly nose and the same gap between the two front teeth. Nico spent an entire night painting out the gaps and trimming off the noses, and when the husband collected the prints he made no mention whatsoever of the retouching, but he paid two hundred dollars over the asking price. Nico said they should invest the money back into the business and so Evangeline got a new camera from the pawnbroker on the next block.

She loved that camera. She stuck Elastoplast across the back and wrote her name on it in biro and the biro leaked, so she worried that it looked messy and tore the plaster off again. That left a patch of glue that stuck to her glasses each time she looked through the viewfinder. This catastrophe brought on a panic attack of such severity that Nico nearly drove her to casualty at the local hospital. She hyperventilated and her eyes bulged. First she sat down and then she lay down on the floor. Nico put ice on her face and an old woman two doors down suggested a paper bag for her to breathe into. The bag did the trick. Ten minutes of inhaling her own carbon dioxide and the colour came back to her face.

'My dog is just the same,' the old woman said, walking off.

'Your mongrel has panic attacks?' Nico asked. He didn't laugh then but they both laughed later on, when Evangeline was feeling better. Nico solved the problem with black masking tape and a silver pen. Evangeline printed her name more carefully this time and then leant back to admire the results.

Evangeline Castelli, she read. Nico's pen hovered above the photo he was retouching.

'Castelli?' he asked. 'I thought your name was Klippel.'

'It is,' Evangeline said, 'but if I lose the camera in New York no one will recognize the surname.'

Nico went back to the picture. She couldn't tell if he was smiling or not. She scribbled the names onto a scrap of paper: Klippel-Castelli – Castelli-Klippel – it was the worst double-barrelled combination she'd ever heard. One day she'd have to decide whose daughter she was. Nico had sort of grown on her as a father, although she still felt as though Darius was the real thing.

Nico paid for her to attend classes in photography, even though she said she didn't need to.

'Anyone can learn,' he told her. He was right. The tutor was a thirty-year-old with a smile to heat toast on.

Evangeline fell in love with him straight away. She stopped biting her nails and she almost stopped chewing her hair. She also drove Nico so crazy he started getting home late on purpose.

'Your hormones are leaking all over the apartment,' he told her. 'The man is too old for you, find someone your own age. Besides, he's your tutor. He has rules – he will have signed documents promising to keep his sticky hands off your little butt. How d'you think he feels with you gazing at him goo-goo-eyed all the time, eh?'

'I don't gaze at him,' Evangeline said. She could hear herself sounding tetchy.

'Whatever,' Nico said.

'Yeah – whatever.'

Stephen Salford was British and Evangeline liked listening to his accent as much as she liked watching him work. He had long curling brown hair and he wore baggy corduroy trousers and white shirts with checked waistcoats. His manners were elegant, too; Grandma Klippel would have approved. Everyone in Evangeline's class was charmed by him.

Nico had taught Evangeline how to earn a living with her camera but Stephen showed how it could be used to create in a different way. He had an artist's view of the world; he never saw things how they were but how they could be on film, and in a way he changed Evangeline's view of the world, too. Sometimes ugly was good, he told her. Nico was used to removing all imperfections from his sitters' features, but Stephen sometimes magnified them to create wonderful images. He brought old men into the studio to sit for them – ugly men with wrinkles and lines – and Evangeline was taught how to find beauty in the texture of their faces.

'You'd never sell these shots,' she told him.

'Forget your sitter, Evangeline,' Stephen said, 'don't always aim to think of them as your customer. Just take great shots, if you can. Take your time, work out what you

142

want to do. Look at that nose, Evangeline. Can you see those pores in the skin? How about the lines around the eyes? Think how many smiles it took to create those lines. Show that, Evangeline, don't just show the pretty bits.'

Evangeline wondered how some of her businessmen's wives would take to having their pores and wrinkles magnified in such a way. Stephen's hero was Bailey. He showed her shots of his that made faces look like pieces of seasoned oak.

She showed him some of her own work.

'Who retouched these?' he asked. She watched him lean over them. He smelt of Old Spice. Nico said all Englishmen wore it. He had small ears, she noticed. His neck looked thin. She wondered how he would look in a tie.

'My father,' she told him. When he looked up she could see the faint ring of the contact lenses around his pupils.

'He's virtually repainted them,' he said.

'It sells,' Evangeline told him.

'You wouldn't recognize your own mother like this,' Stephen said, whistling.

'My mother's dead,' Evangeline told him. If she could have sucked the words back into her mouth she would have. Why did she say that? She knew why she said it. To get sympathy, that's why. The cheapest shot she had ever heard of. Stephen looked back at the pictures.

'I'm sorry.' He sounded embarrassed. She watched him push the shots quickly into the folio again and her face burnt as he handed them back to her.

'They're good,' he told her politely. She could tell he didn't mean it.

'They sell for a hundred dollars each.' She could think of nothing else to say. 'People are vain,' she added. Even he was vain. He wore contacts.

'How old are you, Evangeline?' he asked.

'Sixteen, almost seventeen.' He also wore a wedding ring. Did he have children too? She looked for sick-stains on his shirt. 'Why? Why do you ask?'

He smiled and rubbed at his eye. 'I don't know — you just seem to have a very real view of the world, that's all. It's good you found a market for your work, it's just . . . it's just that I think you should try a few alternatives, too. Experiment a little, see how it turns out. Don't stick to one aspect until you've tried a few others. You're young. Don't waste your talent — I suppose that's what I'm trying to say.'

'But I'm good at this,' Evangeline said.

'Being good isn't everything. Being bad can be good too, sometimes,' he said.

She told Nico. He said he wanted to meet Mr Clever-Smart-Ass in person. Evangeline said she'd rather die first. She showed him some of Bailey's work and he said he doubted the sitters would pay half a cent for the results.

'Look at that nose!' he said about one of them. She could tell his hands were itching to get to work on the retouching. It would have been the challenge of a lifetime for him.

Stephen took Evangeline to a photographic exhibition in a vast studio in SoHo. He said very little about the pictures, just watched her face quietly as she studied each one and then asked her opinion after a few moments.

She liked most of what he showed her. She wished she didn't — she wished she could appear more adult and critical, but she could never act and her admiration showed in her face. A lot of the pictures were nudes and she wondered how there could be so many angles to the human body. She liked the ugly ones but she liked the attractive ones better. She chewed her hair as she studied them but Stephen pushed the hair out of her mouth with his hand. He had long beautiful fingers and clean, white nails.

They drank white wine in the café and Stephen ate a salad. She couldn't eat. She wasn't hungry.

He had a mouthful of beansprouts. He pulled a photograph out of his wallet and pushed it across the table towards her. He sprinkled more dressing onto his salad as she looked at it.

The shot was of a woman with long hair and two small children. One of the children was a baby and the other had food around its mouth. They all looked happy, all three of them. A family. No dog, though – no Patrick.

'Your children?' Evangeline asked. Stephen nodded. He seemed to be watching her face for expression. A small piece of beansprout stuck out from between his lips. 'They look . . .' What in hell did they look? Boring? Normal? '. . . they look like great kids. Your wife must be very happy . . .' Evangeline's voice ran out – she just ran out of words. Lying wasn't good. Grandma Klippel would have been pleased with her for feeling that way.

Stephen nodded slowly. He took the photo from Evangeline's fingers and put it back into his wallet. Then he finished his meal.

They went back to the studio after the exhibition. The place looked solemn in the darkness and Stephen lit a candle.

'I want to photograph you,' he said. It wasn't a question; he went off to set up the lights. Evangeline followed him. He explained what he was doing, just as though she was in class, 'I'll use tungsten to get a more natural effect. What film do I need, Evangeline? Good, go and get me some. How do I take a reading? Right. Good. You do listen in class, then.' Of course she listened. She listened to every sound that issued from his lips.

He worked quickly and smoothly. She admired his confidence. It made her feel secure.

'Are you ready?' he asked at last. She stepped out in front of the camera. It felt strange. She hadn't been photographed since she was a child. She suddenly remembered that she was ugly.

'No,' Stephen told her. He walked in front of the camera

145

himself. She was tall but he was a good six inches taller. 'Not like that,' he said, 'I want to photograph you in the nude. Take your clothes off, Evangeline.'

She stared at him.

'Is that a problem?' he asked. She shook her head. No. She began to unbutton her shirt. Stephen disappeared again. She pulled her boots off and then her jeans. She stood before him with her arms by her sides, covering nothing. She had no idea how her body looked, only her face. Her nose was wrong and her teeth were too big. She wished she was beautiful, like the women at the exhibition.

'Sit back,' she heard Stephen tell her, 'relax.'

She sat on the covered stool they used for posing. She looked at her feet. They were pink where the boots had left marks.

'I've got lines on my feet,' she told Stephen.

'Rub them, then,' he said. She did. He took the first shot. She looked up, startled.

'What exposure?' he asked. She guessed. 'Wrong,' he said, smiling. She loved his voice. It made her feel comfortable.

'What do I do?' she asked.

'Do exactly what you want,' he told her.

The studio was warm. After a while she just felt comfortable. She leant back and closed her eyes and listened to Stephen talking. Sometimes he asked her to move and sometimes he asked her a question, to check she was still learning. Suddenly she felt him beside her. She opened her eyes.

'Now me,' he said.

'What?'

'You're learning, Evangeline. You can't learn if you just stay on that side of the camera all night. You can do some shots of me now, just to see if you picked everything up.'

He pulled his shirt over his head without unbuttoning it. His chest was slim and hairless, like a boy's chest. He

146

undid his belt and stepped out of his trousers.

She had only seen one naked man in the flesh before, and that was Nico. Even then it had only been a glance while he was busy fucking the babysitter. She'd known he was naked but she hadn't seen anything. She'd seen pictures; all the girls at school had. Most of them had screwed a few guys, too, but not Evangeline. She felt sick with curiosity and braced herself to be shocked.

Stephen wore white shorts. As he pulled them down the elastic made his penis bounce. He was circumcised and he had a lot of hair. His balls looked soft, like two mauve cushions. He stood over her, his hands on his hips.

'Well?' he asked. Evangeline stood up and he sat down on the stool.

'Check the focus,' he said. She walked across to the camera and looked through the viewfinder. She used his cock to focus on. Each pubic hair was pin-sharp.

'Meter reading?' he asked. She became busy now, checking lights and depth of field while he relaxed on the stool.

'Are you ready?' she asked when everything was right.

'Don't ask that,' he told her, 'it makes the model tense up. Just start shooting – it doesn't matter if the first few shots are crap.'

She thought his body was beautiful and prayed she could make it appear so on the film. She was more nervous taking the photographs than she had been posing.

'I hope you don't intend letting your father retouch these,' Stephen said lazily. 'He'd give me muscles like Mr Universe and a prick a foot long.'

Evangeline laughed. He was probably right.

They didn't have sex. When the shoot was finished Stephen walked over and took her face into his hands and kissed her and she could feel how badly he wanted her from the way his erect cock pressed against her legs. When the kiss was finished he laughed in a nice way.

'Go home,' he said, 'I'm married.'

*   *   *

Nico found the shots of Stephen, or rather he found the negatives, which was much, much worse, because he made Evangeline print them up while he watched. She had never seen him so angry before.

'You screwed him!' he said, with disbelief in his voice.

'I didn't screw him, Nico,' Evangeline told him, 'I just photographed him.'

'Like this?' Nico held the photograph up to her face. 'You *just* photographed him like this? With all his tackle *just* hanging there? Then you *just* chatted and went home? Jesus, Evangeline, don't give me that crap – you screwed him. The guy should know better. I can't believe he allowed this to happen. You're just a kid, Evangeline – he must have his brains in his balls. I'll talk to him. He's your tutor, for christsakes. You're a kid and you got screwed by your own tutor. Jesus!'

Evangeline chewed at her nails. 'I'm sixteen, Nico. I'm not a child.'

'Yeah, look at you.' Nico said.

'You won't talk to him,' Evangeline told her father, 'I don't want you talking to him. We did nothing. Nothing happened. So what if it did? All the other girls at school do it. What are you going to say to him, anyway? Are you going to force him to marry me, like some old Italian father? Go ahead, then, but I think you'll have a problem persuading him. He's already married, Nico. That's why we didn't make love.'

Nico's face darkened. 'Don't talk to me like that, Evangeline,' he said. 'I'm your father, for christsakes. Show a little respect.'

Evangeline laughed a nasty little laugh. Stephen had rejected her and that made her mad and now she was taking her anger out on Nico, even though she knew it was wrong.

'You're not my proper father, Nico,' she said, 'you just happened to fuck my mother. Darius was my proper father – he adopted me because he wanted me. You only came

148

back when you thought there was some money involved. You got stuck with me, Nico – my grandmother called your bluff and you got the booby prize – admit it!'

She thought for an instant that Nico was going to hit her. Then a terrible sadness came into his eyes and she thought for an awful moment that he might cry. She didn't know what would be worse – the blow or his tears.

He sat down slowly on a stool. 'You're at a difficult age, Evangeline,' he said. 'I thought we were doing OK.'

'Maybe in your eyes,' Evangeline told him. Something horrible had been let loose inside her and she couldn't stop it, however hurt Nico looked. She hadn't thought he'd give in so easily – she'd thought he'd fight back. It was like jumping on a kid in the school playground and then feeling guilty when they collapsed without a fight. Nico was shaking his head in the way a boxer tries to shake off a punch. Evangeline couldn't bear to watch him any more. She walked off into her room and started throwing things into a sports bag.

'Where are you going?' Nico had followed her.

'To Stephen.'

'I thought you said he was married.'

'He is. His family are miles away. He only goes home at weekends.'

'So he can fit you in during the week.'

'Shut up, Nico.'

He followed her to the door. 'How long are you going for?'

'For good.' She had no plan, no idea, she was just saying what sounded right, though it didn't sound so right once she had said it.

'Evangeline . . .'

She looked her father straight in the eye and the worst came out of her mouth: 'Christ, Nico, how could they do it to me? I mean how could they just go and die like that and leave me all alone with someone like you? How could they, how could they, *How could they?*' Her voice had risen to

149

an hysterical scream. She didn't mean it – not all of it – but then she did mean most of it as well.

Her childhood rose up like a wave in her mind. She looked at where she was living now: at the stupid apartment with its stupid little darkroom where she processed stupid little shots that Darius would have pitied her for taking, just like Grandma Klippel pitied her. She thought of how happy they had all been before, of the family they had all made. Life seemed to her to have been perfect then. Her grief was unbearable and made all the worse because it had been kept cramped up inside her for so long.

The misery was like real pain; it doubled her over and made her breathless. Maybe Stephen loved her, maybe he could give her everything she was missing.

She waited until the pain had subsided. When she straightened herself again Nico was standing at a distance, staring at her. She couldn't bear to see the expression on his face. When she walked out she slammed the door so hard she could hear the walls rattle inside the apartment.

17

Stephen opened his door the minute she rang the bell, almost as though he had been waiting for her to come. When he stepped back into the hall she could smell hot aromas of garlic and tomato paste. Neither of them spoke but she saw his eyes move without expression towards the bag she was carrying as she moved past him.

His taste was unexpected. She had imagined he lived in an absent-minded sort of a mess, but everything in the place was tidy and almost clinically clean. The apartment was painted mainly white, with bare boards, and there were chrome lamps on the walls. No photographs, either; she had expected a miasma of framed prints. All this was realized slowly, though; at the time her pain was so acute she saw nothing save Stephen's wise-looking face.

'I want to stay,' she said. He half nodded. She'd had no idea she would feel so relieved. On the way to his address she had been anticipating a disaster: that he would be out, perhaps, or that his wife might answer the door. He was alone, though, and he had allowed her inside without asking questions first.

A feeling of delayed panic overtook her and she thought she might faint in front of him. He saw her face turn white and led her into a small side room filled with bookshelves.

'I'll get you some water.' She heard his bare feet padding down the hall and the sound of a tap running in the kitchen. Most of the bookshelves were starkly empty. One had a clock on it that told the wrong time. She set her breathing by the rhythm of its ticking. Slowly, slowly. In the end she could sit up again.

There was a small lipstick stain on the rim of the glass he gave her.

'Do you feel better?' he asked. He was wearing cotton jeans and a striped shirt. She nodded and closed her eyes. When she did she saw Nico's hurt face in front of her. She opened them again quickly.

'Are you hungry?'

She shook her head.

'I was just about to eat,' he said. He took her into the kitchen where she sat on a painted wooden stool and watched as he ate his supper. He ate quickly and greedily, although always somehow managing to look elegant. He poured her a large glass of cold white wine and she drank it all. When he was finished he wiped his mouth on a paper napkin and leant back in his chair.

'What happened?' he asked.

'Nothing.' It was a stupid lie.

Stephen sighed. 'You mean nothing you *can* tell me or nothing you *want* to tell me about?' he asked.

'I don't know,' she muttered through her hair. He leant forward and pushed her fringe off her face.

'Well, let's go to bed then,' he whispered.

She looked shocked. 'You've just eaten,' she said. 'Never sleep on a full stomach' – it was one of Grandma Klippel's favourite adages. Stephen found the concept highly amusing. He laughed until his face turned red and then, when he had finished laughing aloud and was smiling again, he picked up the half-full bottle of wine and led Evangeline into the bedroom.

The bed was a large one, swathed in white linen sheets.

'What do you want to do?' Stephen asked as he undressed.

'Anything,' Evangeline told him, 'anything you don't do with your wife.'

Stephen laughed again. Then he kissed her.

'You mean you want the bicycle pump and the wet suit?' he asked. He kissed her again, more gently this time. 'What

152

say I just take your virginity in a reasonably civilized and gentlemanly manner instead?' he whispered.

Evangeline nodded. She wanted to be good at sex. She wanted things to be perfect. She lay back and opened her legs. Stephen laughed and pushed them gently together again.

'There are a few preliminaries to go through first,' he said.

'Like?' she whispered.

'Like I have to get an erection. Small details like that.'

'You don't want me, then?' she asked.

'Of course I want you, you silly girl. It's just that I need to get warmed up. Men don't walk about with permanent erections, you know – they'd have to redesign the shape of the trouser if we did. I want you but I want to take you slowly – is that O K, or are you late for some appointment or other?'

He tried for an hour but she couldn't relax. After forty minutes he stopped for wine. His hair was plastered wet to his forehead with the effort of trying. He poured ice-cold Chablis over her nipples and licked it off but, to her great embarrassment, it just made her bored. So bored that she even yawned.

'I think we'd better give up for now,' Stephen said.

'No!' Evangeline protested.

'Look,' Stephen rolled onto his side and pushed her hair back onto the pillow, 'not all men are studs, Evangeline, despite what you may have heard. I'd be only too delighted to keep trying all night, even after I'd bored you to sleep, but I'm afraid my poor old chopper has its own limitations.'

'One more time?' Evangeline asked.

'Are you sure, Evangeline? Maybe you're just not ready yet?'

'I'm sure.'

So he tried once again and this time they made it. Evangeline thought there would be pain when he entered her but instead there was just a gnawing soreness. She enjoyed the way Stephen's body changed once he was inside her. She liked the feel of urgency that overtook him and the way she could tell he was enjoying himself at last. He came almost immediately, then fell back onto the bed.

'I told you,' he panted, 'not all men are like stallions. Sorry.'

She inspected her body while he slept. There was a small stain of blood on the sheet; not much, really, though it looked stark and symbolic against the pure white linen. She ached and she throbbed but the hurt wasn't bad compared to the pain inside her own head. Stephen began to snore — not a deep, comfortable sound, but an uneven rattling that was difficult to listen to.

Evangeline rose from the bed and walked naked through his apartment. She knew she had no right but she didn't care. She felt strange, disembodied. A breeze blew through the open window and it was like balm on her hot flesh. She felt as though she had got her own back on Nico, now. She looked across New York and wondered how she could make him know.

'Stephen screwed me.' She had never imagined it would be such an awkward, unrewarding process. Nothing about it fitted, nothing felt right.

She thought of her parents. She felt dead too, now, suddenly, standing in that empty room when it felt like the whole of New York was asleep. Maybe her life was wrong. More than anything she wished she had died with them. They should never have been killed but — worse than that — they should never have left her alone. Had another car hit them? The idea had not occurred to her before. Maybe they had been victims of a hit-and-run who had forced them off the road.

Thoughts like that were bad. Anger welled up with the grief. Maybe there was a trial. Maybe someone was in prison right now for their murder. Maybe there was someone she should have been hating all her life.

She tried to remember how she must have been as a

child. She tried to think how bad she must have been for them to have gone without her.

Did they discuss it? Why had they gone out without her? Couldn't they stand her any more? What had happened?

She began to shiver. What could a small child have done that was so, so terrible? Why had they rejected her in such a way?

She resented them all for dying without her. How could they have hated her that much? All of them? They didn't even leave the dog behind to keep her company.

Her legs ached and she sat down on the bare floor. Nico. She hated him too, now. Her head was full of aching with big thoughts that were going nowhere. She felt good, though, she felt stronger than before. She wasn't a virgin now. She had had sex with a man she loved. Her life would be good now, it was all part of a new start. Her head ached, too. She stood up and went to the kitchen for an aspirin.

There were tampons in the bathroom and a Ladyshave in the wall cabinet. What were they there for – a courtesy for any unexpected female guests? Or in case his wife stayed over? Evangeline drank the last of her water and rinsed the glass.

She finished her tour of the apartment. There was a large lounge to the right and opposite it a smaller room filled with metal filing cabinets. She opened a few drawers and found them stacked with unopened boxes of photographic paper. There was a portfolio lying on its side nearby. She dragged it into the middle of the floor and undid the tape that tied it.

The first shot inside was of her. She had never seen a shot of herself naked before. She looked strange but not uncomfortable. Her breasts looked a little too heavy for her ribcage and her body a little too long for the length of her legs. Stephen had done well with her face, though. Her eyes looked large and clever and luminous and he'd made her smile without showing her teeth. Her hands looked large and raw, like a boy's hands.

The folio was full of nude shots. Evangeline recognized most of the students from her course, even the older women. There were men there too, young men with bodies like athletes. Stephen had made them all look beautiful. She wondered whether he had fucked them all, too. She stared at their faces, trying to discover an answer. Something in their eyes told her he had.

She took her own shot out of the pile and tore it up carefully before throwing it into the bin. Then she turned out the light and climbed back into bed. The sheets had grown cold and smelt musty, from their sex. Stephen still continued to snore.

Evangeline arrived back at Nico's a week later. He looked relieved to see her, but angry too.

'D'you get it off your chest?' he asked.

'Sort of.'

'Are you intending to stay?' He watched her as she threw her bag down onto her bed. The bed looked small after Stephen's and the sheets didn't look so white. Stephen washed his sheets by hand every morning. She had watched him while she drank juice and ate toast.

'Maybe,' she told Nico. She had to stay; she had no choice. Stephen had told her that his wife was due to pay a visit. She'd noticed the tampons and the Ladyshave vanish from the bathroom. So they weren't his wife's. She didn't think she cared, though. There were other things that still hurt more.

'Do you want breakfast?' Nico was in the middle of cooking eggs.

Evangeline tossed her head. 'I don't eat breakfast any more,' she said.

'I see,' Nico went on frying. 'New life, new habits, eh?' he asked. She couldn't see his expression.

'I suppose so,' she said.

'Anything else I need to know about?' he asked.

'Like what?'

'Like how you like your newspaper ironed or what time in the afternoon you usually take cocktails?'

'Don't be stupid.'

'Then get that snotty tone out of your voice, Evangeline.'

'I don't know what you're talking about .'

'D'you want me to tape it, eh? Play it back so you can hear yourself?'

'I'm sorry.' She truly was – sorry about everything.

'That's better.'

Things were all right then – or almost all right, because she knew she would never feel the same about her father again. Whatever easiness there had been between them had gone from their relationship. They became like working partners, nothing more. Nico never asked about Stephen and Evangeline never told him. It was like a cloud that had passed and gone, leaving only a shadow behind.

Miss Clayburg phoned and said Grandma Klippel was in hospital and then she phoned back and said she was fine after all, and that Evangeline was not to be bothered. Then Grandma Klippel wrote herself and said there was no problem, Miss Clayburg had just been fussing. Evangeline told Nico she thought Miss Clayburg was her grandmother's lover and Nico just laughed.

'As long as she has someone to bother about her,' he said. 'I always thought that big house was too lonely for one woman. Maybe she can achieve the impossible and get a smile back onto the old girl's face.'

Grandma Klippel sent a thousand dollars for Evangeline's seventeenth birthday. She spent the lot on a new camera. Nico didn't know whether to weep or be proud.

18

Budapest 1987

Mikhail discovered that he did not suit regular work. The newspaper offices reminded him of a prison and the other men there drove him mad with their petty concerns and conversations.

Because he was the junior he was given only the most menial tasks to do, things a man should never have to be troubled with, like filling in forms and making the tea. When he tried to argue, though, they all laughed at him and called him 'son'. He thought of all the stunts he had pulled when he lived on the streets and all the people he had conned, and being ridiculed by these idiots in the office left a sour taste in his mouth.

One thing he discovered was how good-looking he had become. When he studied himself in the mirror he saw only a dark, surly face with thin lips and cold-looking eyes. However several women at work had made passes at him, as well as a couple of the men. The prospect of his looks brought him no obvious pleasure. If it attracted types like the animals he worked with then he saw it as a curse, rather than a blessing.

He still met up with Tincan, though it was obvious they had less and less in common as time went on. They would meet in a café when Mikhail had finished work and Tincan would rib him for having a job, while he pitied his old friend for the tricks he had to pull to stay alive. But Tincan still had a good head on his shoulders; he suggested Mikhail stage-manage a few shots to impress the bosses. Mikhail followed him around for a couple of hours and pretty soon he'd got on-the-spot pictures of muggings and fights – all arranged courtesy of Tincan himself.

'Only make sure you don't get my face in focus,' he told Mikhail. 'I don't want my mug staring down from every police board in town.'

The shots amazed everyone and Mikhail stopped making the tea. The person who was most interested in them was the man who did his printing.

'Tell me just how you got these shots,' he asked, with a strange smile on his face.

Mikhail checked his watch. He'd been asked the same question by most of his colleagues and didn't feel like wasting time with this guy, too.

'I just wandered around,' he told the man. 'I happened to be in the right place at the right time, that's all.' He was getting annoyed at the man's expression, and at the way he wouldn't give back the prints.

'Sure you did,' the man said, grinning. Three of his front teeth were missing and the rest were bad. He smelt of the cough lozenges that he continually sucked.

'What does that mean?' Mikhail asked.

'Look at these contacts, son,' the man said, 'I processed them in the order they came out of the camera, right? These are in sequence, no question of it. So look at this fight here – what is this? The mugging of some innocent passer-by, right?' He pointed a stubby finger down the photos. 'There he goes, poor sod – biff, biff, ouch, ouch – he's on the ground and out for the count while the desperate young perpetrators run off with their pockets full of his money. But look at the next shot – what's this I see? By some miracle the same poor victim on his feet again and about to be pounced on by the self-same gang! A very unlucky sod, don't you think, Mikhail, getting roughed up twice in a row like that? Get the exposure wrong the first time, did you?' When he laughed, Mikhail stood back to escape his vile breath.

Mikhail's wages took a drop from that week. He had to

pay the man a proportion of his bonuses to keep his mouth shut about his methods. The man also tried to become his friend, into the bargain. Mikhail didn't mind the money so much but he did object to befriending such a lowlife. Then Tincan gave the man a quiet talking to in the street and he kept away from Mikhail after that.

Winter came and Mikhail offered Tincan a bed in Elise's place again, but, to his surprise, the boy refused. He seemed untroubled by the cold that year and, judging by the state of his clothes and his skin, he could not have been sleeping rough. His hair looked cleaner than ever before and he even smelt good, too. Mikhail recognized the smell.

'Claude,' he said, 'you're living with Claude!' Tincan nodded.

'You don't mind, Mikhail?' he asked. His face had turned pink and he couldn't look his friend in the eye. Mikhail had never seen him look bashful before.

'Why the hell should I mind?' he asked. Tincan blew smoke from his nostrils.

'Well, you two were lovers at one time, Mikhail. I just wondered if you might get upset, that's all. I dunno, you never know how people are going to feel about things, do you?'

'I wasn't Claude's lover,' Mikhail said.

'That's not what he says.'

'I don't give a flying fuck what that man says – he screwed me, that's all. It was a way of getting a bed. It was better than freezing to death.'

Tincan pulled a face. 'He still cares about you, Mikhail. He's got your photos out everywhere. He told me to ask if he could have his camera back.'

'What did you say?' Mikhail asked.

'I told him I never saw you these days.' Tincan grinned, 'You don't think I wanted him mooning about after you again, do you?'

There was a fire the following week: Mikhail read about it in the paper he worked for. Claude's flat was gutted and

Claude and Tincan were both burnt to death. The police suspected the fire was caused by the owner's invalid father smoking in bed. They said the flames were made worse by the rolls of film and piles of photos in the flat, which would have gone up like tinder. Tincan never stood a chance; if the flames hadn't reached him the thick smoke would have choked him to death.

Nobody could name him, he was described merely as an 'unidentified youth'. There was no mention whether the old man had also perished in the fire — maybe the police were having trouble counting all the bones. Mikhail hoped that he had; if not he would have wanted to kill him.

He showed the newspaper cuttings to Elise and she started to cry silently as she read them. Mikhail told her to stop — after all, she had hardly known Tincan. He wasn't a person to cry over — his life was going nowhere and he would have ended up dead sooner or later, whatever happened.

Mikhail went to Claude's flat later that day nevertheless, flashing his press pass at the cop outside so he could be allowed in. The place stank, of course. He took a few photos to make it look as though he was working. It was hard to recognize anything there; it was all black and gaping empty, like a mouthful of rotted teeth. Where had Tincan died? He tried to pretend it didn't matter but he still kept searching and guessing.

Some things hadn't been touched by the fire. There was a low vinyl-covered table Claude had used as a footstool. It looked hideously beige and normal amongst the mess. There was even an ornament on top of it, a glass bowl full of silk roses that Claude had bought from the market. Mikhail photographed it, then picked the thing up and threw it against the wall so that it broke. It was a good shot — he didn't want any other photographers getting it.

He walked along to the old man's bedroom. The door was still closed. He pushed it back, half expecting to see him still in his bed and staring towards Mikhail with one blackened, baleful eye. The room was empty, though; not burnt, but grimy enough to show there had been a lethal amount of smoke in there. One window was broken, near the ledge. Maybe Claude's father had crawled across from his bed and put a fist through it to get some air. The gap was just big enough to get a head through. Mikhail looked out of it.

What had the man seen as he died? Kids playing football in the courtyard below? A tree? The back of some other flats? He took a photograph of the view. If the shot was good he would exhibit it some day: 'The Last View of a Dying Man' would be the title. When he had finished he sat down because his legs felt funny. Once he was sitting he cried for Tincan. He made loud noises, like a child, and he hated himself all the while because Tincan had taught him to be a man always.

He submitted a couple of shots of the burnt-out flat to his newspaper. He got called into the editor's office the following day. The room was smaller than Claude's studio and there was a photograph of a nude girl hanging behind the desk. The girl had huge tits and a stupid smile.

'You seem to have a taste for the gruesome, my friend,' the editor said. He looked up at Mikhail over the top of a pair of black-rimmed glasses. His skin was like orange peel, covered with open pores.

Mikhail shrugged. 'If you can't use them . . .' he began.

'It's a shame you didn't get there earlier, while the fire was going on.'

'Yes, they forgot to tell me they were organizing it,' Mikhail said, 'my invitation must have gone to the wrong address. Otherwise I would have turned up on time.'

'They?' the editor asked.

'The people who died.'

'Don't cheek me, son.'

'Sorry.'

The editor leant back in his chair. There were sweat-stains under the armpits of his shirt. Editorial was the only office in the building that was properly heated, so sweat-stains were known within the ranks to be synonymous with power.

The editor cleared his throat. 'Anyway,' he said, 'I thought you had a habit of arranging those kind of stunts yourself, a sort of house speciality, so I hear.'

Mikhail stared at him. He would kill the printer when he got out of the editor's office – the man had probably talked him out of a job. He would get Tincan to . . . but he remembered that Tincan was dead and a big emptiness threatened to engulf him.

'That's a fucking lie,' he began, but the editor held his hand up to stop him.

'Look, son, to be honest I don't care how you get the shots as long as they look OK – understand? You won't be the first photographer to mock one up, so don't give me all that "What, me?" crap. Now, how do you fancy trying your hand at some more action stuff?'

'Action?' Mikhail echoed.

'Yes. The students' rally tomorrow.'

Mikhail looked blank.

'March the fifteenth,' the editor reminded him, 'every year the same thing, remember? They congregate in the square in front of Petofi's statue before they begin their march. Only this time I hear there might be trouble. The police have been accused of going too easy on drugs. They may choose tomorrow as a day to flex their muscles a little. There're a few old-time communists turning up to shout the odds, too. Hang around and see what happens, will you? With your long hair no one will know you from the students and you may get some good shots. If they're up to scratch we'll be able to sell them abroad, too.'

'Do I get a bonus?' Mikhail asked. 'I mean, I might get my own head broken open.'

'Sod off,' the editor told him. He was whistling a cowboy song as Mikhail left the office.

*   *   *

Mikhail checked Claude's camera over and over before he left home the next morning. Elise laughed at him but he ignored her — what did she know? He had been singled out by the editor himself and he did not intend to blow this important assignment. The sky was clear but the pavements sparkled with frost. He put on two jumpers.

He packed twelve canisters of film around his body. It was more than he would need but he didn't want to get caught short. His hands were shaking with nerves as he took the subway to the embankment.

The crowds were in good humour when he arrived, the students stamping their feet and smiling and chatting in the cold, while a huddle of police smoked their last cigarettes before the off. Mikhail hid his camera beneath his jacket and joined the students. A pretty girl smiled at him and handed him a leaflet, which he refused.

Then the old folk began to arrive, not more than twenty of them, mostly over sixty years of age, their heads held high and carrying the red flags proudly in their hands. When the march took off Mikhail ambled along slowly in the thick of it. A couple of the old folk began haranguing some of the scruffier students as they walked, and the kids jeered back at them in a good-humoured way.

After only a few yards the police started picking on some of the noisier students, throwing them against walls and checking their pockets for drugs. Mikhail stole a few shots but a policeman spotted him, so he tucked his camera back under his jacket.

An old woman fell in alongside him. She was short and bent but she kept pace without wheezing. A small dog trotted beside her, attached to her wrist by a length of old string. Mikhail brought his camera out again and her walk turned into a proud march as he rattled off some shots. She marched well, despite her age, and her black eyes glittered with moist pride.

They went over the Margaret Bridge in a wide arc and reached the other side of the Danube in scattered, disorderly groups. The police continued their policy of picking out the loudest types and the crowd's mood began to change. Some students started running as the police moved in, and Mikhail and the old lady got caught up in one of the faster-moving groups.

He didn't see what happened, but some of the police must have started a charge. Students were still smiling and laughing as though playing some sort of game of tag, but they began to move more swiftly and push at anything that stood in their way.

Mikhail looked back as the crowd ran at him. There was no real danger for him – he was big enough to stay on his feet – but the old woman was less fortunate. No one struck her but the sudden speed of the others as they hurtled past caught her off balance and she fell. Mikhail saw her go in slow motion and he had his camera pointing at her before she hit the ground. It was all over in seconds.

As the students passed, the old woman's skull hit the pavement with a sickening crack. She landed daintily, her arms clutched to her narrow chest and one gloved hand still gripping the dog lead. When Mikhail moved closer she looked as though she were smiling and then blood started to leak out of her head and he saw brains there too, like grey jelly on the kerbside. The little dog sniffed at the blood as though he might lick it. Mikhail pulled him away with one hand and carried on shooting with the other.

As he looked through the viewfinder to check the focus he suddenly saw to his horror that the woman's eyes were open and she was looking at him. A groan came from her lips. He stopped shooting and stared down at her. If she had been a wild bird he would have stomped on her head. He looked about for help but everyone had gone. The eyes still stared. He had a job to do, he remembered. You put yourself first. Others came second. This old woman had just come last. He raised his camera again and carried on shooting. He was a photographer, not a medic.

The woman died. He let the dog go and photographed it

sitting pathetically by her corpse. The two of them to-gether told an even better story. The string slipped out of the old woman's hand at last and, when the police moved in and Mikhail moved away, he found the dog was following him, leaving a trail of tiny bloody paw-marks in the frost.

Mikhail did not go back to the newspaper that day. Instead he went to the printer and pushed the man around until he printed up the shots for free. Even he whistled through his front teeth when he saw them.

'These are good, Mikhail,' he said, trying to be friends again. 'The boss will be delighted when he sees them.'

Mikhail took the prints and pushed them into his jacket. When he got home he took them straight to the light. Elise was there, reading a novel. She watched him over her glasses.

'Are you OK, Mikhail? Did you get good shots? I hear it got a bit rough. I was so worried I nearly went out looking for you.'

Mikhail barely heard what she said. He felt hot; his face was sweating. He peeled off a jumper and threw it onto the floor. Mikhail stared at the shots. A death: start to finish. The old woman, marching proudly, then tram-pled by students, her pride suddenly replaced with shock. Her thin body, curled up on the pavement, and then – *the exact moment of death*. There were two shots, taken only seconds apart. In the first her eyes were gleaming, plead-ing for help. In the second they were filmy and empty.

Suddenly, they were Andreas's eyes, the eyes he had seen on the mortuary slab. Accusing eyes. Eyes that knew the big secret. He wiped the sweat off his forehead with the back of his wrist and when he looked again they were just the eyes of the old woman.

'Get a pen,' he told Elise. He dictated the story to her and she wrote it down for him: the proud old communist and the drug-crazed students who attacked her for her beliefs. Her red flag lay beside her on the pavement like the pool of her own blood. Elise toned the story down a little and then read it back.

'Is this true?' she asked. She had tears in her eyes. 'Did this really happen, Mikhail? Did they attack her?' She was a student herself – she couldn't bear to think of it happening as he had described.

'Look at the pictures, Elise,' Mikhail told her. 'What do you think?'

She studied the shots and then she wept for real. 'I wouldn't have believed it!' she gasped.

'Believe your eyes,' Mikhail said. 'The camera can only show the truth, after all.'

Mikhail took the shots and the story to a big news agency on the right bank, flashing his newspaper pass at the doormen until he was shown to the press room. The place was packed and nobody noticed him. He stopped the first man that walked past and, when he explained his business, was directed to an unattended desk in the furthest corner of the room.

'Where is Peter Kobal?' he asked a secretary.

The woman looked at her watch. 'At the baths,' she told him. She didn't stop typing long enough to look up.

'Which baths?' Mikhail was getting impatient.

'Gellert, of course,' she said. She glanced up quickly and her expression changed. She actually smiled. 'He goes there for his back,' she said.

'Of course,' Mikhail answered. He could feel the woman's eyes watching him as he walked slowly out of the room. When he reached the door he turned and gave her an idiotic wave, then saw her blush and get on with her work.

The baths were modern, but built to look like something from the Middle East, with turquoise tiles, gilded pillars and marble walls. Mikhail found the picture editor in the sulphur baths, basking in the steam with a chessboard in front of him. The man was fat and naked. His glasses were taped to his nose to prevent them slipping down in the condensation.

When Mikhail introduced himself Kobal asked for a towel and wiped his hand before shaking it.

'Special glass,' he told Mikhail, pointing to his glasses, 'made so they don't steam up. Exported from Japan – they cost me a fortune and they still don't work. Do you want a game of chess?'

Mikhail shook his head. 'I came to show you these.' He pulled the photos out of his jacket. The man wiped his glasses on his towel and peered at them.

'The March fifteenth rally,' he said. 'I didn't know this had happened. Why have you brought them today? Why not yesterday?'

'I had to get them printed,' Mikhail explained.

The man stared at him. 'This is old news,' he said.

'How can it be,' Mikhail asked, 'since no one else covered it? Do you want to buy the story or not?'

The man sighed. 'I take it you're new to this business?' he asked.

'Not so new you can screw me,' Mikhail said. He spoke loudly now; several other bathers had started to stare.

The picture editor smiled. 'You were a friend of Claude's, weren't you?'

Mikhail swallowed. 'Claude?'

The man nodded. 'I sold a few of his shots for him – not to the newspapers, of course. I'm sure I saw a couple of you. What a tragic waste his death was, eh? Terrible, terrible. He used to come down here a lot, you know. Most of the chaps knew him. How much do you want for these?' he asked, turning back to the photos.

Mikhail barely heard the question. The picture editor offered him as much as he would earn in a week on the newspaper.

'Do you take commissions, too?' he asked.

Mikhail nodded slowly.

19

'You're leaving me!' Elise was screaming, crying, nearly vomiting with grief as she tried to prevent Mikhail from going. Snot streamed from her nose. He had had no idea that she would behave in such a way. He continued to pack what few possessions he had into a canvas bag.

'No, Mikhail, *no*!' She wrenched the bag away from him and it rolled onto the floor behind the bed. He waited, hands on hips, embarrassed by her emotion.

'I have a job abroad, that's all, Elise – a foreign assignment. It happens all the time. I'll be back in a few months.'

'You won't come back, I know it!'

He shook his head slowly. 'So?'

She became still suddenly – so suddenly that he looked up. She was panting like an animal, staring at him. There was a stain on her blouse and the skin on her chest was red, like a rash.

'I'm pregnant.' she said.

He laughed. 'Don't be stupid.'

'It's true.' Her eyes had become crazed, boring into his face.

'You're lying,' he said.

'You think so?' she was smiling now. 'What do you know, you bastard?'

'Elise, this is ridiculous . . .'

'I'm pregnant, Mikhail.' He could hear her breathing – quick, short pants. Fuck you, Mikhail, fuck you to death.

He walked across the room slowly and bent to pick up his bag. The smile died from her face. She looked comical, like a little animal. He could see her thoughts written on her face: What now? What can I try next?

'Do you realize how old I am, Elise?' Of course she did, she had bought him a gold bracelet for his birthday. He was going to sell it the minute he got to the station. 'I'm nineteen, Elise, that's all.' She could not meet his eyes. Her face turned pink. 'Tell me again,' he said, quietly, 'tell me you're pregnant.' She could not sustain the lie. Her face crumpled.

It didn't matter; what counted was the job. He was off on his first trip abroad, his first proper commission. He'd worked hard for the chance, harder than most people could ever have imagined. He was getting away from the streets at last; that was the only truth that mattered.

20

New York 1982

Nico had bought Evangeline a Louis Vuitton case and giftwrapped it in silver foil with a pink bow on top.

'It's a turkey,' she said, 'I didn't know it was Thanksgiving already.'

Nico beamed and puffed on a cigar. He smoked all the time now – fat Havannahs that he got from the other guys down at the club. He was slowing down a little these days, but not too much. What few grey hairs he had he dyed and forgot about. He was a few inches thicker around the waist, but so what? His clothes still hung well enough. A fat belly meant affluence where he came from. Even Tony Curtis looked like he wore a rug these days.

His friends were always congratulating him for having such a clever daughter, and the cigars were poked into his top pocket like fountain pens as part of the compliment. He knew why they did it: he had a daughter of twenty-two and she was still unmarried. It was out of embarrassment that the compliments of her work were always flowing like wine. Nobody mentioned the lack of a husband and children. She was good at her job – it was something nice to say.

'That girl of yours, Nico, she made my wife happier than I ever managed! Did you see those photographs! We have one over the bed, believe me. I don't know what I'm seeing any more – my wife the film star who hangs on the wall or my wife the cold cream queen I see on the pillow beside me. How does she do it? She worked a miracle!'

Evangeline had been earning enough for a full-time career but she'd still insisted on going to a proper college.

'You're good enough.' Nico told her when she enrolled.

'I want to be better,' she said, 'I want to be perfect.'

'Nobody's perfect, Evangeline.'

'Maybe nobody tried hard enough yet.'

Evangeline tried.

Two weeks after her graduation she came home with a contract.

'It's my own job, Nico, the first one I got myself.'

Nico screwed up his eyes as he studied the sheet of paper. It was typed badly, he could see that, with a few spelling mistakes here and there, too.

'The college arranged this for you?'

'Hmm-mm,' Evangeline nodded. She was trying to look busy at something else, bending over the sink scraping the mark off a cup with a scouring pad. There were no marks on the cups – Nico had just washed them himself. She was wearing some old trousers with a t-shirt that had bleach stains on it. Nico wore tight, snow-white cotton jeans and a black leather flying jacket. It was what all the guys wore, including Tony Curtis. Their wives still wore frocks and had their hair teased up like candyfloss. Their daughters, if they had them, mostly wore designer-label suits, apart from the handful that dressed like punks.

Nico didn't like the punks' look with their pink hair and safety pins, and he commiserated with the parents when they wondered what things were coming to, but at least those kids had a sense of their own style. At twenty-two Evangeline just looked like the usual thrift-shop disaster. She wasn't a pretty girl, but not plain, either, when she tried – but the clothes she wore made her look ugly. He thought her hair looked like a mane and he liked it better up, like her mother had worn it when he had first met her. She could have doubled for Thea if she'd tried, but it appeared she didn't want to.

Nico had bought her nice clothes over the years, but

172

she'd always laughed and looked embarrassed and he'd never ever seen them again.

Baggy slacks, waistcoats, cardigans and clogs – that was all he ever saw her in. If she had a good body then no one would ever know. Her hair was just pushed back into a selection of rubber bands and she stuck things into it absent-mindedly; things like biros and bulldog clips that would wobble around in there for hours, if he let them. It had a life of its own, her hair – it wasn't his hair and it certainly wasn't Thea's. Sometimes he wondered whether Thea had cheated on him when he looked at that hair, but then one look at Evangeline's face was enough to assure him that she could only be his daughter.

Her nose was too big and her chin too pointed and her mouth had the same stubborn look about it that he saw in the mirror every morning. Her eyes were grey with flecks, like Thea's. When he caught her off-guard they were so big and so full of pain sometimes that he didn't notice the nose and the chin at all. It was why he didn't spend too long looking at her, if he could help it. He felt some of that hurt was his responsibility.

It amazed Nico that she always seemed popular with the boys, despite her appearance. If she went out on dates she never dressed up; she just slung an old navy pea-jacket over her cardigan and maybe swapped her glasses for contacts.

Most of the time she just said she was too busy, though, and Nico was often relieved to hear it. He'd opened the door to too many keen young kids dressed up in gaberdine suits and button-down shirts and silk designer ties and hair-gel and then watched in shame as his daughter lumbered into view with her bird's-nest hair and those clogs on her feet.

Sometimes she took her camera out on dates, too. 'Just in case,' she would say. Nico was worried. His daughter was a grown woman now. In his day women of twenty-two were married with one or two kids. He tried to think modern but the fear still remained that soon she'd be left on the shelf for good if she didn't pull herself together and get her hair straightened, or something.

He stopped staring at her and went back to the contract again.

'Charlie Gregg?' he asked. 'They want you to take photographs of Charlie Gregg?'

Evangeline held the cup up to the light. If she scrubbed much harder the pattern would be gone. 'I'm going on tour with him,' she said. 'They want me as the official tour photographer.'

'Charlie Gregg?' Nico repeated. 'But I've heard of him, Evangeline – I mean *I* know of him. I know who he is. That must date him back to the sixties some time. How old is he?'

Evangeline shrugged. 'I don't know. It's his comeback tour.'

Nico laughed. 'Comeback from where? The cemetery? This guy hasn't done anything for years! What is this tour, "by popular demand"? What, did he finally get a fan letter, or something? Jesus! Hey! Wait wait wait! What's this date, Evangeline? When's this? Next week? You can't. No – no way! This is a joke, right?'

Evangeline turned round at last. Her face looked angry. Her mouth had gone white and she had stopped cleaning the mug at last.

'It's next week,' she said, 'and I'm going.'

Nico shook his head. 'Whoa, wait a minute. Think, Evangeline. Stop and think. The Scalaachi brothers? Mr Andrelli's new baby son? The wedding at the Connaught Rooms? These jobs are all booked, Evangeline. You can't just go off around the country like that! These are important people. You know you can't do this.'

Evangeline bit her lip. 'You can do them, Nico,' she said.

'Me? No.' He folded his arms across his chest to back up his point. 'No, Evangeline. They booked you, they want you.'

'They'd be just as happy with you, Nico,' Evangeline insisted. 'This is important to me, it's the first paid commission I got by myself.'

'Why so last-minute?' Nico asked.

'The other photographer backed out,' Evangeline said. 'They called the college to see who they could get. My tutor suggested me. It's an honour, Nico. I've said I'll go. I can't let them down.'

'You'd let *me* down, though.' Nico sighed.

'I thought you could cover for me,' Evangeline said.

'Well you thought wrong.'

He drove her to the coach station, moaning all the way. She made him park around the corner, out of sight of the others. She wanted them to think she had arrived under her own steam; it was important to her. He watched her walk off, a tall, rangy-looking woman with cameras and bags strapped across her body. In her khaki-coloured trousers and white shirt she reminded him of a Victorian explorer going on expedition.

'Good luck,' he called, but if she heard him she made no acknowledgement of the fact. He watched a while anyway.

The coach was an old hippie-mobile, painted with grey storm scenes and galloping stallions. Evangeline laughed when she saw it and then she felt a bit sick. She wouldn't turn around to see, but she hoped Nico hadn't caught sight of it. The name 'Charlie Gregg' was emblazoned across the side in fluorescent orange and gold lettering. There was a dent in the bodywork in the middle, though, so the letter 'G' looked distorted.

Two roadies were loading up round the back. They worked silently and easily but their expressions said they were agency men who had been expecting better, too. She went round to watch and, apart from a first glance, they mostly ignored her. She thought of taking some shots but she knew Nico hadn't driven off yet and there was a sort of a lazy tension hanging in the air.

175

A dry wind blew up from nowhere, throwing her hair across her face.

'Is Charlie here yet?' she asked. One of the guys half pointed inside the bus. He may even have spoken but it was too windy to tell.

'Pissed as a fart,' the other said out of the corner of his mouth and they both grinned at the ground.

'Right,' Evangeline said.

The roadie stopped work and looked at her, scratching his balls half-heartedly. 'You old Charlie's make-out artist?' he asked and they both sniggered.

'What?' Evangeline put a hand up to stop the dust blowing in her face.

'You his piece or something?'

'No.'

They began to look bored again at that. 'Thought not,' the roadie said, 'we heard old Charlie was a bit of a chubby-chaser. You look too scrawny for that.'

'I'm the photographer,' Evangeline said.

'Wanna take our shot?' They mugged a pose for her. When they smiled the sun shone off one of the men's gold teeth.

She clambered inside the bus carefully. The blinds were down and the place stank like an empty nightclub. Charlie Gregg lay across a row of seats at the back, his boots still on his feet and a big old cowboy hat resting on his face. A fat girl sat beside him, filing her nails. She was naked apart from a pair of men's odd socks, but didn't bother to look up.

'Charlie?' Evangeline walked down the aisle, holding the luggage rail to stop her tripping in the dark. The girl inclined her head but the singer never moved.

'OK, buddy,' Evangeline whispered, and lifted her camera instead. 'Shit!' Not enough light. She leant between the girl and the sleeping form and pulled the blind up slowly. An arc of yellow light poured in, diffused by the thick coating of dust and exhaust across the coach's rear window.

176

She got more than a dozen shots before Charlie woke up. She even managed to prise the hat off his face and shoot him snoring and cursing in his sleep. When his eyes opened they opened suddenly and fully, making her jump. His face seemed to rearrange itself as it came to life and he sat up. The skin was tucked and lifted as tight as a snare drum but it was still a pleasant face: clean as a flannel, sun-tanned, even boyish-looking once the correct expression was finally in place.

'Are you a fan?' he asked. His eyes were a bright, sharp blue. They looked at Evangeline with pleasant speculation, as though he were expecting her to ask for his autograph. The naked girl got up without being asked and he slapped her bare rump as she wobbled off.

'No,' Evangeline told him, 'I'm the official tour photographer.'

'And not a fan.'

'I'm sorry,' she began, embarrassed, 'I didn't mean I don't like your music too, I just . . .'

'S'all right.'

'Sorry.'

'Don't think about it. And stop biting your nails.'

Evangeline laughed. 'You sound like my father.'

'Well then, your father has a point. He sounds like a sound man. Yes.' Charlie's eyes narrowed. 'Were you taking my picture just then?'

'Yes.'

'While I was asleep?'

Evangeline nodded. Charlie stared at her. 'Does that sort of thing sell?'

'I hope so.'

'OK,' he yawned. 'OK,' he repeated, 'OK.'

The tour was a success with the fans, who were mainly women who had grown old along with Charlie and were trying to recover their lost youth. The single he had released to coincide with the tour only reached the lower depths of the top thirty, but it seemed sweet enough for Charlie himself; as long as the wages got paid and the beer still flowed he was capable of having a good time.

He slept a lot and screwed a lot and sang a lot and sometimes swore a lot, and he was happy enough to let Evangeline photograph him throughout. She beat him at arm-wrestling and he taught her how to drink bourbon. She found him good company, even when he was drunk as a skunk. He made a pass at her one day, but he wasn't unduly upset when she told him to sod off. If he'd made the pass when he was sober she might almost have been flattered. When he smiled in a certain way it was possible to see the charm that had made him such a heart-throb in the sixties.

The tour was only planned for three months but they were delayed by the weather and well into their fifteenth week before they turned about and headed back towards New York. Evangeline was getting coach-sore; the air conditioning inside the bus was wilful at the best of times and the seats were only good if you were either drunk or asleep, or – in Charlie's case – both.

He'd stopped whistling along with Lohengrin an hour back and, when Evangeline looked round to check, he was stretched out asleep on the back seats, much as he had been when she first met him. It was a shot she'd done already, but this time a small dog that belonged to one of the roadies had stretched its skinny little carcass out on his chest and was snoring too, so she crept back through the coach and took a few more.

A heavy-duty trucker following the bus had seen the name painted on the side and was hollering Charlie Gregg songs out through his open window and slapping the side of the cab with the palm of one beefy hand. He waved at Evangeline and she waved back and ran off a few shots of him too before returning to her seat.

The coach was airless. She leant back in her chair and

wiped the sweat off her forehead with the back of her hand. She wished she could sleep like the others while they were travelling, but she'd got some of her best shots on the road and she didn't want to miss anything.

Charlie was snoring. She remembered the noise for many years after. They passed a small café by the roadside and someone called out, 'Burgers!' which made them all start yelling like kids as the place flashed by. The driver slammed on the brakes as a kneejerk response and, as the coach shimmied to a snake-screwing sort of halt, there was a screech of indignation from the truck behind before it smashed full into them.

Evangeline was tipped pronto from her seat by the impact and thrown into the aisle like a drop-down drunk. A case was hurled from the luggage rack and thudded square in her back, knocking the wind out of her.

In her mind she reached for her camera but things were twirling like a yo-yo and her body wasn't having any part of it.

As she was thrown over and over she thought she saw Patrick the dog rolling with her, his big goofy paws flailing and his huge pink tongue lolling while his eyes rolled in fear.

'Patrick!' Even in the thick of her own terror she was pleased to see him. Maybe this was it after all, maybe she was just meeting her end a bit later than the others – maybe this was how it was supposed to be. Death was just a cheap little thing, then. It happened and that was all. Over. All the big questions – Why? How? What for? – came afterwards, from other people: people like her. People who couldn't let the past go.

She was alone suddenly. They weren't waiting for her. This wasn't it. Only then did she begin to feel the pain.

She saw guys at the front of the bus looking down the aisle, first with some kind of amusement in their eyes – 'Hey, man, what kind of party's going on back there?' – and then, when they finally saw it, a full rush of raw-eyed horror.

'Jesus Christ!'

She heard glass breaking somewhere and then everything went dark. She was lying flat out on the floor, her fingers dug deep into the scorched-stubble carpet. The coach sighed and groaned and then it stopped moving.

She lifted her head slowly and saw the tableau in front of her: two roadies and the three band members all standing, frozen, in a group. Embarrassed, she tried to get up. She even tried a smile to indicate that she was sort of OK, but it wasn't her they were staring at. They were looking way down the back of the bus, to the spot where Charlie had been spread out just a few moments before.

'Jeeeeezuuus fucking Christ!'

'Holy shit!'

'What the fuck . . .'

One of them almost trod on her as he bowled down the aisle.

'Chaaaarleeeeee!' It was the fat girl from the first day of the tour. She'd rejoined the bus for the trip back, spending most of the time with her head stuffed in Charlie's crotch. Her face looked as though G-force had hit it. Evangeline wouldn't have recognized her. She managed to twist her body round towards where all the interest was. There was no longer any back to the coach; the back of the coach was now the front of the following truck.

The trucker was still in his seat only he wasn't singing any more. Someone had stuck chopped liver where his head had been, and his hand, not slapping the cabin any more in time to some tune, was still twitching, as though the tempo had changed and become faster – but it was inside their coach, draped over the headrest of one of the seats.

Evangeline got up and her leg hurt, but she wasn't dead. There was blood on her arm but she didn't think it could be hers. Her camera was still round her waist. Good.

Charlie wasn't there. The one good thing was that Charlie wasn't there. She didn't know where he had gone or how he had got out, but he had escaped, which had to be a great grade A miracle. Then she heard a noise. A dog's whimper. The little stray's button-snout was there under the wreckage of the truck. She saw it shining in the dark, like a wet black berry.

'Charlie?' She saw it then, the whole picture. What had been the back of the bus was now squished right down flat beneath the truck. It made sense, suddenly. It was all there, all where she had last seen it, only she was looking in the wrong place, she was looking too high. Charlie wasn't at waist-height any more, he was down lower than the floor. Flattened with all the metal. The dog's eyes watched her from the dark. What sort was it? A hound? Too small. Small enough to be still alive.

'Charleeeee!' The fat girl was screaming again.

Evangeline wished she'd shut up. Her head was hurting now. The others had stopped before they'd reached the back. One minute they'd been hurrying and then they'd seen for sure what had happened, and suddenly they weren't in such a great hurry after all. There were strange smells back there – metal and petrol and something else worse. Someone was sick. She could smell the sourness of the vomit.

Evangeline stepped forward and there was an eerie quiet, like a church.

'Charlie?' She whispered his name as though he might still be asleep. There was a whimper from the dog. She held a hand near the gap and a small tongue shot out and licked it.

'Charlie?' she peered into the darkness.

'He'll be dead.' She didn't know who said that.

'The dog's still alive.' It didn't sound logical, even to her own ears.

It made them move, though. They pulled great sheets of mangled metal out of the way, with the same precision as when they loaded equipment. They were working; Evangeline wanted to work too. She squatted onto her haunches and lifted her camera in front of her face. Then she paused. Had somebody photographed her parents like that? She put the camera down again. The shot would be worth thousands, but she couldn't take it. If someone had photographed her family's car crash she would have seen them dead in the morning papers. Her hands shook. She went to help instead.

They lifted a crushed cattle-bar and the dog's head popped out. Evangeline leant forward. Then she saw Charlie, crushed inside the gap. She put her camera back onto her belt and helped with the lifting. The dog wriggled clear and she snatched it up, crying with relief.

'Ssh . . . sshhh.' It licked at her cheek, her eyes, her face. She moved bits of seating as they pulled Charlie out. They passed his body through the window. They laid it out on the scrub by the roadside, where the blood vanished quickly into the dust, leaving a rust-coloured stain. They laid him beneath his own name, painted in fluorescent orange and gold, only now the bus was crushed it didn't read 'Charlie Gregg' any more, just 'Charlie Gr', and then some mess. There was a roadie to lie next to him, too – the guy who had owned the dog – and the trucker, who they left in the cabin.

They stood around in a silent group. It was sunset and the sky overhead was a vast cowboy sky, swirling ochre and purple. A John Huston sky, glorious and full of adventure. Their faces darkened as the light failed and they forgot out of shock to call the police, who turned up anyway. And then they took Evangeline to hospital.

21

1989

Mikhail understood very little about his life as a freelancer. The picture editor had taken him for one good meal and then screwed him a couple of times, which was no worse than sex with Claude, somehow; it merely concerned turning your mind off, and then none of it mattered. After that the man lost interest in him sexually and began to pass him on work instead.

The jobs scared Mikhail. He thought when he quit Hungary that he would be going abroad to something better, but the places he was sent to were closer to hell itself. The photographers he worked with were rough professionals, hardened to the horrors, and laden with state-of-the-art equipment. Mikhail had only the old camera he had stolen from Claude. It was battered, but not in a good way. Sometimes it broke down altogether and he had no idea how to fix it properly.

He was not scared for his life in those countries he was sent to, but he was scared of letting himself down. He felt like the worst kind of amateur. The only good things about the job were the money and the passport arranged for him.

He lost track of the places he worked in. He had thought his geography was good – he read newspapers, after all – but he became confused by all the wars and the fighting. He had no money for drink or drugs and so could not socialize with the other photographers in between assignments. His English was improving but he was not familiar with a lot of the slang the Americans used.

There was one American who found the time to make

friends. The guy was a legend among the other journalists he worked with and Mikhail was breathless with gratitude that he even bothered to speak to him. He was older than Mikhail – about thirty – and he'd been shooting wars since he was twenty-two.

His name was Arthur. His parents had called him after the ancient English king, and he pretty much looked the part, too: tall and rangy, taller than Mikhail, maybe even six feet four, with long straggling red hair and a fine, wispy beard.

They worked together first in India, jostling side-by-side during some local disturbances until Arthur looked down at the lanky young man with the long black hair and wild, frightened eyes and told him to piss off and get his own shots.

Mikhail stuck beside the older man like a deranged terrier, though. He knew Arthur was the best and he shadowed him in order to be near all the most valuable shots. At first Arthur was annoyed but after a while he began to make a joke of his shadow. Whenever they met after India, Arthur would always shout the same thing in a joky, cracked, old-man's voice: 'Jeeesus, Micky-boy, not you again!' It wasn't funny really but it amused them both.

Arthur was wealthy already but that didn't stop him risking his life. He was a respected art photographer; he had had a glossy book of his work published; there was even a popular American film out with a character in it that was based on him; he could reputedly play jazz well on the clarinet and the piano, but he told Mikhail one night when they were drunk that he only really felt alive when his life was in danger. He was not married and he had no kids. He wasn't upsetting anyone by living that way.

He was always joking. Mikhail wasn't sharp enough and his English wasn't good enough always to tell when he was serious. Sticking around Arthur was like buying a ticket to the mortuary, the other photographers told him, but he stuck alongside Arthur nevertheless.

The guy had even been shot a couple of times. He showed Mikhail the wounds. The third time the bullet had been deflected by his Leica, just like in the movies. The camera still worked and he said he was trying to set up a sponsorship deal on the strength of it. There was a dent in the metal, Mikhail saw, but he didn't know whether Arthur was lying. It wouldn't have mattered if the story were true or not; Arthur had already become Mikhail's hero, much as Andreas had been many years before.

Getting shot didn't hurt much, Arthur said. Mikhail knew he was lying about that.

They motored through Asia looking for trouble-spots, keeping clear of the pack always and sniffing out their own pictures. When he couldn't get the shots he wanted Arthur became agitated and flagged down a local funeral procession, giving them twenty dollars to unscrew the lid of the coffin so he could take a shot of the corpse.

It was the body of a child, grey as dust in death. The family were dirt poor and starving. Arthur bribed them with great sums of cash to turn their backs as he carried the corpse from the coffin and laid it on the kerbside, as though it was the victim of recent violence.

'This will make the front pages tomorrow,' he told Mikhail, matter-of-factly. Mikhail watched Arthur climbing over the coffin and he didn't want to ask why, but Arthur must have read his thoughts anyway because he looked up briefly: 'Because it makes a great picture, Micky,' was all he said at the time. Later, over a bottle of Scotch in the hotel, he became more talkative.

'You must only think of the shot, Micky,' he said. 'The shot is the one important thing. It only takes a second and it doesn't hurt anyone. You go in and you do what you're paid for, just like any other fucking employee from any other fucking country.' He always got a strange look in his eyes when he was shooting scenes like that. His coldness was almost palpable. The look was there that evening, too, as though the shot stayed in his mind.

'D'you think the stupid assholes working in banks and offices have a conscience, Micky?' he asked. 'D'you think they ever stop to work out where the money they're always shuffling around comes from or goes to? No, of course not. They don't give a flying fuck, so why should the likes of you and me care how we get our pictures?' He was like a comic drunk, blurred and indignant.

They met again in South Africa and hired a motorbike each day to take them to the disturbances. Police shot at marchers during a demonstration and Arthur pulled Mikhail into the crowd, towards the guns. They stood there, photographing the corpses, bending over the bodies like carrion crows. One was still moving but Arthur screamed at Mikhail to keep shooting. It was their job to record, not to help.

Mikhail took the shots. He was excited and terrified.

'It's the photographs that supply the help long-term,' Arthur told him afterwards. 'Let the public know what is happening. Make them throw up over their breakfast pancakes, if you can. Then you get a reaction,' he said, 'then they put their hands into their pockets or their dicks into the air to be counted, and they help. What do you think does the most in the end, Micky?' he asked. 'Your bandaging skills on someone who will die eventually anyway, or your shots of them that will get the politicians sweating? Eh?'

They got separated at a small riot. Mikhail stopped to shoot a kid who had fallen in front of him, and when he looked up Arthur had vanished. There was too much dust to see where. He called out but could not even hear his own voice above the din. Someone struck him, not a hard blow, but enough to almost knock him over. He flailed out angrily with his fists, but there seemed to be no one to hit at, so he ran like hell instead.

The crowd came with him; they became a herd. He had no idea where they were going, he just wanted to be away from the bulk of it, to find a space so he could take some more shots. Blinded by the dust he turned to stop but there were so many behind him he was forced to keep on running. There was a smell of burning rubber that choked the back of his throat.

Then there was a building, a wooden door. The door was ripped open and he fell inside with a few dozen others. Someone lay on his leg and he swore at them in English. He couldn't move, he was trapped beneath the bodies, and so he waited instead.

When it got dark he squeezed his way out. Some of the bodies on top of him were so cold he wondered if they were corpses. There was a terrible stench everywhere, an animal smell of fear and death. Cursing to himself he went outside and looked around for the motorbike. It was peaceful again out there. The night air was cool and fresh, and the sound of the crickets had a soothing, rhythmic quality.

He rubbed his legs to get them moving. One of his shoes was missing and that was very bad news. He thought of going back into the building to look for it but he was frightened of waking the pile of people in there. The whole area was painted quicksilver by the moonlight. He wanted to shoot it as it was but he needed Arthur's advice on the exposure.

He limped about silently, looking for something and nothing. The bike would be stolen. Then he found the keys in his pocket and became more hopeful.

He almost fell over Arthur. At first he was pleased and cried out with relief, but then he saw that the American was dead, hacked to pieces, butchered like meat for market. He stared at his friend in disbelief. He heard a buzz, like a plane engine, and he looked up, but the sky was empty and he realized the buzzing came from the flies around the corpse.

He wanted to vomit at what he saw — the sourness crawled up the back of his throat — but he closed his eyes until the nausea lightened. Arthur: the big man. The one who knew everything. This time his camera couldn't save him.

When he opened his eyes and looked back again it wasn't Arthur any more, though. To his crawling horror it was Andreas who lay there dead by his feet. He screamed into the night and then he stuffed his hand into his mouth before his yells caused trouble and someone came to get him.

He was unable to move. Andreas was looking up, grinning at him. His mouth started to open and in a minute he would talk. Mikhail shook his head from side to side.

'No, no!' But he knew the corpse would speak. He knew it would tell all. Andreas, his brother, spilling blood and terrible secrets. Mikhail looked around in a panic. He lost his fear for his own life and screamed out loud in utter terror at the sight of his brother's face on another man's corpse, and his scream sounded like an animal cry as it echoed around the nearby hills before returning to him again.

Andreas. He was haunted still – a haunted man. His hands shook. The flesh of his face seemed to shrink back around his ears in horror, and his mouth hung open because suddenly there was not enough skin there to close it. He was twelve years old again, a kid in the mortuary in Budapest. Andreas was lying in front of him and any minute his head would turn slowly and his eyes would fall open and he would stare at Mikhail to accuse him of all the terrible things he had once done.

'Andreas?' He loved his brother every bit as much as he feared him. His voice was a whisper, made hoarse by his scream. He desperately wanted to run but he made himself look instead. He stared until the darkened features of the corpse's face squirmed and altered, and it was Arthur there once again. Arthur the clarinet player. Arthur the hero.

Mikhail waited until the shaking stopped and he was in control once more. Then he bent down silently and lifted Arthur's camera – the good one, the expensive one – gently from around his neck, shaking it by his ear to check it wasn't broken.

There was blood on the camera, blood from Arthur's face. He replaced the good camera with his own cheaper one. Had Claude ever imagined where his pride and joy would end up?

He studied Arthur's corpse for a while, calmer now that it had Arthur's face again. Then he did what he had to do – the thing he was employed for, the thing he needed to do for his own survival in life. He took photographs of his friend's body. He had no choice, really, not if he wanted to get on.

He soon became engrossed in his work. It wasn't Arthur any more, or Andreas, it was subject matter to be photographed; a riddle of light and angles to be worked out. The shots would sell well; the whole world would want to see them.

Make them throw up over their breakfast pancakes if you can, Micky. Arthur's intestines lay on the dirt beside his stomach. Mikhail pushed them with his toe so they stood out more. He still needed an angle, though. Then he remembered Arthur's wallet. The guy had carried a selection of happy family snaps in there, to place at air disasters or murder scenes, just to add a little pathos to the shot.

Mikhail pushed his hand inside his friend's jacket and pulled the wallet out. There were six shots in all, two of black families, a couple of grandparents and a few assorted others. Mikhail picked the one with kids that most looked as though they could have been Arthur's, had he had any.

'Is this OK?' he whispered before crushing the photo into Arthur's hand as though it had been the last thing he'd looked at as he died. It would make people cry. It was easy, really, all he had to do was capture it on film, then he could sell the pictures and get out of this filthy place before he too was lying there dead.

189

When the shots had been taken he took the film from the camera and tucked it into his pocket. Then, once he had looked around to make sure he was truly alone and not being watched, he allowed the tears to take over, crying loudly and violently, for Arthur, for Andreas, but also for himself and his life, which was not a life at all, just a series of repayments for the terrible sin he had committed as a child.

He worked by himself after that, but it was never the same. Arthur had had a nose for the trouble-spots and a talent for negotiating fees. Mikhail lost his commission through his own surliness. When his editor refused to syndicate the shots of Arthur, he swore at the man until he hung up the phone. He wrote to Arthur's agency but was considered too high a risk to add to the payroll and, besides, he didn't have the right papers. They could have even published his shots without his knowledge – he had no way of finding out.

He carried on as a freelance for a while, but the job continued to unearth his own ghosts and sorrows. He punished himself with danger to purge his own guilt but it didn't work, the secrets of his childhood stayed with him, haunting him. Andreas was always there whenever he was close to other deaths.

When he started weeping openly whenever he saw a corpse he knew he had to quit the job altogether. In his nightmares he was a carrion crow, flapping around piles of gleaming entrails. He would wake screaming in his hotel room.

The other photographers avoided him because they could sense he was on the brink of a breakdown and they didn't want to see what might happen when things went wrong for them. In the end they clubbed together and gave him the money for his air fare home. Mikhail was angry and grateful. He could never go back to Hungary, though – he was more afraid of his home country than he was of any of the war zones. Going home might only make the memories and the guilt even stronger. He would have to try another country.

'Why not bum your way around Europe?' the guy who presented him with the money suggested. 'Try the UK – London is good. You speak the language and there's plenty of work there – not the best paid in the world, but you should make a decent living easily enough.'

Mikhail shrugged. Anything. Anything had to be better than the situation he was in now.

22

New York 1983

Evangeline discharged herself from hospital after a week. She had spent her twenty-third birthday waiting in a queue in physio and she knew when enough was enough. She told Nico it was because she couldn't stand to see him moping over her bed each day, but in fact she wanted to get out to see to the dog.

It was her puppy now. She called it Paddy after Patrick and at first she wept shamelessly every time she picked the grateful little scrap up.

'It's the accident,' Nico told her. 'It's the delayed shock making you emotional. You should've stayed in the hospital. The bill would have been cleared either by the insurance or the old lady, and the boys at the club all offered to contribute.

'They want you back taking their portraits, Evangeline. I've got a list of bookings as long as Ernie Patoolie's ass waiting for when you're up again.'

'I'm not going back to portraits, Nico,' Evangeline said. Her eyes looked dark and wet, like shiny grey stones. Any beauty her face had was in those eyes. Her hair had got sandy streaks in it from the sun on the tour. It was wildly frizzy and almost full-way down her back. Nico thought it looked like mattress-stuffing. It hid most of her face, which was a pity because the features were on the turn now, from ugly to attractive-in-a-strong-kind-of-a-way. She was looking a lot like his grandmother on his father's side, which he would never have told her for fear of his life. She wouldn't put the little dog down. Their eyes looked the same to Nico: bruised and helpless.

'You're not thinking straight.'

'I'm thinking fine, Nico.'

'Give it time, it's delayed shock – you don't know what you're saying . . .'

'Fuck the delayed shock!'

'Evangeline!'

'I'm sorry.' She rubbed a hand across her eyes. 'Look, Nico, I'm moving out of here. I'm getting my own apartment. I need . . .' she paused, wondering just what it was she did need. She needed to get the sight of Charlie's ripped-up body out of her mind. She needed to move on, to escape a few memories. She wished she didn't hurt so much. The doctors said she might have a permanent limp if she didn't go to physio . . .

'What the hell will you live on?' Nico interrupted her.

'What?'

'Money, Evangeline. Where will it come from? The old lady? You think so? I thought she was down to two gifts a year. You said –'

'Money's not a problem, Nico.' She sounded so sure. She hoped she was.

They had started bugging her straight after the operation, while she was still woozy from the anaesthetic; calls from editors and agents, all keen to get the rights to her shots of Charlie Gregg.

When she refused all calls they turned up in person at the hospital, bearing gifts and smiles, clutching armfuls of flowers, beaming like old friends, full of concern for her health and full of offers for the rights to publish her photographs.

'Why all the fuss?' she asked. 'Charlie was pretty much a nobody by the time he died.' Then she discovered exactly what a facelift death can be for a sagging music career. Charlie had been turned into a rock legend by the press.

The TV was full of clips of him at his peak. The record he previously couldn't sell for trying moved straight up to number one. Charlie had achieved cult status at last. Of course they all wanted her shots of him.

There were a dozen or so press hanging about the ward when a tall, grey-haired man who had been visiting a young woman in the bed opposite finally stood up with a shake of the head and walked across. He wore a suit and a good suit, at that – Nico would have got high on the smell of the flannel alone. He was tall and broad with a youngish-man's body and his shirt was as white as the ones in soap-powder ads.

'I hope you'll pardon the intrusion, but you look like you may need some help,' he said softly, handing Evangeline his business card. She loved his eyes; they had the kindest expression. After the accident Evangeline craved kindness like a dying plant craves water, only she was too tense to admit it.

She couldn't place his accent so she read his card instead: *Stuart P. Carlisle* – the letters after his name meant very little to her. She hated people who used their middle initial. He looked legal but, in truth, she didn't care – she would have given her blessing to anyone who could give her a few moments of peace. She rooted in a bag by her bedside and pulled out one of her own cards: *Evangeline Castelli, Photographer. Weddings and portraiture a speciality*. Nico had had them printed on the cheap soon after she'd set up in business. She was embarrassed by them now. Nico had been so pleased with them.

'You must have something those gentlemen want rather badly.' Stuart was staring at her, watching her expression. Evangeline nodded. 'Is it something you want them to have?'

'No.'

'Would you like me to get rid of them then?' Stuart tucked her stupid card away in his breast pocket.

'You'll have your work cut out.'

He smiled at her then and winked. Evangeline was enthralled by his confidence. She grinned back without intending to look so grateful.

She watched him walk to the end of the ward and call the posse of press men around him. She couldn't hear what he said to them but she could hear his tone of voice. It wasn't angry but it was the sort you don't argue with, all the same. A woman journalist tried and he just shot her a look and that obviously did the trick too.

She saw him handing out cards all round, like sweeties to kids, and then she watched as, by some miracle, they all shuffled off without a word of complaint.

She searched for any trace of smugness on his face as he came back to her bed, but found none; if she had she would have hated him. His eyes were blue and still gentle-looking. She wondered if they had looked the same when he dealt with the press. He had had a cold, business-like tone to his voice.

'You gave them your cards,' she said. 'Why? Do you want to be my manager or something?'

Stuart laughed politely. 'And manage what?' he asked. 'Your wedding photography? What did you do, land a star?'

Evangeline nodded. 'Charlie Gregg,' she said.

Stuart whistled softly. '*The* Charlie Gregg?' he asked. 'The recently deceased Mr Gregg?'

'The same.'

'You'll need professional help,' Stuart said. His voice was soft now. He had an unusual accent that she couldn't place.

'And I suppose you're just the person to give it.' She hadn't meant to sound quite so sarcastic. She wondered what she looked like; bare-faced, bitter-eyed, wild-haired. She'd had a visit from the charity hairdresser who serviced the ward on a Friday. She'd been too ga-ga with drugs to say no. The guy had told her all about his boyfriend while he teased her mane up into a chignon. She'd slept on it twice since then. She didn't need a mirror to see how awful she looked. She knew, she just knew.

Stuart shrugged. 'Not really my field,' he said.

'Oh sure, you surprise me.' Maybe he'd engineered the whole thing – Jesus, she could be so stupid sometimes!

'I'll just leave you to it.' He was backing away, still smiling politely. He was kind and charming – what was she doing?

'Yes, your wife must be feeling pretty neglected by now.' The brunette in the bed opposite was staring with a look on her face that spelt 'attitude'.

'My daughter,' he said.

'Sorry.'

'Don't worry, I'm flattered.'

She went home at last to Nico and Paddy but she looked for a new place to live. She was twenty-three, a woman with a career and not the Italian princess Nico wanted her to be. She found a small apartment and was immediately overcome by acute loneliness.

She missed Nico and their arguments. She missed his noise and his funny stupidity. She and Paddy were like two war veterans, both terrified that another accident would happen. She had nightmares about turning over and over in the crashing coach. She spun with her whole family now – Thea, Darius, baby Lincoln and Patrick – even Charlie Gregg was in there somewhere, grinning and singing as he twisted to his death.

When she woke from these dreams Paddy would be standing on top of her, licking her face, looking scared too. She would pick him up and hug him until he stopped shivering. 'Sorry, little Paddy-pads,' she would whisper into his ear, 'was I yelling again? You have to excuse your mommy, she's a crazy lady all right. Eh? Eh?'

He'd be fine again after a handful of biscuits. She kept them by the bed now, just in case.

She sold the magazine rights of Charlie's tour photos to

Rolling Stone and then negotiated a deal for an exhibition at a gallery she liked in SoHo. The money wasn't spectacular – she was constantly told how high she could have negotiated – but she was planning her career carefully; she wanted to use the shots to get the maximum exposure for her own talents, rather than the biggest payroll.

Rolling Stone did a feature on her to accompany the shots. They printed to a good standard, too. The pictures looked like art, rather than the bad quality reproductions of newspapers. The magazine insisted on shots of her for the feature and when she saw them she laughed; she looked wild, like an unruly kid. Her hair filled the frame. Her eyes stared out from behind the wire-framed glasses. She wore a man's short-sleeved shirt and cut-offs and boots. Her legs looked thin and her nose looked huge, full-frontal like that. She hadn't thought. Grandma Klippel would have a seizure. She cut the page out carefully and posted it to the Cape with, *My first spread* scrawled across the top.

The big names started nibbling. She was approached by Stein and Miles, one of the top photographic agents in New York. They asked her to lunch, which had to be a major event, and she even bought a suit, which would have made Nico orgasmic with pride.

The suit was green linen with cream silk piped around the edges. She'd forgotten she'd need tights. She looked in the mirror and pulled a face. She also needed things like shoes and a handbag. Maybe lipstick, too. A facial? Eyebrow wax? Highlights? Who was she impressing with this fuck-you, Wall-Street look? The suit was a serious mistake but she'd paid a fortune and had to wear it. She found some slip-ons and a big canvas shoulder bag her camera would fit into. No make-up. A couple of pins to hold her hair up off her face. She twisted it into a knot. Strands fell loose as she looked at her reflection in the mirror.

The agent was in slacks and a t-shirt. She was a short, hyperactive woman who moved and thought at the speed of light, throwing brochures across the desk at Evangeline while she tied up two deals on the phone, using the words 'balls' and 'dick' a lot, as in: 'Where are your balls, Norris?' . . . 'We have them by the balls now, Cynthia,' . . . and 'The guy is talking with his dick, Andrew.' All this was peppered with smiles and winks in Evangeline's direction to show what a tiresome play-act all these business deals were.

They ate sushi for lunch and the woman still chattered into her portable as she chewed. At one stage she pulled a sheaf of papers out of her briefcase and knocked a bottle of Evian over as she threw them across to Evangeline, nodding and pointing out a dotted line at the bottom that lay in wait for a signature.

'Ten per cent,' she mouthed at Evangeline, then: 'Holy shit, Cyril, is that kosher? A hundred and eighty thou? Is that supposed to be an insult? My God!'

Evangeline mopped mineral water off her linen skirt. Would it stain? At those prices she guessed it would. Cheap stuff never stained, it knew its place.

'We have to do something about image,' the agent was saying. Evangeline realized with surprise that she was talking about her. 'You look a little like a secretary right now, but that's not a problem. We need something a little more chi-chi – something with balls, if you know what I mean? Black leather, maybe?

'Do you have any camouflage? Something a little distressed? Do you smoke? No? Could you? Do you bite your nails? Good. Photography is still a man's profession, sweetie, and you want to look tough if you're going to get taken seriously. Where's the accent from? Boston? Pity. I thought you'd be more, you know, Bronx, or something. I mean, a tour with a rock group! Can you do a little something with it, d'you think? OK-OK-OK.'

Evangeline looked around the restaurant. Nobody was

eating the food. She'd finished her fish and now she felt embarrassed as well as a little sick. It seemed the trick was to just shove the stuff around your plate with a fork while you talked. She pushed her seat back.

'I'm sorry, I think I'll leave it.'

The agent looked surprised. 'No cappuccino?' she asked.

'No nothing, thank you,' Evangeline replied, handing the papers back across the table.

The agent took them, open-mouthed. 'If you think you're going to fuck me around for the odd per cent or two you're wasting your time,' she said. 'Not even my top guys pay less than ten so you can scratch that idea from the menu . . .'

Evangeline walked out of the restaurant and into the street. Her skirt stuck to her legs where it had been drenched in the mineral water. She walked about for a few minutes, letting it dry out in the sun. There was an old man sitting by the side of the road warming his bare feet in the steam from a subway. She pulled her camera out and took his shot and he smiled at her. She'd expected the usual curse at the intrusion. Maybe it was the suit.

When she got back to her apartment she phoned Nico. 'How would you like to be my manager?' she asked.

'Shit.' She could hear his grin through the phone line.

'I think ten per cent is the going rate,' she said.

'Twelve,' Nico said.

'Eleven.'

'Done.'

'Just one thing, Nico,' she added, 'absolutely no portraits and no weddings, OK?'

Nico began to complain. 'Evangeline, you have to look to where the security is. Those guys loved your portraits and their wives –'

'No, Nico. I got enough money from the sale of Charlie's shots. I intend to keep control of my own career. I'm not that desperate just yet.'

'Maybe now and again, just to keep your hand in,' Nico insisted. 'Money runs out, Evangeline – we don't want to find ourselves begging our old contacts for work once it does.'

'No.'

'Maybe just the Banana King.'

'*Especially* not the Banana King, Nico.'

There was a big sigh from the other end. 'OK, Evangeline, if you're sure you know what you're doing.'

She did know. She had a plan. She was going to be the best, so that she could please her dead parents and win their approval. Paddy was jumping at her leg. She picked him up. He smelt meaty, of dog food. She looked around the apartment. It was a small place – cheap but not scruffy – just two rooms, a kitchen and a small roof garden. She could have afforded better but she wanted a good studio, too.

'Oh, and another thing, Nico,' she said, 'no suits. Absolutely no suits. I am not dressing up for anybody, understand?' She laughed at her father's sigh.

As yet her apartment was empty save a Futon, one whiskery wicker chair and Paddy's huge quilted dog-bed. It was too big for him, but she figured he deserved spoiling after what he'd been through. Maybe he was even claustrophobic after being trapped in the tiny gap in the wreckage for so long. She'd filled the bed with doggy-toys to stop him feeling lonely while she was out.

A bed and a chair. She knew she ought to buy more but she spent any money she had on photographic equipment. There were a dozen rolls of colourama stacked by the door and some lights standing in the kitchen. She was still using Nico's darkroom but when the next cheque came in she intended setting her own one up in the bathroom.

She loved working in the darkroom. It was silent and warm and wonderfully exciting. She felt like a magician still, conjuring pictures out of sheets of bare white paper. Each print had to be perfect; sometimes she would spend hours getting them just right.

Charlie's shots had been a revelation. She had the whole story there on film: Charlie relaxing before the tour; the crew messing about; the most faithful fans — middle-aged, smiling women who had followed the bus around from town to town; Charlie getting drunk; Charlie performing in a variety of venues; and then Charlie asleep with Paddy on his chest, the trucker that killed him waving cheerily behind.

The photographs had made her breathless and panicky so she'd had to step outside the darkroom and sit down until she was calm again.

'Shit, shit, shit!' she punched the arms of her chair and Paddy came running across to see what was up. 'Look, Paddy,' she whispered, holding a shot up, 'look — who's this then? Who's this?' He stared at his own image and she laughed. 'Bad day, Paddy, eh?' she asked. She sucked at the sleeve of her jersey and rocked backwards and forwards in her chair. Paddy trotted off and returned with a dribble-coated plastic bone in his mouth, which made her laugh again.

'Thank God for you, Paddy,' she said, 'thank God for you.'

Nico made a surprisingly good agent — better than Evangeline had hoped. He styled himself on the Banana King of Manhattan and sounded like a fifties hood, which the clients absolutely adored and considered frightfully chic. He was afraid of no one because he knew no one in the business — names were just names to him. The only people Nico Castelli was in awe of were Tony Curtis and Antonio Corelli. For the rest of them he didn't give a flying fuck. If they were good for work he would call them and if they didn't call back it was their loss. Evangeline was made speechless by his attitude but when she discovered it worked she just sat back and took the shots.

Cheques came in for the overseas syndication of her photos of Charlie Gregg and she moved into a better apartment and rented an office for Nico to work from. He liked the office but he didn't like her apartment.

'The place is too bare.' He stomped around the stripped boards uncomfortably, his hands dug deep into the pockets of his suit.

'It's minimalist,' Evangeline said. She liked bare. Bare meant clean. Bare meant no heavy clutter to move every time she dusted. She cleaned twice a day as it was. The air reeked of beeswax and pine. When Nico sat on the one settee she was down the other end, straightening the cushions. Even Paddy had a little 'Doggie-Odor-Oh-No' stuck above his basket.

'What, does the mutt wear rubber shoes inside the apartment?' Nico asked.

'He's not a mutt,' Evangeline corrected him.

'My apology,' Nico said, 'I didn't quite make out the pedigree. Must be my eyes. From here he looks like a mongrel.'

'He's a Jack Russell,' Evangeline said, 'White with brown and black markings. I looked it up.'

Nico raised his eyebrows. 'Jack Russell?' he asked. 'You sure about that? Do you know he has food on his chops? Smells like liver from here. How come I get the cushions rearranged the minute I look at them and that mutt is allowed the run of the place with chopped liver all over his mush?'

Despite his moans Nico managed to get Evangeline two good magazine commissions within a week. She looked at the money he'd negotiated and told him it wasn't enough. The top guys get more, she told him. Sure, but you're right down the bottom, Nico said. He thought she was mad. She thought he was too negative. She went to visit the editors herself, just to see. The first guy threw her out, which made her fighting mad by the time she'd got to the second.

'We already booked you,' the editor said, rocking in his leatherette chair.

'I know,' Evangeline told him, 'but you're paying me bottom rates. I came to sort it out, that's all.'

The guy smiled at her. Smiling was bad. They usually smiled before they asked you to leave the building.

'Why should I pay you more?' he asked. 'You going to sleep with me, or something?'

Evangeline smiled back. 'Why, would you like to?'

The guy nodded carefully. 'Maybe.'

'Do you screw all your photographers?' Evangeline asked. 'Or just the women?'

The editor picked up his phone. 'I think you'd better leave,' he said, 'I got work to do.'

Evangeline stood up and placed her fingers across the receiver. 'What if I do these first shots for free and, if you use them, you pay me top rates the next time?' she said.

'Top rates?' the guy laughed. 'You're talking Bailey and Lichfield if you're talking top rates.'

'Next rung down, then,' Evangeline told him. 'Your magazine's good but it tries to be art too, doesn't it? Art means lots of awards but élitist readership and minimum ads. If you give me a big enough credit with the shots I'll settle for less. The by-lines cost you nothing and you get a discount from me. If you don't like my work you don't use it. What's the problem?'

They used her work and they liked it and they paid better rates. Evangeline got her name alongside the shots in large type and she used it as a free ad to show to the other editors. They didn't know she'd done it for nothing; they thought she was hot. Even Nico was impressed.

Soon she was up to four jobs a week. When she rented her first studio full-time Nico insisted she hold a party there. It was good for business, he insisted. He invited clients and would-be clients and he also invited Antonio Corelli and his colleagues, which was the masterstroke. Guests thought the Banana King and his cronies had been hired from Central Casting for trendy effect. They took one look at the suits and the shiny hair and thought they had walked onto the set of *Goodfellers*.

The Banana King relished all the attention and started

203

passing around the shots Evangeline had taken of him in the pink make-up robe.

'It's bringing in business,' Nico whispered to Evangeline, 'I've had three enquiries about portraits already.'

'No portraits, Nico,' Evangeline said. She hopped about nervously, watching the guests and their reactions to her pictures. They were strange people, she decided. Ghastly-arty she called them, all pallid-skinned with dung-coloured clothes and grief-stricken faces.

'Tough,' Nico whispered, 'they pay well. They pay tops, in fact. This arty stuff of yours might look good but you've got to eat. Trust me, Evangeline, with just a couple a week you can keep that mutt of yours in truffles if you want.'

Evangeline tried to summon a stubborn look but her father was right – the money would be welcome. She agreed to do portraiture and Nico kept to his word: no more than two a week.

She did well for a couple of years; not wonderful, but not badly, either. The portraits brought in the money, which left her free to indulge herself with the sort of work she liked. In a way she grew to enjoy the portraits, too. She took time and she experimented with different techniques. Her shots were original and people got to hear of her.

Commissions came in from magazines. She photographed a few famous faces and word spread. She flattered her sitters, but she did a good shot, too. She made them look good in a way that made it appear they would look good in real life. They looked natural but they looked better.

She enjoyed making things perfect. She wished she could do the same with her life. If Nico could have retouched that for her she would have been happy. Or maybe she was happy already, she wasn't sure.

Then Nico gave her a new booking.

'It came in just before I left the office,' he said. 'I quoted a ridiculous price and they accepted. You're booked for six a.m. tomorrow.'

'For a portrait?' Evangeline complained. 'At that hour?'

'For a *corporate headshot*,' Nico corrected her. He read through his notes. 'Big bores for big money, Evangeline. Mr Tycoon here is busy the rest of the day – the rest of the year, come to that. It was either six in the morning or you would be shooting him sleeping in his bed at night.'

The next day was a cold one. Evangeline cursed as she packed her equipment away. The stuff was heavy. Her heating was erratic and her fingers were blue.

'These people should come to the studio,' she growled to Paddy. The air outside was good, though. She wondered how it got to smell so fresh in such a short space of time.

Nico had phoned her at five to check she was up.

'What are you wearing?' he asked.

She looked down at herself. 'A grey shirt,' she said, 'brown Shetland over the top. Knitted leggings . . .'

'The ones with the holes?' Nico asked. 'You should get changed,' he told her.

'Why? Is it fancy dress?' she asked.

'It's Wall Street,' Nico said.

'I know,' she told him, looking at the paper, 'you gave me the address.'

'They wear suits,' Nico whispered.

'And I wear this.' Paddy scampered after her as she went out, carrying the leather-clad Filofax Nico had bought her in his dribbly little mouth.

The address Nico had given her was a large suite of offices on the top floor of a tinted glass tower. Paddy enjoyed the lift ride so much that they went up and down several times until she almost made herself late.

The receptionist was a Versace-Gucci girl who had been programmed to greet anyone who fell through the doors with the same rigidly corporate smile. She must have been up at four to look the way she did.

'May I help you?' she asked, with a pre-programmed tilt of the head. Her eyeshadow was exactly the same shade of deep puce as the scarf she wore tied around her neck.

Paddy leapt onto the cream calf-skin lounger beside the door and sat there panting.

'Mr Carlisle,' Evangeline said. The name hadn't sounded familiar until then.

The girl checked a list on her desk. 'Ah yes,' she smiled, 'Stuart is expecting you.'

'Stuart?' Evangeline asked.

'We're a first-name-terms-company.' The girl could speak through the gaps in her teeth without moving her lips.

'No, I mean is that Stuart *P.* Carlisle?' Evangeline asked. The name rang bells. Maybe he was famous. Names stuck in her mind sometimes, for no reason.

The girl's eyes looked professionally blank. 'Of course.'

He was waiting in his office in front of a night-speckled view of New York. The whole room smelt of Gucci: a sea of monogrammed leather and light-reflecting lead crystal.

He offered his hand. His shirt looked whiter than snow and he had cufflinks engraved with his initials.

She knew him now. She'd never forget the face from the hospital. If the face, then definitely not the eyes.

'Stuart,' he said.

'Or do I call you "P" for short?' she asked.

He grinned gracefully. 'Whatever.' He pointed a chair out for her. 'Are you OK now?' he asked. So he remembered her, too.

'I should hope so,' she told him.

'Good.' He was polite, charming – everything she remembered him to be. She was smiling at him without speaking, looking stupid. She made herself stop and looked around the room instead. It was like being inside a vast mahogany cocktail cabinet.

'You're rich,' she told him.

'No,' he corrected her again, 'I'm *filthy* rich.'

'And I thought you were after a job when we met in the hospital!' She grinned. 'Sorry.'

He was immaculately dressed again. Nico would have

wept to see the way his wine-coloured tie co-ordinated with his shirt and the butter-soft leather of his hand-made shoes. His hair was maybe a little greyer but it looked good. She tried to calculate his age and stopped when she got to fifty: older than Nico, nearer the age Darius would have been if he'd been alive.

'That's OK.'

'What do you do?' she asked.

Stuart looked vague. 'Oh, you know,' he said, 'develop property, build things. Own things. Play around with other people's money.'

She frowned. 'Is this just coincidence?' she asked.

'Sorry?'

'Me,' she said, 'here. Today. For the shots.'

He shrugged modestly. 'I needed pictures. I found your card in my pocket. I keep things like that, if that's what you mean by coincidence, or did you think it's taken me two years to arrange this little happenstance?'

She smiled and walked across to the windows. 'The light will be good enough soon. I could work by available. Is that OK?' She had her camera out already and was clicking off an opening salvo before he could reach for a mirror.

'Available light? Is that good?' Stuart asked.

'It's softer than flash – more flattering.'

'Well, that sounds splendid then.'

'I didn't mean that you need flattering or anything.'

'Of course you didn't.'

'Can I move this?' she asked, pointing to his desk with her foot.

'By yourself? I suspect not,' Stuart told her. 'It's solid mahogany. May I get someone to move it for us?'

'I can manage,' Evangeline replied. He sat down to watch her. It took her half an hour to move it half a yard, but she was satisfied that she had made her point.

'Anything else?' he asked when she was finished.

'No . . . I . . . think . . . that's . . . about . . . it.' Her hair was stuck to her face and her pectorals were complaining.

'Do we have time for some breakfast before we start work?' Stuart asked. Evangeline glanced at her watch. She was starving.

'I thought you had other appointments,' she said.

'I do,' he smiled.

'It'll have to be somewhere that takes dogs,' she told him.

'Francesca can mind him for an hour,' Stuart said.

'Francesca?'

'On reception.' The one who got in at six, just to keep her boss happy.

'OK.' She had no choice. Moving the desk meant that now she could hardly stand straight. She needed a break.

Francesca used the same smile on Paddy that she used on all the clients. He growled at her, which made Evangeline laugh. 'Oh,' she said as they left for lunch, 'give him this if he gets noisy, will you?' She tossed an old chewed plastic bone across the desk. Francesca caught it with the sort of enthusiasm she might have used on a dead rattlesnake.

Stuart took her to the kind of small, quiet, discreet place she would have guessed he lunched at each and every day of his life. The maître d' knew him and the waiters danced an elaborate quadrille in their efforts to lavish the maximum show of attention upon their table.

'You must have booked,' Evangeline said. 'This sort of place doesn't open for breakfast. Is it all supposed to impress me?'

Stuart grinned at her. 'I didn't think I needed to impress you,' he replied. 'If I did, I could have pointed out the fact that I own the place. I already told you I'm as rich as stink. What more do you need?'

Evangeline shrugged. 'You could tell me you are also a vegetarian and that you give at least a third of your vast wealth to feed Third World countries,' she said.

He didn't answer. When she looked up he was pointing to a wild mushroom sauté the waiter had just placed in front of him.

'And I suppose the cheque for Bangladesh goes off this afternoon,' she said. She was trying hard not to laugh. His eyes were even more beautiful than she remembered. She wondered how she could capture them in black and white. She was staring again. He smiled back.

'A professional assessment, I take it?' he asked.

'On the nose first time,' she told him.

'Should I be embarrassed?'

'Only if you want.' She had just realized he'd chosen her food for her. And the coffee. She asked for mineral water instead, as a point of principle.

'You're English.' She thought she'd finally placed the accent.

'British,' he corrected her. 'My parents came from Scotland.'

'And you have a daughter.'

'Catherine, yes. And a grandson, Paul. Two years old. Catherine was just back in the hospital for a final check-up after the birth.'

'Your wife must be proud.' Evangeline couldn't believe she'd just said something that sounded so obvious.

'My wife died of cancer five years ago.' He said it well enough, just sort of slipped it in without making a number out of it. He was still smiling at her in a kind sort of way, almost as if he were apologizing for mentioning it.

'I'm sorry.'

'She was a lovely woman.' He said it in a matter-of-fact way, his eyes full of intelligence, but with a calming effect. Eyes she could trust – honest eyes. He offered no false pity when she told him her parents had died, just listened intently and without interruption.

'So how was Mr Moneybags?' Nico asked when she phoned him later.

'I liked him,' she said quietly.

'Jesus!' Nico said. 'I must meet the guy and find out his secret. How were the shots?'

209

Evangeline looked down at her camera. There were no shots, apart from the few she had taken before breakfast. They'd spent the rest of the morning at the restaurant and then the chauffeur had driven her home.

'They're fine.' It was a lie. Grandma Klippel would never forgive her.

The following day a parcel arrived by courier, wrapped in bright pink tissue. It was a collar for Paddy, wonderfully tacky — green velvet with diamante studs. The card that came with it said: *To Paddy, with love and thanks from Francesca*, in Stuart's handwriting — she could tell from the cheque he'd used to pay her. Evangeline phoned to thank him but he was in a meeting so she left a message instead.

Stuart's company used Evangeline several times over the next year but Stuart was always busy and did not appear at the jobs, which disappointed her. He was often abroad, evidently. She wondered what sort of countries he visited and what he did there. He seemed to own companies everywhere. She photographed new buildings for him all across the East Coast.

She was working on a site in Washington when she saw Stuart again. She had spent all day on the twelve-storey building. Its architecture was simple but magnificent and she enjoyed watching the autumn light move across it, changing its shape and colour as it went. In a few moments it would be sunset. She was sitting perched on a wall outside, waiting for the splay of ochre flame that would set the building alight.

'What do you think?' His voice made her jump, even though he had spoken quietly. He was standing behind her. She wondered how long he had been there. She made to scramble to her feet but he held her gently by the shoulders to make her stay where she was.

'Any . . . minute . . . now,' he whispered. The sun dropped and the building lit up. She lifted her camera and ran off a few shots.

He was dressed casually, she noticed with surprise when she finally got to her feet. Casual for Stuart was still smart by most yardsticks, though. She grinned at him.

'What?' he asked.

'You have creases ironed into your jeans,' she told him.

'Fashion victim,' he nodded. His eyes crinkled kindly when he smiled. She was at a loss to know what to make of him.

'It happens with age,' he said.

'Bullshit!' Evangeline laughed. 'How old are you, anyway?'

His eyes went serious suddenly. 'Old enough to be your father with a bit extra to spare,' he said. They studied one another in silence for a moment.

'Not too old to buy you supper, though,' he added.

Evangeline smiled.

She got drunk over dinner and decided to have sex with Stuart in order to get him out of her system. The strange thing was that he wasn't even her type and she wasn't his. His charm was seductive, though. She'd had a handful of lovers since Stephen, but nothing important, and Stuart was different; it felt unsettling. When he halted things after a goodnight kiss she was disappointed.

Flowers arrived the next day. Evangeline rang the head office but was told he was in a meeting. Francesca almost purred as she spoke the phrase. She phoned him again the following day but was told he was in Scotland with his daughter.

He phoned after a couple of months and she was pleased and relieved to hear from him.

'How are things?' he asked. His tone sounded the same: charming, polite, concerned, affectionate, all rolled into one.

'Fine.' She meant it. She'd had two new magazine spreads, pictures of a couple of film actors – not big names but talented new hopefuls, still happy to pose patiently, which was just as well as the last shoot had taken eight

211

hours of studio time before she was happy with the results.
'How was Scotland?' she asked.

'Cold. Fearsome. Historical.'

'Did Catherine like it?'

'A little. In parts.'

'Will I see you again?' Evangeline asked.

'Do you want to?'

'Maybe.'

'Twelve noon,' he said.

They ate lunch, then walked back to his office via Central Park. Francesca looked agitated when they arrived.

'Mrs Gottlieb is waiting to see you,' she told Stuart.

'Catherine?' he asked. His daughter was sitting in his chair in his office. She smiled when Stuart walked in but the smile froze slightly when she saw that Evangeline was with him.

She had lost weight since the hospital. She had her father's steel-blue eyes but the expression in them was different, colder. Her hair was dark and rolled into a tight French pleat. She wore a tight-fitting green silk suit that was several years too old for her and carried a quilted Chanel bag.

She stared across at Evangeline as Stuart kissed her fondly on the cheek and greeted her with a wan smile as they were re-introduced.

'You work for my father now, then?' she asked as Stuart slipped off to speak to his PA.

'Sort of,' Evangeline said, 'strictly freelance. I do shots for the company. We're kind of friends, too.'

Catherine raised one eyebrow. Her accent was pure public school English. Evangeline wondered how long she had worked at perfecting it. Flat-chested and round-hipped, she acted like a pretty girl who thinks she is beautiful.

Catherine was staring at her. 'My mother was quite gorgeous, you know,' she told Evangeline suddenly. The implication was obvious. Evangeline pushed her hair off

212

her face with her hand. She was pleased there were no mirrors in the office.

When Stuart returned with coffee Catherine's expression softened and became quite girlish again.

'I wasn't expecting you,' he said, smiling at her.

'Yes you were,' she told him, pouting, 'you promised me lunch. I hope you haven't forgotten.'

Stuart looked across at Evangeline. 'Of course not,' he lied. Two lunches, then. He and Evangeline had just eaten their fill some fifteen minutes before. It was the sort of thing Darius would have done just to keep everyone smiling. 'Would you like to come with us?' he asked Evangeline.

'No, no thanks,' she said quickly, 'I – I thought maybe I'd skip lunch today. No real appetite for some reason. Thanks.' She smiled politely at the look of relief that crossed Catherine's face.

'Just the two of us, then, Daddy,' she said brightly, staring at Evangeline for long enough to let her know that, at that point, she was expected to leave.

23

Stuart arrived unannounced at Evangeline's apartment late that night. She was in her pyjamas – huge, baggy things printed with pictures of dogs, that Nico had bought her for Christmas. Stuart, of course, looked smart, though he smelt as though he had been drinking heavily.

'Do you mind?' he asked, filling the doorway. Evangeline stepped back with a shrug.

'Make yourself at home,' she told him. He stopped inside the lounge, looking about the place with an expression of bewilderment.

He sat uncomfortably on the only piece of furniture that could be described as a chair. The rest of the stuff had cost a fortune but was highly dysfunctional. Gallery pieces, Nico called them, things to be looked at, rather than used. Paddy's basket was the only thing in the room with any comfort-factor in its design. Evangeline liked it like that, though. Everything looked clean and perfect, which was what she wanted. Paddy jumped onto Stuart's lap and curled up into a ball there. Evangeline found some brandy in the kitchen and poured some into a large glass for him.

'Thanks.' She watched as he swallowed it in one.

'It's Catherine,' he said quietly, 'Drake – her husband – is screwing around.'

Evangeline sat down on the floor.

'The little bastard – she was still nursing his first child when it started.' His lips were pale with anger. He stared into his empty glass shaking his head.

'Catherine told you?' Evangeline asked.

Stuart nodded. 'Over lunch. I knew something was

214

wrong. It took me an hour to get the truth out of her. She'd been telling me little Paul was ill but all the time she was covering for Drake acting like a prat. She couldn't face me, Evangeline, she didn't want to tell me.' He looked at her curiously. 'How old are you?'

'Twenty-six.'

He nodded. 'Catherine is only a few years younger.'

'Is she going to forgive him?' Evangeline asked. Stuart looked at her as though she were mad.

'Forgive him? Are you kidding? After what he's done? Oh no. He should be grateful he's still alive. When I've finished with him he might wish he wasn't.' Stuart stood up and Paddy dropped onto the floor.

'I'm going to break him, Evangeline – he'll never work in this – this –'

'– this town again,' Evangeline finished for him. 'That's the cliché, isn't it?' She smiled but Stuart looked deadly earnest.

'Stuart, you're drunk...' Evangeline began. She helped him back onto the chair again, where he sat with his head in his hands. She made him a black coffee and when she came back with it he was already asleep. She loosened his tie instead and left him to sleep it off in the dark.

She woke to the sound of her own shower but by the time she had roused herself Stuart had gone, leaving a note by the phone that read: *Sorry – thanks*. She screwed the note into a ball and kicked it into the bin.

Evangeline never heard what happened to Drake the philanderer but Catherine moved back in with her father for a while, so she heard less from Stuart over the following weeks. When he did call her she could hear the child screaming in the background.

He invited Evangeline for dinner soon after Catherine finally left. It was the first time she had seen Stuart in his own home. The place was vast and cleverly decorated; a blend of modern and antique furniture and subtle lighting to set it off. She expected to find that the meal had been catered, but instead it was Stuart who did the cooking.

'I didn't know you could cook,' she said.

'Do I take that as a sexist comment?' he asked. He was throwing things into a blender. Clever things. Evangeline watched, impressed.

'I can't,' she said. 'Cook, I mean.'

'Maybe you never tried. Here.' He threw her two eggs and proceeded to teach her how to crack them together in one hand without getting shell in the bowl. After ten goes she could almost do it. She gave up, laughing, and sat on a high stool to watch the rest of the meal.

The food was exquisite. Evangeline ate greedily and Stuart watched her, smiling.

'You're beautiful,' he told her.

She grinned and looked away. 'And you're extremely smooth,' she replied.

'Christ!' Stuart laughed. 'Do I slit my wrists now or later? Too slick? Is that what you think? So what do I do about that? Eat with my hands? Belch a bit? Dirty my clothes up?'

'You misunderstood,' Evangeline said, 'I said I like you as you are.'

Stuart smiled. She loved his smile.

'I bet you fold your clothes before you make love,' she said.

He didn't.

He smelt good when he kissed her and he tasted of the brandy he'd just drunk.

'You do want me, then,' she said.

'Of course I want you,' he told her, 'I've wanted nothing else virtually since the first time I saw you.'

She unbuttoned his shirt. He had a nice chest – brown and hairy. It felt good to touch. She pushed the shirt back and found a sprinkling of brown moles and little marks – a small scar. She ran the tip of her tongue around it. He crushed his hands into her hair, pulling her head close against him.

'Evangeline . . .' She shushed him. She felt warm and safe so close to him, like a small animal. His hands were hot and strong, she could feel them through her hair. She licked his chest like syrup some more, making him groan. It was nice giving him pleasure and even nicer watching such a powerful man begin to lose control. His head tilted back and she nibbled at his Adam's apple.

'You devour flesh,' Stuart laughed, 'you chew at your own nails and now you're starting on me.'

He lifted her up and kissed her again on the mouth.

'Do we go to the bedroom?' he asked. 'Or would that be too smooth for you? Maybe I should just clear a space on the floor.'

'The bedroom will do fine,' Evangeline said, grinning.

Stuart was a considerate, patient lover. She liked his naked body.

'You have a handsome cock,' she told him.

'Why, thank you,' he laughed.

'Maybe I could photograph it one day.'

'Maybe not,' he said.

She cupped his fat balls into her hand and squeezed them gently. She felt so safe with him, safe to do what she wanted. She lay back onto the bed and stretched like a cat. He touched her body gently and carefully and all the time the heat and mass of his own bulk was there beside her.

She closed her eyes. His hands parted her legs. He kissed her breasts and then her stomach. She felt the tip of his penis brushing against her leg. In an almost dreamlike state she felt his fingers circling her clitoris, desperately light at first but then, as her pelvis pushed upwards for more, his touch became heavier and more rhythmical. She became damp with longing and clutched at his cock to make his need as acute as her own.

He entered her just as she came, so that her shuddering muscles had something to cling to, then he held her until she was still again, rocking her like a parent with a child.

'You didn't come too,' she said.

217

'Don't worry, I will,' he told her. 'I wanted to make you happy first, Evangeline.'

He began to move inside her then, slowly at first so that she tried to hurry him, but keeping the same careful pace until she was almost laughing for more. He was heavy on top of her but she pulled him down further until he was squashing her because she liked the feel of his weight. He came quietly, his face buried into her shoulder. They lay there together for a while before he fell back.

When they were quiet again he stroked her hair back off her face.

'Come to Spain with me,' he said. 'I've got business there but we can turn it into a holiday. I've got to go but I don't want to leave you here.'

'Don't worry,' Evangeline said, 'I have a job in Japan, a month's assignment. So I won't feel you're deserting me.'

'A month?' Stuart looked surprised.

'You know how the work is.' Evangeline smiled at him. It was a while before he returned the smile.

'It's my job, Stuart.' It wasn't a problem, she just needed to make it clear to him. He was a businessman himself; of course he would understand. He was the type of man that would understand everything: mature, intelligent, comfortable with himself.

'Of course,' he said, smiling again, 'you've got a career and that comes first. That's OK. I can wait.'

24

New York 1991

For four years they made no plans together, each as tied to their careers as totally as if it were marriages that separated them. They met regularly but infrequently and Stuart phoned her at least once a day while Evangeline luxuriated in the comfort and security of the sound of his voice.

She dated other men and supposed he saw other women, but they established an etiquette whereby neither one of them asked about details like that.

She and Nico cut good deals together and her career took a steady path upward. He began to understand her methods of controlling that rise – that you didn't just take the best offer, you took the work that would help long-term. She became known for high standards and quality clients. Sometimes the big accounts came a little too easily and she worried that Stuart was behind it, but she was confident enough in her work to suspect she would have got the jobs anyway.

The top names started to ask for her. Some even refused to use anyone else. She used bold techniques: her portraits looked like art and her art shots looked almost too natural and simple.

Her studio lighting was good but she liked using available because everyone else was doing clever things with flash and tungsten. While other people's shots looked posed and artificial, hers shone out as new and natural-looking. It became her trademark, the thing she was best known for.

She also became known for apparently erratic behaviour.

Top-name clients phoned to book her and she would turn them down for badly paid or even free work. She avoided advertisements with big budgets because she said she would have no artistic control over the shots. Instead she did editorial material for the magazines with the best art reputation and the best reproduction techniques.

It was a clever ploy, even if it did turn Nico's hair grey. Her work was always top quality and it was always seen in the best places. She would not allow a shot to be published if she did not consider it close to perfect, whoever she upset in the process. If she felt she was losing control of a shoot because the client starting butting in or an agency man began to hurry her she would down tools and walk out – it was as simple as that. 'I need two things from you,' she would tell new clients, 'unlimited time and absolutely no interference.' Once they saw her work they respected her request and she usually got both.

Nico was almost happy with her, but not quite. 'You need one of these big-name accounts,' he would tell her, 'one of the cosmetic firms, or something. One of those jobs that pay millions that you could do standing on your head. You won't get married. You'll probably never have children. You need something to keep you in your old age. At least put yourself up for one of the pitches, Evangeline.'

Evangeline would laugh at him. 'Find me a campaign that says I can do what I like how I like and I might put myself up for it,' she said.

Then at last he did. 'Imprex,' he told her one day in the office.

'What?' She was picking burrs out of the dog's coat.

'Imprex,' Nico repeated. His grin was about a mile wide.

'Should I know them?' Evangeline asked.

'Only the largest credit card company in Europe,' Nico said.

'What, you want another card?' Evangeline asked him. Nico adored credit cards. He collected them – all of them –

although he never used any of them. It was a standing joke between them.

'Imprex are launching a new, platinum card. The campaign for it is big, Evangeline, one of the biggest ever – look!' He pointed out a page in the financial paper he always read. 'I've put you up for it.'

'What?' Evangeline looked mad. 'You know I don't do ads, Nico! Shit! What is it they want, shots of a guy in a suit getting onto a plane or something? You know I don't do that kind of stuff!'

Nico smiled his smuggest smile. 'It's a new campaign, like I said,' he grinned, 'and it's also major. Big bucks – millions, maybe – if you get it.'

'That stuff's all hype, Nico . . .' Evangeline cut in.

'Total artistic freedom,' Nico said. 'They want quality and class. No crap, just art.'

Evangeline shut up.

'We had a deal,' Nico told her. 'Total control and you were up for it. Your name's on their list. Finito.'

The following month Nico got married to the woman who ran the deli on the corner.

'All this free food is making you fat,' Evangeline told him when they danced together at the wedding.

'Fat but very happy,' Nico smiled. She had never seen him beam so much. His face would split apart if he stayed that happy for too long. 'You should marry your rich businessman, Evangeline,' he shouted above the music, 'you've known him over five years now. How much time do you need to make up your mind? You're over thirty. I want you to be happy like me.'

'It's four years,' Evangeline corrected him. 'He's abroad too much – we barely meet. We're friends.'

Nico rolled his eyes towards the heavens. 'Lucky he gets back now and again,' he said. He turned her around to face the doorway. Stuart was standing there watching her, splendid in his formal wedding suit.

Evangeline stared at him. 'I thought you were in Hong Kong,' she mouthed. Her stomach was doing things — flipping about like crazy.

Stuart shrugged. 'Surprise.'

She went to him and they kissed. He looked like a hero — the best she'd ever seen him — all warm and huge and wealthy and handsome. He'd booked a room at the most expensive hotel in the area and she ran with him there as soon as the reception was over because she felt she would burst with lust if she had to wait another minute more.

He was as passionate as a younger man that night. They threw their clothes off the minute the door was closed behind them and Stuart stood there, magnificently tanned and naked, while Evangeline sank to her knees and took his cock into her mouth.

'No, Evangeline,' he groaned as she kissed at him, pushing her head away and pulling her upright beside him so that he could enter her. She clung to him as he came, her legs around his waist and her hands clutching at his head. Then she came too, and he held her while she shook with pleasure.

They slid slowly to the floor, laughing at their own randiness.

'I'm glad you could make it after all,' Evangeline panted.

'The feeling's mutual,' Stuart laughed.

They were both in the States for December. Stuart scrawled a booking for Christmas in Evangeline's diary because he joked that was the only way he could ever get to see her. Five weeks before the much-planned Christmas he phoned Evangeline's apartment.

'Hi?' her voice sounded dull.

'Evangeline?' Stuart was surprised to hear her at all. 'I thought you were in Paris on a shoot.'

'Why did you phone then?' He thought he must have woken her, she sounded so groggy.

'I phoned to leave a message, that's all. You said you liked to hear a human voice in among all the work calls when you get back. Are you OK, Evangeline?' The kindness in his voice triggered her off. 'What is it?' He could hear her crying.

'Nico, Stuart – it's Nico. He had a heart attack. He died this morning. I didn't get to the hospital. He went before I could get there. I didn't know he was ill. He must have had a bad heart. I don't know what to do . . . I . . .'

Stuart interrupted her. 'Don't do a thing, Evangeline,' he said, 'I'm on my way over.'

He arrived clutching a bottle of malt whisky and a box of tissues, and sat up with her all night, holding her hand when she cried and hugging her until, finally, she slept.

In the morning when she woke he was standing by the bedside balancing a tray with English breakfast tea, fresh orange juice and a bowl of porridge with a crust of brown sugar.

'Oatmeal!' she said. 'I haven't had that since I was a child on Cape Cod. Mrs O'Reilly used to make it for me to ward off the colds when the fog moved in . . .' and then she was crying again, all over Paddy this time, who ate the porridge hungrily instead.

When she had finished crying Stuart poured her tea and picked up the photograph of Lincoln by the bedside.

'Who's this?' he asked.

'My brother – half-brother,' she corrected herself.

'I didn't know you had a brother,' Stuart smiled.

'I don't,' she told him, 'not any more.' She stared into the tea.

Stuart closed his eyes. 'I'm sorry, Evangeline, I don't seem to be doing too well this morning.'

She told him the whole story of her childhood then. It was as though she were drunk; she couldn't stop talking.

'I don't know where my parents were going,' she cried, 'I don't know why they were going off without me. I don't even know where they are buried.' She sounded like a child but she couldn't pause, even for breath.

Stuart stroked her hair.

'You could always find out,' he said, gently.

She shook her head. 'You don't understand – I don't want to know.'

'OK, OK,' Stuart hushed her. She was right; he didn't understand.

Stuart planned the perfect Christmas for her: a log cabin miles away from anywhere, snow, and home-cooked food he had taken days to prepare. A Christmas tree to greet her when she walked through the door with his hands covering her eyes. A pile of presents for Paddy that he could rip his way through the moment they arrived.

He wanted to make up for anything that might have been missing in her life. He wanted to show her it was OK, even if Nico wasn't there any more. She'd told him about bleak Christmases on the Cape, when she'd spent hours staring at the icy black sea and wondering if this year her parents would come back.

There was something else, too. Another surprise; one he might pull off or not, depending how the holiday went. Stuart had decided he would marry Evangeline; when the moment was appropriate he intended to propose. He had told Catherine because he thought it was right that he should do so – she was his daughter, after all. She had held the ring he'd bought in her hands – a subtle-looking ring, the sort Evangeline would like, the sort that cost twelve thousand dollars but was understated enough for her not to realize, he hoped.

Catherine's hands had been shaking as she inspected it and her eyes went cold.

'Aren't you pleased?' Stuart had asked her. 'Do you think I'm making a fool of myself?'

She shook her head. It was a minute or so before she could talk. 'I'm sorry, Dad,' she said, and her eyes were wet with tears now. 'It's just Mom, and everything. I couldn't help thinking... I suppose I remembered my own engagement, too. It's just it all comes back and hits you when you least want it, you know. It's a beautiful ring, Dad. She'd be a fool not to take it.'

Stuart patted his daughter's hand.

Catherine had phoned his office the day before he left for the holiday. She had sounded cheerful enough at first but he could tell something was wrong.

'It's Gavin, Dad . . .' Her new man had left her. 'I'll be OK,' she gulped. She was crying. He had had no choice. He'd had to invite her, too. He had told Evangeline and she had agreed with him. There would be five of them for Christmas, then: himself, Evangeline and Paddy, Catherine and Paul, his grandson.

'It will be good,' Evangeline had told him, 'a real family time.' He had been cheered by that. Extraordinarily cheered.

They spent three days together before Evangeline got the phone call; three days of snow-fights and dog walks and eating so much food they felt sick. It was two days before the great day itself, and when Evangeline came out of the house he could tell something was wrong by the look on her face.

'What is it?' He was panting. He'd been chasing Catherine through the snow while Paul screamed with delight. Catherine came to a halt beside him.

'What is it, Evangeline?'

'Stuart – I'm sorry, I mean you've been so good and you've gone to so much trouble here . . .' her voice trailed off.

'It's a job, isn't it?' He tried not to show how he felt. He heard Catherine beside him. 'Jesus!' she whispered.

Evangeline nodded. 'It's *the* job, Stuart – one that Nico

had me up for, the one he really wanted me to get. You must have heard of it, Stuart, it's the Bell and Layburn account for Imprex, the biggest account of the year. You know all the top names are up for this one, but I've been shortlisted and I need to finish the pitch Nico started for me.'

'Imprex?' Catherine said. 'Credit cards? You're photographing credit cards?'

Stuart shut her up. 'It's more than that, Catherine,' he said, 'it's the artistic freedom Evangeline's after. Everyone in the business knows about this one – it's the most sought-after job since Selznick was casting *Gone with the Wind*. They're going to let the photographer shoot what they like, how they like – it's the quality they're going for. The posters and ads will go all around the world. It would be a stupendous account to get. You'd be famous, Evangeline. Congratulations!'

Evangeline looked at him. 'You don't mind?' she asked quietly.

He smiled. 'I'm proud of you.'

Catherine folded her arms across her chest. 'How long will you be gone for?' she asked. 'Will you make it back for Christmas Day?'

'The interview's in London,' Evangeline said.

Stuart didn't take his eyes off her face. 'If you get the job you won't be back until Christmas next year.'

Catherine clutched at her father's arm, looking disgusted.

There were tears in Evangeline's eyes. 'I can come back for the day itself,' she said. 'They can't interview on Christmas Day, Stuart. I'll be here, I promise I will.'

'Shall I look after Paddy for you?' Stuart asked.

Evangeline nodded. 'Please, Stuart.'

He stepped forward and kissed her on the forehead. 'Go and pack,' he whispered.

When she was gone Catherine rounded on her father. 'Why didn't you tell her?' she asked angrily. 'Why did you just let her walk out like that? You'd planned it all so carefully – you were going to propose! Jesus, Dad, how can you allow her to treat you like that?'

Stuart picked up Paul and placed the boy astride his shoulders. 'She has a career, Catherine,' he said.

His daughter looked back at the house. 'Mom had a career,' she said, quietly, 'but she loved you enough to give it up.'

It was as though Stuart hadn't heard her.

'I can wait,' he said, smiling, 'not too long, but I can wait.'

25

London 1992

Coming to London was the start and the end of Evangeline's life, all in one. She'd left New York that Christmas in a snow-storm, alone. She'd made Stuart promise not to come to the airport and he'd agreed with what seemed like relief.

The snows had cleared once the plane had flown out over the coast and she'd settled back to consider the job that lay ahead. She'd been told it was virtually hers and she was excited. The prestige was good but the potential of the work was even better. It was a job she wanted desperately. She could do what she was best at and get to the top of her business while she did it. Most photographers had to bastardize their art for the sake of earning a buck but this job had no restrictions. They would leave her to do what she chose and pay her a small fortune for doing it.

The first time she saw Mik Veronsky he frightened her. She'd been at the offices of Bell and Layburn, waiting for the big interview, her portfolio balanced across her lap and a hank of hair stuffed nervously into her mouth. The place was quietly opulent, the sort of building that made you want to tiptoe for fear of creating offence. Very English, she thought, though she'd only been in the country a few hours.

She'd put on a semi-smart suit for the meeting and she felt awkward as hell sitting there so dressed up. What had made her do such a thing? Something to do with voices in her head, maybe: Grandma Klippel telling her to sit up straight, and the frown when she'd seen her years ago in shorts and a scruffy coat.

It was a good suit – designer label – but it was made of linen and, in the British winter, totally out of place. She crossed her legs and tried to look bored. Then she gave up and just chewed at her hair some more.

She checked her watch. Two minutes late. The receptionist saw her looking and smiled to reassure her. You didn't get impatient about two lousy minutes; nobody got impatient about two lousy minutes. There were magazines on a table beside her but she didn't trust herself to pick one up. What she wanted to do was get up and walk and burn off some of the adrenalin.

'Do you think they'll be long?' she asked, and then wished to God she hadn't. Who was she, anyway? If they'd made her sit there a year for the job she would have.

The receptionist shrugged.

'Would you like a coffee?' she asked. She'd been reading a magazine she had hidden in a drawer. She kept licking a finger to turn the pages.

'No – no thanks,' Evangeline said.

'Tea?' The woman cocked her head like a parrot.

'Thank you.'

She was alone now, the woman had slipped out through a door behind her desk. Maybe the whole place was a sham. Maybe there was a small filthy kitchen behind that door with an old electric kettle and a jar of instant coffee.

The reception door swung open. Evangeline looked up with mild concern. Would the receptionist be fired for desertion? She smiled at the man who stood there. He was tall and intense-looking, carrying some sort of portfolio, only it was the old-fashioned sort – the type no one had any more.

'Where are they?' He didn't look at her, he looked at the empty desk. He had a heavy accent that she couldn't place. He wore no coat and he looked half frozen. She looked at his feet. His boots must have been made in the seventies. They were badly scuffed and had a hole in the toe.

'She's making tea,' Evangeline told him. 'She shouldn't be long.'

'Do you work here?' he asked. He turned but he had no eye contact. He was either painfully shy or rude.

'No.'

'Then you don't know Mr E. W. Gershon?'

'Eddie?' she asked. 'Not yet.'

'He's the top man,' he said.

'I believe so, yes.' She was sounding snotty but couldn't help it.

He raised his eyebrows. His face was interesting, full of angles and shadows. She began to wonder how she would photograph it, given the opportunity. There was something in it that scared her, though she had no idea why. He looked angry. Maybe he was mad; she had always been a little alarmed by madness in other people.

'I'm waiting to see him now,' she explained.

The man nodded. He was younger than she'd first thought. She wished the receptionist would come back and deal with him because he made her nervous. He was on edge, too. She had a New Yorker's trained eye for incipient violence and this man appeared to display many of the symptoms. There was a muscle working constantly in his cheek and his eyes checked the room ceaselessly, as though frightened they might miss something. His hands were clenched so hard around the portfolio the colour had gone from his knuckles.

The receptionist returned with the tea in a bone china cup and Evangeline relaxed a little.

'Can I help you, sir?' she asked, smiling her professional little smile.

'Eddie Gershon,' the man said. Evangeline narrowed her eyes. Shit! She'd given that one to him on a plate.

'Do you have an appointment, sir?' the woman asked, flicking through a diary on the desk.

'No.' It sounded like trouble. It sounded like a 'No-but-so-what?' type of no.

The guy was scary, but Evangeline's money was on the woman. She rose to full height and hit him with a fossilized smile.

'Then I'm afraid you'll need one before Mr Gershon can see you,' she said.

The man was almost laughing. 'No, you don't understand – he'll see me,' he said. His hands were pale and long and they had risen in an urgent gesture.

'Not without an appointment.'

He paused, thinking. 'What time could I have one?' he asked.

'Wednesday, at the earliest. If Mr Gershon is available.' The receptionist's eyes never left the man's face. She was obviously going to get someone in security fired for this misdemeanour.

'That's no good. That's too late.' He sat down next to Evangeline and the sudden movement made her portfolio slide off her lap.

'I'm sorry, sir –'

'I'm a photographer. Eddie Gershon will want to see me. I've come for the credit card account. Maybe my agent didn't press hard enough – I'm sure if Mr Gershon will look at my work . . .' He unzipped his folder and held it open for the receptionist to see. Then he jumped out of the chair again to hold the book closer. 'Look, do you see this? And look, this one . . . can you just take this through for me? He will want to see me but I think maybe he isn't aware of my work yet . . . look . . .'

Evangeline caught a glimpse of some of the shots he was showing the woman. They were black-and-whites, grainy and raw. They looked ugly, like war shots. She thought the receptionist was going to throw up. In the back of the portfolio were a few yellowing press cuttings from a foreign paper.

'How did you get past security?' the receptionist's voice

sounded faint. She pressed a button beneath her desk. The man didn't notice, but Evangeline did. She knew what that button would be for. Soon someone big and uniformed would arrive to escort the young man to the exit.

He sat down again, running his hand frantically through his hair. 'I know I deserve this job – if Mr Gershon will just give me five minutes . . .' Another buzzer sounded on the desk. The receptionist smiled an apologetic smile at Evangeline.

'Mr Gershon will see you now,' she said. Evangeline rose and the young man rose too. She had heels on but he was still several inches taller. She wasn't afraid physically but she was frightened of his raw earnestness and the desperation in his manner. She thought he might smell bad but he didn't; he smelt of clean, cold fresh air.

When he looked her straight in the eye she was grateful he hadn't done so before. There was something terrifyingly familiar in the urgency there, like waking up with a hangover and looking in the mirror and wondering where you've seen the face before. She knew that look. Nothing else, but she knew the eyes – understood the emotion in them. She looked away quickly.

'Will you take my book in for me?' He pushed it into her hands. 'Let him see it – please. I need a chance. Do you already have work? Then be decent enough. Just give me a fair chance to beat you.'

He walked away and sat down, confident that she would play fair and allow his portfolio to be shown along with hers.

Evangeline stared at him. Then she crossed in silence and laid the book beside him on the floor, ignoring his expression of betrayal and hatred. She wanted no share of what she saw there. She wanted success and this young man stank of failure.

'Fuck you!' His outburst meant nothing. It was aimed at her back as she walked confidently into the offices of E. W. Gershon.

26

Christmas 1992

There were two other photographers in the running for the Imprex account, but Evangeline was the only one who held out to do the whole thing on her own terms and the only one whose work in the past showed no sign of compromise, and so she was already ahead of the field. She had prepared a good presentation and she had turned up in person, which impressed the clients.

When they called her back on Christmas Eve to offer her the job she turned it down flat. Then she handed them a list of her own stipulations and requirements. One of the things she insisted upon was that she did not get paid a cent until the job was finished and everyone was happy with the results. By everyone, she said, she meant herself in particular. If she wasn't one hundred per cent happy then the shots would be binned, however tight the schedule and however many hoardings and ad spaces had been booked.

The clients were amazed and asked for a day to consider. That would take them into Christmas Day, she told them. They phoned back within the hour to tell her she would be spending Christmas Day as their guest and the New Year taking photographs for their account. There would be no marketing man breathing down her neck, no proper brief, just faith in her ability. The success of the campaign would be in creating art for posters, so that the product became identified with quality and innovation.

It was as though the world had suddenly opened up for her. When she got back to her hotel room there was a note

233

saying her things had been moved to the best suite at The Ritz, in Piccadilly. People she had never met or heard of phoned to congratulate her and journalists sent notes up to say they were waiting to interview her downstairs. A nice woman in a suit arrived to take her on a tour of the best London shops and she was given a schedule for the following few days to warn her what sort of clothes she would need.

Almost too jet-lagged to speak, she phoned Stuart a few minutes before midnight.

'Evangeline?' he sounded tired too. 'Where are you? At the airport? Can I come and pick you up?'

'Jesus, Stuart, no.' She was suddenly filled with guilt at messing him up. 'I'm sorry.' It was all she could think of to say.

There was a long pause. 'Did you get the account?' Stuart asked.

'Yes.'

'Then that's all that matters. Congratulations, Evangeline. I'm so pleased for you. Have a wonderful Christmas, you deserve it.' There was no sarcasm in his voice, only unselfish pleasure. Catherine would supply the sarcasm, though, the minute Stuart got off the phone.

'Get some sleep,' he said, 'goodnight.'

Did Stuart care that much? He'd never told her he loved her and she'd never made any commitment to him. They were both work animals: the job came first, that was understood between them and she was comfortable with that thought. They were friends who slept together occasionally and that was good because she couldn't handle more commitment, not yet.

She wondered whether there were other women he'd rather have invited for Christmas. She rarely thought about him with other women but she knew he had to have them. Stuart was a catch in anyone's eyes. She wondered why he'd never married again. As Catherine was always saying, though, his wife had been exceptional and he'd never find anyone who could replace her.

She called him again the following day. Catherine picked up the phone.

'Evangeline.' There was a long, theatrical sigh.

'Can I speak to your father?' Evangeline asked. She was glowing from a hot bath. A picture on the wall of her room was crooked and she lay back on the bed to straighten it with her toe.

Catherine went away. There was a long pause and then the sound of footsteps returning. Evangeline filled the time by whistling 'Jingle Bells' beneath her breath.

'Stuart?' She heard the phone picked up.

'No, Evangeline, it's Catherine again. My father's asleep. I didn't want to disturb him.'

'Asleep?' Evangeline laughed. 'I thought he'd be playing Santa about now. Tell him I called, will you? Tell him I may be in London but my time-clock's still fixed to New York time, so he can ring me when he's finished his nap.'

Catherine sighed again, louder this time. 'Look, Evangeline, you may as well know the truth. My father's got a woman here. She phoned after you left and he invited her round since you couldn't stay. He's known her for a few months and I think things are going to get serious. That's why I don't want to call him to the phone and that's why I don't think he'll be calling you back later. I'm sure you understand. I hope you have good luck with the job. Goodbye, Evangeline.' She hung up.

Stuart walked into the hall as the receiver went down. He was dressed in the full Santa kit, with Paul laughing astride his shoulders. He saw Catherine's face and raised his eyebrows quizzically.

'Drake,' Catherine told him flatly. 'He wanted to wish his son Happy Christmas. I said I could do it for him.' Stuart pulled his daughter towards him and gave her a hug.

'Just the three of us here,' he said, 'you, me and Paul.

It's OK, though, isn't it?'

'Sure, Daddy,' Catherine said, smiling up into his face.

Evangeline toured Britain for a year, taking shots, and in that time she grew to love the country. Parts of it reminded her of Boston and her woolly memories of the place where she was born came back to haunt her with sharp, sweet stabs of recall.

She felt that she had no roots to speak of. She still wrote to her grandmother but the old lady was getting frail and the answers became less frequent. Was she just a painful reminder to the old lady, now? Maybe she should have given her a chance to forget things. She wasn't even blood, after all. Did her letters merely keep stirring up memories of Darius that would otherwise fade? Sometimes she felt guilty, but she still wrote because she needed to. Her feelings for Stuart were almost as complicated. The idea of him with another woman hurt, there was no denying it, although the subject was never mentioned during their weekly phone conversations. She had no right to complain, though. She was in no position to offer him more than she had already. She hated herself for being jealous.

She missed him, but most of the time she missed Paddy even more. She even phoned just to hear his yelps on the line. She almost hated the British for their quarantine laws and would have tried smuggling him, but she was too scared. She missed his eyes, watching her, and she missed his weight on her bed at night.

Would Darius and Thea have approved of her work now? She thought that they would and this made her feel better. She had earned that ride in the car now. She was talented, even though she wasn't beautiful. If they'd known how she was going to turn out they would have taken her with them after all, she was sure of it.

She had no theme to her work, just a set of standards. When she saw something she liked she photographed it, though without realizing it her work began to reflect her

236

childhood. They were lonely shots – simple, no gimmicks or angles – just page after page of beautiful, haunting work.

When she returned with the portfolio she found herself back in the offices of Eddie Gershon, only this time she wasn't kept waiting and was greeted with a cheerfulness bordering on hysteria for bringing them in so close to schedule.

She showed her year's work in slides, on the wall of the office. The blinds were drawn and there was a quiet tension in the air.

No one spoke when the first slide went up so she spoke instead, telling the roomful of men exactly where she had taken it and why. She had one hundred and seventy shots in all and the presentation took nearly two hours. When the lights went up everyone stayed where they were in their seats and looked towards Eddie Gershon, the boss. He was a young guy to be holding such a post, but nice – she liked him. He swung back and forward in his chair, chewing on the end of a plastic pen.

Evangeline was so proud of her work it had never occurred to her that they might not like it. A sudden sensation of cold fear filled her stomach. Her mouth was dry from all the talking. She opened a nearby bottle of mineral water and made a mess of filling her glass.

Gershon turned around in his chair to face her. 'Are you happy with them?' he asked.

'What?' The glass hit against her front teeth as she took a sip.

'Are they good by your standards? Are they what you wanted?' he asked. Twelve anxious faces turned to stare at her in silence. She realized suddenly that at least half of them, unlike their boss, probably had no idea what was art and what was not.

'Yes,' she said, 'yes, they're very good.'

Their faces broke out into smiles and there was even a smatter of relieved applause.

'Excellent, excellent,' Gershon called out, turning his

chair back to face the screen. He pressed a buzzer and his PA arrived with champagne. 'Show them again, would you?' he asked. Evangeline almost wept with relief.

The art department at Bell and Layburn had firmer ideas about what constituted a good shot but even they had had their wings clipped by Gershon, who had insisted that Evangeline have final artistic say on how the pictures were cropped and presented. It took ten weeks to make the final choice and a further twelve before they had been laid out in a style that suited everyone.

Evangeline was pleased with the results. The posters would look good and, when the shots were previewed in a *Times* supplement exclusive the write-up was favourable and the feedback better than she would have hoped. The biggest criticism came when one reviewer called them 'perfect but bland'. The client was delighted, though; it was the first time an ad campaign had been reviewed on the art pages.

Once the posters and ads had come out Evangeline found herself under siege. No longer an anonymous face, her name had become known and she was dismayed to discover all the hassle that went with celebrity status.

The launch was the starting pistol: Eddie Gershon chartered a flotilla of cruisers to take the press and VIP guests up the Thames to Docklands, where he had hired a massive, three-storey warehouse to exhibit the prints.

Evangeline had not been expecting anything quite so lavish. As the boats rounded the corner in front of the warehouse a thousand fireworks exploded into the night sky, spelling out the name of the company, and massive speakers blared out the music from the TV ad campaign.

As the guests walked up the cement drive the vast main door to the warehouse was dragged back slowly, revealing Evangeline's two most commercial shots, painted on the huge walls in laser beams. Eddie looked across at Evangeline and grinned.

'OK?' he mouthed.

'Shit,' was all she could manage. She felt suddenly shy and self-conscious. The pictures appeared to have no connection with her now – they were images conjured up by somebody else, somebody who should have been standing there dripping in Versace, smiling and shaking hands and lapping up all the credit.

She turned to run away but Eddie caught her by the arm.

'Take the praise,' he said, 'you've earned it.'

Evangeline looked at him and he grinned again and she smiled. 'A little over the top?' she asked.

'Just a soupçon,' he admitted, 'but who's worried? It's good for morale.'

He led her into the warehouse and up to the champagne.

'One glass and you'll feel better,' he said, 'I promise.'

After two weeks of press hype in London Evangeline flew back to the US for a break. Paddy was ecstatic to see her, keeping her awake all the first night by jumping onto the bed and licking at her face. Catherine looked after him when Stuart was abroad and Evangeline had to admit she had done a good job.

'How about a little drive, Paddy?' she asked the next day.

She hired a car and they set off north. She pretended to herself that the drive was still part of the break, but in fact she was itching to get to work again. She needed some strong ideas to pitch for the next Imprex campaign, and thought she could combine her holiday with a little location hunting.

It was autumn and the countryside was covered with a layer of rust-red leaves. She sang a lot as she drove and Paddy joined in with his howls. When they discovered a new town or village she would stop off to take shots and to poke around the local libraries or newspaper offices to

239

dig out the special spots the tourists missed.

Two days out of New York she found a small clapboard inn she fell in love with and they booked in for the night so she could mooch about the nearest town. She was recognized at the offices of the small local paper and the editor came out, wreathed in smiles, to invite her on a tour of the place and to share a bottle of malt whisky afterwards.

The paper was small but impressive. Its owner was a wealthy local businessman who had insisted on all the latest equipment for the place and there was a large room dedicated to its computers and historical library.

'We make a lot of money from storing records other people have thrown away over the years,' the editor said. 'You can find anything in these files and yet most of the stuff is stored on something no bigger than the tip of your little finger. We were the first to do it, you know.' When he grinned he had several teeth missing at the front.

'Can I do a little searching through these files myself?' Evangeline asked. 'I'd like to steep myself in a little local history. Sometimes the story of a certain place will appeal to me and I get a shot I might have missed otherwise.'

The editor patted a nearby computer and sat down heavily on the small chair in front of it.

'Sure, sure,' he said, 'it'd be an honour. We could use a little publicity for the town – it's suffering since the big industries moved out. Perhaps you'd like to read about that – there're a few tales in those derelict factories you must have passed on the way in . . .'

'How do I connect up?' Evangeline asked, bending to see the screen.

The editor pursed his lips. 'Let's see now, suppose you want to look through back copies of this paper or, let's say you want to look through another one from somewhere else. Were you born around here? Where do you come from?'

'Boston,' Evangeline said.

'Time and place?'

She didn't specify where she was born, but she told him where she used to live. There was silence as he tapped it onto the keyboard.

'The *Gazette* would have been your local – is that right?' he asked.

'I don't know,' her voice had gone to a whisper. 'I was only six when I left.'

The front page of a newspaper appeared on screen. He banged a few more keys and the births and deaths column appeared.

'No mention of your birth, I'm afraid,' he laughed, 'maybe you lied about your age, though. Most women tend to, as I understand.'

Her head felt strange. The room was too hot and the buzz from a faulty fluorescent light overhead had started to annoy her.

'Let's go on a bit.'

'No, that's OK.' She tried to stop him but more newspaper covers came up. She hadn't meant to tell him where she had lived. She didn't want this – it was like digging up a grave. 'Please, stop.' She put her hand on his arm. 'I think I've got the hang of it now,' she said, trying to sound polite. 'You're busy. I'll get on by myself. I'll give you a knock when I've finished and we can try some of that malt you were boasting about.'

The man grinned and offered her the seat. 'Just call me if you need any help,' he said.

'Sure will,' she laughed. Her hands were shaking.

When he had gone she looked back at the screen. It flashed at her, the light reflected in her face.

Don't.

Her hand raised itself to the level of the keyboard.

Let it go.

'I can't, Nico.'

She pressed the button with the arrow on it and the image on screen slipped backwards. Nothing. Nothing special. Flower shows. Adverts. A plough for sale. A bring-and-buy at the local church. Nothing harmful. Stop now, stop while you're ahead.

She went back some more. The images had slithered by like eels when the editor had been showing her but she thought she'd seen something all the same . . . A plan to widen the main street that got thrown out; a woman who died when her horse fell and crushed her as she was out riding; a local heat of the All-America Twist-Dancing marathon, to raise money for the needy . . . Stop it. Stop it right now. Then there it was: Darius and Thea Klippel, local artists. Smiling. An exhibition in Boston. A grainy black-and-white picture of one of Darius's more well-known works. A photograph of her mother in a frock, standing awkwardly in Darius's studio, looking for all the world like she had just finished baking cakes.

She touched the screen with the tip of her forefinger. When you looked closer the image vanished into a series of black-and-white dots. A pain ran through her body, a pain that was so bad and acute it almost winded her.

'Mother?' she asked. Nothing moved on Thea's face: pinpricks, dots of nothing, Impressionistic; there was nothing there at all, really. They were her mother's eyes, but then they became spots of print. Ugly close up, beautiful from the correct distance.

She printed the page out so she could touch the picture itself. Thea. Darius's studio. She remembered the dustiness and the smells of oil and paint. The great canvases she was not allowed to touch in case they were wet. The excitement of being in that room, like being in a church. There were spiders there sometimes, but she didn't mind, though Patrick went crazy if he got his face into a web.

Were all these memories or fantasy? She didn't know what was real any more and what was not. How much did a six-year-old remember? Yet how many six-year-olds lost their families as she had?

She began moving the pages forward rather than back.

Don't look. Don't go on. The cranberry harvest; someone with a degree from a university out south, smiling toothily in their cap and gown; then the windmill. She stopped, horrified. A front-page shot of the windmill being moved. Workmen standing astride it, smiling. Some children. Was she there? The shot was too blurred and the kids were just dots with grins. She felt the sun on her face, smelt the wild grasses as she ran barefoot through them. The nostalgia was an ache but the pain turned sweet as the memories grew. Lincoln out of his pram, rolling on the lawn. Patrick leaping around barking and licking at him. Her tears appeared suddenly, sprinkling from nowhere.

Stop it, Evangeline.

It was OK, she could handle it. The pain was sweet now. Maybe it was good, after all. Maybe now it was out it would start to go away.

She was sprinting through the pages, tearing past each one, even though her eyes were too blurred by tears now to see. There was a fear inside her but her curiosity was a lot more urgent than that fear.

There was a shot of Darius accepting an award. His smile looked polite enough but she could see the humour behind it. 'What the hell is this supposed to be?' his eyes asked as he held the cup aloft. It must have been an award for his work. He would have laughed about that once he was home.

She printed that sheet out, too. There was a whole pile of them now — copies of all the pages that had had mention of her parents. Some were just articles but she had the pictures, too.

She became excited. The pages slipped and slithered past again, too quick to see. Then she spotted something, and went back. Black and white. More pictures, smiling pictures of Thea and Darius. A shot of Lincoln in his cradle. Three photos at the top of the front page: one, two, three. She touched each one with her finger. Her mother's was the oldest. It must have been taken while she was at college. Darius's was the one of him accepting the award. The baby

243

shot had to be more recent.

She pressed the button again; this was like Russian Roulette. More shots, shots of the outside of the house, with all the cars. A photograph of Thea and Darius on their wedding day, maybe the shot Grandma Klippel kept on her mantelpiece. She didn't read the writing that went with the shots – she couldn't, her eyes wouldn't settle.

Someone appeared at her elbow – a young woman in a smock and trainers. 'Would you care for some coffee, miss?'

Evangeline looked at her as though she were a freak. Her eyes would not shift focus. 'No, no thanks. Some water, maybe – is that OK?'

The girl must have seen something wrong in her eyes because she nodded and edged out of the room in silence.

Evangeline looked back at the screen.

There was a word hanging there, a headline above the photographs. A big headline, thick and important. The word was *suicide*. It was wrong, though, it had to be.

Suicide.

They were killed in a car crash, she knew that – it was what she had been told. That was the truth, so what were all these lies about?

But the car was still there, Evangeline – you saw it – you saw it out in the drive. The confusion in her head cleared and she read some more:

> *Darius and Thea Klippel . . . distinguished local artists . . . police discovered a house of horror . . . three bodies . . . shot through the head . . . two adults and one small child . . . believed to be a suicide pact . . . no sign of a struggle . . .*

She laughed. It was so ridiculous that she laughed until her guffaws became hiccups that turned into sobs. How could a newspaper have got it all so wrong? She scanned the next issue: *Coroner's report . . . Suicide . . . no suspicious circumstances . . . a riddle . . . whole family wiped out . . .*

Someone had discovered Evangeline a few copies later: *One surviving child, Evangeline Klippel, aged six years . . . tragedy . . . came home to find her parents dead . . . cared for by her grandmother . . .*

There was a picture of an open doorway – the door that led to Darius's studio. The door was ajar but behind it you could just see a pair of legs laid out and some dark stuff in a puddle. A man's legs. The feet wore old-looking sneakers. Darius had been wearing sneakers when he shot himself, then.

What had her mother been wearing? Jeans and sneakers – jeans with turn-ups at the ankle, the way he liked them. Sneakers without socks. Thea used to joke how it made his feet smell. Some of the laces were undone. Had he died in agony, kicking them off?

Where had her mother died? Maybe she was behind the door with him, with Lincoln in her arms. Had he shot Lincoln first? Maybe he shot him first and then Thea had picked him up and then he had shot her too, in the back of the head, so he didn't have to look into her eyes. Shooting himself had to have been the toughest part. Getting the barrel of the shotgun and pushing it into his mouth somehow . . .

When the editor came looking for her much later the room was in darkness and the computer screen switched off. He noticed with vague annoyance that she'd switched off without clearing the screen and he hoped she hadn't wiped any of their files.

She didn't turn round when he walked in.

'I hope you got all you wanted?' he asked. There was a sheaf of papers at her feet, print-outs of several pages.

'Thank you.'

He thought it was eerie that she didn't move her head. She was an artist, though. Maybe she was thinking.

She rose slowly and gathered up the pages from around her feet. 'Is this OK?' she asked. 'Can I take these?'

'Sure,' he told her, smiling, 'glad to have helped. Don't forget the local businesses when you're photographing, will you? Do us good to get a look-in for a change. If the tourists come then the money rolls right in along with them, that's what I always say. Did you find the piece about the old water mill down by the river? There's not much of it left standing now but I'm sure you could make something arty of it if you tried. Let me know if you need any more help.'

She walked past him without smiling.

'Thank you,' she repeated.

It wasn't until she'd gone that he realized he hadn't got the lid off the malt, after all.

27

London 1993

Evangeline found offers of work waiting for her back in London – so many that she had no option but to find an agent to handle it all for her. She booked into a small agency in Covent Garden and even she had to admit that it was good to sit back and let someone else handle all the work and PR for her once more.

She rented a vast empty studio in the East End, pacing around the echoing rooms and finally sitting alone for hours on the varnished floor, relishing the silence and the solitude before the phones were connected.

She felt numbed by her grief. The shock of her discovery had been too great. Suicide. The word echoed around her head until she thought she would go mad. Suicide. Why? There were too many questions, suddenly. And then the desolation of her rejection. She was a child again, only now the hurt was worse. They had chosen to leave her – deliberately selected a fate without her. Darius, Thea, Lincoln and Patrick: a band together. Secrets she was never to share. They had waited until she was at school and then . . .

Her mind could take no more. It shut the door on the whole tragedy. The questions were too many now. It was too much to bear. Work was her only comfort. She turned to it in desperation.

She was difficult, she knew that – difficult and picky – but at least now she did all her arguing with Ross, her agent, rather than with the clients, which was much better for business.

Ross was a calm, formally dressed woman with fat legs

and a year-round tan. At thirty-three she was the exact same age as Evangeline, but her poise made her appear much older. Exasperated as she sometimes was by Evangeline's attitude, she nevertheless admired the quality of her work.

'*Elle* want you for a fashion shoot,' she would tell Evangeline.

'I don't do fashion, you know I don't do fashion,' Evangeline would argue.

'Evangeline, duckie, this shoot is different. You have total artistic licence.'

'Yeah, they all say that, and then some designer ends up coming along too, and then the model keeps phoning her agent to complain I'm not shooting her best side, then they can't book the location I want so would Phuket do instead . . .'

'I have a very solid contract sitting staring at me here,' Ross would argue and sometimes Evangeline would give in.

To please Ross she did the odd editorial and even the rounds of the party circuit, to keep her name in circulation. She never made good copy, though. Her clothes were dull and on chat shows she tended to duck out of the make-up and be remarkably lacking in amusing anecdotes.

Ross moved her to the more serious, arty programmes but they kept comparing her to Annie Leibowitz and that made her mad.

'Why not compare me to Herb Ritts instead?' she asked a sweaty young interviewer on a through-the-night arts show, 'Or does it just have something to do with the fact that we are both women?'

Ross saw blood over that one. 'You're too damn tetchy, sweetie,' she said.

'Artists are allowed to be miserable and difficult,' Evangeline told her.

'You're neither miserable enough nor difficult enough to be entertaining, though,' Ross said. 'If you drank it might be different. You just come across as mildly belligerent, which is not good telly.'

Ross insisted on the parties, introducing her to designers like Oldfield and Gaultier because she said it was good for business. She watched how the other top photographers operated, mingling with all the big names, pairing up with the appropriate supermodels, in order to ensure the biggest bookings. Were their shots any better for it? There were a few she admired but a lot whose work had become stale and formulaic.

She tried wearing Comme Des Garçons and drinking iced vodka cocktails, but she thought a photographer's job should be to watch and record, rather than be up there performing with the rest of the animals.

She didn't want to fuck a hairdresser or a model and she didn't want her own personal fitness instructor. *Hello!* did a spread on her and when she looked at the shots she was horrified. She'd used Ross's apartment because her own lacked furniture. Her hair had been styled into fat waves and her lips painted crimson. She was draped across Ross's World of Leather six-seater with a book of her photos spread out across Ross's faux-rhino pouffe.

'Enough,' she announced. She thought the whole thing stank. She wanted control again. She was in danger of losing it. Ross was not happy.

Evangeline lost a couple of magazine contracts and Ross told her it was because she refused to be more innovative.

'They know your work, Evangeline, they know you're good, but you offer no surprises. You're consistent, your standards have to be the highest there are, but you don't create the buzz and frisson that some of the newer guys do. Jerry Moon walked off a shoot last week because the water they supplied for the bath shot was Perrier, not Badoit. Meercampen took a whole crew out to the Gambia for a week just to come back with a close-up shot of a leaf that he could have done in the studio in ten minutes.'

'That's all pretentious crap,' Evangeline said. She looked

serious. Her hair was pinned back off her face and her gold wire-framed glasses were resting on the end of her nose. Her eyes looked tired. She'd spent all night printing up new material – material Ross knew she didn't stand a hope of selling.

'I know, Evangeline,' she argued, 'but the clients love it. They pretend they don't but then they'll book the same guy again. It's a good moan, a good story – see which editor has had the most abuse from which snapper each month. The only thing they complain about with you is that you take too long.'

Evangeline stood up. When she stopped biting her nails and straightened out she could loom in a quite frightening way. She leant across the desk and Ross tipped back in her seat.

'I'm not changing,' Evangeline said. She meant it.

28

'Beautiful, darling, beautiful. Beautiful ... crazy ...
Wild ... Great ... oh, exquisite! Hm, OK ... maybe
not ... so-so ... nearly ... nearly ... closer ... Yes!
That's it! That's it! Right on the button, darling! Wonderful, oh wonderful! Yes! Yes! Yes!'

Evangeline sat in the offices of MP Publishing in their
Docklands chrome-and-glass dome, watching Lavender
Allcock-Hopkins's crushed raspberry cashmere-covered
back heave and hump like a vomiting cat as she bent
excitedly over the light box to examine the latest set of
transparencies for an editorial. The woman was an odd
shape – fat in parts and thin in others. Ten years of lipo-
suction had left her looking like a kebab on a stick that
someone had bitten huge chunks out of.

Lavender straightened, beaming.

'They're delicious, darling, orgasmic. *Gratia placendi*.
Thanks a mill. I hope we can use them.'

'Hope?' Evangeline asked, 'I thought they were commis-
sioned for the July issue.'

'Oh they were, they were!' Lavender said, flinging an
Ozbek brocade-and-gingham shawl up into the air before
binding it more tightly around her silicone-enhanced
breasts. 'Only Stevie Meissel is rumoured to have done
some extraordinary shots of Linda this month and we want
to leave a few pages pending just in case we can get our
hands on them. I'm in for an exclusive for under ten thou.'
She chuckled like an excited child.

Evangeline yawned and stretched. 'What are the shots
of?' she asked.

251

'Linda.' Lavender looked blank.

'Doing what? Wearing what?' Evangeline asked. 'What sort of a setting? Is the quality good? What is the theme?'

Lavender squinted at her for a moment through amber-coloured contacts and then burst out laughing. 'Ohmy-God, Evangeline, you had me going for a minute there, I thought you were serious! Did you see my face! Hilarious!'

Evangeline sighed and shook her head. Lavender bent back over the light box, this time with a magnifier clamped to her eye.

'I'll have to get Betty in on these . . .' she was muttering.

Evangeline thumbed through a pile of discarded prints on the table beside her. One black-and-white looked strangely familiar but she didn't know why.

'Who did this?' she asked. The shot was raw and angry and hopelessly under-exposed.

Lavender looked up and blushed pretty pink when she saw it. 'That one? Oh that's by some Hungarian guy. He's only young. You wouldn't know him.'

'Are you using him?' Evangeline asked, eliciting another outburst of shrill tinkling laughter from the editor.

'Using him?' she laughed. 'Not really, darling – not in the way you mean, anyway. His stuff's far too piss-poor for our pages. I *am* showing interest, though. I believe he could have big potential. The guy is seriously stunning.' She bent closer towards Evangeline, 'Rosie Bradshaw claims he's a good two-hundred calorie fuck and I need to lose a little weight off my derrière. Rosie said he's hung like a giraffe and actually,' she looked at her watch, 'I'm taking him for lunch in a few minutes, darling – why don't you stay around and slobber?'

When Evangeline left the office she saw the guy sitting in reception, staring out of the window. He looked up as she passed.

'Evangeline Castelli,' he said, quietly.

'Do I know you?' She meant it to sound as snotty as it did.

He stood up. She knew him then. The offices of Bell and Layburn. The guy who had been so desperate for work and had frightened her. He looked less unhealthy than when she had last seen him, but much the same, apart from that. A little smarter, maybe; Lavender or one of her cronies must have got their fingers on his wardrobe, because although the image was virtually identical to before it had been replicated using designer labels.

'You stole my job,' he told her.

She laughed right in his face. 'The Imprex? Jesus, you have some nerve!'

He looked agitated. 'Don't you believe in helping out newcomers?' he asked.

'Yes,' she said, 'if they have manners. I don't appreciate being told to fuck off by a total stranger, though. What was I supposed to do when you said that, give you a hand-out or something?'

'I don't take charity,' he said, his voice matching hers, 'I could have got that job. I'm good enough, but my name's not as big as yours. I should have thought you were famous enough to stand the competition. Are you really so insecure?'

She smiled at him and walked out before she said something she might regret. He followed her outside, slipping into the glass lift before the doors closed.

'This must be quite a novelty for you,' she said, 'leaving a building without the assistance of the security guards.'

He stood close to her, staring her straight in the eye. 'You shouldn't talk to me like this' he said, 'I am a great admirer of your work.' His voice was deep and heavily accented. He had a small scar on his face and she noticed a silver locket that hung around his neck.

'What's your name?' she asked.

'Mikhail,' he told her, 'Mik for business – Mik Veronsky.' He glanced nervously at an expensive Cartier watch on his wrist. 'Do you have a few moments? Would you look at my portfolio?'

She checked her own watch. 'Why should I do this?' she asked.

'Because now I am being polite,' he told her. He didn't smile. He had no sense of irony at all.

They went to a coffee bar in a photographers' gallery. She ate alfalfa salad while he smoked three cigarettes and drank two double espressos. She looked through his book in silence.

'Where do you come from?' she asked.

'From Budapest.' He sounded impatient. He wanted opinions, not chit-chat.

'What brought you to England?'

He sighed. 'Oh, work – like you.'

'You have work?' she asked.

'No.'

'Then why do you stay?'

He shrugged as though the answer was obvious. 'I want to get to the top. In America there is too much competition. I came here because other photographers recommended it. I have contacts here now, too. Important people. I'll get there. It just takes time, that's all. You should know, it took you nearly ten years.'

So he had followed her career. She looked away, embarrassed, back down at the photographs.

'What do you think?' he asked.

'They're very raw,' she said.

'You think they should be better?'

'To tell you the truth I find them frightening.' She didn't enjoy looking at them. They were the poorest quality shots and yet the images jumped off the page.

'Why did you choose such gruesome subjects?' she asked. There were corpses, children in pain, landscapes torn apart by bombs. Even the fashion shots were brutal.

'I don't choose anything,' Mik said, 'things choose me.'

He stubbed a cigarette out with an air of finality. 'Can you help?' he asked.

'What?' She had been staring at a shot of a little girl in obvious agony. The child was alone and dirty, clutching a small wooden toy. The shot hurt Evangeline deep down inside somewhere.

'Her parents had just been killed,' Mik explained.

Tears of self-pity welled in Evangeline's eyes. She shut the book firmly. Enough, enough.

'I asked if you can help,' Mik repeated.

She stared across at him. 'Help?' she asked, 'In what way?'

He was becoming impatient. 'I have talent but it needs focusing,' he said. 'Do you have people you could introduce me to?'

'I thought you had a lot of contacts,' she said.

'Can you help or not?' he asked, picking up his book.

She ran a hand across her face and groaned. 'You've got a lot to learn,' she said. 'The quality of your work is poor. Were you ever trained? You may have an eye for some things but you're missing out because you're still making basic mistakes. Look, I'd like to help you but I couldn't possibly recommend you when your stuff's so scrappy. Why don't you do a course, or something – learn your craft right back from the basics. It would liberate your ideas if you could understand a few of the techniques.' She looked at his expression, 'I don't mean to be rude, but . . .'

He stood up quickly, spilling the last of his coffee. 'I'm late for lunch,' he told her. His face had gone tight again.

Evangeline shrugged. 'You asked for my advice,' she said.

'No,' he told her, 'I asked for your help.' He turned and walked out before she could answer.

She threw money down for the bill and ran to catch him up.

'Look, she said, 'you need to learn and I need an assistant. If you could keep your temper in check I could think about taking you on. You'd be learning while you work. How does that sound? Here, take my card. Phone me when you've cooled down and thought about it.'

He stared at her as though she was mad. 'Be a woman's assistant?' he asked. His arrogant expression made her furious.

'Yeah,' she said, 'why not? You don't seem to object to screwing them if you think it can get you anywhere.'

The anger in his eyes almost made Evangeline flinch but she stood her ground as Mik glared at her. A muscle worked in his jaw. He seemed to be trying to control himself. He looked very young. How old was he? Twenty-three, twenty-four? Evangeline was good at estimating ages, it was something that came with the job. She was thirty-three and all his pent-up energy made her feel ten years older and a whole heap wiser.

He'd burn out eventually. You had to, if you wanted to stay in the job. At first you felt like he did, like bursting into offices just to get your work seen, but soon you learnt better. Mik seemed stubborn, though – it was taking him longer to get the message. She felt weary on his behalf, tired, cynical and a little sad, too.

Despite the aggression there was something in his attitude that she recognized and almost identified with. Need, maybe – that was the best word for it. He was driven, too, she could tell by his eyes. She wondered what demons were pushing him. His shoulders were broad and his coat flapped as he walked off without a word.

'Shit!' she whispered beneath her breath, why was she worrying about him? She didn't even know him. She had enough problems of her own to handle.

He phoned her the following evening.

'The job,' he asked, 'how much will it pay?'

'Whatever you're worth,' Evangeline told him.

'Then the money is good,' he said, again without humour.

'Sorry,' Evangeline corrected herself, 'I should have said whatever *I* think you're worth.'

There was silence from the other end. Shit, you bastard, Evangeline thought, don't you ever laugh?

'OK,' he said, after a lot of thought.

'OK what?'

'OK I'll take it.'

'I'll hang the flags out,' Evangeline answered, and then immediately regretted it. This guy took things so literally he might turn up expecting to see them.

He was impressed when he first showed up at the studio, though he was careful not to let it show. The place was bigger than he'd expected, and full of all the latest equipment which was strange, because Evangeline usually used few lights and just her beaten-up old camera.

It was seven in the morning and she was in the middle of the shoot – they'd been at it from dawn, just to get the right mood. No music, just silence. A sweaty client was yawning in the corner. Two stylists giggled as they quaffed Buck's Fizz through a straw.

Someone asked Mik to go out for bacon sandwiches and he told them to fuck off.

'You're the new assistant, aren't you?' he was asked.

'Yeah, but I'm here to learn, not to fetch food,' he snarled.

He walked up to Evangeline and stood behind her. She smelt nice. The set they had constructed was huge: a background of silk, billowed by fans; water, like a stream, somehow in the middle of it. Expensive magic. He peered through the viewfinder. Nothing much showed, apart from the model.

'Jesus, what a waste.'

Evangeline looked at him, scowling. Then she went back to her work. 'Spotlights.'

'I thought you used available light when possible,' Mik commented.

'Not all the time,' Evangeline said. She was chewing her hair, studying the lights. She reached up and moved a spot a quarter-inch.

'Take another reading,' she said. Nobody moved. Everyone stared at Mik.

'Me?' he asked. He picked up the meter, held it to the model's face and pressed a button that made a thousand lights explode. That was bright, that was very bright. The lights settled back to soft and diffused.

'Well?' Evangeline asked. He called out the reading.

'Impossible,' she said. Someone else took the meter from him and a stylist pushed past him to comb the model's hair. Suddenly there were people everywhere, busy checking things.

Mik walked up to the first guy he'd spoken to. 'Where do I get them from?' he asked moodily.

'What?' the guy looked bored.

'The bacon sandwiches.'

After a while Evangeline and Mik made a fearsome double act in the studio, and the more timid clients usually fled to the sanctuary of the nearby pub until their jobs were finished.

Evangeline expected the same intense concentration she had given Nico when he had been teaching her and, in a way, she got it. Mik was hungry for information yet resentful about putting it to use. He thought he was good and saw little need for improvement. If he made a mistake he claimed to have intended it. They argued a lot, even while they worked, screaming across the vast studio like banshees or yelling at one another over the tannoy Evangeline had fitted so she could contact people when they got lost in the furthest reaches of the place.

Mik could not stand being given orders by a woman, that much was painfully obvious. Every time she asked him to do something she was met with a look that told her she had affronted his masculinity.

'Are all Hungarian men such chauvinists or are you the exception rather than the rule?' she asked. He asked her to explain 'chauvinist' and they got into a row about women's emancipation.

258

'Jesus, Stuart, the guy's from the Iron Age!' she complained over the phone that evening. 'He's so bloody stubborn he needs to be screamed at before he'll do things right.'

'It sounds like a case of like meets like to me,' Stuart told her. It was good to be teased. It was good to hear a man laugh. Sometimes Mik was so intense and dour she aggravated him deliberately, just to get a reaction.

'Have you tried being friendly?' Stuart asked. 'It's an option worth considering.'

'Wow, Stuart, I never thought of that.'

'Well maybe you just lack my corporate nose for man-management.'

She laughed, but when she put the phone down she thought about it. Maybe friendliness was something she hadn't tried. She thought back – arguments, aggression, confrontation. Maybe somebody had to be the first to back down and be pleasant for a change.

The next day they had a lucrative shoot for a whisky company. Evangeline allowed Mik to do most of the work and, once the clients were gone, she pulled a bottle of red wine out of a bag and grabbed two glasses from the cupboard in the studio kitchen.

'What's this?' Mik asked. 'Are you going to get pissed?'

Evangeline smiled at him. 'It's Hungarian,' she said, 'and I thought we might get pissed together.'

He approached the table she was sitting at warily.

'Why?' he asked.

She laughed. 'So I can have my wicked way with you, of course.' She looked at his face, 'Oh, Jesus, Mik, I was only joking – can't you take a joke now and again? I just thought we might talk or something – enjoy time together for a change. I'm not trying to get into your pants. I'm not Lavender Allcock-Hopkins, you know.'

She saw him wince and immediately regretted the jibe. 'Sit down,' she said. He sat and took a mouthful of the wine.

'Is it good?' she asked.

'Yes – no – I don't know,' he replied.

'I thought it might remind you of home,' she said.

He shrugged. 'I don't need that.'

'OK.' She leant back in her chair, 'Tell me how you started in photography.'

He looked up at her. It seemed to Evangeline that it was the first time she had ever seen him smile, but it wasn't a cheerful smile – it was sarcastic, almost pitying.

'Oh, I don't think you want to know that,' he said.

'You mean you don't want to tell me,' she answered.

'No,' he said, 'I meant you won't want to know. I don't mind telling. I stole my first camera from a guy that I lived with. He used to fuck me in return for my keep. I beat him and I took the camera and some money he owed me and I got a job ripping off tourists in the streets. How did you start?'

The question surprised her. She leant back in her chair and put her feet up on the desk. She was still digesting the thumbnail sketch he had just drawn of his life. Should she be shocked? She felt too old to be anything more than surprised. There were all sorts in the media business. She felt she'd seen and heard everything sometimes.

'My father taught me,' she said.

'And he bought you a good camera?'

'My grandmother paid for that.' He was making her feel stupid. Her wine was disappearing rapidly. She always drank quickly when she was embarrassed.

'Ah, wealthy relations.'

'No . . .' Evangeline began.

'Your grandmother wasn't wealthy then?'

'Yes, very.'

'I see.' He took another swallow of wine.

'You see what, exactly?' Evangeline was getting confused and irritated by his attitude. 'Is this some kind of a class thing, Mik? Is there no end to the amount of chips you are carrying around on your shoulder?'

'Sorry?' He didn't understand and she couldn't be bothered to explain.

He watched her face. 'And they sent you to college.'

'I went, yes.'

He smiled again. 'Your grandmother – the wealthy one – did she have servants?'

'Not really . . .' Evangeline began.

'Staff, then?'

'Yes. A chauffeur. And some others who used to come to the house . . .'

Mik smiled again.

'Look,' Evangeline began, 'if you think I've had an easy life . . .' she stopped suddenly. How did she get into all this? What was she about to do, compare their suffering? Hold a competition to see who had had the saddest childhood?

Mik reached across and took her hand and she nearly jumped out of her skin. 'I know you haven't,' he said softly. 'I can tell.'

She stared across the table at him. His change of tone had unsettled her. His hand was warm and strong but slender, not chunky like Stuart's. But then what was she doing comparing them anyway? Was he being friendly or sarcastic?

'How can you tell?' she whispered.

'Your eyes,' he said. His own eyes were huge and dark. 'I can see the pain in them and you can see the same in mine, am I right?'

Evangeline nodded, still unsure of whether he was being sincere. Maybe getting pissed had made her gullible.

'I can tell from other things, too,' he said quietly.

'Like?' she asked.

'Like the way you live. No man. No sex. No life, apart from work. How old are you? Thirty-four, thirty-five?'

'Thirty-three,' she corrected him. 'I have sex, too.'

His eyes scanned her face. 'You fuck some of the male models that work for you?' he asked.

261

'No.'

'Why not?'

'Look . . .' she began.

'I just wondered,' he said, interrupting her.

'I have a male friend back home in the US,' she explained. It sounded prim and pathetic; who the hell was she trying to impress, anyway?

'A male friend?' Mik asked. The words came out of his mouth like bad food. 'How often do you see him?'

She pulled her hand away.

'Twice a year?' he asked.

'He's over next week,' she said, although, 'Mind your own bloody business,' might have been more appropriate under the circumstances. This wasn't what she'd intended when she'd planned the evening. She was sure he was taking the piss now; she'd seen the look in his eyes. Bastard, she thought. The trouble was, the drink was making her susceptible to him.

'Are your parents alive?' Mik asked.

'No.'

He nodded. 'I believe mine are still alive. My mother went off to your country when I was small. That's one reason why I don't want to go there, in case I find her. She could never live up to the picture I have built of her. Do you understand what I mean?'

Evangeline nodded, enthralled despite herself. Maybe it was his accent that made everything he said sound so fascinating. He talked quietly and sometimes his words were difficult to understand so she had to listen carefully.

'My brother raised me instead,' Mik said, looking down. She noticed his fingers reached for the locket he wore. His nails were clean and white.

'I loved him more than my parents,' he said. 'He died when I was twelve.'

Death, lots of death. Evangeline downed her glass of wine. The drink was heavy and strong and beginning to make her feel sick.

'Are you going to get drunk?' he asked.

'I might,' she said.

He nodded. 'You should go home then,' he told her, 'it's not good to get drunk anywhere else.'

They caught a cab to her place.

'I was brought up in hotels,' she told him. She opened another bottle of wine, which he drank straight from the neck.

'Then you should buy yourself a proper home now you're an adult,' he said. He handed the bottle to her and she wiped the neck on her sleeve before drinking from it.

'Possibly you're right,' she told him. 'Maybe I should start looking tomorrow.'

They drank until they fell asleep where they sat, on the floor. In the middle of the night she was woken by his screams.

'Andreas!' It was a terrible noise. She sat up at once. He called out again. Totally disorientated she snapped on the main light but Mik still didn't wake.

He was shouting in Hungarian. Evangeline didn't know what to do.

'Stop it! Sssh!' She walked across to him and tried to shake him by the shoulders.

'Mik! Mik! You'll get someone calling the police!'

She pushed his hair back from his face and his shouts died down, so she went on stroking his forehead until he was sleeping silently again.

When she next woke it was morning and she was still on the floor beside him. She looked at his sleeping face and thought he looked handsome when he wasn't scowling.

Her head hurt badly and she felt sick. She staggered off to the bathroom for water, and to clean the thick Hungarian plaque off her teeth.

263

29

The following week Evangeline placed a deposit on a huge, airy flat in Chelsea. She had so much work in the UK she thought she may as well live comfortably while she was there and, anyway, she could rent the place out when she went back to the States.

Buying a place made her feel sad. She missed Paddy badly and putting down roots in another country made her feel she was abandoning him somehow. Catherine was reasonably tolerant of the middle-of-the-night phone calls when she had to get up out of her bed and carry Paddy to the receiver just so Evangeline could hear him make doggy noises to her. It was a nice side to the girl's personality, but then, even Hitler had been a dog-lover.

Mik turned up on the doorstep the first evening after Evangeline moved in. They'd been arguing in the studio that morning and when she saw the wine in his hand she assumed he'd come round to apologize.

She stepped back from the door without a word and Mik walked inside. He looked around and then looked back at Evangeline. She had rubber gloves on and a wet cloth in one hand.

'You have no furniture,' Mik said.

'True,' Evangeline replied. The flat was newly decorated. The walls and ceiling were white and the floors were bare.

'You were cleaning,' Mik said.

'Right again.'

'Doing it yourself?' He seemed surprised.

'What, you thought I had servants for that type of thing, right?' she asked.

Mik shrugged. 'Maybe,' he said. 'It was the way you were brought up.' He placed the wine bottle on the floor. Evangeline picked it up quickly. It had left a small dark mark, which she wiped away.

'I like things to be clean,' she said, glaring. 'I don't mind doing it myself.'

He inspected the spot she had just wiped. 'But you could afford servants if you wanted,' he said.

'Jesus! What is it with you?' Evangeline asked. 'Look, Mik, I have money, yes. I'm not fabulously rich but, as you know, I do well and the pay comes in. I charge a lot but I work hard for it. Yes, I suppose you could say I had a privileged childhood, if you define the word "privileged" as meaning "raised by someone wealthy".'

Mik shook his head. 'You should not be so sensitive,' he said.

Evangeline stood close to him, so close she could feel his breath on her face and almost name which brand of toothpaste he used.

'Thank you for the wine,' she said, 'but I've got a lot to do. Maybe you should leave.'

He looked around the place. 'OK,' he told her, as though it really didn't matter.

She kicked the door shut behind him.

She tried to be patient. She tried to be kind to him in the studio. She wondered why she bothered and then she realized it was because, for some reason, back there in Lavender's office, she had felt sorry for him. He wasn't good but he didn't deserve that kind of treatment.

With her permission he had been doing tests in the studio when she wasn't there, borrowing new models from the top agencies and doing shots for free, for practice.

She thumbed through a few of the most recent prints. They were all black and white – he refused to use colour. She picked one up to hold closer to her face and tutted out loud. He was still making some of the same mistakes as when she'd first met him. She had taught him everything but he selected only the nuggets he wanted – the rest he seemed to ignore.

He never used Polaroids when he was setting up the shot, so his compositions were usually clumsy and flawed. He liked working with one light, maybe because he was lazy or stubborn, or both. Some shots cried out for fill-in flash. He'd got shadows on the noses and he made the girls look almost ugly. In all the shots they were made to look small in the frame, hidden crouched in the corner or only half visible, with most of their bodies out of shot.

Why did he do this? She snapped out the overhead light and studied them again beneath the pool of a spot. Did he hate women so much? Maybe he had hated his mother. Oh God, *she* was going crazy now – she was trying to get Freudian over some badly produced shots.

The last shot made her freeze: the model, naked, on set with Mik, who was naked on top of her. Fucking like rabbits. The shutter-release cable was in the model's hand. She put the photo down quickly then picked it up again. He had a great body, thin but with wide shoulders and muscles that were well-defined beneath the stark light. His head was back and his long hair trailed past his shoulders. His eyes were closed. She could see the outline of his stomach muscles and the line of his dark pubic hair.

She pressed fingers to her lips. Why was she looking? The shot was erotic. His back was arched above the girl's prone body, the muscles in his arse clenched and tight. Evangeline moved in her seat, her insides melting like wax.

'My God, you're getting turned on, you sad, sordid old hag!' she whispered to herself, and laughed.

So, had the camera gone off by accident or had he taken the shot deliberately and, if so, why? And why leave it there? There was a mirror above the table and Evangeline looked in it: pale face, shock of buttermilk-streaked hair, grey eyes smoking with lust. Maybe Mik was right, maybe she had been too long without good sex.

She looked through the photos once more. She was jealous and it hurt to admit it – not jealous of Mik and the model but jealous of the way his pictures had an endless capacity to shock in a way her own never had. That was his strength; that was why she was training him. If he stopped fighting for a second and applied himself to learning instead his talent could be awesome.

He was yawning and stretching when he arrived in the studio the following day but the yawn froze on his face when he saw she had overnight luggage with her.

'What are you doing?' he asked. His voice was like the photo – it stirred something deep inside her.

She was tidying up, picking up mail, scribbling out business cheques.

'I'm going away for a few days,' she said.

'A shoot?' he asked. He was staring at her.

'No,' she replied. She couldn't meet his eyes. 'I'm going home for a while, that's all. A job got postponed because of the strike. I thought I'd make the most of the break.'

She went to walk past him but he grabbed her by the arm. 'To see Paddy?' he asked. She had told him about the dog.

Evangeline looked at him now. 'Yes, to see Paddy,' she said.

'He must have missed you.' His voice was so low she could barely make out what he said, but she could hear the sarcasm in the tone well enough.

'Yes,' she told him calmly, 'I expect he has.'

'By the way,' she added, 'you left this lying about. Anyone could have seen it – you ought to be more careful.'

It was the photograph. Mik took it from her without a word.

'Goodbye,' Evangeline whispered, and she even managed a smile as she said it.

30

Mik walked around the studio that seemed so empty with Evangeline gone. He was angry without reason, mad with himself – the worst kind of anger. His dreams were all of Andreas and his mother again. Nightmares. They both blamed him now, they both hated him. When would it stop?

He pored over Evangeline's work, studying her shots as he would never have done had she been there. He phoned agencies and booked models for tests but each time he called a halt half-way through the session because he could not get the effects he wanted. When he printed the shots he had taken he tore them up, furious at his own incompetence. Evangeline had grey eyes, like a cat. He wanted to see respect in those eyes. He needed to earn that respect badly.

'How was your friend?' he asked when she returned.

'My friend?' She seemed bemused, in a daze.

'Your man friend,' Mik said, annoyed, 'the one in New York.'

'Oh.' She started chewing her hair. 'He's fine.' She didn't tell him to mind his own business. Mik was about to say more but then changed his mind.

Evangeline had asked Stuart about the woman that had stayed at Christmas. He'd told her there was no woman, that Catherine must have lied. She had lied because she was mad, he said, and then he'd told her he had been intending to propose. She'd had no idea. He'd found that difficult to believe and they'd argued. She and Stuart. Married. They'd been together for so long but she'd never imagined it.

Mik was speaking again.

'Did your man friend ask after me?' he said. His eyes were strange.

'Ask after you?' Evangeline said. 'No. No, of course not. Why should he?' But he had, straight after he'd told her he loved her and that he still wanted to marry her; the minute she'd looked to the floor because she couldn't give an answer; the minute the hurt had started to show in his eyes; just before the coldness had come to take its place.

'How are your staff problems?' was what Stuart had said.

'What do you mean?' It was a strange question at such a moment. Stuart's face revealed nothing when she looked up.

'That chap you took on, the Hungarian,' he said. 'You were having problems with him — a clash of personalities? You've said nothing about it since. I take it the problem has resolved itself?'

Evangeline nodded, still confused.

'Good,' Stuart said. He'd given her three weeks to make up her mind about his proposal.

She walked into her office and listened to all her messages on the machine. There were only a couple from Ross and neither of them were urgent. Work was obviously going to be quiet for a while. She didn't worry — it meant she had more time to start thinking about the new Imprex campaign. She had a meeting with Eddie Gershon that afternoon and he'd given nothing away on the phone. They were happy with her first collection but she'd have to pitch for the new contract just like everyone else.

She'd heard a couple of the heavyweight snappers from New York were flying in to pitch for it too. The stakes were higher after the publicity she'd received for the last launch. Even the big fashion boys were willing to come down off their pedestals to turn up with proposals.

The media had got hold of the idea that the account was worth millions, but that was mostly hype. Evangeline knew she must have lost as much work as she'd gained as a result of the publicity, because clients thought she had priced herself out of the market. She didn't care, though. The account was the best. It might have lost her a few jobs, but losing it after one year would make her lose a hell of a lot more.

The meeting with the ad men was held at the Savoy. Eddie was delayed but there were two suits she recognized waiting to greet her with nervous-looking smiles. They'd hired an entire banqueting suite. Evangeline was impressed but tense. The table they ate at must have seated twenty and she sat at the furthest end in isolation, pretending to enjoy roast quail with truffle sauce.

Once the plates were cleared a screen appeared at the opposite end of the room, with 'IMPREX 95' printed across it via back projection. The slide disappeared to be replaced by a blank screen. Evangeline stared at the screen a while, waiting. Nothing happened, so she looked at the two men. They were smiling at her again.

'So?' she said.

'You fill the next slide, Evangeline,' one of the men told her, 'the contract is yours. Just let us know what you have in mind.'

'I got the contract?' Evangeline tried to keep her voice steady, 'Just like that? To do what I want again?' She was glad she'd put Ross off coming. This was turning out to be easier than shaking ripe apples off a tree.

'Almost,' a voice said. She turned around and Eddie was standing there, a sandwich in one hand and a briefcase in the other.

'Almost?' Evangeline provided his echo. He sat down. He was smiling. They were all smiling.

'Evangeline, we need to be honest,' Eddie said. His sandwich looked like prawn mayo on ciabatta – much more tasty than the quail and truffles. 'As you know, we all loved your work for last year's account. The critics loved it too, which is a miracle in itself. Financially the whole launch

270

ran at a minor loss, which was good news for the clients, who were prepared to shoulder a major one just to get the product placement.'

He put his briefcase on the table and snapped the locks back. 'Evangeline, we could be looking at a new name to do the pictures this year – just to generate a little more excitement, you know – but we thought we'd run with a more interesting plan instead. You're good and we like your work. Choosing a new photographer would only detract from the current scheme, which is to use a model for the pictures this time and invest all our energies into searching for the best face.'

He pulled some agency catalogues out of his case and threw them down in front of her. 'I know what you're thinking,' he said, 'and in some ways I agree with you. The idea's a corny one. So? So was the Andrex puppy and so is the Oxo family. Revlon and L'Oréal do it in the States, but it's never really been floated as an idea this side of the Atlantic. If we offer fat enough figures the publicity could be strong. We want you in on the selection process. We start looking today – nothing seedy, no beauty competitions, just a serious search run by you and ourselves. We consider new faces as much as we do the supermodels. Four weeks, too – that's all we have. We're not milking this any further than that.'

Four weeks for a decision. Stuart had given her three. How many days ago was that? Evangeline looked straight into Eddie's smile.

'I don't see these shots with a model,' she said.

Eddie closed his case. 'Think about it,' he answered. The meeting was at an end.

Ross talked her round for the first time in their professional relationship, but then Evangeline had known all along that she had no choice. Eddie's idea was a good one. She needed to keep the account. It all sounded simple when Ross put it like that. Evangeline agreed to help find a face she could

271

work with and she agreed not to be difficult, just to give each girl a fair look.

They drew a blank with the agencies and they drew a blank with the girls the handful of scouts around the country trawled in. They picked shortlists and then worked their way through them. Then one day at the end of the fifth week Evangeline was called into the Imprex head office for a crisis meeting.

They were all smiling again. Evangeline wondered how they looked so cool considering they had gone over their time limit. She'd had enough trouble managing to get Stuart's deadline extended and that was only because she'd explained about how this job was taking up all her time.

Then she found out why they were so cheerful.

'We think we've found her,' Eddie announced. 'We just need your final say. She came with that last batch of cards you sent us. Thank you, Evangeline, we think she'll do nicely.'

They'd got the girl herself there. She walked into the room on cue. Evangeline thought she looked good, though she had no memory of ever seeing the girl's card, let alone sending it. She'd seen so many, though, she was prepared to believe anything.

She was surprised and relieved. The girl seemed reasonably suitable, which was better than she was hoping for, under the circumstances. She had intelligent eyes. She was not a beginner but her face was not so well known as to be associated with other products. What's more she seemed nice and easy-going. So many of the top girls had such serious attitude problems that Evangeline would have refused to work with them.

Evangeline didn't want to be prissy. The girl was the most suitable they'd seen – there was no point pretending otherwise just to gain points.

'Would you object to a few tests in the studio, just to see how we work together?' Evangeline asked.

'Sure,' the girl smiled. And so she should – the account was worth a million dollars to her, at least.

It wasn't until she got back to the studio again that Evangeline started banging doors.

'Mik!' He was there, hunched over a camera. He lifted his head slowly.

Evangeline threw the model's card down in front of him. 'Deeta,' she said. 'Does the name ring a bell?' She walked across to him, until she was so close she could smell him. 'This was the girl you were screwing in that shot!' she shouted.

He raised his eyebrows. 'Does it matter?' he asked.

'Did you send her picture to Eddie?' Evangeline said.

Mik sighed. 'Again, Evangeline – does it matter? Did they like her or not? If they didn't then forget it and if they did I have done you a favour.'

'It matters, Mik,' Evangeline shouted, 'it matters because you didn't tell me first and it matters if you're still screwing her.' She paused for breath. 'The girl they're looking for is supposed to be sensual but unobtainable, Mik,' she said, 'you'll have to stop fucking her if you want her to get the job.'

'I already did,' Mik said quietly.

Evangeline did some tests of Deeta in the studio and her unease lessened when she found that they clicked. The clients fell in love with her. Everyone breathed huge sighs of relief. Shooting proper started the following week.

Mik was hanging around the studio late one evening.

'Can I speak to you?' he asked Evangeline. She was packing rolls of paper but she stopped at once, surprised by the politeness of his tone.

'Sure.' She sat down on a stack of cases. Mik seemed agitated, more like when they had first met.

'I've got some ideas for the credit card photos,' he said.

Evangeline smiled. 'Right.'

'Are you interested?' he asked.

She waved her hands in the air. 'Go ahead.'

He opened a portfolio. Inside were some rough shots and some sketches. He talked her through the ideas excitedly.

'Great,' she said when he was finished.

He looked her straight in the eye. 'Great and we can use them?' he asked.

'No,' she corrected him, 'I meant great that you have gone to so much bother. Great that you are getting the hang of how the business works.'

'I thought we might at least do a couple of them,' Mik said.

'We?' Evangeline asked.

'We could work together on them,' Mik said.

'I thought we did work together anyway.' Evangeline was beginning to feel awkward.

'No,' Mik said, 'I work *for* you at the moment, not *with* you. There is a difference.'

Evangeline smiled and stood up. 'They're good ideas, Mik. I'm pleased you did them and I'm pleased you showed them to me. The thing is I've already got ideas of my own and they've been discussed with the clients and the marketing men . . .'

'I could do them by myself,' Mik interrupted her.

Evangeline sighed. 'Look, the client is my client and I know what they want. Even if I let you take some of the shots – even if you were good enough – we'd still need client approval.'

'I already asked,' Mik said.

'You what?' The studio suddenly seemed very quiet around them.

'While you were away in America with your lover,' Mik went on, 'I phoned the client and asked if I could do a couple of the shots for them.'

'You phoned the client?'

Mik nodded.

'And what did they say?' Evangeline asked.

'They saw my book,' Mik said. 'They told me to speak to you.'

Evangeline turned and went back to her work. 'Well you've done that,' she said. 'The answer's no.'

Mik put a hand on her arm. 'Evangeline, I think you must listen to me –' he began angrily.

Evangeline span round. 'Don't you *ever* phone up a fucking client of mine again, understand?' she shouted.

Mik's eyes narrowed. 'Why will you never give me a chance?' he asked.

'I've given you all the help I can, Mik!' Evangeline yelled. 'I brought you in here and I have tried to teach you about the business, but I guess I forgot to teach you some of the etiquette, too! You behave like shit, you don't listen to what I teach you, you are arrogant beyond belief, you waste my studio time arguing and now you try to poach my work! Shitty behaviour, Mik – understand?'

Mik's face darkened. 'I said we could work together, Evangeline,' he told her, 'I didn't try to take anything from you.'

'And why should I want to work with you?' Evangeline asked.

'Because it might do you good,' Mik said. His voice dropped. 'Because your own work is getting stale. Because you are losing clients, or haven't you noticed? Because you need a fresher angle, Evangeline. I thought I might bring that to your work, that's all.'

She wanted to hit him for his arrogance and she wanted to hurt him so much he would never recover and she wanted to scream at him, too – in case what he said was right. Stale work, clients going away; Ross had warned her, only she hadn't listened. Surely it didn't matter as long as she had the biggest account? What the fuck was she supposed to do? Her work was perfect. She could not bear to think what would happen if she failed now.

'Why do you want all this so badly?' she asked Mik.

'Money,' he answered flatly.

'You don't care, do you?' she asked. 'You don't give a shit about anything else.'

'I came here to work,' he told her, 'I came here to make a living. If I didn't work I starved, it was as simple as that. In a way the same is still true. Did you ever have to screw someone you hated just to stay alive? After a while it doesn't matter who you fuck, you know – they are all the same if you can be in the right frame of mind.'

'You'd fuck me too, to get what you want, wouldn't you?' Evangeline asked.

'Not in the way you mean,' he said.

'I mean in a business way.' Her voice was still but her eyes huge and staring.

'I told you I would work *with* you,' Mik said.

'And I told you to get stuffed.'

The photo flashed into her mind just then, the shot of him screwing Deeta. His face had looked beautiful. His naked body so intense. She thought about marriage to Stuart. She'd say yes, she needed his integrity and his honesty. What she didn't need was shit from bastards like Mik. Marriage scared her, though. She was thirty-four but she still felt too young to commit.

'Are you sacking me?' Mik asked. She couldn't tell if he cared or not.

'If that's what you want,' she said.

'It isn't.' He moved closer, so close she could feel his anger.

'What *do* you want then?'

'I want to work here,' he said, 'I need to learn from you. I still need your help.'

She followed him home after he'd left for the day – she didn't know why. There was a squat in a back street in Notting Hill. She'd never thought about it before – how he lived, where he stayed. She knocked on the door and a woman answered with a baby strapped around her waist. She let Evangeline into the house and she went up to the second floor, where Mik slept. He was shocked to see her, though he didn't let it show.

His room was the sort of room kids create when they first leave home, just to annoy their parents: posters that looked as though they'd been put up by someone else, a mattress on the floor with a rug thrown over it. There was nothing that looked as though it belonged to him.

'What did you want?' he asked.

Evangeline looked up at him. 'I thought you might like to come for dinner,' she said.

'When?' he asked.

'Tomorrow?'

He nodded.

It was just to make up, because she needed to understand him and because she didn't like being beaten. She needed him in the studio, too. She liked having him around. He was dour and he was angry most of the time but she wanted him there, all the same.

She bought a frock in a shop in Chelsea, a flimsy, ankle-length shift in crinkled blue-grey silk that made her look like a wraith when her hair was down.

She shaved her legs. She bought ingredients for a Hungarian goulash and she put patchouli oil in her bath and soaked until her skin wrinkled.

She lit candles and then she extinguished them in favour of side lights and then she turned those out and lit the candles once again. She had money now – too much, maybe – but she'd never furnished her flat. She liked it bare. She'd had to borrow a dining table from the elderly woman in the flat downstairs and the woman had insisted she use one of her antique lace cloths, too, to make it look nice and protect it from scratches.

The woman also brought up china and a cut-glass vase for the table decorations. When Evangeline asked her what she meant she kept repeating the word 'centrepiece' as though Evangeline were a little soft in the head. Eventually she disappeared and came back with a handful of plastic roses which she arranged in the vase before placing it in the centre of the tablecloth.

When the woman had gone Evangeline surveyed the scene. An empty room, vast, white and varnished; two Bill Brandt photos framed on the wall; a halogen lamp in the corner and, in the middle of all this space, a faux-Regency drop-leaf dining table complete with hand-embroidered cloth and mauve plastic flowers. She laughed at the scene and she laughed at herself for acting like a big kid. What was this, a first date? She felt nervous, though. It was Mik – Mik could make anyone nervous.

She tried shoes on with her frock but discovered that Timberlands didn't go and so opted for bare feet instead. Maybe she should have worn make-up. She found some mascara among the bits in her box and sat down on the floor to try it.

She saw the door open behind her in the reflection of the mirror. 'No more plastic flowers, thanks,' she called out to the old woman from downstairs. It was Mik. He stood behind her, taking in the scene with his dark, suspicious eyes. She knew what she looked like, at that moment. She looked like Lavender Allcock-Hopkins and all those other bloody women who had been after his body from day one – and probably all the old men he'd shagged in Budapest, too.

She stood up and faced him, feeling stupid and childish. He stared at her frock and her bare feet. The casserole started to scent the room. He glanced over at the table with the floral centrepiece.

'I'm sorry,' Evangeline said, 'I didn't mean . . .'

She was thirty-three. He was about ten years younger. She was ashamed of herself, ashamed of her age, ashamed of what the young man in front of her must be thinking.

He frowned but then he always frowned; black brows, black lashes, a black shadow where his beard would be if he grew one. Long dark ragged hair and a neck she wanted

278

to bite. Badly. Despite her shame and her embarrassment lust was still a major player. He wore a shrunken, faded sweatshirt and black jeans and boots.

'I cooked dinner,' she said, 'traditional Hungarian goulash.'

'You used too much paprika,' he said, and then he walked across in a rush and kissed her.

Mik's lips were dry and soft. She felt his teeth with the tip of her tongue. His hair fell against her face and it was thick and heavy and damp against her skin. They kissed without holding. They were tall together; their height made them evenly matched. The melt-down began with that kiss – there was nothing solid inside her any more. Her bare toes touched against the heavy leather of his boots.

Did he want her? She didn't know. There wasn't a thought in his head that she imagined she could read. They parted faces. Mik looked serious. She waited while he stared at her. He didn't move any more. What was he thinking, what was he thinking? God it was aggravating. If any other man had kissed her she would have known, but with Mik . . . she smiled a grin that felt inane and padded off to serve the food.

They were careful as they ate; careful not to discuss work in case they argued. Not discussing work meant not having a conversation unless they discussed themselves.

'So, you have no parents?' Mik asked.

Evangeline shook her head. 'No.'

Mik sighed.

'What happened to yours?' she asked. And then he told her. He told her in a tone that lacked any emotion and which had her in tears before his story had ended.

'My mother was an actress,' he began, 'and my father was in the same profession also. Sometimes she sang, though she began life as a dancer. Mimi and Chico – if you were a Hungarian then those names would mean something to you, or maybe you would be too young – they were famous a long time ago. Mimi was my mother's stage

279

name. Can you believe I never knew her real one? She was ugly as a child. Skinny legs. Strange eyes. Her mother sent her to dance classes to try and mend her knock-knees. Her mother wanted her to be a classical dancer. With her face and her legs, though, she turned instead to comedy. By the time she was eighteen she was famous. Her manager paired her off with my father. He was a good actor – very grand, rather serious – his work was less frequent than when he was younger, though. They made a good double-act. He would appear on stage in cravat and gown and start doing the classics and Mimi would come on with her mad eyes and knock-knees and mess the whole scene up.

'Then there was some scandal about Chico that had to be hushed up. He was a good-looking man in his fifties but he had never married. The police arrested him one night with a young man. The agent got things hushed up but it was arranged that Mimi and Chico get married, to clear things up. Andreas, my brother, was born soon after. Having a son changed Mimi. She stopped doing the slap-stick stuff and started getting into satire instead. She had a son to care for and his future to think about. She became serious about things – things going on in her country that worried her. Chico got wary for his own future. She was getting a name as a dissident. He pulled out of the act, which made her worse. Some of her jokes were too strong for anyone's taste.

'No one was sure how it happened but my mother got taken to prison. She was accused of many stupid things but I think the state just wanted her out of the way.' He paused and his head dropped. 'I was born in the prison,' he said, quietly. 'She kept me for a few months but then I had to be moved out. Chico had vanished to save his own skin. Andreas had been fostered and I was placed with a family, too. When he was old enough Andreas came and found me and took me away to grow up with him. I loved him for that. Can you understand – a young man, as he was, seeking out a kid like myself and taking him under his wing? How many boys would do that? How many could be bothered? Andreas was my hero, Evangeline. In many ways he still is.'

Mik pushed his food around his plate. His voice was quiet and his accent heavy, but Evangeline was mesmerized by every word. The candle guttered and, in the pause that followed, she went to light a new one.

'Andreas was the only person I ever cared about,' Mik continued. 'He loved me and he taught me all I knew. He was wild but he looked after me. Then one night he took too many drugs and he died. I was on on my own then, but I didn't care. The only thing I cared about was my brother's death.' He tapped his chest. 'In this locket is fabric from a coat of his that I used to wear,' he said. 'No one else knows about him. The memory of Andreas is my secret.'

Evangeline wiped her eyes on her sleeve.

Mik looked across at her.

'Sad story, isn't it?' he asked.

Evangeline nodded.

Mik lifted a forkful of food to his mouth. 'You shouldn't cry for me,' he said, 'you should save your tears for your own life.'

'Yeah, well,' Evangeline whispered, 'it's amazing how you can still find a few more to go round when you need them. What happened to your parents?'

'They both pissed off,' Mik said. 'Chico went back to his old name and the serious stage. Maybe he is dead, I don't know. Mimi was let out eventually and went off to start a new life in your country, I think. Good luck to her. I never knew her, except in my imagination and from a few things Andreas told me. I don't need to look for her. It's all shit,' he said. 'It makes me angry. All of it.' He lifted his glass in a silent toast.

'Do you miss Budapest?' Evangeline asked.

Mik laughed. 'Not the town. Maybe the countryside, where I stayed when I was fostered. I remember there were mountains there – hot enough to grow grapes for wine on

281

the south-facing slopes. I remember how clean and perfect the mountains always looked. The town is just filth, nothing to get nostalgic about. How about you?'

She told him the story of her own childhood then. She spoke as he ate and the telling of the story brought her comfort somehow, because she had never told it in its entirety to anyone else before. She didn't even know how much he was listening; she told the story as much to herself as she did to him.

The candle burnt down as she finished her tale and she did not bother to relight it this time. When she looked up he was staring at her, face-to-face, across the table. He watched her in silence for a long time and she could not read the look in his eyes. Then he rose to his feet and she wondered in a detached kind of way what he would do now that they were both sated with misery and self-pity.

Mik leant across with his long arms and she found herself stretching out to meet them needily. She had never felt so greedy for someone before in her life.

The table was wide between them. She clambered up onto it like an animal, on all fours, and he reached to part the plates with two quick sweeps of his arm.

Evangeline watched dishes of food fall to the floor and a plate break with a crack that must have had the old woman downstairs praying for the safe return of her rose vase.

The vase itself staggered and teetered on the edge of the table but Evangeline leant out calmly and caught it before any damage could be done.

She was still clutching the plastic roses when Mik lifted her up by her armpits and dragged her bodily towards him across the lace cloth.

Pieces of crockery still fell like lemmings. Some just took more time to make their mind up than others. A knife rocked in a see-saw over the gulf. The rest of the goulash hit the floor with a sickly wet plop. She wondered in the back of her mind whether paprika would stain varnish. Maybe there would be a red mark on the wood down there, like stigmata, for all to see afterwards.

Mik pushed the frock up to her neck and she was pleased the fabric was so flimsy because it meant she could see over the top of it. He studied her naked body like a surgeon about to operate. She wondered what it was he saw. She had no angles or bones in her any longer – every conceivable, recognizably solid particle had achieved full meltdown, like quicksilver in a thermometer, in the heat of her lust.

He pressed the palm of his hand against her groin and she let out a small gasp as his fingers dug greedily into her puff of pubic hair. He bent and kissed her belly softly with his lips.

She parted her legs hungrily and he stood waiting between them. She felt the lace cloth against her back and wondered whether the stains they were about to make would wash off better with Ariel or Daz. Could you soak semen off an antique cloth or did it rot? Maybe a hand rinse, then, to see if the worst would dissolve. He had two fingers inside her now, probing gently. Her back arched slowly, like a bow. Oh God. The fingers retreated.

She watched as he took off his sweatshirt. The body was the same – the same as in the photo – better, maybe, in the flesh. Better in the golden candlelight. She saw a scattering of dark hairs across his chest: broad-bodied at the shoulder but slim around the ribs, each rib-bone defined by a small ridge of muscle; meaty ribs, not fat or skinny. She wanted to bite and suck at each one.

His stomach was flat. He watched her face with everything he did. Her legs parted wider, dangling from the knee so that her toes dipped into the leftover goulash on the floor like crudités into guacamole, and she could paint pictures on the floorboards with her toenails.

'Do you want me?' he asked. What was she to say? If she had wanted him any more badly she would have Hoovered him up inside her altogether. Words were not ample. There

283

was no point pretending otherwise. She nodded her head once.

His penis was large – very large. She was surprised and charmed by the size and the shape of it. Shining and circumcised it bounced and prodded politely at her entrance until he took it in his hand and pressed it slowly into her a little at a time.

'Evangeline,' he was whispering at her, 'feel me, it's there.' He lay still inside her savouring the ecstasy as she massaged him with her muscles until he could stand the stillness no more. As he slid deeper inside, their bellies touched and parted with a wet sucking noise. His arms were on either side of her, supporting his weight. She lifted her head and kissed him on the mouth. She felt the muscles of his body begin to tense.

Mik plunged again into the sweet slime within her, plundering her, making her drip and trickle until their bodies squelched in the damp and the wetness they had created between them. The lamp on its long black flex swayed above them, turning them into a French art movie. The whole flat seemed to move like a crazy house. Losing control too quickly, Evangeline tore the antique lace cloth with her fingers in frustration at her attempt not to come. She clenched herself together and she squeezed inside her brain. Wait. Wait. Another second, another minute, another hour or two of anticipation. Anything.

She ran her fingertips down Mik's back and felt the muscles there as he worked above her. He felt good. Her fingers explored him, the row of round bones of his spine, the dents at the top of his buttocks, the softer skin around his waist. She slid a hand between their stomachs and felt the downy dark hair there. She felt for his balls and squeezed each one gently, making him groan. She ran her hand around the wide base of his cock as it entered her. Then she felt the first triggered mechanism of her own body and she knew it was too late. Her head tilted back and her eyes closed. She would come now – she had to.

Mik grabbed her face roughly in his hands. 'No,' he said. He had felt it too, then.

'Not yet, Evangeline.' It was a command – an order. He pulled his cock out of her and began to kiss her neck and throat instead. She dragged at his hair in frustration. He ran his tongue between her breasts and down past her ribcage and her stomach until he was nibbling gently, like a guppy, at the soft, delicate flesh of her inner thigh. She called out for him and he turned to straddle her, so that the head of his penis bobbed against her mouth.

She licked at the large purple vein that ran along the length of his cock and watched the head expand still more and a crystal of liquid appear at its tip. She felt his tongue work at her. Oh God, not yet. She bit her bottom lip until it hurt. Her hips pressed against his face and she, in turn, took him into her mouth, sucking and kissing at him until she could feel she was making him burst.

Jesus! His loss of control inspired her. She let go of her own body then, turning towards her orgasm and embracing it with a smile of welcome and open arms – and it was all the better for being made to wait. An acute orgasm – sharp pulses of the most intense, endless pleasure, so good she almost laughed out in delight at her fortune.

Mik's body swooped and spasmed above her and the warm salty liquid squirted out of him and down the back of her throat. She swallowed. Her mouth was wet, dribbling – did a bigger cock produce more fluid? They twitched and splashed together for a while like landed fish.

Oh. Coming down was hard. Whoa. Did lust always bring guilty questions trailing in its wake? I can't believe we just did that. I'm sorry, but we just spoilt a good professional relationship. Did I tell you I had a lover in America, a wealthy man I have known for years and who has just done me the honour of proposing? A decent man. A man I could live with. She wanted to go to the bathroom to clean up but was afraid the lace would have left imprints on her bottom.

What happened to men like Mik after you'd screwed your insides out with them? She braced herself. Whatever else, she knew he wouldn't offer to stay and wash up.

She went to sit up but he pulled her firmly down beside him.

'Wait,' he said, quietly, 'wait.' He put his arm around her and pulled her close until her body was pressed to his side. She studied his head. Beautiful bones. Why were some skulls so much better than others? The flesh of his face clung around those exquisite bones, leaving dips and curves her eyes could have found pleasure in exploring for hours.

Wait. Wait. She felt drawn to him in every way. If the rest of her life had not existed she would have clung to him for ever.

After a few moments he took her hand in his and placed it on his cock. It was soft and curled but, as she held it, it began slowly to firm and grow. A miracle.

'Mik?' she asked.

He kissed her quiet.

'I wanted you more than that,' he whispered, 'more than just one time.'

And then he fucked her once again.

That was their first day together – the first of five. If she'd known she would have been counting.

31

It was still dark when she woke. At first she couldn't move, her bones wouldn't allow it. Face-up on the table still, like a landed and gutted fish, she had lost the feeling in the back of her thighs and her spine felt paralysed. Her head weighed too much as she tried to lift it. She slid along on her back with a groan and the soles of her feet finally found the floor.

She was stuck to the rim of the lace cloth. Sitting up suddenly spoilt her equilibrium. The wine gushed up the back of her throat while other fluids leaked and snaked down her legs. She half ran, half limped to the bathroom for toilet paper.

Her face looked pink and bitten and swollen. She splashed it with cold water and studied it in the mirror. Smug. She looked smug. And a little nervous. Mottled with lust and a little unsure. Good? Yes, good. Guilty? Why should she be? She was single and so was Mik. She looked at her own eyes. She was his boss. Stuart loved her. Stuart had proposed.

What was this, then? Sex, nothing more. She wanted him and he had wanted her and they had both been sad enough and drunk enough . . . Lies, though, she told herself. Worse lies. Stupid lies. Nothing was what it seemed to be and she felt she was walking on quicksand.

He was behind her in the bathroom, framed in the mirror that she looked into over the sink. Reflection stared at reflection. He was still naked and so was she. This was the moment when he would have asked a client for money. How much would someone have paid for what he had just done? A lot, she thought – he was good, very good. She had a thought that he would ask her for money now, and her face turned scarlet with shame at the idea.

'What are you doing?' he asked.

She looked down into the sink. 'Washing. Maybe I should shower.'

There was a long silence. She picked up some soap and put it down again. Then she began to tidy her hair with her hands. Anything.

'Do you want me to go?' he asked. His voice sounded deep and unreal.

'I think maybe you should,' she said. Straight of back and prissy of tone. Grandma Klippel would have been proud of her.

She watched him turn and then turn back again. 'Do I still have a job?' he asked.

'If you want.'

Reflection studied reflection some more. His eyes had become feral and dangerous. She looked away.

'Thanks,' he said.

She winced but he didn't slam the door behind him.

Mik worked one more day in the studio before he disappeared. He was there before Evangeline arrived and he set up the shoot without being asked. Ross was on a visit and she watched with surprise.

'You have him housetrained now?' she asked. Evangeline didn't answer. She had been watching Mik as well.

'Evangeline?'

'What?'

'Mik,' Ross repeated, 'he seems a little more keen to get on with the job. Did you two stop arguing?'

'Oh, I suppose,' Evangeline replied. She was chewing at a lock of her own hair.

'Well, good,' Ross said.

Evangeline followed Mik onto the set. 'Thanks,' she told him.

He turned to face her and she thought she might wilt under the intense stare he gave. 'For what?' he asked.

She looked through the viewfinder to check the lights.

'For setting up like this,' she told him, 'it looks good.'

'It's my job,' he said. 'It's what you pay me for.'

The insult was implicit in his tone. As they looked at one another she felt that they were both treading around a rim, balancing on the edge. She sighed.

'Maybe I was wrong,' she said. He looked up. 'Maybe we can't work together after all.'

He didn't stop. She suspected he had been waiting for her to say it. She watched as he packed and left without a word. Ross watched too.

'Did you fire him?' she asked.

Evangeline shrugged. 'Maybe,' she said. 'I just said things weren't working – is that the same thing?'

Ross turned to face her. 'I think you made a mistake,' she said, looking genuinely concerned. 'Mik was good, Evangeline – not good technically but good in a raw sort of a way. I think he might have been good for you, too. I think he might have brought some excitement to your shots. I think you needed a little fresh young blood in here. You may have hooked the biggest account but you need to keep on top. Your work is always good – technically you're the best, but fashions come and go and your style never changes. Mik is a new mind with some new ideas – maybe you should ask him to come back.'

Evangeline's face closed up.

'You don't need to change all that much,' Ross said, 'you could just update your ideas a little. Get out and mingle a bit, too. When did you last get your face in the glossies? We need the mags, Evangeline; even if they don't bring in the best money they do bring kudos when you put their latest spreads before a client.

'What about that feature *Tatler* wanted on you and Deeta? Eh? Three pages unveiling your new find? You said

289

you were too busy to do it so they shot some new guy who's just done *Elle* instead of you.

'I love your work, Evangeline – everyone does – but you must help me keep your name hot if you want to survive.'

Evangeline stared at the empty set in front of them, still chewing on her hank of hair.

'I won't wear funny hats, I won't go posing at some nightclub and I don't want to see myself plastered all over some colour spread with a face full of Estée Lauder and my hair cropped off by John Frieda,' she mumbled.

Ross shook her head. 'What do you want, then?' she asked.

Evangeline didn't answer. What she wanted most at that moment had just walked out of the studio. She could still smell him in the air. She could still feel the ghost of him inside her own body. There were parts of her that still ached and stung from what they had done. 'Damn you, Mik,' she whispered when Ross had gone and she was finally alone again.

She phoned Stuart. His voice sounded good – it made everything else seem like a bad dream.

'I miss you,' she told him.

'Badly?' he asked.

'Badly,' she replied.

'How badly? Quite badly, very badly or so badly it hurts?'

'Um –'

'If you have to think about it then it can only be quite badly,' he told her.

'No,' she laughed, 'I was just trying to work out how bad the hurt was – slightly painful, very painful or exquisitely painful.' She listened to herself lying.

There was a pause.

'I don't have an answer to your proposal yet, Stuart,' she said.

'And I didn't expect one,' he told her. 'Take your time – I only set you the deadline to scare you.'

'Ha,' Evangeline said. She felt smothered by her own guilt.

It was almost an entire week before she finally snapped and went round to Mik's room. The same woman answered the door with a different child strapped to her hip. She motioned Evangeline inside with a tilt of her head. There was no answer when Evangeline knocked at Mik's door.

'He's in,' the woman told her when she went to leave, 'he was playing music earlier on. I told him to keep it down because it woke the youngest. He's there, though, I'd have heard him go out.'

Evangeline climbed the stairs and knocked again.

'Mik,' she called out, 'I know you're in there.'

He looked as though he had been sleeping or drinking heavily, or both. His eyes were bloodily evil and he needed a shave.

Evangeline stepped inside and looked around the room like a health visitor. 'Jesus, Mik, you look like crap!'

He sat on the bed and rubbed his hands across his face.

'What do you want, Evangeline?' he asked.

She sat on a chair opposite. 'I came to ask you to come back to the studio,' she said.

'You want me back?' he asked, yawning. 'Why?'

She leant back in the chair. 'Because I miss you.'

'Oh.'

'Yeah – I miss the arguments, Mik. I only get to argue with Ross these days and she's not nearly up to it. She always lets me win.'

'And what about us?' Mik asked.

'Us?'

'Yes,' he said, looking at her, 'what about the sex we had the other evening?'

'Oh,' Evangeline answered. She inspected her nails prior to chewing them. 'We can forget about that if you like.'

291

'Forget it?' Mik asked. 'Is that what you want?'

She found it difficult to look at him. 'If it compromises our business relationship then maybe . . .' she began.

Mik stood up, towering above her. 'I said, is that what you want, Evangeline?' he repeated. 'Do you *want* to forget it?'

She did not reply.

He was close to her now. 'Do you want to forget it?' he asked again, more softly this time.

A buzzing filled her head, like a thousand flies let loose. She looked up and he kissed her.

'A third time,' he whispered as he held her and she nodded, yes – a third time. One more fuck and maybe she would be sated. One more time and then maybe she would be free to marry Stuart.

The plan wasn't foolproof. As they fucked a great sense of tenderness welled up inside her, making her throat hurt with wanting and neediness, and when she examined what she knew to be impossible she realized she was in love. In love with Mik. Despite everything. She kissed him and allowed the feeling to liquidize in her veins like a slug of malt whisky.

I love you. She could never have said it. He would have turned from her immediately. It was his brother's love he missed, not hers. He whispered to her in Hungarian. Did he tell her he loved her? She didn't know – it was barely important. Her own love was the only thing – it was more than she was capable of dealing with.

Mik took her hand with great tenderness, as though she were something special and precious to him, and he twined his own fingers between hers until it was hard to tell which belonged to who. Then he kissed her knuckles.

'You know, you should go back,' he said softly.

'Go back?' she asked. 'Go back where?'

'To Boston.' She tried to pull her hand away but he wouldn't let her.

'There's nothing there now,' she said in a distant, breezy

voice. She didn't want the reality. She wanted the other stuff, the love and its soft cocoon.

'There are still questions for you, Evangeline,' Mik said. 'You told me, there are things you never knew. Don't live with secrets, they destroy your life, I know. Go back to where you came from. Speak to your grandmother while she is still alive. When people die doors lock to you for ever. Find the little girl you left back there – she is trapped inside your memory, Evangeline – set her free for good. Do you understand me, Evangeline? Do you see why this is important to us?'

She looked at him. He was asking too much – speaking to her grandmother meant reviving all the old pain.

He said something in Hungarian.

'What does that mean?' Evangeline asked.

'It means, "You think I am talking crap."'

Evangeline laughed a little.

'How is your man in America?' Mik asked, suddenly.

'America again?' Evangeline echoed.

Mik's face was serious. 'Do you love him?' he asked.

Evangeline looked away. 'Of course not.'

Mik nodded. 'Why not?' he asked. 'Because you love me?' he held her face in his hands.

'You frighten me sometimes,' Evangeline whispered.

'That's ridiculous,' Mik said.

'No, it's the truth.'

He took her hand again. 'You think I would hurt you?'

'I *know* you will.'

Mik raised her fingers to his mouth and sucked the tip of each one in turn.

'You would have to let me, Evangeline,' he said.

'I don't know how I can stop you.' She stared into Mik's dark eyes. Something was wrong, she was running out of control.

'I want your love,' Mik said quietly.

'Why?' Evangeline asked.

'Because it is what I need the most,' he told her. 'Do you love me?'

Evangeline was unable to answer him and she watched the hurt and the anger grow in his eyes at her own indecision. In the end he could lie there no longer.

She watched him rise naked to his feet, his face no longer tender but hard with hurt and anger.

'Only return to me when you have reached a decision,' he said. 'Only come again if you love me. If not you are killing me – do you understand?'

She found a bar to get drunk in.

'Do I look like a mad woman?' she asked the bartender.

'No, lady – you look perfectly sane to me,' he told her, grinning.

'Then you are a very poor judge of character,' she said. There was some Western song on the jukebox – slow, mawkish guitars with a woman yelling something about 'standing by your man' every few bars. Evangeline put her head in her hands and groaned. She had it bad; even the words of the song seemed to make wise sense tonight. It could have been her anthem: 'Stand by your man. *Stand by your fucking man.*'

She was about to behave in the maddest of ways. She was drinking to give her the courage to tell Mik how much she loved him.

As she stood by his door again her head suddenly cleared. Her mouth felt dry and her heart was thumping about all over the place.

'Jesus!' She was angry with herself. There had to be some way to calm herself down. When she was a kid Nico had given her brown paper bags to breathe in to. She closed her eyes instead, listening to her heartbeat, willing it to slow down to a mild rhumba, at least.

She knocked at Mik's door and it opened so quickly and suddenly that she let out a yell. He looked wild, truly insane with worry and then relief. He came out towards her and took her face roughly in both his hands and looked deep into her eyes.

'Yes?' he asked softly.

'Yes,' Evangeline said. She was happy to lose herself, then – happy to be stupid. *No good will come of it* – she could hear her grandmother's words in her head. She was working on instinct now, not intellect; grabbing what she could while it was still there on offer. Greedy and selfish. Stupid. She didn't care much, though, and when Mik kissed her on the mouth she cared even less.

32

There was something inherently wonderful about doing what was so patently the wrong thing. Evangeline loved the look she got from the make-up artist when he caught her kissing Mik on set the next morning.

I can't help it, she thought to herself, there is nothing I can do about it. I'm happy. So what?

Who are you kidding, Evangeline? a voice in her head asked. You're thirty-something, a professional woman. Intelligent, even. Of course you had a choice. No, she replied, cheerily, it was all out of my control. I had no say in it. It just happened. She started referring to star signs and fate. She even began reading the horoscopes in the papers, she was so head-over-heels, loopy in love.

They worked together well now that he was back. Mik was quiet but business-like. If she needed anything doing out on a job he had already done it. No demands, so no confrontations. Why hadn't it always been like that? When she had a problem she even asked his opinion. They made a good team and Ross was right, he did bring a freshness to her work.

She knew it could never end like that, though. She wasn't stupid, she had just put her brain on hold for a while.

Ross was surprisingly nervous when she found out about the relationship.

'I only meant you should keep him on, Evangeline,' she told her, 'I didn't mean you should share your bed with him too.'

'It's OK.' Evangeline told her, 'it's nothing serious.' She looked tired and she sounded a million miles away.

Ross leant forward. She had large eyes that got magnified by the lenses of her glasses. Her hair was cropped short in a way that used to suit her when she was younger.

'Look, duckie,' she said, 'call me an interfering old cow if you like, but I'm just not sure about Mik, that's all. I don't know that you should trust him.'

Evangeline looked at her. Her eyes were moist, as though she had a cold. 'He's not like he seems, Ross,' she said, 'not once you get to know him. He's had a terrible life, really awful. I think I understand him now. It just took time, that was all.' She was fiddling with some pens in a tub on Ross's desk. The agent moved the tub out of her reach.

'Is this a proper relationship then?' she asked.

'No.' Evangeline said. Three days as a couple, that was all. She needed to speak to Stuart. Things with Mik were running out of control; she needed him now – she had even learnt to trust him. Three days and all that much had happened. Her body belonged to him.

'He heals some of my wounds,' she told Ross, 'and I hope I heal some of his.' It sounded like a line from a Charlie Gregg song.

She had to think of Stuart – she had to force herself. Thinking about him was like opening a deep gulf of guilt in the middle of all her happiness. She had a job back home in the States – just a couple of weeks – but it would force her to confront the situation and explain things to him. She told Mik she needed him to stay in London, to finish a job they'd got booked. Mik didn't argue but she could see he was worried. The night before she was due to leave he held her to him, rocking her like a child.

'You will come back?' he asked. His voice sounded level but she could hear the fear in his tone.

'You will come back to me, Evangeline.' It wasn't a question this time.

Stuart was in Japan on business. She felt relief at first, and then a sinking of the heart that she couldn't end their

297

relationship after all. She visited Catherine just to see Paddy.

'Are you back for good?' Catherine asked straight away.

Evangeline could barely talk for all the licks she was getting. It was Catherine's only good point, the way she looked after the dog. Her son loved Paddy and she treated him like a puppy prince. He had a collar with real fur and diamante that made Evangeline want to puke.

'No,' she said, eventually, 'I have to get back to the UK soon to start the new credit card job.'

'Is that your home now?' Catherine asked.

Evangeline shook her head. 'No,' she told her, 'well, maybe for another year – once the new contract's been signed. The account's sort of taken over my life. It's my main source of income now – I can't afford to turn it down.'

Catherine nodded. She seemed happy enough that Evangeline might be out of the way for another year at least.

'Maybe Dad will visit you over there,' she said.

'I hope so,' Evangeline replied. She felt sick with guilt. What was she doing? Then she tried telling herself it would be all right, Stuart had to have other women. They'd always been casual enough about that sort of thing. Only now Stuart had proposed, and that made things different. She was shit. Worse than shit. She was the worst scum on the planet for what she was doing to Stuart. He was a good man, a nice man. She had to tell him, it wouldn't wait, it wasn't fair.

She looked at Catherine. 'When does your father get back?' she asked.

The girl shrugged. 'Next week or the week after. Who knows? You know what he's like.'

'Do you have his number in Japan?' Evangeline asked. Catherine found it for her and she scribbled it onto the back of her hand. 'Thanks.'

'Is anything wrong?' Catherine asked.

'No,' Evangeline told her, 'I just need to speak to him urgently, that's all.'

She phoned Stuart at the wrong time. There were hours between them and he sounded like he was on another planet. He was in the middle of a meeting. Evangeline swore underneath her breath. She could hear the other voices in the background, doing business in Japanese. Stuart muttered something in the same language as he took her call.

'Evangeline?' he asked. 'Is everything OK?'

She drew a deep breath. 'Yes, Stuart, I just . . . I'm sorry, I picked the wrong time. It's nothing urgent — nobody died.' She stopped. It was still good to hear his voice. When she heard him speak it was as though everything else had been some sort of strange dream. 'I'll call you later,' she said.

'Evangeline!' He stopped her before she could hang up. 'Don't go yet,' he said. She closed her eyes. There was a pause. Silence. She could hear him breathing. He was a million miles away and she could hear the breath in his lungs. 'You didn't phone to tell me you're accepting my proposal,' he said.

Little hairline fractures began to appear on her insides. 'No,' she told him. The voices in the background grew louder. This was not the time. This was definitely not the time.

His tone became business-like. 'OK,' he said.

'Stuart?'

'I have to go,' he told her, 'I'll be in touch.' His tone was dead now — there was no emotion there, nothing at all.

'Goodbye,' Evangeline said, but he'd already hung up.

Mik phoned her that evening. 'I need you, Evangeline,' he said. His voice was close to the mouthpiece — her need for him was intense and instant.

'Did you look in your camera bag?' he asked before hanging up.

She felt inside it, then into each of the pouches. There was a small wrapped package inside one of them, a present from Mik. She pulled it open carefully and a silver locket fell out, a little like the one Mik wore, though more delicate and ornamental.

Place something precious inside it, the note with it read.

'Jesus!' she looked around in despair. She had nothing, no scrap of fabric or lock of his hair. She'd get a shot of Mik once she was back – a sort of gimpy, corny, smiley shot that would make her grin and go wobbly when she looked at it. She hung the empty locket around her neck anyway. It was cold, but she breathed on it until it became warm.

'It looks good,' she said to herself in the mirror.

What did they look like together, she and Mik? She imagined their faces close. Alike but unalike. Sad eyes but defiant mouths with comical jutting jaws. An absolute hairfest, hers wild and pale, shimmering across her breasts and down her back; his dark and heavy and straight.

Five days in love. They had parted on the fifth.

He didn't phone her after that first time but she knew he was busy and she was, too. She was amazed to discover how big her name had become in the States. Paparazzi followed her in the evenings and journalists phoned for interviews during the day. She found the interest funny and in some ways flattering. They took their photographers more seriously out there – they were news items, personalities, big ones – so while her photos were less well known in her homeland it treated her more like a celebrity. At the airport, though, as she was leaving, the press coverage seemed to get out of all proportion, even by US standards. There was jostling as she walked through departures, and an airport security guard appeared from nowhere to push the snappers back so she could get through in comfort.

'Sorry about the job,' one of the journos shouted. 'Do you have any comment? Any plans?'

'What the hell was that all about?' she asked when she got on the plane, but she was just met with glassy smiles from the air hostesses.

It was the same at Heathrow: not as many snappers, but a lot, all the same. Too many just for her, she would have thought. She wasn't a news item – not at the moment, anyway. Ross was standing to the side of the scrum, smoking nervously. She caught Evangeline by the arm and led her to a waiting taxi. As the cab pulled away Evangeline fell back into the seat, laughing.

'Christ, Ross, how did you pull that one?' she asked. Ross wasn't smiling.

'Evangeline, ducks, you've lost the Imprex account,' she said.

Evangeline looked at her. She had forgotten to stop smiling. It was like a moment of suspense after a bad wound or an accident – the few split seconds before the pain comes, but when you know it is coming and you wonder how badly it will hurt when it does. The smile became a rictus.

'What?'

'The credit card, darling,' Ross said, 'they decided to use someone else, after all. They love you but they wanted new blood. Christ, I'm sorry, Evangeline.'

Evangeline swallowed. The smile still hung there on her face, stretching its way to a bravery award.

'Evangeline?' Ross sounded worried.

Evangeline's hands began to shake. Shock. Violent shock. Unbelievable shock. She wanted to laugh – it was wrong, it had to be a joke. 'I went to the meeting, Ross,' she said, trying to keep her voice steady, 'Eddie Gershon told me the job was mine for another year. We chose the model together. There's some mistake. There was no one else in the running.'

Ross sighed. 'No mistake, I'm afraid, ducks,' she said,

'and Eddie appears to have resigned on the strength of it. I hear that even he couldn't take all the behind-the-scenes crap. He's been headhunted by a big operation in New York – it's amazing how quickly these things happen. A new guy called Norris or something has taken over Eddie's job. The guy's a snake, Evangeline, an ex-lawyer from the States and as tight as a drumskin. I couldn't even get through to him to find out exactly what happened.'

Evangeline felt sick suddenly. Her head ached. She called to the driver to pull the cab over into a lay-by and she got out to get some air and try to clear her brain.

It was just a job, that was all.

She wanted to cry so much she was gasping for breath but she didn't want to lose face in front of Ross. The woman was looking out of the cab window at her, her face full of concern. Even the cabbie looked bothered.

She fingered the silver locket around her neck: Mik. She'd been so excited at the thought of seeing him again. She needed him now – badly. Worse than that, though, was the need to speak to Stuart. He was the strong one, the one who would always sort things out. The one she had always gone to in a crisis.

'Get a grip on yourself, Evangeline,' she whispered, 'Stuart isn't an option any more. You can't lean on him all your life.'

She climbed back into the cab. Ross flashed a smile of relief that she hadn't actually done anything embarrassing like throw up out there.

'Can we go straight back to the studio?' Evangeline asked. Ross nodded.

'Can we sue?' Evangeline asked, quietly, after a while.

'I don't think so,' Ross said, 'nothing had been signed yet – I got my boys to look at it. There are grounds, of course, but Imprex is a big organization. They said you'd run out of money long before they did if it came to a fight in the courts. The publicity would be bad too, Evangeline. I don't think . . .'

302

Evangeline looked at Ross. She didn't want her agency associated with that sort of mess. It was understandable.

'Shit!'

'Don't get too angry, Evangeline,' Ross said.

'It'll ruin my name, Ross,' Evangeline said. 'Maybe I had better go over to Imprex and speak to them. Maybe there's just some sort of a glitch. Perhaps they're playing poker with me, or something – trying to keep my money down . . .'

'No, ducks,' Ross said, touching her arm, 'they mean it. It was in the *Standard* and they even got it on the front page of *Campaign*. It's a news item, Evangeline. The press have got their teeth well and truly into it.'

Evangeline ran her hands over her face and through her hair. 'I don't understand, Ross – I know these things can happen, but they were all so positive! They weren't even looking at other photographers! Jesus!' Her head ached badly now. She felt suddenly tired. 'Someone else must have poached it, Ross,' she said. 'Who got it? Lichfield? Meissel? Jesus, who was it?'

Did Ross look embarrassed, or had her anger made Evangeline paranoid?

'I'm not sure, Evangeline,' she said, 'I don't know if they've decided yet. It's all a bit confusing at the moment. There're enough rumours, of course, but, who knows?'

Another sigh.

'Look, I'm sorry, Evangeline, I'm bullshitting you and not doing a very good job of it, to boot. Mik got the contract. I'm sorry. The guy's a prize bastard. I won't say I told you so but I think you knew it yourself, too. I suppose neither of us realized just how big a bastard he might be.'

Evangeline laughed in a quick burst. 'Mik?'

'I'm sorry, Evangeline.' Why did Ross keep saying that?

'Mik got my job?' Evangeline asked. '*My* job?'

'Evangeline . . .'

'He poached *my* client? No. He wouldn't do that. Ha. Why would they take him, anyway? He's just an assistant – my assistant. They wanted the best – you know that, Ross!

303

you must have heard wrong. Who told you? I bet you were just on the wrong end of some gossip.' She laughed again, a horrible laugh this time.

'Ask him yourself when you get back.'

'Ross, he wouldn't do that to me . . .' He loves me, was how she was going to finish.

They drove on in silence. Ross glanced at Evangeline's face. She was sitting bolt upright, staring straight ahead, fingering a locket she wore around her neck.

'You know, it's all so breathtakingly horrendous you could almost admire him for it,' she began. 'I mean, there is always something terribly attractive about beastly men, isn't there – I mean I know what he's done to you is the pits and everything, but . . .'

Suddenly Evangeline knew. Mik would do it – of course he would do it. He had thought that job should be his all along. Maybe that was why he'd screwed her; maybe all the time he had been planning . . . She'd been stupid, blindly, overwhelmingly stupid. Clever Evangeline, the one who had always held control over her own career, had been conned by a sad story and a pretty face . . .

'Shut up, Ross,' she said to her agent, 'for pity's sake just shut the fuck up.'

Ross dropped Evangeline at her flat. When she got back to the agency her phone was ringing.

'What about Deeta?' Evangeline sounded cool enough.

'What about her?' Ross asked.

'Have the clients jettisoned her too? I thought they were using her for the year. They said they loved her.'

Ross sighed again. 'I'm sorry, duckie,' she said.

'Sorry?' Evangeline asked. 'Sorry? What? What is it now, Ross?'

'The guy's a complete shit, Evangeline,' the agent said.

'What?' Evangeline asked.

'She's with Mik,' Ross said. 'Look, Evangeline, you have to know the talk is that they're an item now. I may as well tell you, because you'll read about it in the papers soon enough. There was a shot of them together in *Harpers* last week. I suppose you didn't see it, or something. I tackled Mik about it at the time and he said it was just a fake shot, a paste-up job, and made me swear not to tell you. Now Deeta's agent says she's signed to Imprex for the year, so I suppose Mik's poached her, too. Maybe that was how he got the job in the first place – maybe he screwed her so silly she signed an exclusive with him and he took that to the client as a *fait accompli*: if you want her you have to have me too.'

There was a long silence the other end.

'Do you *want* to sue?' Ross asked.

'Oh, Jesus, no, I want to kill, Ross.'

'Murder might be cheaper than suing. You know that.'

'Shit.'

There was a pause. Ross could hear Evangeline breathing at the other end.

'Are you OK, duckie?' she asked. Evangeline had always seemed tough enough. A little anxious about things, maybe, but Ross didn't have too many worries about her. She'd known Mik was a no-go, even if she did have a fling with him. She'd be mad, of course, and maybe get pissed a few times, but it had happened to snappers before and it would happen again.

This business had always been dirty, but it was getting dirtier now the financial stakes had gone through the roof.

'We can sue if you like, Evangeline,' she said slowly, 'but the publicity would be more likely to damage you than those two. The client might even pay their legal bill, who knows? I don't want you in the press as the failure who lost the account, either.

'Think about it, Evangeline. Do what you think's right and I'll back you all the way, but there have to be other ways of getting even. Evangeline?' she said, raising her voice. 'Are you still there, duckie?'

'Shit!'

'Do you want some time to think, sweetie?' Ross asked. She wasn't good with histrionics. The ash on her cigarette had grown three centimetres and she was not within reach of an ashtray.

'Yeah.' What did Ross detect in Evangeline's tone? Anger? Upset?

'Do you want me to come over and sit with you?' she asked, praying the answer would be no.

'No,' Evangeline replied. 'No – leave it, Ross. I might . . . I might go away . . . I don't know. Shit, I can't think straight. Look, I'll call you, OK?'

'Sure,' Ross cooed, 'take your time.' She flicked through Evangeline's diary on her computer screen. There was no need for her to rush back – she didn't have any urgent bookings, after all. Besides, Ross was just about to get Mik to sign on with her and she wasn't sure how she was going to break that one to Evangeline, exactly.

Evangeline tracked down Eddie Gershon's new number in the States.

'Eddie?' she asked. 'What the hell is going on?'

'Evangeline,' his voice sounded friendly. 'I'm sorry about what happened – you know I quit because of it. I won't have any part of those sort of dealings.'

'What sort, Eddie?' Evangeline asked. 'What happened?'

Eddie sighed. 'I can't say, I'm afraid. There were very big and very sudden changes in the company. You've heard about the new man who came in when I left? Somebody there's got it in for you, Evangeline – I don't know why and if I did I couldn't say because they've threatened me with an injunction if I mention anything they consider detrimental.

'I'm sorry, Evangeline. Your work was good and you know I was going to use you. Maybe you should find out whose toes you trod on, because whoever it is is very anti, that's for sure. You understand my position, I'd like to help but I couldn't afford the flak.'

'Sure, Eddie,' Evangeline said, 'you've been more help

than I expected. Thanks, I'm truly grateful. It's nice to know not everyone in the business is a shit.'

'Any time,' Eddie said. 'What will you do, Evangeline – get mad or get even or both?'

'I don't know,' she sounded tired and confused.

There was a long silence.

'Evangeline?' Eddie was worried she might have hung up. 'Look – I know I said I had no idea who's got it in for you, but I do know one thing, they're a major league player. I suggest you think hard before you take them on. You'd stand to lose everything, Evangeline.'

There was a cold laugh down the other end of the line. 'I think I already did, Eddie,' she said.

She took a cab to the studio and found the place locked and empty. The phone was ringing inside but she ignored it. She pulled out the portfolio of work she'd done for Imprex and looked through it. At the back were the tests she'd done of Deeta.

Jealousy: that was all she could feel when she looked at the girl's face. She had Mik and Evangeline didn't. Her eyes looked mocking, but that was just the imagination. Evangeline had lost the biggest account of her career in a publicly humiliating way and all she felt was schoolgirl envy because another woman was screwing her man.

Not her man, though. He never had been her man. She was forced to keep reminding herself – what she'd had with Mik was nothing, just a ruse on his part so he could screw her in business.

She caught sight of herself in the mirror. The locket gleamed in the glow from the desk lamp. It had all been an act. She hated Mik, but she couldn't take the locket off. Did Deeta wear one, too? The idea appalled her. She shook her head but she couldn't think straight. Crying, she ran out of the studio and took a cab to Covent Garden where she talked a newsagent into finding her the previous week's copy of *Harpers*.

307

The shot of Deeta and Mik together was on the gossip page. She didn't bother to read the copy — she couldn't, her eyes were too cloudy with tears. She just had to see if Deeta was wearing a silver locket around her neck. Of course the shot was taken at the wrong angle. She could have ripped it out there and then.

What the hell was she doing? She felt her breathing go out of control and clutched at her chest. Panic, panic. She had to calm down. People were staring. She had to go, she had to get away. She had credit cards and her passport still in her bag. She hailed a cab and told it to drive to the airport. She might get a stand-by. She couldn't stay there any longer, she had to get home. It was only once she was on the plane that the panic subsided a little and she was able to sleep.

She slipped back into New York unnoticed and rented a car before driving off into the country. She barely knew where she was herself. She bought a camera on the way and got it out of its case a few times to try and take some shots, but her heart wasn't in it.

Most of all she missed her dog. After a couple of days she phoned Catherine and begged her to send Paddy out to be with her, but she couldn't remember what it was Catherine had said to her. She phoned her back a few hours later and Catherine recited some details about couriers and where she could meet them. She told Evangeline it was expensive but Evangeline didn't care — she just needed her dog there with her.

'Paddy!' It was a miracle he still remembered her at all. He flew at her like an arrow so she supposed her scent couldn't have changed much, to a dog's nose anyway. It was good to be licked and slobbered over and she wept unashamedly.

She slept in the car a lot and she bought a couple of blankets because the nights were getting colder. What was it now? Autumn? She looked at the trees around her. Maybe late summer. A note had arrived with her dog:

Phone me. It was from Stuart. There was a list of numbers, just in case. She spread the paper out on the dashboard. Where was he? She recognized some of the codes. New York a lot. Japan, maybe. A couple she didn't know. Stuart felt like a million years ago. Everything felt like a million years ago, apart from the pain. The pain was current. The only way to stop it from killing her was to not think, not at all. She ate, she slept, she talked to the dog.

She didn't think of Mik. She didn't think how stupid she had been. She didn't worry that maybe she had lost everything now. It was OK, she just had to close up part of her mind like an old attic room, that was all. Throw all the junk up there and forget about it. Maybe browse through it when all the hurt was gone.

Maybe one day.

Maybe the next century, or the one after that.

She wanted to kill him. She wanted to kill Mik.

33

Mik sat in front of what had been Eddie Gershon's desk, glowering with anger. Randall Norris, Eddie's American replacement, sat uneasily behind the vast obelisk. Up until five minutes ago he had thought Mik was going to attack him. He'd had his finger on the security buzzer beneath the desk for the past two hours. Mik had only just been persuaded to sit down but he sat like a coiled spring, ready to pounce.

Mik was muttering something in Hungarian. Norris thought the guy was cracked. He'd worked with many psychos during his time in the US courts and he thought he knew the symptoms well enough when he saw them. If it had not been his brief to keep Mik on the account at all costs he would have had him thrown out of the building the minute he arrived.

Randall wondered whether Mik was running out of steam. 'Deeta is giving us grief,' he told him, reasonably enough, 'she says you're screwing her about. We thought we had bought you two as an item. Explain.'

Mik just glared at him.

'She says she did some stuff with *Hello!* or something,' Randall went on, 'some sort of publicity thing about you two being a couple. Mik? She says you were in the papers the same day with some other model? Comprendez? Can this be sorted? Was it some kind of a mistake?'

Mik looked across at him. 'I screw who I like,' he said.

'OK, OK,' Randall held up the palms of his hands, 'OK. So?'

'So what?'

'So what happens now? She says she won't work with you. She says she'd feel humiliated. We need her for the campaign. She is the face that goes with the product. Speak to me, Mik, tell me what happens next.'

Mik stood up. 'What happens next is easy, Mr Norris,' he said. 'Either you get Evangeline back on the job with me *now* or you'll lose her. As far as Deeta goes, well, that's easy, too – if you use her you find a new photographer and if you use me we find a new face. It's not difficult, anyone can see that.'

Randall's face flushed and he examined his nails. 'We can get Evangeline in on this again later,' he said. 'If you walk out now you'll lose the account for both of you. I already explained this, Mik. As far as Deeta is concerned – well, maybe we can compromise.'

Mik's attitude bored and annoyed him. He was not used to being spoken to in such a way. He did not like feeling threatened, either.

He leant forward across the desk. 'You think you can find another face?' he asked. 'Just like that?'

Mik shrugged. 'Maybe somebody better,' he told them.

Norris thought for a while. Deeta had been made to look stupid in the press and they had never wanted their name linked with anyone, anyway.

Norris nodded. 'You can find someone else?' he asked. 'A new diva?'

Mik smiled at him. 'No problem,' he said. 'So what about Evangeline?'

Norris shrugged. 'Have you managed to contact her?' he asked.

Mik glowered again. 'You know I haven't,' he said, 'she's not responding to any calls – she may even have left the country.'

'So how do you expect us to, then?' Norris said. He hoped Mik was incredibly stupid because there was no way this little charade could go on much longer.

*   *   *

It had begun to snow. Freak weather. Everyone was surprised. Locals kept apologizing to Evangeline when she stopped off for petrol. The snow was OK, it reminded her of Boston. Then it got too bad to drive and she booked in at a small hotel in the middle of a small town slap-bang in the middle of nowhere at all. Her credit card had bounced at the gas station and she had no other way of paying for the room, but they didn't ask for a deposit and she thought she might just sit it out until she could think a little straighter. She was confident her brain would clear if she just gave it time.

Her room was empty, save for the bed, a wash-basin and bidet that were hidden by a Victorian screen, and an ancient cupboard for her clothes. She sat on the bed, curled up her legs and looked out at the snow.

Had she forgotten to pay the card? She was wealthy enough, she supposed, so that had to be the reason. She felt that she was waiting, but she didn't know what for. The lace curtains at the window reminded her of her grandmother's house. One night she woke up and imagined she could hear the sea.

She wrote a letter to Catherine to thank her for looking after Paddy but the letter sounded mawkish when she read it so she tore it up and began again. The woman who owned the hotel posted it for her. She went back into her room to wait.

Mik phoned Ross.

'Have you heard from her, has she called?'

'No, Mik, nothing.' Ross's voice was like syrup on sponge.

'Is she OK?' he asked. He sounded angry.

'OK, duckie?' Ross sounded surprised. 'I suppose so. Why? Do you think she might not be?'

'If she rings ask her to call me,' Mik said.

Ross laughed. Mik hadn't signed up with her after all. She didn't know who he had signed with or whether he was handling things himself – either way she was miffed about losing him. 'I shouldn't wait by the phone, Mik,' she said.

'I need to speak to her,' Mik's voice was on the brink of a shout.

'I'll pass that message on,' Ross told him, coldly.

When the snow stopped Evangeline went out for a walk. It was warmer and the ground had thawed already. A freak blizzard in the Antarctic was what the locals were saying. Paddy leapt about joyfully. She watched him race off through the fields, cutting a small swathe through the snow in his wake. She looked around her. The light was perfect. She pulled her camera out of its bag, just to get a look through the viewfinder.

The sun was low enough to bathe the snow in corn-coloured light. The air was sharp in her nostrils. There was a country smell that reminded her of her childhood. It was a smell that she loved – a million miles away from the dead scents of the sea on the Cape.

A sprinkling of snow powder blew up with the breeze. She loved the calmness of the place. Paddy bounced back towards her, stopping to leap up into the air to chew at the new flakes that had started to fall.

She waited until he got close and then made a snowball to throw for him, pitching it as high and as far as she could to give him a good run. He shot off in wild pursuit, leaping up to catch it as it dropped. It broke on his nose in mid-air and he did a little victory twist and landed and then vanished.

'Paddy?' She was still smiling.

'Paddy!' Evangeline banged her hands together. Making the snowball had frozen them because she wasn't wearing gloves. She only had a coat because she'd picked one up in a sports shop en route.

'Paddy?'

She thought she'd heard a whelp.

'Paddy?' Had he landed badly? She started to run, not panicking, but concerned all the same.

The blood was like a ruby wine-stain on the white snow, a small mark in such a big field, but no less shocking for that.

313

'Paddy!' She yelled his name out now, dropping her camera in her haste to find him.

He had fallen into a poacher's trap. When she tried to lift him his head rolled because his neck was broken. There were teeth-marks around his throat where the trap had cut into him. Paddy was dead.

'Oh sweet Jesus, no!'

Evangeline fell onto her knees in an attempt to comfort him, even though she knew it was too late.

'Paddy, sweetstuff, no-no-no, come on, boy, come on.' She held his lifeless head close to her own and rocked him as she whispered into his matted ear. 'No-no-no, Paddy. Come on, come on, come on. Chopped liver indoors, Paddy, minced steak if you like . . .'

She wrapped him in her jumper and laid him on the car seat beside her to drive him back to the hotel. She even switched on the heater to keep him warm and sang softly with the radio to prevent him from being afraid. She knew he was dead but she couldn't stop herself. Paddy, sweet Paddy. She remembered his first accident – the round wet black nose sticking hopefully out of the wreckage of the tour bus. If he'd had nine lives, like a cat, he must have lost at least eight of them then.

The snow was getting heavy again when they drove up to the hotel. Evangeline clambered out of the car and picked Paddy's limp body off the passenger seat. She was half-way up the path before the snow seemed to blind her and then she lost her way stupidly and only then did she collapse.

There was a doctor and an injection and then blissful, ignorant sleep.

When she finally resurfaced she found herself still in her room. The truth hit her all at once, about ten seconds after consciousness, and she groaned with the pain of it and looked around for her clothes. There was a spare pair of jeans she'd bought, lying by the bed, and she pulled them on groggily. Someone had put a nightshirt on her, which she stuffed into her jeans, and she walked across to the window.

Stuart was there, walking about outside. She didn't understand that, it was wrong, it had to be the sedative making her confused. She closed her eyes and rested her head on the cold pane. She looked again. There was a tall, smartly dressed man walking about in the garden outside. He wore an expensive-looking overcoat but was not dressed for the snow. He had his back to the window and she could see his breath coming out of his mouth in frosted clouds.

She knew it was Stuart, even though she knew that it couldn't be. He should have been in Europe. She needed him. He was exactly what she needed. She pulled the French doors open and ran out behind him. When he turned she could see the concern on his face.

'What are you doing here?' she asked.

He smiled at her. 'I was just passing,' he said.

Oh God, she wanted to hug him. He looked good – solid and honest and sane and wholesome. His tanned face looked unbearably handsome and kind. Strength radiated from him. She felt that, if she clung to him like a limpet to a ship, she could feed off some of that strength.

She stood her ground. 'You look good,' she told him.

'You look like shit,' he said. She did, too: matted hair, a face drawn from self-pity, indescribable clothes.

'I wasn't expecting guests,' she said.

He grinned and she smiled back. What the hell had she been doing? He was a loving, caring man – a man she could trust – and she had been off playing with matches until she had been badly burnt.

She walked towards him. 'Jesus, Stuart, how did you find me?' she asked. Her voice broke. He held out his arms and she fell into them hungrily, grateful for the warmth and the expensive, clean smell of him – and the feeling of another body close to her own again.

'A small cry for help,' he said. 'When you contacted

315

Catherine you left enough clues for any self-respecting private dick to track you down.'

She looked up at his face. 'You paid a detective to look for me?' she asked.

He stroked her hair gently and kissed her forehead. 'I've had the bill forwarded to your London address,' he told her.

'Paddy's dead,' she said.

'I know, I've taken care of him,' Stuart whispered into her hair.

He took her to her room. He sat her down on the bed and rubbed her hands and blew on them, just like Darius used to do when she was little and had been playing out in the cold.

'No tears, Evangeline,' he said, kissing them away.

'It's not that easy,' she told him, and they spilt out anyway. He let her cry for a while and then he sat down next to her and looked at her seriously.

'What else happened?' he asked.

She shook her head. 'Oh, Jesus, I lost the Imprex account, Stuart. I was stupid . . . I trusted people . . . I mean I should be old enough and clever enough by now, I thought I was so bloody smart and in control, but I guess . . .'

'Did the job mean that much to you?' Stuart asked.

She couldn't bear to look at him – she couldn't bear to let him see the expression in her eyes. 'More than I thought,' she whispered. It was Mik as well, though – she felt bruised by him, so sore she could barely move or speak. And now Paddy.

The words of all her conversations with Mik flooded into her head, all the things she had told him about herself and all the things that he had told her. So many secrets, so many confidences. But now so many lies.

Mik was screwing Deeta. He had been stealing her job all the time he had been screwing her. Lies, endless and stupefying. Grandma Klippel would have had a seizure at the thought of such lies. 'When you tell a lie you kill a little

316

angel in heaven, Evangeline.' Heaven must have been strewn with dead angels after Mik had got through.

She felt crushed and flattened, like a character in a cartoon fight. She'd need a spatula to even get herself up off the floor. She didn't want to fight back, though, she just wanted to lie there.

She must have slept, somehow. When she woke up Stuart still had his arm around her. It was dark and the room was cold.

'Stuart?' she whispered. She felt his lips on her forehead.

'Come back to New York with me,' he said. 'Come back now. You don't have anything to pack. I can just pick you up and take you home. Forget London, Evangeline, forget everything that happened there. Let it go, just let it go.

'You can have a break – we might even take a holiday, if you like. Get strong again and then get back to your work, if you want. You need a rest, Evangeline – you need looking after.'

'Why are you so good to me, Stuart?' she asked.

'You know why,' he said, softly.

'But I walked out on you,' she wept, 'and then I fucked up your proposal . . . Jesus, I don't know.'

Stuart stood up suddenly and she looked at him.

'What are you doing?' she asked. He had her camera bag in his hand and he was throwing a few other things into a carrier she had used for Paddy's food.

'Taking you home,' he said in a tone that left no room for negotiation.

Evangeline hugged her knees to her chest. She looked out of the window. It had stopped snowing again. The tears had returned the moment she thought of her dog. Had it ever really snowed, or had she imagined it? Things were dry out there now, dry and green. Staying here alone with her thoughts was killing her. Home sounded OK. She sighed and got up to help with the packing.

On the trip back Evangeline broke out of her misery long enough to speak sensibly to Stuart.

'I need to tell you something,' she began. 'Stuart, over in London . . .' She looked into his face. He was kind and generous. She couldn't hurt him. She couldn't tell him everything – not yet.

'Mik,' she whispered silently to the clouds outside, 'Mik, where are you? What happened?'

It was finished. All over. Mik was gone from her life.

34

Finding a model was easy. Finding a model who was special was a little more difficult. Discovering the hottest face to hit the scene since Naomi and Claudia and Kate was virtually impossible, Mik discovered. The agencies had no one suitable. He drank endless cups of espresso as he flicked his way through a mountain of portfolios and after a while each face began to look the same and he started to curse the fact that he had made the suggestion in the first place.

Ross was a bitch. She had stopped taking his calls altogether now and he had no idea where Evangeline was. He had to speak to her – he needed to explain. Nothing had gone according to plan. Then he saw a copy of the *New York Times* with Evangeline on the cover, clutching at Stuart's arm. She was hiding her face from the cameras but she looked beautiful, all the same. Stuart was smiling and protective-looking. Mik stopped searching after that.

Evangeline would come back eventually, he was sure of it. She had work to do in London, and Evangeline prized her career above everything. He wondered if she still wore the locket he had bought her. He pulled the shot of her he had torn out of the paper from his pocket and stared at it. Then he picked up the phone and punched up her New York number again.

Mik was on the books of a guy called Baz who worked as an agent, but who insisted on being referred to as his publicist. All big-name snappers had publicists, Baz told him. It was cool – it was the thing to do. Without Baz, Mik's career would have been on a serious downturn, according to Baz himself. He was going to make Mik stellar.

Baz inhabited state-of-the-art offices on a third floor in Soho, a minimalist barn of a place that had laser art on the walls and choir matting on the floor. Baz pretended to be a Buddhist so he could opt out of unwanted meetings by getting his PA to say he was tied up with his chanting. He was legendary in the business – the best in London and more famous than most of his clients, despite being a prize asshole.

Baz took over Mik's life. He sent him off to Covent Garden to get his hair styled and his wardrobe sorted. Mik came back looking scruffily the same, but in a more expensive way. Baz rocked in his chair as he studied his latest client. Mik was a publicist's wet dream come true. Surly, good-looking and with minimal talent, it was the classic rock-star combination, only this time applied to the photographic business.

Mik's business didn't worry Baz. He knew sod all about taking snaps but he knew a successful face when he saw one. Scandal, too – every day he prayed that Evangeline would cause more of a fuss about Mik's betrayal.

Then the publicity began.

'Photographers in the UK are treated like tradesmen,' Baz told Mik. 'In the States they call them supersnappers and treat them like a breed apart. The guys are gods – they command the fees and they call all the shots. Over here you get paid late and if they don't like your face they won't pay you at all.

'Do you know what happened last week?' he asked, fanning his face with a copy of *Campaign*. 'One of my snappers showed up thirty minutes late for a shoot to find the client had got the fucking hairdresser doing the shots for them instead! No more of that, mate. No fucking more. I want them creaming themselves over you, Mik. I want them fighting over who's going to book you for the next session. Understand? Yeah? They'll be booking the name and the concept, not just the hairy-bollocks that comes along to press the shutter. Understand?'

Once Mik was gone Baz pulled a large quartz stopwatch out of his desk drawer. How long to make someone famous? He liked to time himself – it was better than sex. He was ringing the magazines as Mik climbed into a taxi in the street below.

The initial publicity was easy: Mik was an unknown who had landed one of the biggest accounts in the country and he was seeing one of the newest top model names into the bargain. The fight between Mik and Deeta sounded interesting and Baz saw a lot of mileage in it. He took Deeta's agent to lunch and found her pleasingly co-operative after a couple of Camparis and a bottle of lukewarm Moët. Soon the gossip columns were full of news about the two of them.

Baz went through his books. There was a royal premiere the following week. Lots of top Hollywood names were arriving. He scanned the list for any female stars who had just split with their partners and might need a good-looking escort. He circled at least two of them and set about phoning their agents.

Next on his list was *Vogue* for the new talent page and the *Sunday Times* for the same. He'd have to get a profile written *tout de suite*. He cracked his knuckles and set to work. He was enjoying himself; creating people from nothing always turned him on. God must have got a mega kick out of making Adam and Eve, he thought.

Stuart took Evangeline to New York and booked her into a hotel. She asked him to book the one she had lived in years ago with Nico but he thought it might be too poignant for her and put her into a suite in the Carlyle instead.

'It's too ritzy,' she told Stuart. 'Besides, it's much too expensive. All I want to do is sleep, and I can do that pretty much anywhere.'

Stuart smiled at her as she paced around the rooms.

'The staff are too charming,' she said.

'So? Let them charm you,' he told her. He held out the room key and she took it.

'Thank you.'

'That's better,' he smiled.

'Stuart?' she began. He put his hand up.

'No questions, Evangeline, and no pressure,' he said. 'I'm at home if you need me but I'm invisible if you don't. You need rest. Call me when you want to.'

He hugged her one last time before he left and she wanted to stay wrapped inside there for ever, but she knew she couldn't.

'There's more I have to tell you, Stuart,' she said.

'Not now,' he told her, kissing her face, 'everything can wait.'

He was wrong, though – this couldn't. She needed to tell him, and as soon as possible; she must be fair to him, and she didn't want the weight of the guilt hanging around her. She was tired, though – too tired. She watched in a daze as Stuart left and then fell down onto the bed and slept.

When she opened her eyes again the room was dark and her head felt woolly, like a hangover.

'Paddy!' She scrabbled for her watch. 'I didn't feed you, I didn't walk you . . . oh, Jesus, Paddy, I'm so sorry!' She checked the time. She must have slept half the night and an entire day. She tried to get up and her stomach pulled her over double. Paddy. He was dead – she was confused with sleep. The hurt was like a real pain inside her again, making her feel sick. No Mik. No Paddy.

Eventually the room was still again and she rose unsteadily to her feet. There was a note from Catherine propped against the fruit bowl. She had been in twice to check up on Evangeline. Stuart must have given her a spare room key. It was obvious from the tone of the note that she didn't approve, but Evangeline was past caring. There were also fresh flowers from Stuart – two vases full of white roses – and a ridiculously frothy dressing-gown hanging on

322

a quilted hanger next to her bed, which she also supposed to be from him.

She crawled into the robe and looked at herself in the mirror. The sight made her laugh out loud. She looked sick, like a recovering consumptive: whey-faced with mauve eyes and a pinched expression and greasy hair that hung in damp snakes about her neck. And then swathes of pink satin and frills, courtesy of Stuart.

Where the hell had he bought the thing? She looked at the label: Ora Feder. Expensive frou-frou, then. She smoothed it respectfully with the palm of her hand.

She thought of the last time she had looked at herself properly. Mik had been standing behind her then and they had both been naked. They had made a beautiful pair. The tears started again and she knew she wept out of grief at her loss and mortification at her own dull stupidity.

'I'll lose Stuart, too, once he knows,' she whispered, miserable with self-pity. 'I have to tell him about Mik. I owe him that much. Oh, Jesus, how the hell did I get involved in all this?'

Catherine called once more the following day. She looked well and full of confidence and spite. She had changed her image, Evangeline noticed. This time she looked like a presidential wife, in a suit and high heels, with her hair pinned up in a chignon.

'You're better, then,' she said, bending to clear some newspapers off a seat. She was also wearing gloves. Cute, Evangeline thought, very cute.

'Yeah,' she told Catherine, 'I suppose I am.'

Catherine straightened. 'Dad was really worried about you, Evangeline. He even hired a private eye to find you when you disappeared.'

Evangeline rubbed her hands across her face. 'I didn't mean to worry anyone,' she said, 'I just needed some time to think, that was all.'

Catherine's eyebrows rose. 'I believe the general consensus is that you had some kind of minor breakdown, Evangeline,' she said.

Evangeline smiled. 'Oh dear,' she said softly, 'is that so?' Maybe she had, she didn't know.

Catherine brushed invisible dust off her cashmere coat. 'I suppose you'll let him take care of you now?' she asked.

'Him?' Evangeline said. She was being a bitch, but Catherine brought out the worst in her.

'My father,' Catherine sighed.

Evangeline looked at her. 'I didn't ask for his help,' she said.

'But you always get it, don't you?' Catherine's mouth became thin with suppressed anger.

Evangeline closed her eyes. 'I'm sorry, Catherine,' she said quietly, 'I know how things must look to you. You must hate me quite a lot – I think maybe I would if I were in your shoes.' She looked down at Catherine's feet as she said this – no chance, she thought, she could never have squeezed herself into heels that high and toes that narrow.

'I don't hate you, Evangeline,' Catherine said. Her face had recomposed again now, and her eyes looked blank and vacant as the polite smile was held into place. 'I just wish my father didn't care about you quite so much, that's all. I can see it hurts him and I can do nothing about it.' Her lipstick matched the shade of her coat perfectly. Maybe there was a shop where you could buy them both hanging off-the-peg together.

Evangeline rose unsteadily to her feet. 'I don't believe I'll be hurting him much more,' she said.

Catherine's eyes filled with hope. Maybe she thought Evangeline was about to tell her she was dying. The little light snuffed, though, when she realized Evangeline had said all she was going to. She breathed in hard and pulled her gloves straight.

'There are fresh snacks in the refrigerator,' she said. 'I know you won't want room service seeing you looking like that.' The look she gave as she left would have curdled milk.

Stuart took Evangeline to dinner a couple of weeks later, when he considered her to be properly rested. He turned up like a young man on a date, smartly dressed and nervous-looking, with a bunch of garden flowers tucked underneath his arm. Evangeline smiled when she saw him but the sight of him hurt, nevertheless.

'You look wonderful,' he said. She did look better, she knew it. She'd had her hair trimmed and styled in the hotel salon and pampered herself with a manicure and a facial. She felt scrubbed and fresh and defenceless and horribly, horribly guilty.

Stuart moved towards her to kiss her and she turned her head a degree so that the kiss landed on her cheek, rather than her mouth.

'Do you feel up to going out?' he asked.

'Sure,' she smiled at him reassuringly. His face looked so good. She wanted to bury herself inside of him and never come out again. That was stupid, though. She was a grown woman. She had plans to make, things to take care of. Nobody could burrow themselves away all their lives, although with Stuart the idea seemed very tempting. But she had no right. Even Stuart would no longer want her once she had told him the truth.

They ate at Four Seasons and Evangeline allowed herself to relax for a while and bask in the comfort of the place. There was something very good about classy hotels and swanky restaurants when you needed comforting, she decided. Once you stepped inside the door you found everything was taken care of for you. She even allowed Stuart to order her meal and then she ate it voraciously, because she found to her surprise – and to Stuart's obvious delight – that she was starving.

As she came to the end of a large raspberry and chocolate dessert she realized he was just sitting there smiling at her.

325

'You know you look like a child when you eat,' he said.

She wiped her mouth with a napkin. 'Only an older man could say such a thing,' she said, smiling back. He took her hand and she felt awkward again.

'Stuart,' she began. He was watching her, waiting to hear what it was she had to tell him. Her voice dropped. She felt as though just about everyone in the restaurant would be listening to her. Suddenly paranoid, she looked around the other tables nearby. People were eating, talking, laughing. She looked back across the small table. Stuart had a worried frown on his face.

'I was in love with Mik, my assistant, back in London,' she told him. 'We had an affair. Not a long one, but very intense. I'm sorry, Stuart, I think you ought to know. You were waiting for an answer to your proposal and I was screwing another man.' There was no other way to do it. She felt his hand contract and pull away.

'Do you still love him, Evangeline?' Stuart asked her.

'The affair's over,' she said.

'That's not what I asked you, Evangeline. I asked you if you still love him.'

Evangeline looked down at the table. 'Yes.' There was no point in lying, except to herself. Grandma Klippel would have applauded her honesty – no angels died that day because of her, at least. She did love Mik – still. She couldn't turn it off. She wanted to kill him, too, but she didn't tell Stuart that. There had been enough revelations; she knew when to stop.

She watched the light of affection turn off in Stuart's eyes, as she had been expecting – as she had known it would. One day it had to happen. It had taken her years to achieve it. Congratulations, she told herself, you just lost the best man you were ever likely to meet.

He wasn't looking at her, he was looking at the waiter who had just arrived with their coffee. 'I see,' he said, once the waiter was gone.

Evangeline studied his face; it looked stranger now the

love had died out of it. She had forgotten how much affection can change someone's features. She realized how long Stuart must have loved her, for she felt as though she had never seen this newer, colder expression before. He looked like what he was, an intelligent, sophisticated, very successful and astute businessman.

She thought there was nothing more for her to say, and so they sat together in silence a long while. She drank her coffee but he did not touch his. She felt that her whole world had been picked apart, bit by bit. Nothing was right any more. In a vast wave of self-pity she realized that she had no one now, no one at all. Then she looked across at Stuart's shell of a face and her self-pity was instantly replaced by guilt and shame for what she had just done to a man who had loved her.

Was she any better than Mik? She doubted it and the idea appalled her. What did that make her, then? He had always told her they were alike and she had never believed him. Did the scars and bruises of childhood make you such a monster later on? Was she like Mik – incapable of love? Yet she knew she had loved him intensely and she had thought that he loved her.

She thought of the nights they had spent together, and of how the sullen, stubborn man had slowly turned into a sad but tender lover. She had understood him, she thought. Battered and bruised, they had slowly reached out and touched one another's hearts. Had the intimacy frightened him as much as it had her? He had betrayed her, though, she reminded herself. He had planned to steal her best job. He had taken her model and fucked the girl into the bargain. He was a liar and a bastard. She had been singed by him and now she was allowing him to torch her life completely.

She could have kept Stuart. She could have married a man who loved her. She could have lied to him about Mik, but it wasn't in her nature. He could have read about them one day in the papers, anyway. Maybe he already had.

Maybe it wasn't the sex between them that worried him, but the fact that she still loved him.

Stuart deserved better – he didn't deserve the same fate she had suffered. He should have a woman he could love and trust without question. She knew she could never have lived a lie with him, the guilt would have been overpowering.

What did Mik think of guilt, then, she wondered. Was he suffering from all the pain he had caused her? When he slept with Deeta did he ever once wake to wonder where she was sleeping now? He had spoken the word so many times when they had been together, she had known him to be riddled with guilt over something, but what?

Stuart was watching her again. Some of the remoteness had slipped and been replaced by – what? Hatred? Disgust? He had proposed to her and she had come back with her reply – an affair in London that had left her gutted.

'Stuart, I'm sorry,' she said.

There was another long pause. Stuart was polite to the waiter. Evangeline wanted to be away from the restaurant so badly that it almost hurt. Why had she eaten so much food? What had she been doing, dressing herself up for a date when she had known what she had to do that evening? She tried to think positively. Things might get straight again, somehow. In the meantime she just wanted to die.

Stuart suddenly looked very sad and very old. She had never noticed the years in him before but now she did.

'I'm sorry,' she repeated quietly, 'you have no idea *how* sorry, Stuart.'

He seemed to find her pity the most wounding thing of all. He dusted invisible crumbs from the tablecloth. She wanted to take his head into her hands and kiss it until everything was better, but most of all she wanted to cry. Stuart had been the central pivot of her life for so many years and yet she had never noticed it until the moment he had been removed.

What was she to do now? How had she become this

pathetic and helpless? She watched him settle the bill. He was a gentleman to the last, calling her a cab and paying the driver once she was safely inside.

'Call me if you need anything,' he said quietly, through the open window, and then the cab pulled away and his face was gone.

35

Baz got Mik a four-page deal with *Vogue* and a six-page spread with *Elle*, on the proviso he use Deeta for the shoot. Mik told him where to stuff the job but when Baz explained it in terms of cash and kudos he finally, reluctantly, relented.

'The Deeta story is a good one, Mik,' Baz said, 'shit-hot, just like the punters love. They'll buy the mags just to see if her hatred for you is showing through her eyes – you know the sort of thing.

'I can't remember the last good chance they had to see a marital spat in full glorious Technicolor – now they have the Mik and Deeta story. I've got an exclusive lined up in one of the Sundays and I charged the magazines double up for the human interest angle.'

'We weren't married,' Mik said, leaning both hands onto the agent's desk.

'That's OK,' Baz said, cheerily, 'no one is these days. You screwed her, mate – that's good enough for anyone.'

Mik still looked agitated. 'I need an efficient assistant,' he said.

Baz grinned. 'Nuff said,' he replied, 'consider it done.'

Mik knew his limitations, at least. Studio work was not a forte of his – not when there were big clients involved. He needed someone with technical knowledge. That was OK – there were many great photographers who wouldn't even know how to take off the lens cap if their minions didn't do it for them.

Deeta arrived at the studio looking pale and feisty and

immediately started complaining about the lack of heating. Mik's assistant — a kid called Adam whom Baz had found fresh out of college, wearing a combination of Gap and Benetton — managed to coax her out of her whingeing and got down to the job in hand. Adam was a good ploy; not only was he technically brilliant in the studio, he was also polite and pretty and earnest. He fetched and carried until even Deeta had no cause for complaint.

They painted her face with crimson lipstick and twisted her hair into long, tight curls. With each stroke of the brush she became more beautiful and more mollified. The stylist bound her up in clothes from Versace and Comme Des Garçons and in the end she looked so wonderful she was happy again at last.

Mik worked quickly and instinctively, with Adam supplying the final, more technical points. The client wanted snow and sheep in the shot so Mik's PA had hired an industrial fan and sacks of polystyrene she was busy grating into flakes, while Adam had just taken delivery of two elderly sheep, on hire from the zoo.

'Sheepshit!' The PA screamed when she saw the animals, 'It'll fuck up my fucking snow!'

'Jesus, forget the shit, those animals are too old!' Mik yelled. Adam set about washing them and the stylist primped their fleece and sprayed it white until they looked cleaner and a little less elderly.

Deeta needed few directions on set, which meant barely a word passed between photographer and model during the shoot. The make-up artist and stylist stood watching, soaking up the electric atmosphere. When it was over they all breathed a collective sigh of relief and regret. They had been hoping for a wobbly of epic proportions — something with which to regale the rest of the glitterati over drinks that night at the Groucho.

Vogue and *Elle* were delighted with the results, but when Deeta saw them she went utterly ballistic.

'*My fucking face isn't in any of them!*' she screamed at

331

her agent. '*The sheep get a better fucking look-in than I do! The bastard! Just who the hell does he think he is?*' She was so mad and her language so profound that two of the booking agents were assigned the job of removing any under-age models who might be hanging around to a place well out of earshot.

Deeta's humiliation was public and complete. Baz was surprised and delighted but Mik said nothing, and his agent wondered whether it had even been intentional.

'I don't want to work with her ever again,' Mik told him.

'A remote possibility, even if you did,' Baz said. 'The words "hell" and "freezing over" spring to mind. I should think the chance of you and Deeta working together again rate about as high as that of the royal family taking their holiday in Blackpool this year. Still,' he added with a chortle, 'nice one, Mik, if I do say so myself. Brilliant little coup. Did you find someone to replace her for the credit card ad?'

Mik nodded. He looked tired, but then he always looked as though he had a permanent hangover. Baz admired his client's style now that he had been booted and suited by the finest in the land. He looked like a fashion spread himself, if you were a fan of the Gothic look, that was. Baz tilted his head to one side, wondering whether he could talk Mik into a drop earring, to go with the ethnic charm of the embroidered hat. The hat had been a masterstroke. All the supersnappers wore them in the States and it was an easily-recognizable gimmick.

Mik pulled a small photograph out of his bag and threw it onto Baz's desk. The agent picked it up and studied it. It was a black-and-white, three-quarters of a girl. Mik must have taken it by telephoto – the shot was grainy and the girl in it looked as though she was running.

'Yeah, well,' Baz said.

Mik stared at him. 'I spotted her coming out of school. She's good. She's the right one.'

36

Flora packed her cello away and stuffed an Extra Strong mint into her mouth. Three sucks later she spat it out into her handkerchief. That way she got through over a packet a day, but with only ten calories the lot. She had a Kit-Kat for her lunch. She wiped the smears off the lenses of her glasses with the hem of her skirt, then she brought Mik's card out of her pocket for the thirty-first time.

It was still unbelievable: Mik Veronsky. Mik-Mak, as he was called in the press now. She had pictures of Kate Moss and Linda Evangelista taped up on the walls of her room. She knew more about Kate than she knew about herself — what she ate, who she was seeing, what her day was like when she was doing the shows. Now she was going to be one of them.

Mik had stopped her on the way out of the school gates. She'd been with a group of friends, on their way to the local shops for stamps and some magazines. She hadn't noticed him right away but when she had, his look had been electric. He'd singled her out, too — walked straight up to her and asked if she wanted to be a model.

She held Kate's picture up alongside her own face and looked in the mirror. Who was she kidding? They were from different planets. She stuck the picture to the mirror with spit and looked again. Then she lifted her hair up from the sides of her face. Mik Veronsky must need glasses. She remembered how she looked in family snaps — shy, gauche, awkward, a little demented, even. Fingers stuck away down the sleeves of her jumper, shoulders slumped, skinny legs with gawky great feet.

She glanced at her watch. She had three hours of Art History homework to do. Then she would ring her father and tell him about the appointment she had in London at the weekend.

There was a soft rhythmical ticking noise from outside the open window. It had started to rain. She watched the long grass twitching as the first drops hit it. There was a low rumble in the distance and then later a glimmer of silver, like a spark flashing across the sky.

Flora put her head out of the window and twisted it painfully so that her face caught droplets of rain. She loved storms. She loved her family. She loved her life. But soon it would become even better — unimaginably better. Her stomach flipped and curled in anticipation. Like a child before a birthday, she could hardly bear to wait.

The appointment was at Mik's rented studio in World's End. He was photographing another model for Italian *Vogue* when Flora arrived. The girl was famous and the jewellery she was modelling took second place to her luminous, exquisite face in the viewfinder.

Flora was pink with embarrassment. Her father had insisted on driving her up and he'd come inside, too, to talk to Mik and 'sort things out'. She had never really argued with her parents before. They didn't understand. To them modelling was not a career, it was something pretty girls did if they were too thick for university. They were worried that she would be gang-raped or ripped off. They couldn't believe that someone like her could even be interested in such a fatuous job. She told them how much the top girls earned and they laughed at her. Flora would have been miserable if she hadn't been so excited.

She watched Mik working in reverential awe. He was so goregous he made her feel physically sick and she wished her father hadn't made her eat that slice of baguette in the café earlier on.

Mik had ignored her since she arrived but a young guy

called Adam had greeted them and got them two bottles of Perrier from the fridge while they waited. It turned out that her father knew Adam's father from some connection in the City. Flora began to relax a little once her father started chatting.

The studio smelt of joss-sticks. There was some strange music on the sound system. She loved it. She loved the smell, too – patchouli mixed with dust and a warm, burning smell as the coloured gels heated up over the lights.

'Can I look around?' she asked Adam. He nodded.

'Yeah, only keep away from the set itself.'

The room was vast and dark around the edges. Only the model was clearly visible, posing in the middle in a pool of blue-tinted light. She barely moved; she even blinked in slow motion. Her features were lit to look as though they had been carved out of ice. The effect mesmerized Flora. How could anyone sit still for so long? The girl's mouth was slim-lipped and wide and painted a shade of deep ochre. Her eyes were pale, like a cat's eyes. There was movement from near the camera and the girl's focus changed as she looked towards the floor.

'Shit! Jesus Christ! What the fuck are you playing at?' It had to be Mik as the rest of the abuse was finished in Hungarian. Flora looked quickly across at her father to see if he had heard, but Adam must have taken him off to the waiting room.

The model did not move or look upset. Her eyes flicked back to the camera and a flash went off.

'OK,' Mik said, quietly. The model rolled down off her stool and cracked her knuckles noisily.

'Ciggie!' she yelled to no one in particular and the make-up artist ran out to stick a lighted cigarette into her mouth.

'Watch the lips,' he murmured, 'just watch the bloody lips, won't you?' The model nodded and took a deep drag with her eyes closed.

Mik turned away from the camera and saw Flora watching. 'Hi.'

She nodded in reply. Her mouth was dry suddenly. She wanted to sniff to check her deodorant was still working. She'd used two that morning, a double-protection first and then another brand on top of it to mask the first smell, which she'd discovered she didn't like. She'd also shaved her legs, which she had done only once or twice before, and then worn a long skirt to cover the nicks and cuts.

'Do you want a go?' Mik asked, pointing towards the set. She would rather have died – she truly would rather have died.

'My father's here,' she said.

Mik grinned. 'I didn't ask you for sex, I asked you for a photo,' he said.

Mik held out his hand and helped Flora onto the set. The other model returned and stood watching, drinking Budweiser through a straw.

Flora was dazzled by the lights. 'I don't know what to do,' she said. She heard the other model snort in the darkness that surrounded her shimmering world.

'Do nothing,' Mik said. There was a pause. 'Do more nothing that that,' he said, 'do nothing at all. You look too tense.'

She tried to relax. A flash went off and she jumped.

'OK,' Mik said, 'fuck off.'

She smelt of sweat now, for sure. 'You want me to go?' she asked.

No one answered so she climbed out from behind the lights unaided, being sure not to knock any of them over. When she got to the darkness she had to wait a moment for her eyes to clear. When they did she saw Mik standing beside her, holding out a Polaroid. She took the shot from him and held it back in the light. She looked like a prisoner in a line-up, rigid and unsure, as though suddenly impaled by the spotlight.

Her father appeared out of nowhere and took the photo from her.

'You look like a terrified little rabbit trapped in the headlights of an oncoming car, Florrie darling,' he said.

Flora looked across at Mik. He was staring at her.

'I guess that's just about what she is, too, poor innocent little cow,' the other model whispered to the make-up man, who giggled as though she had just made a major joke.

Evangeline looked at the note the bellhop had just given her. Her mind was fuzzy with sleep and painkillers. She tried to think straight but the thoughts she reached out for slipped away just as she grabbed at them. Her grandmother was dead. She knew it the minute she opened the note the boy had given her. The death wasn't a jolt like the others had been. Grandma Klippel was old now, in contrast to all the others who had gone too young. Would she be old when she died? Maybe that was the worst punishment, staying around when all the others had gone on somewhere else.

The boy was asking her if she wanted anything. He had a small pillbox hat on the side of his head, held on with a thin leather chinstrap. She wondered if the strap left a mark on his face all night. She fished in her bag for some cash to give him and then she couldn't think straight enough to count it all out properly. He did it for her and she was grateful to him. What would he think was wrong with her? Maybe that she was drunk or drugged. Perhaps he would report her to the concierge as a guest to keep an eye on.

She phoned Cape Cod. Miss Clayburg sounded sad but not weepy.

'Evangeline? Where are you?' she said in a voice breathy with relief. 'Oh, I've been trying to contact you for weeks and nobody knew where you were.'

Grandma Klippel had died a few days before. If Evangeline hurried out there she could make it just in time for the funeral. Miss Clayburg's relief was so intense Evangeline had no chance to say she couldn't get there. She was shivering when she put down the phone.

The Cape was at its most threatening when she arrived for the funeral. She had no time to go to the house, so she drove straight round to the churchyard in her rented car and ran into the toilets to change into a black suit she had managed to buy in the shop at her hotel. It was a size too big but it looked OK when she stood up straight. Miss Clayburg was waiting for her when she stepped outside.

'The Cape is so beautiful at this time of the year,' were her first words. Her face looked lined and eroded by the winds. Her hair was short, now, cut like a boy's. In a strange way, though, she looked almost beautiful. Grief gave her a sort of pride and dignity that had always been lacking before. She hadn't worn black, just a red knitted coat over a brown crêpe frock. Her eyelashes looked stuck together, as though she had been crying. She had a ladder in her stocking and that made Evangeline sadder than anything else.

She took Evangeline's arm, as though they had been close. 'She'd have been pleased to know you came,' she said, smiling.

The air on the Cape tasted sour: salt again. No wonder Grandma Klippel had never served it at meal-times. The grey skies looked frosted and fringed with mist. The church seemed to be in the loneliest spot on earth, with its crazily leaning headstones and its bow-backed trees that bent still further each time the sandy winds blew up.

Evangeline felt haunted and lonely and her body felt hollowed out inside. Her arm, with Miss Clayburg's hand upon it, felt numb to the touch. The wind whipped around her head and her hair spun. Strange thoughts nuzzled at her head. She imagined she was a child again, and that her whole life was just beginning. She saw herself standing between the gravestones, a small girl of six, stubborn and hurt and lonely as a buzzard.

338

The funeral was a big one. Grandma Klippel had wanted to know few people but many had wanted to be associated with her. There were limousines the full stretch of the road and a crowd of over a hundred and fifty standing waiting as Evangeline walked inside the porch.

Many were family, too — Darius's cousins and their kids — a whole posse of unlikely looking blood relations from the South, and a whole two rows of well-behaved and fussily overdressed grandchildren.

Miss Clayburg settled for a pew seat next to the aisle, more than three rows back from the altar. She wore gloves, Evangeline noticed, and her hands were primly crossed above Grandma Klippel's old leather-bound prayer book. Evangeline wondered whether the woman still painted. She had asked Evangeline to call her by her Christian name but Evangeline, to her shame, had no idea what it was.

When the service was over they walked together in the mottled daylight.

'You know your grandmother left me the house?' Miss Clayburg asked. She sounded hesitant, as though she had no right to it.

'Will you sell it?' Evangeline asked. Her old tutor smiled and the smile made her face look younger again.

'Oh, no,' she said, 'I love it here. I like the solitude. I was the youngest of ten, you see. You can't imagine how good it feels to have time and space of your own. She left all her money to charities, you know,' she added. Evangeline said nothing for a while and Miss Clayburg let out a tiny laugh. 'Money,' she said, 'at a time like this. Who could imagine? But you know what your grandmother was like, she would have wanted everything to be clear right away. You do understand, don't you?'

Evangeline smiled at her. 'She wasn't my grandmother,' she said, 'not really, not by blood. I wouldn't expect anything and I don't need anything. I suppose some of the real family are pretty sore, though.'

She had seen the way they'd looked at her. Families had long memories. She was Thea's girl, the one kind Darius had adopted. Poor Darius, that poor, poor family of his, all dead now, all except Evangeline. Why not her? Evangeline could see the question in their curious eyes: why all the others but not her too? She was the one that had survived. The one that had been rejected.

'Your grandmother spoke about you a lot, Evangeline,' Miss Clayburg was saying.

'I frightened her,' Evangeline said. She hadn't even known it before she said it. Miss Clayburg looked up in surprise.

It began to rain – great stinging needles that pricked the grey marl surface of the sea. They were walking down to the beach and Evangeline could do nothing to stop them. You didn't say no to the bereaved. You listened when they talked and you went where they wanted. If Miss Clayburg wanted a shore-walk straight after the funeral then that had to be fine. She hadn't noticed the rain or, if she had, it didn't bother her. Maybe the soaking was therapeutic for her. Maybe she would have thrown herself into the sea if she hadn't been wearing her best clothes.

Miss Clayburg sat right down on a grassy grey dune, just as though it were summer and they were out for a picnic. Her wide-brimmed hat had lost its shape and hung jokily about her white, salt-dried cheeks. Evangeline pulled off her shoes and took a seat beside her.

The rain had blurred the sky and the sea into one threatening mass that was hemmed with a curling border of white foaming surf and studded with a bleached sun the colour of lemon-rind. Evangeline felt scared, just as though she were alone and a child once again. The sea had nearly killed her.

'You're right, Evangeline,' Miss Clayburg said, 'your grandmother was afraid of you. She was afraid pretty much all of her life, after you came to stay.' She picked up a handful of wet sand and patted and shaped it like a snowball with her gloved hands. 'She loved you too, though,' she added. So that was all right, then.

Evangeline sighed. 'She had such grand expectations for me,' she said. 'I knew I was a disappointment to her. She wanted someone to live up to everything Darius had been and all she got was me. Whatever I've done in my life I've always heard Grandma Klippel's evaluation of it in my head.' She laughed quietly, 'You know I still can't tell a lie – even a small one – without hearing her disapproval in my mind. Do you think she knew how long-term all her teaching would be?'

The sand-ball disintegrated between Miss Clayburg's fingers.

'Evangeline,' she began. She looked even older out there in the unkind light. Her eyes looked nervous. There was a good picture in her face in that light, Evangeline thought. Maybe she should have brought her camera, but then no idiot would go taking snaps during a funeral. She realized all the guests would be back in the rented hall, swilling tea and the special reserve her grandmother had laid down for her own wake. Would they be missed? If they were it would have to be with relief – Darius's unwanted stepdaughter and Mrs Klippel's Bohemian lover.

'Evangeline, I want you to sort some things at the house,' Miss Clayburg was saying. 'There are some papers and bits I think you should go through.' Her hands were shaking now, the sand was falling at an alarming rate. 'Would you mind very much? Would it be too upsetting?'

Evangeline shook her head. 'No.' She didn't know. She couldn't say how upset she would get. How sad could you be over a grandmother when you had too many other wounds already? On the Cape, though, it was like nothing else existed. It was like a time vacuum. She was steeped in the smells and sensations of her childhood and it was hard to imagine that much else had happened since then. The place was salt on the old wounds but a balm for the fresher ones.

'Of course I'll go back with you,' she whispered. The fear inside her hadn't stopped. 'Although it's not really my place . . .'

'There are things you should read,' Miss Clayburg said, sounding stronger now, as though a decision had been made, 'things about your parents. Things you should have been shown a long time ago.' She pressed her hands over her face. She was crying now. The sand would get stuck in her eyes. Evangeline sat with her while she cried but she didn't feel fit to try and comfort her.

Mik had told her to go back and sort things out. He had advised her to discover her past, instead of leaving it buried. Ghosts loomed up out of their graves at her. She didn't want to know – she didn't want to know anything. The pain was almost at an unbearable level. The scars were bad but she had learnt to live with them.

'Maybe it's better I don't though,' she said. Miss Clayburg looked up, her face a sandy mess. Grief was horrible, like raw meat. Evangeline didn't want to see any more of it. There was a shot of silver on the horizon and a low growling that seemed to shake the dunes around them.

'There's a storm brewing,' Miss Clayburg said, standing up, 'we'd better get on back to the house.' She was dusting her skirts and picking things off her gloves. She rearranged her hat as though the brim was not sodden and hanging down and then she looked at Evangeline with her head cocked, waiting.

Evangeline studied the sky. She had no real alternative – either she went back with her old tutor or she just sat out the storm. She stood up and dusted herself off, just as Miss Clayburg had done, and then they ran arm-in-arm along the beach before the lightning could reach them.

37

Mik called Flora in for further test shots and then sat watching while Adam, his assistant, took them. There was a huge, pink-painted cherub on set that she had to pose with. Adam told her it was left over from another shoot Mik had been working on. It was polystyrene but it looked like painted stone.

Adam was talkative and encouraging and good with all the lights. He worked quickly while Mik watched, setting up flats and great walls of diffused light to either side of her. He took readings and he smiled at her as he corrected the settings.

Mik was the coldest man Flora had ever met. His stare made her pale flesh turn to goosebumps. He didn't smile and he rarely spoke. People had been nice to Flora all her life – she was that type of girl. Mik's indifference made her shiver, like walking past the fridge on a hot day when the door is open.

Because he didn't show his thoughts she imagined he was thinking the worst. Every kind of self-criticism flowed through her mind. She was too fat, she was too ugly, she was too stupid. In blind panic she tried to look like someone else, pulling faces that she had never pulled before and poses she had never used. Adam stopped shooting.

'What's wrong?' he said. He stepped into her pool of light, so that she could see him. He was quite young and sounded like one of her brother's friends. Adam had a nice face, open and friendly. He was shorter than Mik but not short. Tanned, with a fresh look about him, as though he played sports. Brown hair, wavy, not curled. He looked out of place in the studio. Too public school, too normal.

'Nothing,' she said quickly. Everything, in fact, was wrong, but she was too afraid to tell him. Her stomach growled with hunger and she blushed at the noise.

'You looked uncomfortable,' Adam said.

Flora smiled. 'I'm fine.'

'Relax.' It was Mik's voice, from somewhere beyond the shadows. Why was it so hot? She could feel herself sweating. The spotlights blinded her and she couldn't stop squinting.

She flapped her long arms and giggled. She wanted to cry but her face was thick with make-up. She looked about twenty. She felt humiliated. Why had she ever thought she could do this job? Adam went back behind the camera again and she leant against the cherub, taking care not to topple it. It was leaning but not leaning; self-supported. It made all her muscles ache.

'Tell me about your horse,' Adam had been chatting to her before the shoot. Her face softened soppily. The flash went off. 'Better,' Adam said.

She spoke for a bit and he took another shot. Some blood returned to her feet and hands and her face felt normal again. Adam cracked a joke and she laughed. Another shot. Each one went off with a soft popping sound and an arc of light that made her blink.

'Laugh, don't giggle.' Was that Adam or Mik? The lights felt warm on her bare back. She was wearing a dress she liked, even though it was too old for her.

'Lie on the floor.' She lay down, feeling strange. It smelt of dust. More flashes. She stretched like a cat. Phones in the distance were ringing incessantly. The soles of her feet were dirty. She sat up at once, licking a finger and wiping the dirt off. She didn't see Mik take the camera from Adam's hands. A volley of flashes – she looked up, startled, into more shots. She shielded her eyes from the lights, her foot still clasped in her hand. He didn't stop now. She clambered onto all fours.

'Stop!' Her voice sounded little. Mik continued to shoot. Her dress had fallen off at the shoulder, just the strap, but she clutched the bodice to her in fright.

'Stop shooting!' She must look a mess. Nobody answered her, though, just the relentless flash of the lights, like a Photo-Me booth. She'd had shots done for a passport the year before and the camera had worked when she wasn't ready, just like now. She'd looked crap in the pictures – all the girls had laughed at them. She didn't want that happening today. She wanted to look good – she wanted these to be special.

'Stop taking my picture, please!'

She'd shouted – frightened herself into the bargain, actually. The flashing stopped. Mik walked onto the set, leaving footprints. As she looked up from the floor he appeared huge to her.

'You want to stop?' he asked. She could smell him there – some sort of strange, spicy cologne she'd never smelt before. She'd shouted. Shouting was rude. He held out his large hand. 'Let me help you up.' His hand was warm against her cold one. Her fingers had turned blue with fear. Her legs were mottled red and white. There were veins on her arms she hadn't known she'd possessed before. Her body looked like a diagram in the biology department.

'That was OK,' Mik said. His eyes were dead – deader than anything she'd ever seen before. Her hand was still held in his. He dropped it suddenly and she shuddered. His eyes transfixed her. They were like the eyes of Jesus in the painting of the Resurrection at church. Sad, unfathomable eyes, like a bottomless lake. She fell in love with Mik at that moment. There was no helping it. It just happened.

She felt she could help him with her love. She thought she could make his eyes come to life if she cared about him enough. The thought made her breathless, like asthma.

345

He'd told her what she'd done was OK and so she felt that next time she could do better.

'Do more with Adam,' he said. She smiled at the boy, she was warmer now. She could do anything.

'Can I try some without the cherub?' she asked.

Adam shrugged, so she pushed it away. They worked for the rest of the afternoon and it was only after they'd finished that she realized Mik was gone.

Mik spoke quietly into his portable. 'Well? What do they think?'

The clients were sitting around the computer screen in an office three miles away. Flora's shots came up one after another, for their approval. The office was dark and the clients were silent.

'Is she OK for the account?' Mik asked.

There was silence from the other end. The clients carried on looking.

'How would she be with a fringe?' someone asked.

Mik sighed. 'Try her with a fringe,' he told Adam. Adam worked quietly on the computer for a few moments and a fringe appeared on Flora's forehead.

'She looks a little too young,' another voice suggested.

'Adam, paint a few wrinkles in, will you?' Mik said, exasperated.

'Jesus, Mik, give us a minute, will you?' one of the ad men shouted down the phone. 'Keep the shots going, with a fringe in each one. We'll call you back when we've decided.'

Mik paced by the screen while Adam replaced each shot one at a time. After a long pause the phone rang again.

'We'll use her,' the ad man said. Mik almost smiled with relief.

Mik took Flora's shots to the biggest, state-of-the-art model agency in London, but then he got pissed off when they kept him waiting fifteen minutes and strolled into the

346

offices of a smaller establishment instead. The agency was new, but good. The woman who ran it had been a supermodel herself only two seasons before and she'd poached a handful of bookers from some of the more established perches. Mik knew the word was that she'd soon be selling out to a top American agency and that meant more money and better links with the US.

'This girl's good – she needs an agency,' he told the booker, a skinny black girl called Diaz. 'I want two per cent finder's fee,' he added.

Diaz stared at the shots and then she looked at Mik. 'She is good,' she agreed. The shots were a haunting combination of rough camera techniques and a beautiful, ethereal model. 'Any without make-up?' she asked.

Mik threw a Polaroid across the desk. The girl was staring straight into the camera, with no make-up or posing. She had wild features, startled eyes, a funny nose, a wide slash of a mouth.

'When can she come in?' Diaz asked.

Mik scooped the shots up and threw them into a satchel on his shoulder. He seemed to be in a hurry. 'Either you want her or you don't,' he said, 'I can take her to Elite, only you happened to be on my way.'

Was it his accent or his attitude that made him sound so rude, Diaz wondered. Either way, she could see why all the girls were after him. The guy was a prize shit, but good-looking with it. She suddenly felt sorry for the kid he was trying to promote.

'Get her to call me,' she said, firmly. Mik might be hot but she took crap from no one, not even the clients. She could feel Mik's glower on her back as she swung around in her chair to answer a ringing phone.

Flora arrived at the agency the following day, looking awkward and nervous and almost as good as she had in the shots. Mik phoned ten minutes after she'd left to say he wanted her on an exclusive for six months. Diaz tried to negotiate upwards, sideways – any way but down, but that was the way she could feel the deal going if she didn't agree with Mik's first offer. In the end she held what ground she had and smoothed out a few smaller details in their favour.

When she put down the phone she was sweating as though she'd just done two rounds with him. She smiled and looked in the mirror. Mik Veronsky was hard but she could be harder. There was a full-length poster of Michael Bolton on the agency wall, and a spud-gun, in case of emergencies. Diaz picked up the gun and loaded it slowly before landing a shot right in the crotch.

'Bullseye!' she shouted. The other bookers looked up and blew raspberries into the air.

'Shafted?' another booker called. 'Stitched up like a kipper by young Mik-Mak there?'

'No fucking way,' Diaz told him with a smirk, but she knew inside her head that it had been a close-run thing.

Evangeline dragged her feet across the shingle to get the mud off before entering her grandmother's house. Only it wasn't her grandmother's place any more – it was Miss Clayburg's.

It looked just the same as it always had, only older and maybe a little smaller, although it was still huge. Evangeline wondered what one small woman would do alone with so many rooms. There was a shudder as she entered the dark hall: polished wood, flowers. No flowers visible, but the room was still haunted by the perfume from all the wreaths that must have been delivered that morning. There were leaves, still, on the floor. Miss Clayburg kicked at a few of them, embarrassed by the mess.

'Evan will be here by tomorrow,' she said. 'His mother died, you know.'

Poor Evan. Evangeline wondered how he was doing, still wheezing over his dusting and still chasing planes along the beach.

'Would you like tea?' Miss Clayburg asked, and then rushed off without waiting for an answer.

348

Evangeline pulled off her jacket and hung it over a chairback to dry. There were no fires in the place and most of the shutters were closed, out of respect. The air felt warm and damp. She stared across into her grandmother's parlour and saw that the photograph was still there on the mantelpiece, the picture of Thea and Darius. She walked across the hall, her shoes clicking on the floor.

She felt strange, entering the room without her grandmother's permission. There was a bowl of fresh anemones standing next to the frame. Miss Clayburg would keep the job on, then. Keeper of the dead. Respecter of all the lost souls. Fresh flowers in the bowl and a daily dusting for the picture frame. She went to lift it and started. Alongside it was another frame with a picture of her grandmother in it; Grandma Klippel on her wedding day. It was a shot Evangeline had never seen before. She picked it up instead, and still had it in her hand when Miss Clayburg returned with the tea.

Her eyes became rheumy at the sight of it. 'She made a lovely bride, don't you think?' she asked Evangeline. 'I found the picture in your grandmother's room. There're other things up there – memories I thought should be kept in the family. There are locked cases, too. I imagine if your grandmother had wanted me to see inside them she would have opened them to me in her lifetime. Here,' she fished in her pocket and brought out a fistful of small silver keys, all joined by thin string and with small markers stuck to the top of each key.

'I thought you might stay the night,' Miss Clayburg said. Evangeline looked at the keys in her hand. Secrets: the keys would unlock secrets. Don't you want to know? she asked herself. Aren't you just plain curious? Curious, yes, but of what? Her grandmother would have no answer for the sort of questions she wanted answering. The cases would be full of legal documents and papers, she was sure of it. Miss Clayburg was just being over fussy. Grandma Klippel was

349

an honest woman, a church-goer. Her life held tragedy, yes, but no secrets.

'I'm booked into a hotel –' Evangeline began.

Miss Clayburg just stared at her with hurt in her eyes. 'I got your old room ready, Evangeline,' she said.

Evangeline smiled. 'Thanks.' She wanted to be away from there. Mik had been wrong, there was no point in going back unless you wanted to be battered with all the memories. She felt them pressing in on her, stopping her breathing. The noise of the sea still scared her. Foghorns, calling out like the drowned dead. She remembered the waiting.

She walked into her old room and saw herself at the window, a small girl with paint on her clothes, waiting each night for the sound of her parents' return.

She sat on the narrow bed and stared at the keys. They were luggage keys, small and silver and unimportant-looking. She tried to read the labels, though the print was small and the light not good. An insect buzzed against the painted window-blind, making her start. Some of the labels had years written on them. A couple had things like 'tax' and 'electric'. So why did they scare her so much?

She pushed her feet into slippers and walked up to the landing outside her grandmother's rooms. Would Miss Clayburg be sleeping there still? There was no light on, though. She tried one door and jumped when it opened. The smell of her grandmother's scent was sudden and shocking. The room was full of it – maybe Miss Clayburg had been spraying it to stifle the smell of death.

'Grandma?' The impression was so strong she almost called out for permission to enter. She imagined the old lady stretched out on the bed, as she had been during the migraines. It seemed wrong to go inside without her say-so. Like grave-robbing. The room was empty.

The floorboards creaked as she walked on them. She started out on tiptoe but then told herself that was stupid. Someone had hung a shawl over the dressing-table mirror as a mark of respect. She pushed the shawl back and sat down on the padded stool.

There was a small light on the dressing-table and she switched it on. Before her lay all the powders and perfumes that went to create her grandmother when she was alive. The stuff was old-fashioned and wonderful, glorious round cardboard tubs full of pale face-powder that created its own cloud as the lid was pulled off, sixteen lipsticks, all the same favourite shade, some utensils for curling eyelashes and creams to ward off the effects of the sea and the sand on her face.

Evangeline buried her face in the powder and smiled. Oh sweet Jesus, it was as though the old lady were in the room with her. She remembered all the things that were good about her – her honesty and her integrity. She had tried to love Evangeline and in all probability failed, but that wasn't solely down to her because she had been grieving too.

Had she been a lovable child? Evangeline closed her eyes and thought back: stressed, irritable, impatient, bewildered. An odd kid, bruised, like fruit. She fingered a row of creamy pearls that hung from a cut-glass candlestick on the table. No other jewellery was laid out. Maybe the pearls had been a present for her grandmother's wedding. The pearls rattled against the glass. There were two dried flowers in the hole where the candle should have been. Evangeline smiled.

She got up from the stool and approached a wall of mahogany wardrobes. When she opened the first door the smell of camphor escaped, making her cough. The rail was crammed with clothes – suits, dresses – few of which she had seen her grandmother wear. Some were still in the original bags, with price tickets still hanging.

One of the cupboards was half empty. Wooden hangers rattled like teeth as she pulled the door back. There were only half a dozen outfits there, three men's suits and some women's dresses. The clothes had a familiar look to them.

She pulled one of the frocks out and held it against herself: too small. Too small for her and too small for her grandmother. She pulled the neck down and read, Thea Klippel. There was a hand-made label in the back of the neck. The dress had belonged to her mother. She even recognized the label and the black, marker-pen writing, because she had had labels just like it in her own clothes when she was a kid. Thea had a passion for them; hats, scarves, shoes and baby clothes all had the same identifying tags stitched inside them somewhere.

She pressed the frock against her face, praying for a trace of the smell of her mother, but there was none – just the stench of the mothballs that rattled like marbles in the pockets. She had never known her grandmother had these things. Darius's suits and her mother's dresses. How long had they hung there? When had the old lady had them collected from Boston?

Some of them looked rumpled, as though they'd been worn recently. She punched a hand into the pocket of a pair of trousers and there was one of Darius's handkerchiefs and a handful of small change. She checked the other pocket. There was a small toy, a cheap plastic thing, the sort that came free with cereal packets. The toy had to have been hers. He'd picked it up for her. It was a small red clown with swivelling eyes. She flicked through her memory for more of the good times, but so little came – so much was forgotten. She'd thought she was loved, but she'd been wrong. All that six-year-old arrogance and confidence, assuming she had parents who loved her and who would be there for her. The best fighter in the school with a mean streak a mile long. The knowledge that she could do anything – anything she chose to. How did you get all that back once it was gone?

She closed the wardrobe door. There was no point in wishing. They had chosen not to take her with them.

Evangeline knew that the cases Miss Clayburg had spoken of would be in the dressing room, to the right of the bedroom. She picked up the bundle of keys and stepped through the door.

The room smelt of wood and air freshener. Miss Clayburg must have been cleaning up already. She'd put bowls of pot pourri in all the rooms that had been empty and gone spraying herbal stuff around too, just in case. The room was dark. Evangeline pulled back the shutters and the moonlight flooded in. She didn't want to switch on the lights because she still felt like an intruder, somehow.

Miss Clayburg had placed the cases out in a neat row and she must have dusted them off, too, because there was a smell of beeswax when Evangeline got closer. She fingered the top of the first one. The surface was raised and bumpy. Crocodile skin. She pulled a face and took her finger off. There were luggage labels on each one that corresponded to the labels on each of the small keys. With a sigh she began to unlock them and read through the papers that were stashed neatly away inside.

Flora walked straight into success like a hedgehog hit by a speeding car. Her very first casting was a big one – there was no apprenticeship once she was on the agency books. It was chocolate ice-cream whirls: the company had a new campaign every two years and the girl they used became a face overnight. She turned up at the agency prior to the audition and they put her in something short and tight that made her legs look a mile long and her face as red as a number nine bus. She kept trying to pull it down and they kept trying to stop her.

She had matching shoes and a short leather bolero. She thought she looked like a tart but they told her it was all by Versace and therefore OK. They kept her face clean of make-up but got someone in to trim her hair and tidy her eyebrows. She only had Mik's photos to take with her but they put them into an agency book and said they'd be fine because his name was like a passport anyway.

She was so nervous that she almost bottled the audition.

When her name was called she had Polaroids taken and was asked back for a second casting the following week. Then she went and threw up in the loo because she thought her stomach looked big in the dress. She was so weak afterwards she had to go home by taxi, even though she had no cash to pay the fare.

Six days later she was told she had the job. Mik was in there too – he had to be, he'd got an exclusive on her. The agency were ecstatic. Flora was too busy being sick to care. The other models she had seen had all looked so thin. By making herself sick she lost four pounds in as many days. Then she felt in a position to celebrate.

Mik told her to insist he did her shots for most of the broadsheets and she was happy about that because she was scared of working with other photographers. It was Mik who had discovered her. It was Mik she was besotted with. He took her around London, to all the top clubs and restaurants, and the paparazzi were there to photograph them when they emerged at the end of the evening. Then Mik would make sure she was put in a cab for the long drive home. He never touched her and he never kissed her. She wished he would. She wondered what was so wrong with her.

She started taking the pill, just in case. Her agency sent her to a private GP because she was getting too thin and the GP gave her tranquillizers because he said she was hyperactive. She enjoyed the tranquillizers because they made her less afraid when she went out on jobs and castings. She had her hair dyed jet black for a magazine feature and her navel pierced for a one-off spot in a Paris show. She liked the way she looked, now. She looked great.

The credit card clients were still unsure at first but Mik blew up shots of Flora to life-size and took them along for a presentation and they fell for her at once when they saw how she could look. They liked her for her youth and for her innocence. Even with black hair she still had a very

English freshness about her. The new campaign went under way immediately.

For the launch the press were flown around the world to take tea in each of the six locations the shots would be done. It was a public relations coup – nobody missed a single flight, there were no delays at airports and not one piece of baggage went missing. They tasted the last cuppa in Paris and came back to London via the Channel Tunnel. Nobody got raging drunk and no fights broke out mid-journey. Everyone emerged with a smile on their face, despite being paralysed with jet-lag.

The only sour note came when Mik was interviewed by someone from GQ and told them he would be doing the job with Evangeline. Baz got hold of the journalist and refused to let him have the story unless he dropped all references to Evangeline and used Mik's photo on the magazine cover. Apart from that one hairy moment, though, Baz considered the whole thing an unqualified success. The interest in Mik and Flora was becoming manic. Baz was good at his job and once the pack had been unleashed there was no getting them back into their cages.

Adam hung around Flora a lot in the studio, looking after her and spoiling her when he could. Mik was happy with that – they made a nice pair.

Things were going well. Mik should have been happy, but he wasn't. He still thought about Evangeline. She hadn't been in contact – not even to slag him off. He knew she would have been angry and thought she might have screamed at him or something but he hadn't expected this: nothing. No word at all. He'd thought she was a fighter. He didn't understand.

38

The first bundle of papers were legal documents, confusing with all the jargon and nothing to do with Evangeline, as far as she could see. Her grandmother's husband must have had shares in some ancient companies. The share certificates were so elaborately decorated they should have been framed and sold in a craftshop.

Evangeline pulled sheath after sheath out onto the floor. Solicitors could be paid to go through them in detail. Most of them looked too old to be worth bothering with. Perhaps Miss Clayburg could make a bonfire of them, out on the beach.

The third case she opened rattled as she picked it up, which meant it could not be crammed with old papers like the others. She pulled the lid back carefully. The insides smelt musty, like rotten apples. She was looking at what appeared to be mementoes. She got the same buzzing in her ears as she had had in the newspaper offices. Her hands started to shake.

There was a small parcel of faded tissue, like a nest. She pulled the top layer back gingerly. There were baby shoes in there. She picked them up carefully, barely breathing, as though they were made of cobwebs. They had to be Lincoln's. They were so tiny she could just get her fingers inside them, yet they were made of cream suede, soft and perfect in every tiny detail.

Tears began to swell up in her eyes. She tried to speak his name but her voice cracked. How long had her grandmother had these? Maybe they had come with the clothes in the closet. She held them up closer. They looked new.

'Lincoln!' She could whisper his name now. Memories engulfed her – real or imaginary, she didn't know. She kissed the little shoes and pressed them against her cheek before placing them back in the tissue.

Beneath them was an album of photos. She tried to turn the pages but it hurt too much already. They would be smiling. They would be there as a family, perfect and happy and alive. She wiped tears off her face with the back of her hand. She couldn't stand the photos – not yet, not now. She pushed the album to one side and dug deeper.

There was an old cigar box. Inside were a man's things: a school tie-pin; gold cufflinks with initials; a small trophy for sporting achievements; a shot of a grinning boy, cut out of a newspaper, yellow and faded. She smoothed the shot flat on the top of the case. It was Darius, she recognized him by his eyes. She smiled because he looked so cute yet so wicked. Darius and his things. She tried to get the scent of them but it had faded long ago, like the newsprint. She replaced the precious objects in the box along with the photograph and closed the lid.

She found a cuttings book and opened it. The clippings had been torn out clumsily and stuck in place just as badly. Her grandmother must have compiled them herself and each page must have hurt more than the last. The cuttings were reports of her parents' deaths. Some of them she had already seen, on the computer. There were shots of the house and copies of the same shots of Darius and Thea. One paper even had a photo of Evangeline, taken from the school year-book. Bug-eyed and buck-toothed, her shot stood out in painful contrast against the beauty of her parents and half-brother.

Survivor – Evangeline Rebecca Klippel, aged six, the caption read. She looked startled in the shot, and her hair was wild. Why did they go without her? Maybe the shot said everything that needed saying. She was the cuckoo in the nest; plain, lacking in talent. Did she really think all those years as a photographer could make up for that? Had she really thought her parents would forgive her, just because she took a few snaps?

Forgive her for what, though? It was what she needed to know, it was why she was searching through her grandmother's papers. What had she done to make them do this to her?

She read through the reports quickly but discovered nothing new. Then she stopped: her grandmother had known, then. To collect these cuttings she must have known all along. It wasn't possible that she had lied to her – yet she had told Evangeline that she had only discovered the truth later on.

'Shit!' She was confused. She rubbed her forehead with her fingers. Lies. Her grandmother never told lies. Maybe they weren't her cuttings. But they had to be – nobody else ever came up here. Her eyes were too blurred with tears to read straight. So many lies, then. Her tears were wetting the cuttings.

She sat on her heels and tried to think logically but it was like unravelling knots. Nothing came right. Exactly how long would her grandmother have known for? From the beginning? Had she known when she came to Boston to collect Evangeline that her son and his wife had killed themselves and taken their baby along with them? She had known they lay inside that house with shotgun cartridges in their heads.

'How could she have told me?' Evangeline spoke out loud now. 'I was six years old – what could she have said?' She had been trying to shield a small girl. She had even moved her to a smaller school to keep her away from gossips. She'd done things for the best.

The lies, though. Grandma Klippel had brought her up not to lie – ever. All that time, then; all that time she had been keeping such terrible secrets. She replaced the cuttings book. An envelope fell from the back as she did so.

She picked the thing up absent-mindedly. It was a large envelope of creamy vellum, unstuck at the top and crinkled along the edge, as though it had been steamed some time, maybe years ago. Evangeline turned it in her hand. The writing on the front was familiar: 'TO MY DAUGHTER EVANGELINE'. It was Thea's writing, her mother's spidery scrawl, printed out to make it easy to read. It was as though her mother had spoken out loud to her. She felt her heart stop.

There was one sheet inside. She tried to read it but became confused. What was she reading? The moon had gone behind a cloud. She stood up and switched on the bedside light, no longer afraid of the intrusion.

'TO MY DAUGHTER EVANGELINE' her mother had written to her. When? She tried to hold the paper steady but her hands were shaking too much to see. She closed her eyes to calm her breathing. Then she looked again:

> My darling Evangeline,
>   Please, please forgive your mummy for all the crying she has made you do. Try to understand that your daddy and I had to do what we have done and please, darling, know that we both love you very, very much.

Evangeline paused. She couldn't breathe. Her grief and her sadness were like two choking hands around her throat. She went back to the note.

> I must try to explain things to you, darling, even though I know you will find it difficult to understand. You know Darius, your daddy, to be a great artist, but the truth is he has done no proper work for many years. Talent is a strange thing, Evangeline. It can be affected by confidence and that is what happened to your daddy. He was so successful early on that people came to expect great things from him – so great that he became afraid he could never live up to

his own reputation and other people's expectations of him. He paid a student — a young man from Baltimore — to do his work for him. Nobody knew, darling, and at first we thought it would be just for one exhibition, and that the talent would come back after that. Unfortunately the deception went on longer — too long — and the lie became something we could no longer live with.

We were naïve, Evangeline. The young student asked for more and more money and threatened to expose Darius if we did not give it to him. The money has run out now, darling. We have nothing left, nothing to leave to you, and that thought breaks my heart.

We are leaving you our reputation, though. This way the secret is kept, for we do not think the student is a bad enough man to start talking once we are dead. I believe he has enough goodness in him, Evangeline, so the name of your family will stand you in good stead for the rest of your life.

Forgive us for forsaking you, darling, but we have no choice. Lincoln is too small to know what is happening, but we love you too much to take you with us. We have faith in you to do good things, Evangeline, and we know you will be cared for. Please understand us if you can, but we are cowards and too weak to bear what would happen if our secret got out. We pray you will not hate us for what we have done.

You are a clever and strong girl, Evangeline, and knowing that makes us happy. Go on being clever and strong and go on knowing we loved you more than we could ever say.

God bless you, Evangeline. Forgive us, please.

It was signed by both Thea and Darius.

It takes a long time to change a lifetime of thoughts and emotions. This letter had been written by Thea to be read by her. Grandma Klippel had kept it from her, and it had lain there all these years. She wept profusely, now, great racking sobs that shook her entire body.

Her parents had loved her too much to take her with them. They were not the golden couple her grandmother had led her to believe, they were human, just like anyone else. Grandma Klippel had known of her son's deception all along and still allowed Evangeline to feel the stinging failure when she couldn't live up to his name. She had known, but she had not stopped any of it.

Thea had asked *her* to forgive *them*. Evangeline took the letter and walked with it through the house. Miss Clayburg was in the parlour, sitting staring at her grandmother's framed photograph in the half-light. There was a glow from a cigarette in the ashtray by her arm. Evangeline had never seen her smoke before.

'How much of this did you know?' she asked. The tutor did not look up.

'I loved her,' she whispered. Evangeline walked nearer. The whole house seemed different. The parlour wasn't special any more, it was just a room, like any other in the house. She no longer felt she had to tiptoe everywhere. She wanted to open up all the windows and let her grandmother's ghost out of the place, to fly down to hell.

She held out the letter. 'Did you know about this?' she asked.

Miss Clayburg nodded. 'She told me most of it just before she died. I read the rest while I was going through her things. She was wrong, Evangeline, but she loved her son fiercely and she couldn't bear the shame if his secret ever leaked out. She couldn't trust you to keep it, you see. You weren't blood. Those things were important to her. Her family always came first.'

She lifted the cigarette to her lips and took a heavy drag. 'She paid the student off, you know,' she said, 'once she read the letter she tracked him down and paid him to keep silent. He died soon after, in a rail crash in China. I suppose it was some kind of retribution for all the damage he had caused. I know she wished him dead enough times. Maybe wishing can work. If it does she'll be coming back through that door any day now.' She broke down then, covering her face with her hands as she had done on the beach.

'Why didn't she give me my mother's letter?' Evangeline asked. 'Why did she tell so many lies?'

Miss Clayburg looked up. 'I told you, Evangeline,' she said, 'your grandmother felt her first duty was to her son. His name had to be saved, whatever. He was a great artist to her and must always remain so to the public. Her pride was the thing, Evangeline. She didn't mean to be cruel. She thought you were too young for it to matter.'

Evangeline crouched down in front of her. 'She made me try to be as good as him!' she said. 'I thought they didn't love me! I thought I'd done something wrong!'

'Your grandmother was good to you, Evangeline,' Miss Clayburg said. 'She took you in and she did her best for you. She couldn't stand to let you know the truth. It was hiding things that made her so ill. She was terrified you'd find out. She didn't deserve to live with that sort of fear, Evangeline. Try to understand her, she was a good woman.'

Evangeline stared at Miss Clayburg. It was as though there was a mile of empty air between them. Arguing was pointless. She wanted to kill the woman for her blind loyalty and lack of understanding. She no longer felt sorry for her, alone in that haunted mansion. Let her live there with all the mad, scheming ghosts. Let her listen to the sea all night and watch poor Evan polishing things all day long. Surely the most pathetic of the spirits there would be the little six-year-old kid, who sat in the top bedroom by the window, watching for her dead parents.

'I can't stay here any longer,' Evangeline said. She went to her room and pulled on her coat. The door to her grandmother's room was still open. Should she take the case with her? Lincoln's shoes were in there, alongside

Darius's things. She still had her mother's letter in her hand. She walked quietly into the room and replaced the letter in the cuttings book, where she had found it. Then she closed the case carefully and locked it before leaving it there. She couldn't take any of those things, they had been there too long. It would have been like robbing a grave.

She was crying as she left the house. The dawn was breaking and the sky was alight with ribbons of scarlet. She wondered if the small plane still flew over, and then she heard its engine. She waited on the sands as it passed overhead. Evan had thought his father was the pilot. Did he still think so? Was he happier, believing that lie? She held her hair down in the wind and the pilot waved at her.

Two gulls fought in the sky, over a piece of dead meat. Had Nico known, too? Her own father, her father by blood – the liquid Grandma Klippel had cared so much for, the fluid she had thought it worth ruining a child's life over.

She stared back at the old house. It didn't look so awfully menacing now. The wind dried the tears on her face and she almost started laughing instead. Grandma Klippel, with her rules about how life should be led. The many ways she had tried to please the old lady before she'd finally given up and gone off with Nico. All those tiny, tortuous little drawings and that prissy, pained look on Miss Clayburg's face when she studied them. Shit! Too many illusions – she couldn't bear to be around them any more.

She tore off her coat and threw it out to the winds. Then she ripped her shoes off her feet and left them standing in the middle of the dunes. They looked quaint, all alone there. She realized they might think she'd killed herself if she left them, but she didn't give a toss.

Darius and Thea: just human, after all. Darius so God-damned permeated with his mother's good words and high ideals that he preferred to kill himself and his family rather than face a life of shame. Shit! The concept was too, too

363

stupid. Some geek rips you off and you give him all your money and then you kill yourselves, into the bargain. What would have been so wrong in being poor? How long would people have been bothered that he'd lost his nerve for painting and got some creep to do it instead?

She punched the air with her fist. 'Jesus, Darius!' she shouted. 'Was that all it was over? All dead because you couldn't stand a little helping of public shame and humiliation? I loved you – didn't that count for anything?'

She tried to remember; maybe he had been driven mad by it all. Maybe something had cracked from the strain of the secret. She could only ever remember him happy, though. Darius, Thea, Lincoln and Patrick, all playing together on the lawn in the sun. She could add her name to that group, now. She wasn't excluded. They had wanted her to live. It wasn't her fault, after all.

She started off up the beach. When she got to the phone box she'd make a call to see if she could hire a car. She had to get out of there. She couldn't stand the place a moment longer.

She phoned Stuart from the phone box, while she was waiting for the car. He sounded surprised to hear from her, and then relieved to hear that she was sobbing from joy, not grief.

'All those lies for all those years, Stuart,' she sobbed, nearly incoherent. She had to ring him, she wanted to hear his voice. She needed his strength and his sanity, even if it was over the telephone line.

'Where will you go now?' he asked, when she was finished. She paused. She couldn't go back to him, not after all she'd done to him.

'Boston,' she said, quietly, 'I need to go back to the house I lived in as a kid. I could never stand it before, Stuart. I want to see it now.'

He was quiet. 'I hope you find what you want,' he said. He sounded concerned, not bitter. She wanted to say more, but she hung up instead.

39

There was little evidence of her parents left in the house. The place had been spruced up: the paintwork retouched and the lawns manicured, and there was a chain fence flanking the sides of the long drive as well as an angry black guard-dog tied, barking, to the very spot outside where Patrick's old kennel had been.

Evangeline drove slowly up to the front door before switching off the engine of the rented car and sitting, hunched over the wheel, staring for a while. The place was owned by a TV actor now. He had a regular spot in a series and used the house only when he was in between episodes. He was not there now. He was famously married to a much younger actress but allowed his ex-wife the run of the place when she was in New York. It was the ex-wife Evangeline had made the appointment with. She'd told her she wanted to do some shots for a feature on New England architecture.

The woman answered the door in full make-up and a kaftan and a small white dog padded out from between her feet. She looked pleasantly drunk and was happy to give Evangeline the run of the whole place. Evangeline walked about, taking shots. There were things she had remembered and things she'd forgotten until she saw them again. Everywhere was redecorated, of course, but when she half closed her eyes there was a lot that still looked familiar. The nursery was a box-room now. Lincoln had smelt so good. She'd thought they could grow up together, with her teaching him all the things a kid around there needed to know. Her own room was still a kid's room. She remembered the actor had two young girls of his own. She looked out of the window at the tree. There was some old rope tied to it, for swinging on. She photographed it all, in case she forgot any of it again.

The ex-wife lurched back in. 'You know this place used to be owned by a painter?' she asked.

Evangeline smiled. 'Really?'

'Yeah,' the woman said, 'quite well known in the right circles, too, by all accounts. Come see.' She led Evangeline up into the master bedroom suite. The bed was in a different place to where it had been when her parents had slept there. It didn't hurt so much, then. She smiled at the woman again.

'Look,' the woman said. She gestured towards two large paintings on the wall above the bed. 'He did these,' she said. 'We bought them when we bought the house, they were the only two we liked – the rest were too abstract. These are nice, though.'

Evangeline looked up at them. The one on the right was of her mother: beautiful, half naked and laughing, she sat upon the bed that used to be there, her youngest child held between her arms. The face held half-memories for Evangeline. It filled in the blurs better than the photo on Grandma Klippel's mantelpiece, but it wasn't quite the same face she'd been trying to remember for all those years. It was right, though – it had to be. Darius had painted it.

The other painting was of a small, skinny-legged girl standing alone in a field of burnt corn-stubble. The girl's hair was the same colour as the burnt corn and it flew about everywhere, as though a wind was up. Evangeline looked closer. She didn't remember Darius doing it. Had he made her sit for him? Had she minded keeping still for all that time, or had she fidgeted and complained as she usually did?

Looking at the painting filled her with hope. She knew he'd loved her, now – she could tell from the picture. She

366

wiped her eye dry with the sleeve of her jacket. Then she wondered, had Darius painted these, or the student? Nothing was as it seemed any more. Maybe they had been painted by a total stranger.

'Would you mind if I photographed these, too?' she asked the ex-wife.

'Go ahead,' the woman said. She sat down heavily on the bed. 'He killed his entire family, you know,' she said. 'Shot them through the head – the old woman up the street told me. Suicide pact, apparently. Poor, demented souls, eh? Some religious sect, in all probability. I never told the kids, you know, because I'm sure that it would spook them. What a crazy family, eh? The whole lot of them.' She shook her head slowly, tutting.

Evangeline packed her camera away. 'I guess I'm about through, thank you,' she said. The woman looked disappointed. She saw Evangeline to the door. 'Come back whenever you want,' she said.

Evangeline didn't bother to wave.

40

Evangeline stayed a couple more nights in Boston. She walked about the place, relishing the memories and the feeling of solitude. She went back to her old school and watched the kids leaving at the end of the day. She had been loved, not abandoned. The anger she felt at her grandmother for not showing her her mother's letter slowly turned into a new kind of grief for her parents and a growing confidence in herself and her abilities. Things looked new to her: the lost child inside her became slowly exorcized and she felt it leave with wonder and relief.

She ate well and she slept through the night, untroubled by nightmares. She caught up the threads of her life for the first time and was able to knit them into some form of shape. She was talented and she was successful, but she had never fought. All she had wanted in her life had been to prove herself worthy of her parents. And all that time there had been that letter lying there begging her forgiveness for their weakness and their shame.

She had wanted Mik, too, but he had turned out to be valueless, like Grandma Klippel's platitudes. And all that long time Stuart had been waiting for her.

She saw herself at the school gates, with the others, a runty-looking kid with bruised legs and cunning eyes — and this time the eyes didn't grow wider and wider with fear because this time she saw Thea, speeding down the driveway, leaping from the car even before the dust had settled, and throwing out her arms as she apologized for being late. Mother and daughter were held in an embrace that never happened. Evangeline photographed the scene in her mind and locked it away in her memory.

An elderly woman came puffing through the school gates as she sat on the bonnet of the hired car. The woman shielded her eyes from the glare of the sun as she stared. The white light lit her round glasses so they gleamed. Her legs were fat and her feet overflowed her shoes.

'Are you missing a child?' she yelled out. She walked a few steps further, her arms swinging with the effort. 'Did you fail to collect?' she asked. She was within range now. She stopped abruptly and her hand flew to her mouth in shock.

'Oh my!' Her fat legs held her aloft as she started to sway.

Evangeline held her camera up. 'I'm just here taking pictures, if that's OK,' she asked. The woman's face had turned from raspberry to ash.

'Miss Starmount?' Evangeline asked. 'Miss Starmount, is that you?' She had no idea how she had remembered her old teacher. She had only been six, but six felt like twenty-six when things happened as they had on that day. The teacher's face was one of the photographs her memory had taken and she had not been wrong. Older and wider, it was still the same face.

'Oh my!' Miss Starmount appeared to be about to run. She looked longingly back at the school behind her and when she turned again her face was distorted by anguish.

'I'm sorry . . .' Evangeline began, 'I didn't mean to frighten you, only I used to be a student here a long time ago. You were my teacher . . .'

The woman raised her hand again. Some of the blood returned to her face. 'Dear God, I thought you were a ghost,' she said. She stepped closer again. 'Dear God, I thought you were poor Thea Klippel come to pick up her child at last. I – I – I'm so sorry, I am shameful. You must take no notice, I'm an old lady now, and my eyes are not what they were, and these glasses are not prescription . . .'

She took them off her face and began rubbing them furiously on the sleeve of her cardigan.

'Thea Klippel?' Evangeline asked. 'You thought I was my mother?'

Miss Starmount pulled her glasses back on again quickly. 'Evangeline?' she whispered. 'Evangeline Klippel?'

Evangeline nodded.

The old teacher waddled up to her and took both her hands in her own. 'You look just like your mother,' she said.

Evangeline smiled. 'My mother was beautiful.'

The old lady nodded. 'Yes.'

They both sat against the bonnet of the car.

'We said prayers for you, you know,' Miss Starmount said quietly, 'every day during that week and then once a year at Christmas time.' She looked crumpled, as though she might cry. 'I thought about you a lot, wondered how you were faring. The others missed you badly, you poor little soul.' She looked up keenly. 'You did well, though? Despite everything, you did well?'

Evangeline studied the dirt on the ground. 'Sure,' she said, 'I did really well. Despite it all.'

The teacher smiled. 'Good,' she said, patting Evangeline's hand, 'good.'

Her old apartment in New York smelt fusty when she opened the door. Evangeline pushed back the shutters and the smoggy air filtered in. Someone had been in and cleaned. The mail was in neat stacks on the floor in the hall. Evangeline squatted down to rip her way through it. There was something from London – a postcard, with the wrong stamp on the back. Some words were scrawled diagonally next to the address: *Contact me soon – Mik.*

Her head fell back against the wall. She dropped the card slowly. She didn't want this any more. Her life had patterns now. Mik was wrong. She closed her eyes and thought. He had stolen her job, betrayed her. She tried to

370

discount her own stupidity in trusting him and loving him. Her stupidity was her own fault, not his.

She sliced the story up into segments. He had planned to screw her up. He had planned to screw Deeta so he could take her with him and make sure he got the account. She had run off licking at her wounds like a scalded cat. She spliced the business from the emotional; cut out the love crap. See what he did to you as well: he took your work – your reputation.

She had something to fight for now. Years of hard work and talent; years of knowledge. She hit the darkroom before she had even unpacked, printing up the roughs all through the night: shots of the Cape, shots of Boston, her childhood in pictures, her parents' house – her house, rooms she had lived in. The room they had died in.

Darius had given up. One puff and he had keeled over, taking the others with him as well. She loved him still, but she knew now that he had been weak. Was that what she was like? Was that the trait she had inherited from them? No talent to pass on, but a remarkable flair for defeatism.

Mik had hurt her hard and she'd given up, just like Darius. Jesus! She ran out of the darkroom and punched the nearest wall until her fist bled. *Contact me soon – Mik*: she tore the postcard into shreds.

41

London 1994

'I think you're pushing Flora too hard.' It had taken Adam the entire morning to spit out these words. At first it appeared that Mik had ignored them. He was bent over some contacts, studying them with his magnifier.

'I think she might crack up, Mik, she's too young,' Adam went on. He'd grown fond of Flora – he had a sister about the same age and he knew how their minds worked. He hated Mik's attitude towards her. He hated the whole set-up.

'She's not well,' he said. He'd seen what she ate and heard her throwing up. She'd started to get like all the others – nervous and highly strung – and now she was trying to learn how to smoke to keep her weight down. She'd be doing drugs next. The thought sickened him.

'She looks fine to me,' Mik muttered. He pointed to a particular shot on the contacts. Adam bent over the frame to see and his lungs seemed to skip the next breath.

Mik had photographed Flora half naked, stretched out over a pile of boxes, all bearing the logo of the Imprex credit card. She looked pale and beautiful and impossibly long-limbed. Her head was thrown back and her eyes closed, as though she were asleep or dead. A wisp of pale blue chiffon covered her body.

'What do you think?' Mik asked.

Adam swallowed. 'She looks . . . she looks amazing,' he whispered. She looked too special. He looked again, closer this time.

'Get her up on the computer, Adam,' Mik said.

Computer enhancement: Adam had done a whole course in the techniques. He flicked into the programme with Mik bending over his shoulder. Flora appeared on the screen. Adam gazed at her, waiting for instructions.

'Take her colouring up a little,' Mik said. Flora's skin tones warmed slightly. Mik grunted approval. 'Get rid of those two small bruises on her arm . . . her feet look too big, I want them smaller, and watch the big toe – it looks ugly.'

Adam frowned. There was nothing ugly about Flora, nothing at all. He shortened her big toe by about an inch.

'Can you stretch her legs out longer?' Mik asked.

'Shit, Mik, she'll look like a freak!' Adam complained.

'That's what I want,' Mik spoke quietly but angrily, 'she has to be special, Adam, then we can make her famous. Point up her lashes, make them longer, too.'

'She's starving herself, Mik,' Adam argued, 'she's too thin. I think she's got problems. Look at her ribs.'

Mik's eyes never left the screen. 'Tone some of them out,' he said, 'make her look a little less scrawny.' He smiled, 'See? She's not too thin here, Adam. That's all that counts. get rid of that stray hair that is going across her face.'

Adam turned back to the screen. An hour later the shot was perfect. He printed it up and faxed it across to the client. The reply was immediate: a large exclamation mark on the first sheet, followed by, 'WOW!' on the second. Mik read it but didn't smile.

'You see?' he said, showing it to Adam. 'You see, it works. That's all that matters. You don't understand the business yet, but when you do you might do well for yourself. Stop caring, Adam, just worry about the shot and whether it will sell. I sold shots of corpses in India because they made a good shot.

'Flora is alive and she is young. She will make a lot of money and she will be famous, which is what she wants. Once she's done that she can pull out and sod off back to university, or whatever it is she fancies. If she's unhappy she can stop any time she feels like it. I wouldn't hold her to the contract, I'm not some fucking monster.'

Adam stared at his boss. Wasn't he aware that Flora was in love with him? The possibility had probably never crossed his mind. He thought everyone was like himself – driven and obsessed with success. He didn't know anything else. He'd never met anyone he wouldn't walk over to get where he wanted to be.

Mik went into his office and threw the shot of Flora down onto the desk. He sat down in the canvas director's chair and thought for a few minutes in silence, fingering the silver locket about his neck as he did so.

Nothing of his conversation with his assistant had registered. He picked up the phone and dialled Evangelines number in New York. Why hadn't she replied to his card? Maybe she hadn't been back there yet, though the phone had been engaged when he had rung the past three evenings, so somebody had to be living there. He listened to the number connecting. It rang three times before it picked up. His heart contracted as he heard Evangeline's voice and then a cold disappointment washed over him as he realized he was listening to a recorded message.

She was back, then. She only set the machine when she was living there. He hung up without speaking. Then he leant back in the chair and studied the clock. What time was it out there? Maybe he should be like some of the assholes he saw in Quaglino's and wear two watches, with one set to New York time. Why not, he wondered, he'd done everything else necessary to look like the walking style guru his agent had wanted him to be. If he wore two watches he could guess where she was at any time of the day and contemplate what she might be doing.

He opened the locket around his neck. The small square of coat fabric was still in there but so was something else. He held it up to the light. It was a small shot of Evangeline, taken while they had been together. Her hair was blowing out in the wind and she was smiling at the camera – smiling at him. A muscle worked in his cheeks as he studied it. He looked at the time again. Where was she? What would she be doing? He replaced the phone with a scowl on his face and went out to give orders to Adam for the setting-up of the next shoot.

Evangeline spent the next three weeks in the darkroom, printing all the shots she had taken in Boston. There were also the shots she had taken of the Cape – heavy, moody pictures taken on overcast days when the dunes looked rank, with their sparse bristling grasses and the storm flats hanging overhead like slabs of granite. Looking at them she could smell the dead scents from the sea. She thought of Miss Clayburg alone on the beach and alone in the great, salt-stained house and she shuddered.

There was a portrait of Miss Starmount, red-faced and frightened when she thought she'd seen a ghost turn up to collect its abandoned child. The light was there on her glasses, making her eyes hidden behind two round circles of white light, but you could feel the fear in her posture and see the indecision in her awkward, fat legs and slippered feet.

Evangeline printed them all and then she phoned an old contact, a man who owned a gallery in SoHo. He came round to the apartment and studied the shots in silence.

'Do you want to exhibit or do you want to sell them to magazines?' he asked at last.

'I want a three-day exhibition,' Evangeline told him. 'I've got some other ideas lined up for magazine features.'

'They're a new style for you, Evangeline,' he said, sipping at the glass of wine she'd poured for him. He looked up at her. His glasses magnified his eyes, making him look permanently startled. 'You know, I've never heard you say what you wanted before, Evangeline,' he continued. 'You were always so unsure. You seem to have made plans at last. I always thought of you as the last of the Bohemians,

375

wandering the world in the permanent furtherance of your art.' He smiled. 'Just when did you get so worldly?' he asked. 'In England? Is that what they taught you? Did all those pounds they threw at you go to your head?'

Evangeline grinned. 'Let's just say I learnt to gain a little confidence,' she said. 'Now are they good, or what?'

'They're wonderfully evocative,' the man said. He smiled again. 'Of course they're good, Evangeline, you know they are – look at that smug grin on your face. Can I show them? Good grief, listen to me, I'm begging. Eight weeks, then – I'll need that time to arrange all the marketing.'

Evangeline pulled out her diary. 'I'm showing in London that week, too,' she said. 'I've been booked for a retrospective at a leading gallery.'

'My, my!' The gallery owner looked suitably impressed. 'What brought this change of approach about, Evangeline?' he asked. 'I haven't known your career move so fast since poor Nico passed away. Did you marry a hustler or something?'

Evangeline shook her head. 'No,' she said quietly, 'I just decided to start fighting back, that's all.'

The exhibition was a critical success and the show in London brought her further publicity back home in the States. She went across for the press launch but she flew back the same night, without waiting to see the reviews. Her appearance at the gallery was rapid and unexpected. She dressed up and she was charming to the press, but she wasn't hanging around to see if Mik would turn up.

At night in her apartment she left the answerphone on. Sometimes she sat by it when the calls started coming through. Three rings and then the sound of her own voice, giving the recorded message. Then the bleep. Then silence for a few seconds or longer. Sometimes she could hear him breathe. She imagined things from his breathing. She imagined that he sounded angry. He never spoke, he never once left a message, yet she knew it was him. She knew it was Mik.

Mik's shots of Flora for the Imprex account made her a serious name on the modelling scene. She became so much in demand her agency were turning work down. Her rise had been rapid, even by modelling terms – a mere six weeks stood between the gawky schoolgirl and a face the public was beginning to recognize.

Her agency's publicist got onto the newspapers and there were several features about her being the next Kate Moss. She got her first cover and the agency rewarded her with a room in a flat they rented for their girls in Putney. Flora was frightened by the place, with its empty rooms and cold, bare decor. She was to share with another model, but the girl was rarely there.

They were on the ninth floor. Before the Imprex fame Flora would spend her spare time gazing out of the window at the clouds. When she was working, though, she was rarely there either. Sometimes she would be too busy to think and when she did stop for a few hours she found herself sitting naked on the empty floor, sucking her thumb.

Her father phoned a lot and she bought an answerphone to hear his voice. He was proud of her, now. All the neighbours said nice things. The other girls she worked with looked like they were having lots of fun. Flora couldn't. She was too afraid.

The fear grew daily inside her and she had no idea where it had come from or why it was there. She had never been frightened like this before. If she wasn't working she was afraid; if she had bookings she was even more terrified.

Her hands began to shake a lot of the time, even when she was supposed to be relaxing. Adam took her out a few times and she tried to listen to what he said when he spoke to her, but she couldn't, her mind wouldn't concentrate. She told her agency she didn't want to do so much work and they looked startled and concerned and sent her home for a week to rest.

Home was strange. It was all the same, just as she had left it, but she found she couldn't manage life there any more. It was like picking up toys she'd outgrown – she'd forgotten the games in such a short space of time. She tried to mix in, but they all treated her as though she were on a visit, as though she were special.

She missed the bitching and the sassiness of the other models. She missed the designer clothes and the background smells of expensive scents and cigarette smoke. At home they nagged her to eat and arguments began. Her father asked stupid questions about her job and so did everyone else. She turned up at the agency two days early.

'You sure you're OK to get back?' the booker asked.

Flora nodded.

'*Sure* sure?' he asked. She looked tired to him, or maybe it was the light in the office making dark rings around her eyes.

'Yes,' Flora said.

He pulled out her card. Her schedule was packed: there were three colours: black for the bookings, pencil for the provisionals and red for any break days. There was a red line for that week but the few weeks following were thick with black felt-tip. She looked at the pencil words upside-down and hoped they would never be confirmed.

When she got back to the flat it was empty. She didn't put on the light, even though the darkness scared her. She wanted to ring her father but it was too late. The next morning she had shots with Mik. They were behind on the credit card job and he was going apeshit because she was so busy. She sat on the floor until the sky became pink and then she walked into the bedroom and fell down onto the bed. She had three hours left for sleep. She had to rest. She had to look good for Mik.

42

'Christ, Flora. Get a move on!' Adam stood in the doorway of her flat, punching numbers into his portable phone. 'Mik?' he called. 'Mik, she's here. She's been ill. She's OK, though, I'll have her with you in about twenty minutes.' Flora could hear Mik shouting from the other end. Adam disconnected and grinned at her. 'You'd better get your finger out,' he said.

She looked a mess. Her eyes were blearily unfocused and her hair needed washing. She wore some sort of an old checked kimono and her feet were bare. She looked beautiful, though. He went to the kitchen and hunted in the fridge for some orange juice to wake her up. There was only water, so he handed her a cup of that instead.

'Are you OK?' Adam asked.

She smiled back at him. 'I'm fine, really, I'm just tired. Do I look terrible? Is Mik really mad with me?' She sounded suddenly tearful.

'He'll do,' Adam told her. 'He's always in a mood. Get ready. Have a shower. Throw some of that iced water over your face. Thank Christ you're only fifteen – if you were any older you'd be unusable this morning. What were you doing? Clubbing or partying?'

Flora yawned. 'I was just sitting here,' she said.

'By yourself?' he asked.

Flora nodded. 'I like it. I can think properly.'

She was wiping a pad soaked in witchhazel across her face. She looked young – even younger than fifteen.

'Do you want breakfast?' Adam asked. He was pacing around the flat, getting angrier by the minute. The place was a mess. There were clothes over everything and travel bags strewn across the floor with their contents spewing out. He smothered an urge to tidy up. According to the luggage tags, most of the bags appeared to belong to Flora's flat-mate. He bent down to push some of the contents back inside so he could throw them into one of the cupboards. His hand hit something hard in one of the bags.

'Flora?' he shouted. She walked into the room. She was half dressed, in her underwear, with one leg in a pair of jeans.

'What the hell is this?' Adam asked in a whisper.

Flora performed an annoyingly slow blink. 'That's Chelsea's' she said.

'Chelsea?' Adam asked.

'My flat-mate,' Flora told him, 'She got given it on a trip to the States last year. They said she needed it for protection while she was staying out there. I don't know how she got it through customs. She could have been in trouble if they'd found it, eh?'

'Flora, it's a gun!' Adam said. 'Shit, you shouldn't have this lying around here!' He slid the barrel out. 'God, it's loaded too!'

Flora shrugged. 'Chelsea nearly got raped when she was younger,' she said, 'she says she likes to have it around, just in case. It's OK, she's not often here. Nobody else knows she's got it. I'll put it away, just in case.'

She took it from Adam and dropped it into an empty shoebox before putting it away in the top of her wardrobe.

They drove to the studio in silence. Mik was hopping with anger by the time they arrived.

'You have to learn to be punctual!' he told Flora. Adam hurried her away into the changing room, where the make-up artist was waiting.

An hour later she was ready. Adam struggled with the lights as she walked out onto the set. He'd arranged fill-ins to get rid of some of the darkness beneath her eyes and filters to warm up her skin tone.

Mik walked in with the phone in his hand and carried on an angry conversation as he bent to look into the view-finder.

He paused. 'She looks like shit!' he called out. Evangeline's recorded voice droned its interminable message out into his ear: 'I'm sorry, I'm not available to take your call at the moment, but if you'd like to leave a message . . .'

Flora's face crumpled in shock but she didn't cry. Adam could see how hard her legs were shaking. Mik threw the phone down and stormed into the changing room.

'She looks like shit!' he repeated. 'What the fuck have you two been doing to her . . .'

Flora walked into the room with Adam following. Her face was like a white mask. She looked up at Mik, her eyes full of pleading.

'She turned up like that,' the make-up guy replied. The stylist was throwing her things into a case.

'I'm not staying around to be spoken to in that tone,' she said, 'you can go to hell, Mik, I don't care what you think. I was at *Vogue* yesterday and *Marie Claire* the day before. I don't need your fucking job and I . . .'

Adam chased her out of the room, on the usual damage-limitation exercise.

'You're a charming boy, Adam,' they heard the stylist's voice echo down the corridor, 'and I know that is why he keeps you on, to schmooze all the poor sods he's been a bastard to. You also have more talent than he has in his little finger, and I say that having worked with all the top names . . . I understand what you're saying, Adam, but I am not staying here to be treated like a piece of shit . . .'

They heard Adam speaking but couldn't hear what it was he said. Then there was silence and the stylist returned, flushed and shaking with anger, her eyes firmly to the ground as she unpacked her things and laid them out again.

Mik looked from her to Flora before walking out.

Adam was waiting in the studio. 'You'll destroy her,' he

said, quietly. Mik raised an eyebrow. 'Flora,' Adam went on. 'She's only a kid. She's fifteen, Mik. You're pushing her too hard. She can't cope.'

Mik's eyes were like two cold stones. 'Do you want to know what I had to cope with at fifteen?' he asked.

Adam stared at him angrily. 'She's not you, Mik!' he said.

'She's got a contract,' Mik told him, 'and she helps us earn our wages. She's young but she is intelligent. Do you think she is an idiot? She will stop when she wants to. Now get on with your job in the studio – we have to make up for lost time.'

Later on that session Adam heard Mik apologizing to Flora for his tone. The relief in Flora's face made him sick. She even started humming. Her face lit up and the shots began to work again. Adam stared at her from the periphery of the dark set. She was pathetically happy now that Mik had spoken to her.

He felt he wanted to protect her. He would have liked nothing more than to wrap her up and carry her off back to the security of her home, but Mik was right – she could quit any time she wanted. He wondered how long it would be before she did.

43

It was December and the streets of New York were coated with grey slush from the snowfall of two days before. Evangeline wore Timberlands and a parka and a tartan scarf Nico had bought her years ago.

Evangeline had been working for six months and she'd finally installed herself near to where she used to be. She wasn't the star turn any more because she wasn't new, but her reputation gave her a kind of kudos that some of the younger photographers lacked.

She got pulled in when a major star needed photographing. She could deal with their moods and they trusted her to do good quality work, with no real surprises. If she provided shocks with her shots they were the professional kind of shocks that her sitters liked, not the ugly kind, where a photographer carves his reputation at the expense of the model.

She had three shots to do that day and the addresses were screwed up in her pocket. She preferred studio but someone at *Time* wanted location. The streets smelt good – hot and friendly – from all the steaming food bars. She liked to walk; sometimes she found good shots along the way. She would have bought Paddy a hotdog had he been with her. She missed him; it still hurt like it was yesterday.

Evangeline had planned her Christmas as she planned everything in her life now. Two days in an hotel close to the Canadian border and the rest of the time flat on her back in the apartment, eating and watching movies. No work, no printing. Well, maybe just a little, when she got bored, but hobby stuff, nothing serious.

Miss Clayburg had written from the Cape, asking her to visit for Thanksgiving, but she had written back to say she had other commitments. She had wanted to explain that she would never go back there again, but she didn't find the time she needed to put her feelings into words that would not seem too wounding.

Her exhibition had been a success and all the prints were sold for excessive amounts. She had looked at them the night before the opening, alone in the empty gallery, her feet echoing on the varnished floors. All her childhood was there on those walls – all the places, from her old room at the house in Boston, to the wintry beach on the Cape. One hundred memories, all framed and captioned and hung in careful order.

She'd folded her arms as she walked around them. The memories made some sort of sense when she viewed them all like that. She looked at the driveway in Boston and she could feel the dust in her mouth from the day her parents had died. She looked at the sea and she could feel it falling over her waders as the chauffeur caught her up and saved her from drowning.

Her grandmother was there in the shot of the house. The place sat to the right of the frame, a dark sky above it and a cold sea behind it. A slither of moon hung overhead. The house seemed to be waiting for her. When she looked at that photograph she thought her grandmother was still there, inside it.

The park was nearly empty as she crossed it on her way home. Around the perimeters she could see the coloured Christmas lights winking from the shop windows. Some cute-looking kids were throwing sticks into a frosted puddle and she stopped to shoot them. They saw her taking photos and started yelling: 'Hey, fuck you, lady! You take shots we want paying! Hey!' They couldn't have been more than seven or eight, at the most.

She thought about Mik and how his life had been at that

age. She thought about his brother dying and how he had grown up alone after that. Was she making excuses for him? Did the suffering of the child excuse the bastard it became later on? She ran a bit, to warm up and clear her head, then she sat down on a bench, the breath billowing from her mouth in plumes of white. She'd lost her tartan scarf — it took her a few minutes to realize it.

'Shit!' She did up the neck of her parka to keep warm.

Someone sat down beside her. Evangeline looked up in surprise. 'Stuart?'

He didn't look at her, he just sat down beside her. She could feel the warmth emanating from his body. He wore a smart charcoal wool overcoat and his hands were stuffed into the pockets. Evangeline stared at him.

'Stuart?'

He inhaled deeply. He appeared to be watching the wind blowing the muddied leaves about. She felt his strength. He was solid and real, like he had always been. He looked handsome and honest. He pulled one hand out of his pocket. It had her scarf in it.

Evangeline took it from him and they sat a while in silence before Stuart finally spoke.

'You haunt me, Evangeline,' he said, 'you haunt my memory. You won't go away.' He sighed. 'I loved you for what felt like a lifetime and maybe it nearly was. Old men shouldn't care so much, it's not comfortable to live with. It's not becoming, either. Loving someone who doesn't love you back is humiliating. I have everything, Evangeline, and what I don't have I can get. I have the power to achieve most things yet I don't have the power to make you love me.

'I've given you time, space, and patience. I could give you almost any material thing that you want. Yet all you wanted was friendship. Do you understand how that has felt for me all these years?' He stretched out his legs. His shoes were finely polished. He still talked to the open space in front of him.

'You are an enigma to me, Evangeline, and I believe that

is why I love you so strongly. I believe I know you better than you know yourself, yet I don't understand you and I know I never will. This intrigues me. My own vanity intrigues me, that I should keep on trying after all these years, after all these rebuffs.

'I imagine that one day you will love me, Evangeline, and that we will be married while I am still young enough to make a viable groom. I continue to believe that we make a good pair, though God knows I have been shown enough evidence to prove my belief is little more than pig-headedness.' He sighed again. 'I never spoke of my first wife, did I? Though I suppose Catherine has mentioned her to you many times. She loved me as much as I love you, Evangeline, only that time it was I who was unable to return the love in the same degree.

'If she felt as I do with you, then maybe death was the only thing for her. There's no pleasure in feeling as I do, Evangeline, and this confession may be the most painful thing I have ever had to do in my life, short of burying my wife.' He shook his head slowly. He smelt clean, of soap and subtle spiced cologne. 'I don't ask you to say anything, Evangeline,' he added, quietly, 'I only wanted you to listen, to understand how I feel and how I have felt all these years. In case you didn't know. In case you were in any confusion.'

He stood up slowly. 'I'll go now,' he said. He still hadn't looked at her.

She let him walk off, watching his back, wide and solid in the cold air. You must be stupid, she told herself.

Evangeline ran up behind Stuart and slipped her arm into his. 'I don't know what you see in me,' she told him.

'No,' he said, smiling at her, 'neither do I.'

He kissed her then, in front of everyone walking through the park. He put his arms around her and she felt protected and happy and safe.

'Come back with me,' he whispered.

'I can't,' she told him, pulling the screwed-up addresses

out of her pocket, 'I've got some jobs to do.'

Stuart took the paper from her hands and screwed it into a ball. Then he flicked it into the nearest litter bin. 'No, you don't,' he said, 'the jobs were phoney. I booked you up, just in case.'

She was so close to his face she could see the veins that ran beneath his skin.

'Will you marry me, Evangeline?' he asked her. If she said no she wouldn't see him again.

To love and not to be loved in return. She knew how that was. Stuart would love her, it was a truth in her life. There had been so many lies; it was the lying that had nearly destroyed her. He offered her strength and the truth at last. But what was she to offer him in return?

'I want to love you,' she whispered. Maybe she almost did. She knew she couldn't bear to give him up. Maybe that was love, after all. 'What can I give you, Stuart?' she asked him. 'You always offer me so much.'

He smiled at her. 'We'll start with the basics, shall we?' he said. 'A pain in the neck when you're off on your jobs. Earache when you're in a bad mood. We'll start with that, shall we? The rest can just happen. I can make you love me, Evangeline. I just need the chance.'

'OK, then,' she said. It seemed the only way possible. Losing Stuart was too awful an idea to contemplate. She'd missed him badly over the past few months, he was everything that could be right in her life. She had to say yes. She felt happy for saying it. It sounded right.

Mik was in his agent's office, pacing the floor like a panther in a cage.

'Get me out of this fucking deal with the credit card,' he said.

Baz looked at him as though he were half mad. 'No way, Mik,' he said, 'no fucking way.'

Mik leant across his desk and Baz had an urgent desire to press the button that would fetch security. Mik frightened him. The guy had psycho eyes. He smiled. Passive body language – it worked with dogs, maybe it would work with crazed-up Hungarians, too. He clenched his hands and leant forward helpfully in his seat.

'Why?' he asked reasonably. 'What's wrong with the job? It's the best, man. Your reputation depends on it – you get chucked out or you quit and everyone thinks you are crap. Is that what you want, Mik? Is that the way you see things going? What happened? Tell me, why this desire to self-destruct all of a sudden?'

Mik ran his hands through his hair. He looked ill, even by his own standards. 'We had a deal,' he muttered, 'and they broke it.'

Baz frowned. Was the guy raving or did he deserve serious consideration? Was he on something? A lot of them were. Most of them managed without it during daylight hours, though.

'They were going to take her back,' Mik rambled on, 'we were going to work together on the job. She was never supposed to disappear. Jesus! I can't fucking stand it!'

Baz tapped his fingers on the desk. 'Was this whatever-it-is written into the contract?' he asked. There were no fancy clauses that he knew of. He didn't pass anything he didn't understand. Baz liked his contracts to be clean and simple – no jargon, no double-meanings. He could recite each one on his files by heart, so he knew Mik had to be raving.

'In writing?' Mik asked. He looked confused. Baz wished he would just go off somewhere and dry out before the next Imprex photo session.

'Was this just something they told you?' Baz asked him. He tried to sound patient but irritation was frothing beneath the surface.

'We talked about it,' Mik said, 'they agreed. We agreed it all before I took the job.'

'Was it money?' Baz asked.

'Money?' Mik shook his head. 'No.'

388

'And they never wrote it into the contract?'

Mik shrugged.

Baz leant back in his chair. 'Well, a verbal contract could be binding of course, Mik, but with the state of your English I suppose there would be room for manoeuvre if it ever came to court, old son. Maybe you just misunderstood something. Best to forget it, if I were you – doesn't do to go ruffling the feathers too much, if you know what I mean, they are only the biggest fucking account you and I or anyone else, come to that, are ever likely to get our hands on – in terms of prestige alone, Mik, and there's the money, too. That account made you, Mik – you'd do well to remember that fact. If you lose it through some petty whinge you'll lose everything we've built up for you. Do you know how quickly reputations can be broken in this business, Mik?' He snapped his fingers dramatically. 'That quick – that's all it takes. Especially when the talent is not quite on a par with the hype. You want my advice, Mik? Shut up. Put up and shut up, whatever it is.'

He could see the anger had gone out of Mik and so allowed his voice to rise to a shout. He was in a foul mood, anyway, his hairweave was hurting and what he didn't need was further aggravation. He had no idea what Mik was on about but he wanted it over, dealt with. Gone. He got his wish. Mik stormed out without another word.

Evangeline was floating, buoyed up on a tide of affection and attention. Stuart was spoiling her and she was allowing herself to be spoilt. He took her on holidays, he bought her presents. She found herself swaddled in his love, and in return she was happy. 'Contented, even,' she told Stuart.

'You?' he looked amazed.

Evangeline nodded. 'Being with you is like being permanently stoned. You sort of take over, Stuart, did you know that?'

Stuart smiled: 'Me?' he asked. He kissed her. 'Do you mind?'

'I don't think so,' Evangeline told him. Life had become very easy. Suddenly most of her work seemed to be in New York. She slept a lot, she ate good food, at the proper times, she often got up late. She even went shopping, but only when Stuart made her. She tried on nice clothes to please him and was surprised at how good she managed to look in most of them. She thought it was funny. Her work became regular again, but the hours were comfortable.

She'd never had a life outside business before but now she did, and she liked it. They went to the theatre and to baseball games, though often they sat alone in his apartment and talked. Stuart made her laugh a lot. He was also a touchingly considerate lover. Regular sex with her suited him.

'You improve with time,' Evangeline told him.

'I love it when you talk corny, Evangeline,' he laughed, 'tell me some more.'

One day they got back to her apartment and she flicked on the answerphone by mistake.

'Phone me, Evangeline. Why won't you speak? Call me, just once . . .' She had walked into the bathroom and couldn't get to the button to switch off Mik's voice in time. When she came back into the lounge Stuart had the machine in his hand and the jack was hanging out of the wall. He had his back to her. When he turned she saw the desperation in his eyes, just before the intelligence slipped back in again.

'I broke it, I'm sorry,' he said, putting the machine down on the table. 'I'll buy you another one.' He forced a smile. 'Do you get many calls like that?' he asked. 'I'll get the number changed. Your other calls can be re-routed. I'll take care of it, don't worry.'

Evangeline opened her mouth to argue but then she changed her mind. It couldn't go on – Mik's voice was like a knife each time, cutting into her soul. Once he was gone for good she could be really happy at last, she was sure of it.

She hated the hurt in Stuart's eyes. He'd waited for her. He deserved this much. The following day he took her out and bought her an embarrassingly large engagement ring. An hour later they went back and changed it for something she could wear. That night she took Mik's locket off from around her neck and placed it into a box, which she shut away in a cupboard in the darkroom. She would never put the locket back on again. It was all over, finished. If she'd been stronger she would have thrown it away and she hated herself for not being able to.

Five months, Stuart had said. They would be married in the spring because he was romantic and he wanted it all to be perfect. He also wanted his daughter there. Catherine was away until May. Evangeline couldn't wait to see her reaction when she found out.

44

Mik was half-way through the Imprex account shots when Flora's agency expressed their concern that she was having a breakdown. He took her to dinner at a bar on the Thames to discuss the problem. They were photographed going in and they were photographed again coming out. Flora looked happy enough and Mik thought the agency were over-dramatizing, as usual. She'd dressed up for the dinner and was wearing something short in black that looked like bandages. She looked all wrong in the outfit, like a kid dressing up in a tart's clothes. Too much make-up, too. Mik made a mental note to speak to the agency about her image.

They ate Vietnamese food and Mik asked Flora if she was tired or overworked and she said no, everything was fine. When the coffee was finished Mik took her back to her flat in a taxi, which he kept waiting while he went up in the lift with her. When they got to Flora's door she turned and kissed him. The kiss made Mik feel tired to his soul. He pulled her arms off him carefully and watched the blush that started to build from her chest upwards until her face was aflame.

He couldn't bear the look in her eyes. Why? The word was there between them, even though she never spoke it.

'No, Flora,' he said quietly, 'not with you.' The questioning look was still there in her eyes. 'You're too young. You need someone different. We are working on a job . . . I'm sorry.'

He watched his words destroy something important inside her. Embarrassment and disappointment fought for control of her features. He watched the child in her re-surface and he thought she was going to cry.

He ran a hand through his hair. 'Go to bed, Flora, it's late,' he said. She was looking at the floor, now. Her face was burning even brighter.

'Find someone who is right for you,' he said, softly.

'You are right, Mik,' she argued. Her voice had a pleading tone. When he looked at the desperation in her face he wanted to be away from there, he wanted to be gone.

'I have to go,' he said. He felt better once he was inside the lift. When he stepped out at the ground floor someone was standing there. He flinched, believing for a moment that he was about to be mugged.

'Mik?' It was Adam. Mik barely recognized him, his hair was dishevelled and his normal smart-casual clothes were rumpled, as though he had slept in them.

'What the hell are you doing here, Adam?' Mik asked. He looked across at his taxi. Adam's four-wheel was slewed across the road behind it.

'Did you screw her, Mik?' Adam asked. His face looked distorted by some unknown emotion. Mik laughed.

'Did you?'

Mik had had enough for one night. He was tired.

'Fuck off, Adam,' he said.

'She's only fifteen, Mik,' Adam said.

'I know,' Mik told him, 'she's my model, remember?'

'She can't cope with all this.' Adam's voice was breaking. Mik pushed him out of the way. He was a whole head taller than Adam. The boy tottered but tried, unsuccessfully, to stand his ground.

'Neither can I,' Mik said. 'I need some sleep. I'll see you at the studio at seven a.m. Mind how you drive, Adam,' he added as he jumped into the cab, 'I think you're over the limit.'

Adam arrived to collect Flora the following morning. It was a habit he'd got into; he didn't like her travelling on public transport by herself and a couple of the taxis she had hired had been late, making Mik furious.

He had to knock several times before she opened the door. She was dressed and ready but her face looked pale and her eyes were red, as though she'd been crying.

'Are you OK?' he asked. She'd made him coffee. He was touched by the gesture. He watched her nod. 'Yeah, I'm fine.'

Adam looked around as he sipped the coffee. 'Mik was here last night, then,' he said. Flora said nothing in reply. He wondered whether she'd heard him. She didn't even seem interested to know how he knew. She seemed agitated and worried that they were going to be late. She checked her watch for the third time.

'He's in love with someone else, you know,' he told her. Her eyes looked like a doe's, wide and hurt and helpless. 'He's been phoning her constantly,' he added, 'another photographer. I hear him a lot in his office. Evangeline. He used to be her assistant. They had some sort of affair, it was in all the papers.'

'We ought to go,' she said. She sounded destroyed. Adam thought she looked beautiful. The misery in her face broke his heart.

'You look great,' he told her.

She smiled. 'Thanks.' She didn't sound as though she believed him.

There was an envelope full of newspaper cuttings lying on the floor in the hall when she finally got home. Most of the articles called her a spoilt brat, saying she was getting turned down for jobs because of her attitude.

She phoned her father.

'Flora?' He sounded confused. 'Are you OK?'

Why did everyone ask her that? It was as though she were living life behind a sheet of thick glass. They were all there and she was here. Nobody could help her.

'Flora?'

'I'm fine, Daddy, fine.'

'Are you sure, darling?'

'Of course.'

She hung up and dialled Mik's number, pressing the receiver to her ear when she heard his voice. Then she realized that she was listening to a recorded message.

'Mik?' she whispered. 'Mik? Are you there?' If he was he did not pick up. She paused. Swallowed. Licked at her lips.

'Goodbye, Mik.'

She sat cross-legged in the middle of her room, painting her face with the help of a large plain shaving-mirror that belonged to her flat-mate. She was careful with the cosmetics, but some still spilt because her hands would not stop shaking. She tried harder to concentrate. She had to look her best.

She changed lipstick four times until she found the right colour. She looked in the mirror again. Too much blusher. She got some tissue paper from the bathroom and wetted it in the sink before wiping it across her face. She'd made the mascara streak now. She wiped at it with her finger until the streak was gone. The lipstick was good but the line was uneven. More tissue. She steadied her hand on the floor and tried again.

In the end she was pleased. Her eyebrows were heavy with black pencil and her mouth was a slash of glossy red. Her lids were sore from all the rubbing and her face was deathly white, drained of nearly all its blood. She sat back on her heels. It was good. She even started to hum. Then she started on her hair.

Mik listened to her message on his answerphone. He had been there when she left it.

'Mik?' Her voice troubled him. She sounded weak and dependent, like Elise, back in Hungary. Their voices blended and became the same. The same long white arms winding round him, trying to keep him. He couldn't bear their dependence on him. He didn't pick up the phone.

He heard Flora hang up: 'Goodbye, Mik.' He sat with his head in his hands a long time, thinking. Goodbye. What did that mean?

'Shit!' It was Evangeline he wanted to speak to, not Flora. He lifted the phone to dial the US again but then replaced it slowly. Elise had pretended to be pregnant. It seemed that Flora was trying a similar trick now, trying to scare him. He stood up. 'Goodbye, Mik.'

'Oh my God!' He grabbed his coat and picked up his camera, too, in a reflex. It was raining. He would never get a cab in that weather. He went outside to wait for one anyway.

The traffic was heavy and by the time he reached Putney the taxi meter had long since passed the amount of cash he was carrying in his wallet. He took some abuse when he pulled out a credit card but the driver quietened down when he saw the expression glittering in Mik's eyes.

Mik looked up at Flora's floor as the taxi pulled away. There were only a few lights on in the building. There were none at all in Flora's flat.

He thought for a moment that she must have gone out and he cursed himself for reacting so stupidly. She was a kid and kids overdramatized mightily. Models were worse than ordinary kids, they could summon up a disaster out of thin air. He'd never get a taxi for the return trip, he'd have to walk to the nearest station.

Something made him look up again. The picture had changed slightly. There were still no lights on in Flora's flat but the window must have been opened, because a white net curtain billowed from the balcony like a flag of surrender. Mik stepped back for a better view. Nothing else moved up there. Maybe she was watching him. He ran up to the main entrance and tried her buzzer. There was no reply. He leant the palm of his hand against it but there was still no answer.

Mik ran back out again. Looking upwards made him dizzy. He looked away, back at the door, and rubbed his neck, wincing.

He saw her the next time. She was there on the balcony. He watched her standing there, waiting. The curtain blew over her, engulfing her for a second and when it blew back she was climbing onto the balcony rail.

Mik placed his cupped hands to his mouth and called out to her: 'Flora!' He knew she wouldn't hear, though, she was too far up. 'Flora!' he screamed again, nevertheless.

He stepped back, waving his arms. 'Flora!'

She was naked, posed tall and curving upright on the rail like an Art Deco statuette.

'Flora!' He was running now, running backwards and forwards. He picked up his camera and looked at her through the lens. Her image became magnified. He watched her back arch as she threw her arms out to either side, like a crucifix.

She took off into the night air. Her hair billowed like the curtains behind her, streaming in ribbons as her long arms stretched out overhead.

For a moment he thought she could fly. Her arms were like bird wings, slender and brittle. She moved outward rather than down. For a second nothing happened, it was as though her skinny body had caught on an eddy of wind and was floating.

Mik pressed his finger down on the shutter release. He thought she was flying, spreadeagled there above him. It was as though she were posing for him, giving him time to get the perfect shot. Then he realized she was dropping like a stone.

Take the shot. No matter what, take the shot. You are there to record, not to act. Make them sick over their breakfast. Shock them. Make them react.

His reaction was instinctive. He carried on shooting. She looked extraordinary, pale and luminous, with the moon lighting up her body. When she hit the ground he continued to shoot, running across to her body, standing above it. There was screaming, but he didn't stop shooting.

A dog began barking near him, and then there were people. Someone pulled at his arm.

'Shit, man, what do you think you're doing? Eh?'

He was pushed in the back. Someone punched him on the shoulder.

'Hey, fuck off, fucking moron! She's fucking dead, man! What is it with you?'

He was cuffed across the face and then pushed so hard that he staggered.

'Fucking animal! Look at her, man, she's dead! What the hell are you doing?'

'Fucking bastard!'

'Fucking pervert!'

He was attacked from several sides now and curled his body around his camera to protect it. He was pushed onto his knees and felt himself kicked in the ribs, though with not enough force to do damage. Flora's was the main violence of the evening. All of this was just half-hearted stuff in comparison.

Mik waited until they became quiet and then sprang up and ran off without looking back.

They didn't follow him. He knew they wouldn't. He'd seen enough crowd violence to know when it was going to turn lethal or not. His camera was OK and he hugged it to his chest. He stumbled once and he heard them cheer. Then there was silence, broken only by the distant whine of the ambulance siren. Mik shoved his hands into his pockets and carried on walking towards the station.

Adam was waiting for him at the studio the next morning, whey-faced with shock.

'She's dead.' He looked at Mik as though hoping he might supply an alternative to this statement.

'Flora,' he added. 'She's dead.'

Mik looked at Adam and the boy stared back. His hair appeared to be literally on end. His mouth was almost comical, stretched down at either corner in a tragic caricature. His eyes bulged with hopelessness. Mik only realized at that moment that Adam must have been in love with Flora. He shook his head and moved his eyes to the floor.

The phones echoed somewhere way along the corridor.

'Its the fucking press, Mik,' Adam said, 'they've been ringing all morning. She's killed herself! They found her on the ground outside her apartment building. Oh Jesus, no!'

'Does her father know?' Mik asked, but Adam just stared at him.

Mik walked quickly along the hall to the darkroom. Once inside in the cocoon of quiet he locked the door and unloaded the film from his camera. Someone pummelled the door but he ignored them.

He developed the film quickly and then sank down onto the stool with his head in his hands.

'Andreas,' he whispered. He was going mad, he knew that now for sure. When he'd printed the shot of Flora's body lying broken on the concrete ground she'd had his brother's face, instead of her own. It was all he could do to stop himself from screaming.

No matter what else happened there was to be only one tragedy in his life, and that was the death of his brother. He straightened slowly. It took all his courage to pick the shot up again. At first his hands shook too much, then at last he saw it. It was Flora, not Andreas. Her eyes were open, staring out at him. Was it his fault too, her death?

'Shit!' He tore the silver locket from around his neck and threw it across the room. It hit the wall and dropped behind some shelving. Then, with a cry, he threw himself after it, knocking things over, breaking things in his frenzied hunt to retrieve it. He cut himself on broken glass

399

getting it back. His hands were bleeding when he left the darkroom. With a sigh he locked the door quietly and went off to answer the ringing phones.

Evangeline read the story of Flora's suicide in the newspapers quietly before putting them, neatly folded, to one side. The story had been a small one in the *New York Times* but she'd bought some British papers to read the whole thing. Flora's photographs had been on most of the covers and the word 'Tragedy' was included in a lot of the headlines.

Inside were more of her model shots and, inevitably, shots of Mik, who most of them called Flora's 'guru'. Many implied an affair between the two of them and there were several stock shots of Mik and Flora leaving a restaurant together. Several were paste-ups, shots cut out and then reset to make them appear closer than they were in the original.

By the following day everyone was being blamed for Flora's suicide: Mik, her agency, her father, drugs, and the pressures of anorexia and bulimia in the modelling profession. The press must have camped outside Mik's place because there were many shots of him leaving it and one of him losing his temper outside his studio and lashing out at a journalist.

Evangeline removed her glasses and rubbed the bridge of her nose. She felt very tired, suddenly. Had this girl killed herself over Mik? There were other feature articles, speaking out against the twin curses of beauty and early fame, and a couple of the health pages hammered home the perils of excessive dieting. But ultimately they all went back to Mik. Apparently Flora had left a letter saying she loved him, and a hand-written poem with his name scrawled across the front.

'Shit, Mik, what did you do to that girl's mind?' Evangeline whispered. She knew, though — oh yes, she knew. If she had been younger she could easily have done the same thing. Age had been her only protection against Mik – it had given her a perspective that this poor girl must have lacked. She pitied Flora, even though she had never met her. Had Mik said the same things to her as he had said to Evangeline?

Flora's eyes looked wide with hope and innocence in the photographs. She wouldn't have stood a chance against Mik Veronsky. She looked just like a rabbit caught in the headlamps of an oncoming car. Evangeline folded the image away. It was something she didn't care to look at for too long.

Flora's death obsessed Mik, even though he was careful not to reveal his emotions. Another death. This one he had photographed. What was he doing? He felt his life becoming unhinged and falling apart. Emotions that had lain buried since his childhood resurfaced, causing him pain. He was where he wanted to be. He was successful. Famous. He commanded respect now. But he had nothing that he wanted.

He had pretended to be Arthur and Tincan – tough, professional, unfeeling. The photograph was everything, nothing else mattered. Look after yourself, Tincan had told him. Take the shot, don't worry about the consequences, had been Arthur's advice. But it didn't work. Maybe for a while, but not for ever.

He loathed himself for his coldness. He needed Evangeline so much the pain was palpable. It was no good pretending any more, he had needs and desires like the next man. The thought frightened him.

There were only six weeks to go before Evangeline's wedding to Stuart. Stuart had been making all the arrangements – all she had to do was find a dress and organize the place where they would live. She'd found a beautiful apartment facing Central Park and now interior designers were working on it, to designs she and Stuart had chosen.

Her outfit was a more difficult problem. She'd bought three dresses so far and then returned them all after realizing they were unsuitable. The wedding wasn't going to be grand, but it wasn't a small one, either. She wished she were more vain, so that she could conjure up something appropriate in her mind. She didn't feel right in smart clothes. Yet she couldn't let Stuart down by appearing in pants and a jacket.

'Maybe Catherine would help you choose,' Stuart told her. Catherine. They hadn't heard her reaction to their engagement yet. Stuart had faxed her hotel when she hadn't returned his calls, but she still hadn't seen fit to reply. Stuart didn't seem too troubled by this but Evangeline had serious worries. Then a fax finally arrived sending Catherine's love and saying she would be back in the States a week before the wedding. Stuart was full of relief and Evangeline feigned something similar, to keep him happy. He was a wonderful man. She was lucky to have him.

Then she went back to rooting out a frock.

45

Adam sat alone, in the dark, in the rain. His hands had stopped shaking and his breathing was even again. He sat on the ground but nobody noticed him because they thought he was just another one of the homeless who slept out everywhere in London. His back leant against a rough brick wall. His hands were wet, even the palms.

He had found her photos in the darkroom. Mik had barely bothered to hide them – they were lying there beneath some stuff he'd done the week before.

At first he had not believed what he saw: Flora, dying. Flora, lying dead. He thought they must be from a session they'd done for the Imprex account, something new and tasteless – the sort of thing that Mik revelled in. Then he'd looked again, turning the photo around so that her face was the right way up. It was real, she was dead in the shot.

He'd thrown up where he stood at the shock of it. His stomach had just rejected all his lunch, violently and suddenly. When he could stand up straight again he'd started to cry, calling her name as he wept. Then he'd realized how wrong it all was. How terribly wrong that Mik should have photographed her like that. How her death had been Mik's fault and yet he had stood there callously while she did it, taking her photograph as though he were on just another shoot.

He didn't know why he'd done it in front of all the others. It had just seemed right, shooting Mik while all those cameras were around. After all, he'd shot Flora while she was dying.

He'd stolen the gun from her flat for her protection and

now he had used it on her behalf, for revenge. It all seemed right. Only he hadn't thought out what he would do afterwards. He started to cry and then he stopped. Then he folded his arms across his chest and waited for the police to come and find him.

He waited for four hours, until it got light. Nobody came and he heard no sirens after the first few. He was cold and shivering. He felt ridiculous, sitting there. People had started to stare. Someone had even tried to give him a few coins. Fate didn't seem to have a script written for him. He threw the gun over a hedge and went home.

Mik lay in the hospital bed in the darkness, listening to his own breathing. He was not dead, then. The sound of his lungs told him he was still alive. He had been shot — he knew the sound of the gun from his time in South Africa. Maybe he would die now. He knew who had shot him; he knew it was Andreas, his brother, who had come to kill him at last.

Revenge. It was the only way it could all be right. An eye for an eye . . . he tried to move and a pain seared through his back. It was the only way. He lay back to wait for Andreas to finish the job.

Adam shot Mik five days before Catherine arrived in New York. If Stuart had read about the shooting he made no mention of it. Evangeline was stunned. The parts of her that still belonged to Mik, despite everything, wanted to go to him. It was something in her blood. She could feel him calling to her for help and she hated herself for her own weakness at wanting to go. She grew angry and then she became quiet. Would he die? The papers seemed to think not.

There was a time when she would have gladly been the one to have fired that gun. She read that Mik's assistant had been arrested for the shooting and she smiled. Dog eat dog. She had been destroyed by Mik when he was her

404

assistant and now his own assistant had tried to destroy him. She tried not to think of him in the hospital. When she did she always imagined him lying there alone.

She was twitchy and uncomfortable when Catherine arrived. Stuart's daughter was tanned and serenely pregnant, with a new man in tow. She kissed Evangeline and embraced her father before sitting down to join them for tea.

'I am so pleased for the pair of you,' she bubbled. She looked genuinely pleased. Her face was pink with the pleasure of it all. She eased herself into a chair and both Stuart and her new man danced attendance.

'Only a few days to go, then,' she said, smiling. Evangeline nodded, trying hard to be polite but barely listening.

'We could have done with you here earlier,' Stuart said, looking at Evangeline with concern. 'Evangeline needed help choosing her dress. It's a good time to have female company, Catherine. You two could have done the designer houses together.'

'I don't have a lot of time in between jobs,' Evangeline told her, 'I had to slot fittings in when I could.'

'You're still working, then?' Catherine looked surprised.

'Of course.' Evangeline smiled politely.

'Oh.' Catherine looked at her tea. 'I suppose you'll quieten down after the wedding, then,' she said.

Evangeline laughed. 'I hope not.' She looked across at Stuart but he was staring strangely at his daughter.

'I thought Dad would have talked you out of all that by now,' Catherine said. 'I thought with all his money you'd be a lady of leisure, like me.' She stretched and yawned. 'Why work when there's no need?' she asked. 'I thought Dad would have had you chained to the kitchen by now, like a regular little housewife.'

She laughed and then yawned again. 'I need to lie down, I'm afraid,' she said, rising from her chair, 'the baby makes me tired. Maybe we can go shopping tomorrow, Evangeline.'

'I'd like that,' Evangeline lied.

*   *   *

She found herself sitting alone in her studio the evening before the wedding. The place was dark and very quiet and her thoughts seemed as empty and hollow as the room she sat in. Things were packed away. The place was tidy, as though she weren't coming back. She thought of Catherine's crack about Stuart wanting her as a housewife and she grinned. Stuart always encouraged her work. He listened when she discussed it and his ideas were always good ones. Catherine talked a lot of shit, but then she'd been expecting worse.

She put some music on the CD and then turned it off again. She couldn't settle, she felt too agitated. She poured herself a glass of Scotch but it tasted bitter and she winced as it went down. She rubbed her hands through her hair and tried to be happy. She wished Stuart were there to convince her. When he was with her she fed off his strength but when she was alone it was as though the spell were broken.

She walked into the darkroom and snapped on the safe-light. Its red glow made things look dramatic, like a movie. She remembered how Nico would stand behind her when she did her first few prints, watching, sweating for her. He never stopped worrying. He'd be proud of her now, though, proud she was marrying a good man with prospects. Prospects. The word didn't apply in Stuart's case. Stuart had made it. When he offered her everything she knew that he meant it.

She thumbed through some reject prints. Money didn't have much meaning for her. Grandma Klippel had been wealthy but she'd lived in fear of a six-year-old child. Was Stuart frightened of anyone? She thought not, but then she remembered the look in his eyes as he had stared at his daughter, and wondered whether maybe he was, now and again, after all.

Evangeline had her own money, too. She had the sort of studio most photographers would kill for and she sold her work for vast amounts. Not as much as the fashion guys, but then her reputation was more solid now, whereas their careers depended on being name of the month for as many months as they could manage.

Like Mik. That was the sort of life he had carved out for himself. Mik Veronsky: the name on every fashion editor's lips. Had he been happy to get there? Had the fight been worth it? She wondered how he felt now – whether he was busy planning his comeback after the shooting.

Maybe he was going to use the incident as a publicity stunt. His name would be known worldwide, now. That had to be worth a few thousand dollars more per hour.

She began tidying things. She was lucky to have Stuart, he was the perfect antidote to her affair with Mik. She took a cloth from the kitchen and some scouring powder and started wiping down surfaces. The place was clean but she wanted it cleaner. Stuart was her friend, as well as her lover. The phrase sounded so corny, like a line from a Country and Western song, but it was true.

She was on her knees now, scrubbing marks from the floor. She loved Stuart. The scrubbing got even more frenzied, she was cleaning marks that didn't even exist. She was sleeping at his apartment overnight, while he had booked into a hotel. She would have been happy to sleep in the studio. She would have been even happier to have spent all night cleaning and tidying.

There was a lot to arrange. The photos were filed but the stacks could have been neater. The floor needed fresh sweeping – there was dust that had blown in under the door. The higher shelves hadn't been cleaned for months. Her breathing was getting erratic. She sat down on a stool to concentrate. Nico would have given her a paper bag to breathe in and out of until she calmed down. She had no bag so she used her cupped hands instead.

She was OK. Fine, now. She began to feel better. She closed her eyes slowly. Good, good. She was too old for this type of thing. She thought she'd outgrown her panic attacks years ago. She took another sip of Scotch and gasped. Not the right thing to do, but this time it made her feel better, anyway.

When she opened her eyes Catherine was standing there. She jumped with shock and nearly gasped out loud. How could a pregnant woman move so lightly? The mask had slipped now; the smile had gone and Catherine looked serious.

'You forgot to lock the door,' she told Evangeline. She didn't look fragile any more and she didn't look tired, she just looked fat and rather grim. She studied the broom by Evangeline's feet and then she took a general look about the place.

'No hen night, then?' she asked. Evangeline gave her reply with a sweep of her arm that said, see for yourself. Catherine pursed her lips. She seemed to be considering things. Evangeline tried to guess what her next line would be: something like, 'You know I never liked you, Evangeline,' sounded favourite.

She loved the dramatic pause. Catherine walked across to a pile of old prints and started fiddling with them. Evangeline wished she'd stop – she'd just tidied there.

'Why are you marrying Dad?' she asked.

Easy answer. 'Because I love him,' Evangeline replied.

Catherine nodded. The formalities were over then, the fighters had touched gloves.

More pauses. Catherine looked up and smiled. 'You lost that big account in London,' she said.

Evangeline nodded. 'The Imprex account, yes.' It seemed like a long time ago. It still hurt, but she could handle it. It seemed a mean, petty kind of a blow for Catherine to make.

'That must have cut you up,' Catherine said.

'It did, yes,' Evangeline said quietly. It was like the old Perry Mason courtroom scenes: 'Where is this line of questioning leading to, counsellor?'

'You got over it, though,' Catherine stated.

'It's the nature of the business,' Evangeline told her,

'that sort of thing happens – it's that sort of job.'

'But you're an excellent photographer, Evangeline,' Catherine told her, spreading out a few of her shots and gazing at them, 'you couldn't have lost that account through lack of talent.'

Evangeline shrugged. 'They gave the account to someone else, Catherine,' she said. 'I told you, that sort of thing happens all the time.'

Catherine picked up a couple of the prints she had been fiddling with.

'What is it, Catherine?' Evangeline asked. 'What do you want?' Impatience. A bad mistake. Don't let her know she's rattling you. Smile.

Catherine sighed, pressing her hair into place with a gloved hand. 'I just wanted to tell you how sorry I was,' she said. 'I believe people should be awarded jobs through talent and worth and hard work, not politics and in-fighting. I feel very strongly about that sort of thing, Evangeline. I know that might surprise you. I've seen enough of the opposite, though, to realize how destructive it can be. My father is embroiled in that sort of thing, it's a way of life for him and I believe he enjoys it. I just wanted to let you know that I don't.'

'Sisters under the skin, eh?' Evangeline asked.

Catherine smiled. 'Something like that,' she said.

She sat down opposite Evangeline. 'May I?' she asked pointing to the Scotch. She poured herself a hefty measure into a plastic cup and sipped at it.

'You were having an affair in London, weren't you?' she asked. 'Your assistant? Mik Veronsky? He's gone on to make quite a name for himself in the business, hasn't he?'

'I never knew you took such an interest,' Evangeline said. She wanted Catherine to go, yet in a way she was enjoying herself. Nothing she could say could matter now. Stuart knew everything. She was plugging away for nothing.

'Look, Catherine,' she said, sitting forward, 'your father knows all about Mik because I told him. He knows we had an affair. Whatever it is you want to say you're wasting your time, so why not go home and slip into a face mask, or whatever it is a guest of honour does the night before a wedding, eh? I know you don't approve and I know I'll never live up to the standards your mother set, but I'm not exactly asking you to call me your step-mother, now, am I? Whatever your opinion of me I'm sure I could agree with it, and maybe add extra criticism, but for some reason I seem to make your father happy and in return he has provided the only stability I have ever known in my life. Can't we just call a truce? Perhaps we could get drunk on Scotch and arm-wrestle, or something? What do you think?'

Catherine shook her head. She appeared to be laughing. Finally she stopped. 'You didn't love him, then, this other photographer — not really?' she asked.

'Mind your own fucking business, Catherine,' Evangeline said. She annoyed herself immediately. Lose your temper, lose the argument. Another homily from her grandmother's lips.

'You did,' Catherine said, seizing the advantage. 'Poor bastard, you did.'

She paused again, obviously sifting through her vocabulary. Searching for words, putting them in order before speaking. 'I hear he was shot,' she said.

Now the words had begun to hurt. I don't need this, Evangeline thought, whatever else, I don't need this right now. She should have been soaking in perfumed bath-water. She should have been curling her hair with tongs and ironing her trousseau, or whatever else brides did on the eve of a wedding. Maybe getting pissed with friends. Male strip clubs, wasn't that the thing? Or a Chinese restaurant and some good-humoured chat. She'd lock the door of the studio next time. If she'd learnt anything from this evening then that was it.

'I thought you would have gone to him,' Catherine said.

'Then you've been reading too many romantic novels, Catherine,' Evangeline told her. 'Like I said, we're finished. I'm marrying your father.'

Catherine tapped a finger against her lips. 'Why do you love Dad so much?' she asked.

Evangeline looked down at her hands. 'For his honesty, his integrity and his loyalty. For his strength, for his patience. Because he is probably the nicest man I have ever known and because he loves me – will that do for a start?'

'You didn't know that it was Dad who got you taken off the Imprex account, then?' Catherine asked. Her expression feigned concern as she dealt the killer blow. Evangeline's eyes flicked up at her.

There was a silence – an electric silence.

'Don't talk stupid,' Evangeline said.

'You didn't know,' Catherine repeated. Evangeline swallowed. Her mouth had gone dry. Shock. Again. Not true, though. She hated all these lies. Where would she find the truth in the middle of them? She had, though. Stuart was the truth. Honest, decent, a man of integrity. Catherine was the liar – she had lied before.

'Mik stole that job from me, Catherine,' she said. 'It had nothing to do with your father.' Now she had found the truth at last she was clinging to it, defending it.

Catherine shook her head. 'You're not a businesswoman, are you?' she asked.

'Don't patronize me, Catherine,' Evangeline said. Anger was rising now, not sickness, not shock. Anger at the other woman's lies.

Catherine pulled her bag open and rooted for a minute before holding out a sheet of headed paper. 'I'm sorry, Evangeline,' she said.

The headed paper belonged to Imprex. Catherine leant over and pointed to the small print.

'That's the name of one of Dad's companies,' she said. 'He bought into the holding company before you got to

411

work there. That's why you got the job and that's why you lost it. Look at the directors' names along the bottom. The first one is the name of Dad's PA. He put her in as nominal director. I'm surprised you never noticed.'

Proof. Evidence. So they were in a courtroom now, finding Stuart guilty. Not true. No. Catherine would do anything to split them up – anything.

'Stuart got me the job?' Evangeline said.

Catherine smiled. 'At first he only bought enough shares to get you in on the account. In a way he played an own goal. He didn't realize it would mean so much time in London, he just did it to make you happy. Then he found out about the affair with Mik and he virtually bought the company out so he could make sure you didn't get another year with them.

'Giving Mik the job was a great idea because it meant that it broke the two of you up. He didn't know you were in love – that must have been a terrible shock for him. My father's used to getting his own way, Evangeline – you must have realized that much by now.

'Dad told me Mik had turned the job down at first, but was told you'd be coming back in again after a couple of months. They said it was the only way you'd ever get to retain the contract, if the two of you worked together. He must have been wondering why you never came back. And then someone goes and shoots him – I don't know who to feel more sorry for, you or him.'

Sick, Evangeline thought, the woman is seriously sick.

Catherine smiled at Evangeline. 'You don't believe me, do you?' she asked. 'Go and talk to my father, then. He'll tell you the truth. He's the one with all the integrity you love so much. I'm sorry, Evangeline. I thought you needed to know.'

She stood up, her hand resting on her swollen stomach. 'Actually I do know who I feel the most pity for in all this,' she said. 'It's that poor model I hear committed suicide. She was only a child and she got caught up in adult games, didn't she? My father shouldn't have allowed things to go so far. I blame him for that.'

'I know you're lying, Catherine,' Evangeline whispered, 'what I don't know is why. Do you really hate me so much?'

Catherine leant forward. 'I told you,' she said, 'speak to my father. He'll tell you the truth. He's having his stag night at the Plaza. I'm sure he'd like a visit. Why don't you pop in and see how it's going? Only don't be too mad with him, Evangeline. When he sees what he wants he will always fight dirty to get it – it's the only way he knows.'

When she had gone Evangeline sat in silence, staring at nothing.

Her mind was in a maze of its own making. Catherine was lying. Mik had lied to her. The clients had lied. She paced round and round in her head. Then she stood up.

She picked up the sheet of headed notepaper Catherine had left behind and studied it. She could hear her own pulse beating in her ears. It sounded like the sea. She wished it would stop – it was preventing her from thinking properly.

Truth. Hang on to the truth. Catherine was a liar. She'd lied before. She would obviously do anything to stop the marriage taking place – even accuse her own father. She read the names on the paper. Catherine could have had it printed herself. How would she know so much about the business? Then she remembered Stuart telling her Catherine had spent some time in the office, trying to learn all she could. Stuart had been so proud that his daughter had shown an interest. She wondered whether he'd be so proud of her now. She couldn't confront him.

She put the paper down again. She had to, though, before it was too late. She pulled on her coat and ran out in search of a cab.

46

The private room was vast and golden and hazy with drifting smoke. There were congratulatory banners stretched out across the ceiling and a champagne fountain flowed in the centre of the floor. There must have been about two hundred men in there, all friends or business acquaintances of Stuart's, and they all wore black tie.

Evangeline pushed through the tables until she reached the top of the room.

'Evangeline!' Stuart saw her at once. When he called out her name men around him laughed drunkenly, digging one another in the ribs. Evangeline stood still, taking in the scene. Camelot, with Stuart on the throne. Even in a large gathering he was the most powerful and the most in control. He stood up, smiling and surprised, and she thought how handsome and how kind he looked. Shocked as he was he swept her up and kissed her and all the men clapped and slapped their hands on the tabletop.

He smiled at her. 'Isn't this bad luck, or something?' he asked.

'It's OK,' Evangeline replied, 'this isn't my wedding dress. Can we talk for a minute?'

Stuart looked concerned. Without a word he led her through the main area to a quieter room on the side. She watched him hand the waiter some money and then he closed the double doors and they were alone.

'What is it?' he asked.

She turned to face him. 'Catherine came to see me,' she said. She pulled the headed notepaper from her pocket and held it out. 'She brought me this.'

She watched Stuart's face turn white and she watched him age in front of her eyes.

'She told me you arranged it all,' she whispered. 'Tell me she was lying,' she whispered.

Stuart looked at her.

'Tell me, Stuart,' she said, her voice stronger now, 'for God's sake tell me!'

She had never seen him look so sad before.

'Jesus, no!'

'I can't,' he said, after a long silence.

'No, oh God, no!' Evangeline whispered the words and her hand went to her mouth. 'No, Stuart, not you.'

She brought her hand up to strike him but it froze in mid-air. What had he done to her? What had he done to Mik – to all of them?

She couldn't stand the look of pain in his eyes. She went to walk out but he was at the door before her, stopping her.

'At least let me tell you why I did it,' he said.

'I know why, Stuart,' Evangeline said, 'Catherine already told me.'

She pulled the door open quickly and a waiter jumped back.

'I did it because I loved you, Evangeline,' Stuart shouted after her. The room outside fell silent immediately. They all turned to stare at her, the curiosity and amusement in their eyes turning to aggression as they took stock of the situation. The bride turning up at the stag night to jilt her lover. Stuart calling after her pitifully. She looked at them all and then she looked back at Stuart, standing frozen behind her.

'You did it for yourself, Stuart,' she shouted, 'you did it because it suited you and because you always get what you want. Well, not this time.'

And then she walked out.

The phone was ringing when she walked into her apartment. She started to pack without knowing where she was going, only that she had to leave.

She curled up in her seat and slept like a cat on the plane. When she arrived at Heathrow she ran through customs and hailed a cab. It was raining so hard they could barely see the road. Evangeline gazed out of the window, chewing her nails and trying to think.

She booked into The Mayfair, changed into fresh clothes and caught a cab to Covent Garden. Her agent was surprised to see her.

'Darling! Quel surprise! You should have phoned! I have people in London who are dying to see you after that fabby exhibition at the gallery . . .'

'Where's Mik?' Evangeline asked. 'What hospital did they put him in?'

Her agent's mouth pursed. 'Him?' she said. 'You saw it, then? Little turd. What a shame young Adam was such a bad shot, that's what most people are saying. Of course in terms of publicity Mik couldn't have done better for himself. He's refused to give evidence against Adam so I suppose the case will drag on until the money runs out . . . Young Adam's the celebrity now, though, you know. I took him on the books *tout de suite* and he's got two newspapers willing to pay half a million for his story and a Hollywod producer, no less, is bidding for the film rights once the book comes out. We got the publicity shots of him yesterday — he's quite a good-looking boy, don't you think? Maybe an eyelash dye, or something . . . I wonder if he can act? Who knows, if he gets a good lawyer he could be playing himself in his own movie next year . . .'

'Where is he?' Evangeline repeated.

'Mik? Did you try the studio? Someone there should know. He's discharged himself from hospital, I know that. His agent says he's quite unhinged now — he believes he's had some sort of a breakdown, from the way he's been behaving. Did you decide to sue him, or something? You can count on my testimony if so. I know he's got what he's been asking for but one can't help but feel that one final squeeze might just push him right over the edge.' She smiled encouragingly. 'Why don't you speak to Deeta?' Ross asked. 'She's been threatening to sue Mik for a long time now, since he humiliated her in front of every reader of *Vogue*. Maybe she'll supply you with a little inside info.'

'Mik's studio is closed up,' Evangeline said. 'It looks like it's been empty for ages. And I thought Deeta and Mik had an affair.'

'Not since the first time, according to Deeta,' her agent said, 'she says she wouldn't touch him if he was the last man alive.'

'Where is he?' Evangeline asked again.

Her agent sighed. 'He's preparing an exhibition, though heaven knows what about. He won't let anyone help him and the press aren't invited, evidently. Doesn't sound like our Mik, now, does it? I believe he's chosen some dive in Vauxhall to show at, too. He may think he's a big draw now but I can't see the real money making the trek all the way out there if they've no idea what they'll be getting. It was supposed to open last week but the thing's been cancelled three times already. Thinking of popping round to gloat, are you?'she asked. 'Give him my regards if you do.'

Evangeline took the address of the studio and went back to her hotel. It was dark before she came to a decision.

It was the worst part of Vauxhall. Dead country. Bleak, but not bleak enough to be fashionable. The taxi skidded Evangeline past two sprawling, boarded-up estates and stopped in the courtyard of some deserted factories.

'D'you want me to wait?' the driver asked. Evangeline shook her head.

Her boots made no noise as she picked her way across the cobbles. She tucked her camera inside her jacket, just in case, though there seemed to be no one around. Ahead of her, on a dark wall, was a small printed sign advertising the name of the gallery. The entrance was a large grey metal door that seemed to be padlocked, though the lock fell apart when Evangeline touched it.

Inside was a small entrance hall with a mountain of post stacked over an old, unpainted radiator. The bright strip-light made her blink. The bulb was faulty, flickering like strobe.

Evangeline looked about. There was no noise from the place, just the insect-like buzz of the broken light. A sign similar to the one outside pointed down some stairs, towards the basement. Evangeline glanced back at the empty hall behind her and then headed for the steps. She walked down three flights before she finally reached a door. Her agent was right – none of the glitterati would show up to a hole like this. What was Mik doing here?

She pushed the door open and she was facing total darkness. She paused, waiting for her eyes to adjust, but the only light came from behind her. The bulb in the hall failed altogether at that moment and she nearly stumbled down a small flight of steps in front of her.

'Shit!' She could see nothing now. Her hands reached out and she felt along the wall for a light switch. Instead she found fabric – some curtains or drapes – and her hands fell to her sides again in surprise.

She felt stupid, standing there in the darkness, but she had no option. She walked forward gingerly, feeling for more steps, but the ground seemed even and she felt her boots squeak on polished board, so she relaxed a little.

She was in the right place, she could smell enough to be sure. Fresh paint and sawn wood and the smell of the prints in their frames. Only a photographer would recognize that smell in the dark. She reached out for a wall again and this time her fingers encountered cool glass, that moved a little as she touched it. A hanging print. She steadied it carefully before moving on. There had to be a light switch somewhere on the wall. Then she had an idea. Feeling her way back to the door she groped around behind the frame. The light switches were there, outside in the passage. She pressed the lowest one on and stood, frozen, as the room became bathed in a dozen pools of silvery, diffused light.

The darkness was still there, between the pools. Spots had been rigged up to throw light onto the pictures themselves, alone. The effect was extraordinary and eerie. She'd had no idea the room was so big – it seemed to stretch out for ever.

Twelve prints. Mik was showing only a dozen of his pictures in that vast, tomb-like area. Evangeline stepped forward quietly until she had reached the centre of the room. The middle spot was in total darkness. If you rotated slowly you could see all twelve shots from the same place.

She turned, and her stomach contracted all at once, as though she had received a punch. At first she circled slowly then she spun around, hardly believing her own eyes.

The twelve shots were all of her. It was her own face she saw, wherever she looked. She recognized some of them, but not all. They were shots Mik had taken of her while they had been together. Private shots – casual shots – blown up to six feet or more. In some she was smiling, in others she was serious. A couple were posed but most were off-the-cuff. Only one thing was constant in all of them: the expression in Evangeline's eyes.

She stepped a little closer to the largest one. Had she really loved Mik so much? Yet it was there for anyone to see. Cameras lied, though, she knew that much. She placed her fingers across her mouth. Her eyes in the pictures were molten and smudgy, burning their way off the paper. She frowned.

She moved softly on to the next one. She touched the image of her own face with the tips of her fingers. Had it really been like that? She was filled with yearning.

There were footsteps behind her that stopped suddenly. She turned to see Mik's feet in the light. She had known he would be there, like a spider guarding its web. He moved closer in the vast room. He was all shadows, picked out in the brightest of white light that buried his eyes and made his mouth a dark curving line.

His hair was longer, his face even leaner. He had an arm around his waist, as though to protect his wound. His coat hung from his shoulders.

'You bastard, Mik,' Evangeline said, 'you stole my job.' Her voice had an echo in the empty space.

'And you stole my life,' he replied. No regret, then, and no apology. His voice sounded stronger than he looked. It still had power over her — incredible power — to draw her to him and pull her down until all her anger was gone. It was like liquid — molten metal. She shuddered, trying to shake it off.

She looked back at her photograph. She felt so much older than the woman in the shot. 'You missed the focus by a fraction,' she said, 'and you need a bigger format camera if you're blowing it up this big. The grain's beginning to show.'

He came up behind her and slipped his free arm around her. She felt his face pressed against her neck and her eyes closed.

'I need to talk to you, Evangeline,' he whispered, 'I need you to listen to me. I can't survive like this any longer. I have to tell you everything.'

She rested her face onto his. 'It doesn't matter, Mik,' she said, 'I heard about everything that happened. I came back to find you. I would have come for you before but there have been so many lies . . .' He turned her and kissed her and her words were lost somewhere in the heat of his mouth.

She became uncontrollable in her love and her lust, as though everything were unlocked at once. All the fear and the terrible sadnesses and the anger and the mourning were unleashed together and she knew it was only with Mik that she would find release for her passion.

Her arms wound around him and his around her. She felt him flinch and withdrew at once.

420

'Jesus, Mik, I'm sorry . . . I forgot . . . I forgot the wound.'

He pulled her back towards him, though. 'If you stop now I will die, Evangeline,' he whispered.

She sank to her knees and pulled his jumper up. His coat fell from about his shoulders and slid to the ground behind him. There were bandages and plaster and bruises on his flesh. He must have broken ribs as well. She pressed her lips so softly upon him that she heard him groan with pleasure, rather than pain.

'Help me down, Evangeline.'

She steadied him as he lay on the ground beside her and then she undressed him until he was naked before undressing herself.

'Mik, oh Christ, you have no idea how much I wanted you,' she whispered, 'even at the lowest moments, even when I thought the worst – even when I hated you so much I thought I wanted you dead. I still had a need for you and it hurt like hell to admit it, even to myself.'

He was beautiful, even more than she had remembered. Their silver lockets hung about their necks and she straddled him and leant forward so that they touched and glinted in the half-light.

His hips bucked upward and he was inside her and she cried out with the pleasure and the righteousness of it all.

Mik's hands reached out for her thighs. 'Come with me, Evangeline,' he said, 'I can't wait, I want you too much.'

She took him as he came, swallowing him in the depths of her own orgasm, holding him and caressing him and burying him within her for ever.

Long moments passed before she could speak.

'I love you, Mik –' she said.

'No!' he interrupted her violently, turning her around and pulling her chin up to face him, 'No, Evangeline, you have to listen to everything. No more lies, OK? You have to know it all.'

She tried to stop him. She tried to touch him, to tell him that nothing mattered. She had heard enough about his past. Like her own, it was better forgotten.

'No,' he said, 'this can never be forgotten.' He paused, appearing to choke on his words. His eyes looked mad with grief and guilt. 'I killed my own brother, Evangeline,' he said, 'I killed Andreas.'

47

They lay together in the pools of half-light and now they no longer touched. His hand had fallen from her body and she, in reply, had leant back.

She said nothing, just stared. He looked away and she thought he might cry. There was a chair somewhere in the darkness, by a wall. He got up slowly, dressed and limped painfully towards it and sat down. Evangeline lost him in the gloom. She pulled on her clothes, went back to the door and pressed the remaining switches. The overhead lights came on, yellow and painful. Mik winced, but whether from the lights or his wound she didn't know. His coat was wrapped around him now. His head was bowed. He looked like a warrior who had just lost the battle.

She walked down the long room towards him. His eyes were closed. He looked ghastly in the light. He needed a shave and there were mauve circles beneath his eyes.

'Adam blamed me for Flora's death,' he muttered, 'he thought her suicide was my fault.'

'Was it?' Evangeline asked.

Mik shrugged. 'Who knows? He said I worked her too hard. He was in love with her, Evangeline. He saw what was going to happen, I didn't. I wouldn't listen when he tried to tell me. I watched her die, you know. Like Andreas. He was the same. Young. Very beautiful. It will not happen again. Nothing is worth that, nothing. Only my love for you.'

Evangeline stood over him. 'What happened?' she asked.

Mik smiled. 'In Budapest?' he asked. 'I told you, I killed him. I killed my brother and he has haunted me ever since.

423

Can you exorcize ghosts, Evangeline? I almost believe you can.' He looked up at her. 'But I forgot, you have your own to rid yourself of.'

She squatted on her heels in front of him. 'I got rid of mine,' she whispered. 'Tell me about yours.'

He told her the story then, the whole story of his childhood. He told it rapidly, in a monologue, without expression in his tone, but the story was no less tragic for that. Evangeline sat in silence as he spoke, not daring to move and hardly remembering to breathe.

'Chico was never my father,' he said, 'my father was some prisoner.' He paused. 'Do not bother to correct my English, because what I say is right, perfectly right.' His head fell back. She watched his Adam's apple as he swallowed. He ran a hand across his face. His fingers looked thin and long.

'I loved Andreas,' he went on, 'I loved him – that much was true. And the other stuff, my life after he died, what I did with other men. Who would make that up?' He coughed and winced. 'It was the things that happened before that I didn't tell you about, Evangeline. I was trying to forget.'

He pulled himself further up in the chair. 'I told you my mother, Mimi, was an actress, a comedian,' he said, 'famous in Budapest for the act she had with her husband, Chico – Andreas's father. Then she became famous in other ways. There were clubs in Budapest where certain people congregated to plot against the state. My mother told jokes there – political jokes. She was a good mimic, too. Maybe she was too good. She was sent to prison, Evangeline, for nothing more than telling a few jokes. I told you all this, Evangeline – how I was fostered, how Andreas came to take me away. Do you know what it is like to love someone who is a hero to you? That is how I loved Andreas. For me everything he did was a thing to be copied. He was all I ever wanted to be, but so confident and beautiful I knew I could never begin to try. I was proud of him, Evangeline. Just to be called his brother was something special for me.

'He was a musician. He worked at other things but playing music was his special job. I knew he would become famous, even though I was no judge. Sometimes he played in the clubs our mother had played in. He spoke of her a lot and he created a special memory of her for me. She was beautiful, too. She was full of good intentions, a moralist and an idealist. She wanted the best for our country.

'He had a photograph of her, Evangeline, a photograph that lied. In it she was on stage. She was skinny, with funny legs and eyes that almost crossed. The photo showed an ugly young woman, Evangeline, but Andreas told me she was beautiful and I believed him. I also believed his father was my father.'

Mik stopped, paused. Evangeline waited. His story was her story. She became confused at what she was hearing. She still listened, though. Her story was complete now. His still needed telling.

'I followed Andreas everywhere,' he said, 'I must have been a pain to him. He was older – what did he want with a young kid of ten or so? At least I was tall, and ready to fight anyone, just to impress him. He tried to teach me good things. He tried to make me like our mother in that respect, and our father, maybe. I never understood why he had abandoned us but it didn't seem important – Andreas would have told me if it were.

'I knew Andreas took drugs, like a lot of his friends, but he was always careful to hide the worst from me. It was never anything much – when they found his body there were no track marks, no signs of long-term abuse. His friends took more. Andreas smoked; I knew the smell, it has a nostalgia for me, even today. Sometimes he must have taken heroin, too. They all did, it was part of the culture – part of the job of musician. I still thought he was a hero. One day I saw him take some. I shouted – in front of his friends – told him he was stupid, that our mother would think he was crazy. I don't know what I said, I was too mad and scared for him to care.

'Did you ever see anyone take heroin? It is a frightening sight, even for a boy of twelve who thinks he is tough. I was frightened it would kill him. I knew that without my brother I had no life. I thought that without him I would be dead, too.' He paused and swallowed.

'I thought he was going to hit me, Evangeline. His eyes . . . I had spoken to him in front of his friends and made him look foolish. He must have been tired of me – Christ, how did he manage? A young boy to bring up, a job, the desire to be famous, maybe go to America.

'I had said too much. He turned on me, told me some truths. Not in anger, Evangeline, but from coldness, which was worse. I had no right telling him how to live his life. I was nothing – less than that, maybe. Our mother was not perfect, as he had told me. She was no longer suffering in prison, she had been released a year before and vanished without troubling to find us. She was shit. I couldn't believe that he was saying it.

'He started on our father, too. The man was famous and talented. Class – he had class – which was why he had abandoned our mother. One day Andreas would go and join him. Not me, though, I would have no place with them – he was Andreas's father, not mine. I had been lied to. Andreas laughed at me. I had been born in the jail – what did I think his father could have had to do with it? Our mother hadn't been pregnant when she was arrested. I hadn't known. I was too young. I hadn't thought.

'Andreas told me everything, then, and the story made the hair on the back of my neck rise. I could not believe it to be true, though I knew in my heart it was.

'Our mother had been put into the women's prison outside the city. The place was crowded and filthy and unbearable for her. She was used to better; she had been on the stage, she had been famous. The conditions were intolerable. The other women used to laugh at her for all her airs. She told Andreas this when he was allowed to visit her – she told him she couldn't bear it, that she would have to do something about it.

'There was only one way out of the prison, the women told her, and that was to find yourself pregnant. If you were expecting a child they moved you somewhere better. It was the only hope, otherwise you stayed where you were until the day you were released.

'My mother thought they were making a joke of her – it was an all-woman prison. How was one to get pregnant? The men's block next door was strictly segregated. All visits were overseen. The other women told her it could be achieved but she thought they were laughing at her. It was the cruellest kind of joke – she would have done anything to get out.

'Then one woman in another cell got pregnant and she knew it was possible. She had a few supplies, so she bribed the woman to tell her what she had done.

'My father was some prisoner, Evangeline – I told you that at the start of my story and that was how Andreas told it to me. The method was easy. A condom and some string. Can you imagine the rest? Throw the empty condom from the cell window to the windows of the men's cells. A while later it returns full. A good service, evidently, the men were always only too happy to oblige.

'How many of them, I wonder? How many of them participated in the filling? The woman showed my mother how to use what came back. It must have taken several goes, unless she was lucky. Andreas said the men's block held the worst type of criminals – sex offenders, perverts.

'Can you imagine being told that story at twelve years old? I thought my brain would explode. I was disgusted – I disgusted myself. My mother had been perfect. I couldn't believe . . . yet I knew Andreas was not lying.

'I ran away, but then I came back because I had no chance of life without Andreas and, anyway, it was myself I was trying to run away from. I would have been on the streets. I ended up there anyway. Oh, Christ.' He stopped, his head fell into his hands.

'What happened?' Evangeline whispered.

Mik sighed. 'I killed him. I couldn't stand the truth of what he had told me. I wanted it all to be as it was: that my mother was a perfect and beautiful woman, and my father a famous actor, a classy man. I wanted it all back. As little as it had been it was a constant comfort to me. I didn't want the other story. I didn't want to think about who had been my real father.

'After that Andreas didn't care so much about hiding the drugs. One time he was ill and he asked me to buy them for him. He gave me the money – I almost ran away with it but I knew it wouldn't have lasted me more than a few days. I didn't want to buy the drugs. The dealers scared me – Andreas told me they had knives and would cut me if I spoke to them. I was just to give them the money, that was all.

'I met someone else, a girl I had seen before. I told her what I had to do and she took pity on me. She sold me the heroin instead, saying it was a better bargain than I would get from the men Andreas had sent me to. She said it was too pure, though, that it needed mixing. I thought she meant it was good, so I didn't tell Andreas what she had said. Maybe I didn't want to.

'The heroin was too pure, Evangeline, it killed him. I had said nothing – I never told him, I just watched. I killed him – I wanted him to die.'

Mik looked up at Evangeline. His eyes were clear and intense. 'Can you understand that?' he asked. 'I loved him, I needed him for my existence, yet I wanted him dead. Jesus! I wanted him dead because I couldn't bear his knowledge. I couldn't bear to hear again what it was that he told me. I thought it would all die with him. Yet after . . .'

His story was obviously ended. He had run out of the words to tell it. Evangeline stood up, her hands covering her mouth.

She walked to the far end of the gallery. All photographs of her — so many of her faces. It was eerie, staring at herself in such a way. The eyes in those photographs told her that she loved him. What he had said to her didn't matter to those eyes. They didn't believe Mik had killed Andreas. They believed Andreas had done more to kill Mik. Twelve years old. She wondered how he must have looked. She cried tears for him, but she wiped them away with her sleeve before he could see.

'Well, Evangeline?' His voice sounded calm and strong. He merely wanted to know. It was just a question — do you hate me?

She stood in silence. Felt him walk up behind her.

'Why did you do these shots?' she asked.

'For you,' he said. 'I did them for you.'

'How did you know I would come back?' She still didn't face him, kept looking at the nearest picture.

'I knew it was impossible that you would not,' he said. 'Look.' He limped to the end of the room. There was silence and she could feel him watching her in the darkness. She heard a door open and then a scuffling. Whispers and little yelps of delight. Something small shot out of the shadows and threw itself so fast at her legs that it lost its balance and cannoned into her ankles.

'Oh, Mik, no!' She bent down and the last remaining portion of her heart that had not been liquidized turned to mush. A puppy. Not identical to Paddy but with the same goofy expression and the same irrepressible delight at seeing her. She tickled his head and he rolled onto his back with his fat little puppy-belly in the air. The laughter erupted into tears of loss and pleasure.

'Blackmail,' Mik said.

When she looked up at him her eyes gleamed with sadness and gratitude.

'How did you know he died?' she asked.

'We're famous, remember?' Mik said. 'I read it in the papers. Christ knows how they found out.'

Evangeline picked up the puppy and it squealed and licked at her face. She couldn't stop the tears. Blackmail. He was right. How could she mind, though?

Mik kissed her neck. 'I can't stand it,' he said. 'Tell me you still love me.'

Evangeline kept silent.

'Forget everything else and tell me how you feel.'

She turned to him then, and the love in her eyes completely mirrored the love in the eyes in the photographs. Total and so complete that there was no need for words.

No illusions, no false images, it was the real thing at last.

Other paperback titles by HarperCollins include: